THE GIRL FROM
Old Nichol

Betty Annand

Amberjack Publishing
New York, New York

Amberjack Publishing
228 Park Avenue S #89611
New York, NY 10003-1502
http://amberjackpublishing.com

Publisher's Cataloging-in-Publication data
Names: Annand, Betty, author.
Title: The Girl from old Nichol / by Betty Annand.
Description: New York [New York]: Amberjack Publishing, 2017.
Identifiers: ISBN 978-0- 9972377-9-5 (pbk.) | ISBN 978-0- 9972377-8- 8 (ebook) | LCCN 2016941246
Subjects: LCSH Great Britain--History--Fiction. | Women--England--Fiction. | Historical fiction. | Love stories.| BISAC FICTION / Historical.
Classification: LCC PS3601.N5551 G57 2017 | DDC 813.6--dc23

Cover Design: Red Couch Creative, Inc.

Printed in the United States of America

Dedicated to Art, my soulmate forever.

Life isn't about finding yourself. Life is about creating yourself.

—George Bernard Shaw

Chapter One

It had been a good day. The Tunners' cart was loaded with junk and they were almost home. The temperature had fallen below zero and the cobblestones were as slippery as a bed of wet seaweed. Wrapped from head to toe in layers of ragged coats and scarves, Tonnie and Bert were unrecognizable as they pulled their cart through the littered streets. Most of their neighbours, unfortunate enough to live in the district, were huddled in their hovels around whatever heating apparatus they owned. By the end of winter, there would scarcely be a piece of wooden furniture left; firewood being more a necessity than a comfort.

Raising their heads at the same time, the couple gave each other an encouraging nod. It wouldn't be long before their nagging thirsts were quenched, and their cold hands warmed in the nearest pub. Suddenly, Bert dropped her handle and grabbed her swollen belly, almost upsetting the load. "God, it's comin'! We 'as to leave the cart 'ere, Tonnie. Go fetch that Sally woman."

"Can't just leave it 'ere! Some bloody thief'll take it—and the cart as well."

Another pain brought on a scream. "I don't give a damn if they takes the lot! Now go an' get 'er!"

Tonnie left reluctantly while Bert made her way home through Old Nichol Street Rookery as quickly as her condition and the icy cobblestones would allow. Later that evening, the 29th of January, 1829, Bert gave birth to Gladys Tunner, the only child she and Tonnie would have. It was a bleak and unsteady welcome for Gladys, into one of the worst slum districts in London's East End.

Luckily the cart and the goods within were intact when Tonnie returned to pick them up. He didn't dare tell Bert that he'd taken time to find a boy to watch over it before going for the midwife.

Bert had suffered three miscarriages and, convinced that this pregnancy would be no different, was unprepared for the arrival of a healthy, six-pound baby girl. Two years before, both she and Tonnie would have been delighted with such a blessing, but both their lifestyle and personalities had suffered with time, and now neither appreciated the added burden. Sally Tweedhope, who was kind enough to act as midwife in the neighbourhood, hadn't delivered such a beautiful and healthy baby since she had moved to the slums.

Perspiration ran down Bert's face as she raised herself up on her elbows and watched Sally lift the baby from between her legs. She wasn't surprised when it showed no signs of life and for half a second experienced the usual feeling of sadness—even more so when she saw that this little one was fully developed. Then a deep sense of relief overtook her, and falling back on the pillow, she uttered a tired and silent "Thank you."

Suddenly, the infant emitted a loud cry and began kicking its legs and waving its tiny arms. Shocked, Bert bolted back up crying, "It's alive!"

"Of course she is," Sally replied, smiling.

"No, it can't be! It's too late," Bert protested, but judging by the lively sound of the baby's cry, this baby had come to stay. Bert covered

her face with her hands and began to cry.

Sally was too busy tending to the infant to be of any comfort, but when she had the baby wrapped in the cleanest blanket she could find, she carried her over to the bed and laid her gently beside Bert, saying, "There now, Mrs Tunner, you should be happy. You have a beautiful little girl."

Bert kept her hands over her face mumbling, "No, it's too late."

"Of course it is not too late. Just have a look at her." When Bert refused, Sally pulled her hands away from her face and demanded, "I said *look* at her!"

The order was given in such an inexorable tone that Bert didn't argue. Slowly, she looked down at the bundle beside her. A gasp escaped her lips. The baby was so beautiful and perfect she could scarcely believe it was real. Gently, she touched its downy head and then its face; never had she seen such a baby. She was sure there had to be something wrong, and a shiver of fear ran through her as she slowly folded back the blanket. Relieved, she could see that the little body was as flawless as the head and even had the correct number of fingers and toes.

Sally, watching the awe spread across Bert's face, said, "She is perfect, isn't she?"

Tears were running down Bert's cheeks as she nodded. Then she looked up at Sally and tried to make her understand how she felt. "Oh, that she is, but Tonnie an' me—we aren't able to look after a young one anymore. The poor little mite would be better off dead."

Sally was aware of the Tunners' drinking problems, but she also knew they were both hard workers, and she could tell by the house, as humble as it was, that Bert worked to keep it clean. Therefore, she thought that having a baby might be just what the couple needed to help them mend their ways.

Before she could say as much, the baby began crying, and without stopping to think about it, Bert began nursing her.

Sally laughed and said, "There you go. You are already taking care of her. Don't you worry now; I think you shall make an excellent mother."

"Thank you Missus. I 'opes for the baby's sake you're right.

Anyway, I'm going to do me best, I promise."

"That is all anyone can do, my dear. Now, do you have what you need for the baby?"

Bert shook her head, and then explained that, because of her past miscarriages, she had not anticipated the baby would be born alive.

It had been over a year since Bert first realized how dependent she and Tonnie were on liquor, and she knew in her heart they were in no condition to be parents. As a result, she began refusing Tonnie's advances. Luckily, the booze had taken its toll on his desire, and he was easily dissuaded. Then, somehow, in spite of her best intentions, and even though neither she, nor Tonnie, had any memory of intimacy, she found herself with child once more. Although neither had the slightest idea where or when the conception happened, they had no doubt who the father was. Their love for one another, along with their mutual trust, was the only thing that hadn't yet suffered from their addiction.

Certain that she would have another miscarriage, Bert didn't worry too much about things until she could no longer wear her one and only skirt and had to look amongst their rags for another.

It was then that she decided to visit old Murlee, a gypsy woman who lived in the deepest part of the slums and sold herbal remedies for such things. What Bert didn't know, was that the last two women who had received the old witch's abortive herbs had perished, along with their babies. Afraid of being found out, Murlee had disposed of her supply of the tansy root powder that she normally used, and sold Bert a harmless concoction of ground liquorice and aniseed powder, telling her it would have the same effect.

When Sally left the Tunners that day, she prayed that Bert would keep her promise. The child might have a chance if she did.

The filth and sickening stench inside the homes that she visited were in most cases worse than outside, where the sewers ran alongside the streets. There were times when she was forced to leave and run outside to vomit. It wasn't difficult to understand why so many of the babies she helped deliver died within a month or two after they were born. As she made her way through the Tunners' shop, she spotted Tonnie sitting on a stool, sorting junk. He had been at the nearest bar having a drink when the baby was born and hadn't heard it cry. Now he was hunched over with his head down, and although he flinched a little when she touched his shoulder, he didn't look up. Instead, in a low and apologetic tone, he mumbled, "It's not 'er fault, Missus. She's didn't want to 'ave a 'nother go at it. It's me's to blame. Even if she don't want a young'n any more, it still saddens 'er when they comes out dead."

"But, Mr Tunner," Sally replied, "that's just it. She's not dead! You have a beautiful little baby girl!"

Tonnie was having trouble digesting the unexpected news and, looking up at her, stammered, "Are you certain, Missus? I mean . . . Bert . . . you knows yourself . . . she can't 'ave babies."

"Well, she has one now."

Still not sure of what she was telling him, he continued to stare at her until she put her hand gently on his arm and suggested, "I think you had better go in now and be with your wife and daughter, don't you?"

First he replied with a slow and dubious nod, and then, a wide and beautiful grin lit up his dirty, whiskered face. He jumped up, grabbed her hand, shook it vigorously and said, "Thank you, Missus; you're a proper angel, you are!" Her depression vanished as she watched him give a little hop, smack his thigh with his hand, and exclaim, "Jaysus, I'm a bloomin' da, I am!" She couldn't help but laugh as she left to inform the neighbours that Bert was in dire need of baby necessities.

Tonnie pulled back the old, grey wool blanket, so full of holes it did little to separate the bedroom from the rest of the house. In his excitement, he forgot to duck, and the sound of his head smacking the five-foot door frame along with his volley of profanity startled both the baby and Bert, who had dozed off. Rubbing his head, he sheepishly apologized, "I'm right sorry, luv. I didn't mean to wake you."

He knelt down beside the bed and looked at the baby. "Crikey, she's a right keeper, she is! You outdid yourself, Bert, luv. I never laid eyes on one so bonnie. I think we should give 'er the name, Gladys, after me Welsh gran, if that's all right with you, luv. I fancies the name Gladdy, don't you?"

Bert nodded her head in consent. Then she reached for Tonnie's hand and, grasping it, said, "She's too good for us, Tonnie. We'll 'ave to stop drinking so much if we're going to look after 'er proper like."

"I 'opes we can, luv; I 'opes we can."

"We will Tonnie; we 'as to! But I think we deserves a wee nip now to sort of celebrate. Go on now, luv. Go fetch us a bottle."

Tonnie agreed, but before he got up from the floor, he ran his big rough hand over the baby's head. His eyes were so full of love and pride that Bert was tempted to tell him not to go, but her thirst wouldn't allow it. He gave each of Bert's bared breasts a quick kiss, and then with a grin and a wink he left, whistling a lively tune.

The women Sally had visited on Bert's behalf had little sympathy for the new mother. They had even less than the Tunners and hardly owned enough rags to cover their own little ones. Nevertheless, they each managed to gather up an item or two and arrived the following morning with a hodgepodge of gifts: chipped bottles with well-worn nipples, yellow-stained nappies, and a mixture of dirty, shrunken, and matted wool blankets, sweaters, bonnets, and booties.

Being able to donate something allowed them a certain sense of pride and eased their jealousy. As they filed past the newborn, none could deny that she was an exceptionally pretty baby. However, once outside, the ladies pulled their well-worn shawls and cardigans tight to their breasts and huddled together to discuss the birth.

"I hopes now she has a wee one, she'll keep out of the pubs."

"Not that one! She's a lost soul, she is. I almost feels sorry for 'er."

"Well you never can tell; 'avin' a young'n to care for might just change 'er right o' ways."

And so it did—for four weeks. Bert had meant it when she promised Sally she'd try to be a good mother, but as the weeks went by, she began begging Tonnie to bring more and more booze home, and was soon back to drinking as much as ever. Nevertheless, she still managed to keep Gladys fed and clean even when she began going to the pubs again, taking the baby along with her.

Although Old Nichol was considered the most undesirable place to live in all of England, it too had a 'slum' within its slums. This area dwelt deep inside the ghetto, and was so deplorable that no law-men dared visit. Hence, wanted criminals considered it a safe place. It was often referred to as "The End" for a good reason: the death toll being more than twice what it was in the rest of Old Nichol.

Bert had been born in The End, and when she married Tonnie and moved to Nichol Street, she felt as though she was moving to Buckingham Palace. If she had had Gladys during the first four years of her marriage, she may have been content to stay at home and be a good mother, but then again, she may have died from drinking the putrid water from the communal well, rather than liquor.

In every pub she frequented, Bert hung the baby up on a coat peg in a cradle-like sling fashioned out of an old, ragged blanket. Fortunately, the baby's hunger and her mother's discomfort demanded a reunion every few hours or she might have been forgotten as her mother went from one pub to another.

Gladys was far more safe hung on a peg than she would have been placed on the floor. There she was likely to be lost or trampled to death among the broken tankards, spittoons, and other debris. The interiors of the pubs were as littered with rubbish as the streets.

As Gladys grew, so did her lungs, and it wasn't long before customers began complaining about the noise she made. Bert was ordered to leave her baby at home. To solve the problem, she had Tonnie build a pram out of a slatted-wooden box, some odd shaped wheels, and a piece of canvas used for a hood.

When Bert said they would now be able to leave her outside the pubs, Tonnie protested, "Bloody 'ell, Bert; someone's goin' to take 'er if you leaves 'er alone outside!"

"Take 'er? Who do you know what wants another one, eh?" When Tonnie couldn't come up with an answer, she laughed and said, "If you could get rid of them that easy, there'd be 'undreds of them left in the streets."

Bert was right; with conditions as dire as they were in the London slums, children were more of a burden than a blessing since food, clothing, and shelter were almost as scarce as gold. Old Nichol Street Rookery housed over five thousand people, all crammed into a space barely big enough to accommodate a hundred. London was the most populated city in the world and had run out of jobs and room for the mass migration of people who came to the city from rural areas hoping to find employment during the Industrial Revolution.

Tonnie was more fortunate than most because his father had established a second-hand shop before the migration, and it had two shack-like rooms at the back of the building. One room was used as a store room and bedroom, and the other contained a cooker, some boxes nailed to the wall for staples, a table, four odd-shaped chairs, and a well-worn and dirty, flowered divan where their daughter Gladys slept after she outgrew the wooden box that served as her crib.

Many of the families in Old Nichol lived eight or ten to a room, and many of those rooms were in rat-infested cellars that flooded during the rainy weather. For the privilege of living in such hovels, they were forced to pay an inequitable amount of rent to rich landlords with no conscience. Shamefully, some of these landlords were churchmen and politicians.

Children as well as adults were forced to work in order to survive. If you lived on the ground level, you could manage to keep a rain barrel. Otherwise, the only available drinking and washing water had to be carried from a communal pump, which usually meant wait-

ing in line for long periods of time. Due to the scarcity of water, the washing of clothes or bodies was seldom practiced.

Drinking water came from the same shared pump and was piped in from the heavily-polluted River Thames, where it wasn't unusual to see floating carcasses of dead animals, and occasionally humans, bobbing out of the scum that lay on the river's surface. In spite of the hardships and frequent deaths from starvation and disease, laughter and music still played a regular role in the neighbourhood clamour. All it took was a tune on a fiddle, a mouth organ, or another instrument, for an excuse to dance and sing, not only in the pubs, but in the streets as well. If the dancers had no shoes, they danced barefoot. With such appalling poverty, thievery was to be expected, but crime was far overshadowed by compassion and sharing, and bigotry was applied towards the rich and not the races.

When Bert and Tonnie were first married, they were known for their generosity, especially in the winter months when they often donated second-hand clothes to the poorest families. As the water from the pump grew more and more fetid, they began substituting gin or ale, and before long, liquor became their first priority.

Bert was small of stature, but she was blessed with a generous set of lungs. A feisty redhead with a freckled complexion and an hourglass figure, she was the offspring of the poorest of the poor. Therefore, fortune had indeed smiled on her when she married a man who had not only inherited a business, but could also afford to rent a building large enough to accommodate it, as well as living quarters and even a bed.

A bed was a luxury that few people in the slums were fortunate enough to own. The one that Tonnie and Bert owned had an inscription carved into the headboard that once read, "*Love keeps his revels where there are but twain.*" The bed had been handed down through four generations of Tunner junk collectors. The story was that it had belonged to the Great Bard himself, who had bought it for a certain young lady, only to find that she was nothing of the sort;

hence, the bed was sold and bought many times over, until it was eventually handed down to Tonnie and Bert.

By the time they inherited it, three bricks replaced a missing leg, and there was a hole where the word "revel," had been. Since none of the Tonners were acquainted with the works of Shakespeare, one of them had covered the hole with a piece of board and written the word "grog" on it.

Another benefit of Bert's marriage was a sturdy wooden rain barrel outside her door. Even though the rain changed from transparent to a murky yellow as it made its way through the pollution that hung over the city, it was far cleaner than the water from the communal well. To her credit, Bert made good use of the barrel-water and kept her home as clean as she possibly could.

Although illiterate, she had a keen mind and a most remarkable memory. When she discovered that her repertoire of lyrics, her adeptness at carrying a tune, and her dancing skills could earn a few extra coins, she took advantage of it, and most evenings, after work, she would discard her soiled pinafore and dust cap, shake out her mop of flaming curls and, along with Tonnie, make the rounds of the neighbourhood pubs. Her talent also resulted in many free drinks, which had helped her addiction progress.

Not as many women as men frequented such establishments, but the ones who did had little appreciation for Bert's lively dances and flirtations and began to exclude her from their daily gossip. At first, she reacted by shrugging her shoulders, hawking up a ball of phlegm, spitting it on the street, and saying to Tonnie, "That's what I thinks of them dirty buggers. They's just jealous, they is!" But in spite of her act of indifference, she missed their inclusion and friendship.

Tonnie was as noticeably large as Bert was small, thus the nickname "Tonnie." He had a habit of squinting, which was a pity, since his large, bright, brown eyes were his most attractive feature. His nose was straight, but all his other facial features were hidden behind a forest of black hair. He would have displayed an enviable head of thick, black, curly hair if Bert didn't hack away at it every few weeks with an old pair of chipped shears. Tonnie was known for two things: his good-nature and his extraordinary strength—a fortuitous combination. He also had a talent for song and dance and could swing a woman as large as himself—over seventeen stone—off her feet to the tune of a good Scottish Reel.

Along with the business, Tonnie inherited a four-by-eight-foot wooden cart and an old donkey to pull it. Unfortunately, there wasn't much left of the poor animal but bones and hide, and it died soon after the demise of Tonnie's father. Without the money to buy another, Tonnie and Bert were forced to take the donkey's place. As the neighbourhood's population increased, more and more folks were scratching out a living by collecting junk and selling it. So, in response, they had to work longer and harder in order to collect enough saleable merchandise to pay their rent, satisfy their hunger, and quench their ever-present thirst.

Once a week, they pulled the cart more than a mile to "Warehouse Corner," usually arriving there before daylight. Warehouse Corner was the nickname given to a street corner on the very outskirts of the slums where the gentry sent their servants with cast-off clothing, rags, and other unwanted articles to be dropped off for the poor. The servants would take the goods that far, but refused to take it any farther, for fear of contracting diseases.

Whoever arrived at the corner first could claim the most advantageous spot. On the days when no servants came, Bert and Tonnie often pulled their cart up and down the streets, and while Tonnie rang an old cowbell, Bert would call out, "Rags, old rags."

Some days, if they were fortunate enough to have a bottle of ale along, Bert would be in such good spirits that she would make up rhymes and sing them out in a loud voice as she danced around the cart to the ring of the bell.

"Rags, old furnachure, whatever it will be, throw it 'ere, throw it 'ere, we 'auls away for free." Such antics, difficult to ignore, were often rewarded.

For two months after Gladys was born, Bert stayed home, and Tonnie pushed the cart alone, but he complained so loudly that she began going with him, taking the baby along, wrapped in a blanket and laid in the cart. This seemed to please the child since she cooed and gurgled contentedly as the cart bumped along over the cobblestones. As soon as they arrived at Warehouse Corner, Bert would sit on the side of the road, unfasten her bodice, and proceed to nurse the infant while Tonnie loaded the cart. When they were ready to start back, the infant, pacified with a full belly, would be placed amongst the junk, where she usually slept contentedly all the way home.

One day, Bert and Tonnie waited for two hours at Warehouse Corner, but there were no deliveries. Since they were badly in need of money to buy liquor, they began trudging up and down nearby streets calling out for second-hand goods. It took all day before they had enough to earn them a bottle or two, but when they arrived back at Warehouse Corner, they were surprised and delighted to see that someone had left a load of junk while they were gone. Tonnie unloaded the poor stuff he had in his wagon then reloaded it with the better quality items while Bert fed the baby. When they were ready to leave, Bert found a large enough cavity amongst the junk to put Gladys, and they continued on their way.

It was almost dark by the time they came to another junk yard, owned by Bob Tweedhope, the midwife Sally's husband, a pleasant and likeable man who was just closing up for the night. Sally suffered with a lung ailment and was unable to assist in pulling a cart, so Bob often bought his merchandise third hand.

When he spotted the Tunners going by, he called out, "Hi! Tonnie, you're a mite late, aren't you?"

Tonnie, hearing Bob's greeting, nodded to Bert and in unison, they dropped the cart handles to the ground. Wiping the sweat off his brow with a dirty rag, Tonnie called back, "If ya wants to talk to me, Bobby, ya lazy old turd, you gotta bring me a drink."

Bob laughed, then picking up a tankard half full of warm, stale ale, crossed the road, and handed Tonnie the drink before poking around to see if there was anything on the cart worth buying.

Downing the stale ale in one swallow, Tonnie said, "Gawd bless ya, Bob, that there's the worstest drink I ever drunk!"

Bert grabbed the tankard from Tonnie only to find it empty. "'Ere! Don't you ever think of nobody but yerself?" she said, as she gave Tonnie a shove with her arm. The empty tankard had intensified her thirst even more. She threw it back to Bob, and snarled, "There's your goblet; now quit lookin' round our bloody cart. Come on, Tonnie, let's get this lot 'ome."

They were both desperately in need of a drink by this time, but as they started to leave, Bob put his hand on Tonnie's arm. "Hold on now, Tonnie, what if I was to offer you a good price for the whole cart full?"

"It would 'ave to be a good one. This 'ere's the best junk I've 'ad in ages."

Bob had seen enough to know that Tonnie was right, but he started his offer low. They bickered back and forth for a few minutes before Bert, who was so in need of a drink that she was beginning to shake, told Tonnie to take whatever he could get, so they could be on their way. Tonnie wasn't in much better shape, and realizing they could get to the pub twice as fast without the cart, he said, "Tell ya what, Bob; you gives me ten quid and you can 'ave the bloody lot if you unloads the cart yourself an' brings it to me tomorrow."

Bob agreed, and after the cart was in the yard, he counted out the money and handed it to Bert. It had been a long time since she had held that much money, and, looking down at it, all she could think about was the grand amount of thirst-quenching liquor it could buy. She grabbed hold of Tonnie's hand and they hurried off to the nearest pub. By this time, darkness had fallen, and Bob decided to put off the unloading until the next day. Throwing a canvas over the load, he closed the gate behind him and went home to his wife two streets away.

Not long after Bob left the yard, it began to rain. When it turned into a downpour, the noise woke the baby. Although she usually slept through the night, the noise and the confinement of being tucked into such a tiny space under an upside-down, broken rocking chair frightened her. She began to cry, softly at first, but then, when no one came to her rescue, she started to howl and kick her feet. Unfortunately, her struggles shook the cart, causing the untied canvas to slip off the load and onto the ground. After a time, her cries became sobs that grew weaker and weaker until the only noise in the junk yard was the sound of the rain pounding down on an old piece of tin lying on top of a barrel.

In the morning the rain had subsided, but when Bob arrived at his junkyard he could see the canvas had come off the cart, and his merchandise was soaked. He began going through the junk to see what he could salvage, and when he came to what he mistook for a bundle of clothes, he pulled back the blanket, hoping some were still dry. It was then that he found the baby. At first he was sure the infant was dead; her skin was the colour of skim milk, and her lips were purple. For a second, he was too shocked to do anything but stare at the little creature, but then, when he bent over and gently picked her up, she uttered a weak moan, startling him so much, he almost dropped her.

"My God, you're still alive! Why you must be the Tunners' babe. I'd better get you to Sal. Maybe she can save you."

He took off his jacket, wrapped it around the infant and hurried home. Sally was appalled when she saw the baby's condition. "I don't know if I can save her, Bob, she's pretty far gone. You had better go and find her mother. She's far too weak to cry, but she must be starving. I simply cannot understand how any mother could leave her baby like this. What sort of a woman is she?"

Bob said it had to be the Tunners' little one and that they had probably been too drunk to miss her. Sally remembered how beautiful and healthy the baby was when she was born, and she couldn't believe that Bert could abandon such a child. She also remembered the promise Bert had made, and she shook her head in disgust.

"Go on now, Bob, hurry and find her. I shall try to get a little warm milk into her until you come back." After Bob left, Sally took off the baby's damp, soiled gown and wrapped her in a clean blanket, then she warmed some milk and tried to feed her.

It had been two years since she and Bob had lost their infant twins, a girl and a boy. They had died of cholera a year after they were

born, in spite of Sally's expert care. Sally hadn't always lived in the slums. She came from a fairly well-to-do family and had lived in one of the better districts of London where her father, a doctor, was fortunate enough to have a number of wealthy patients. Although her mother objected, Sally often accompanied her father when he made his rounds, and sometimes she would be called upon to assist him in his work, but when she revealed her plans to become a nurse, her father was shocked, and he refused to allow it.

Hospitals were ill kept, and female nurses had almost no training. Most came from the slums and were given the most despicable chores. Because it was practically impossible for a woman to become a doctor, and Sally wanted to spend her life tending the sick, she may have gone against her father's wishes if it weren't for a cruel turn of events that caused him to be sent to prison. One night he had received two calls for help at the same time—one to attend a very wealthy woman, and the other to a nearby factory where a young father of six had his arm caught in a machine. Knowing both parties, he had no trouble deciding who to see first. If the young man didn't survive, his family would be sent to the workhouse. The woman, on the other hand, was a spoiled hypochondriac and was in the habit of sending for him if she so much as sneezed.

Unfortunately, both patients died that night. The woman, who was grossly overweight, suffered a heart attack, and the poor man died of internal bleeding. The wealthy family took the doctor to court on a charge of neglect. Sally and her mother spent all their money hiring lawyers, but they all failed to prove the doctor's innocence. Sally's mother had a brother-in-law who was a lawyer, but he was a stingy and self-righteous man and refused to help the family financially or professionally. After a time, Sally and her mother had nothing left and were forced to move to the slums. A short time later Sally's mother died of a broken heart. Her father passed away in prison two weeks after his wife.

Unable to find employment of any kind, Sally would have had to resort to begging in order to pay her rent if Bob, who lived in the same building, hadn't offered to share his one room with her. They were married a short time later.

Although she'd had no intention of becoming the neighbourhood's midwife, Sally had heard a pregnant neighbour screaming in pain one night, and felt obliged to offer assistance. From the moment she delivered that first baby, there was no turning back. It seemed to Bob that each delivery took its toll on his wife's health, especially if the baby didn't survive. He wanted her to stop, but her conscience wouldn't allow it. After a time, she began to disassociate the loss of her two babies with the ones she delivered, and the job became easier. But now, holding this poor little creature close to her breast, tears ran down her cheeks. She would have said a prayer, but so many of her prayers had gone unanswered that she superstitiously thought it would do more harm than good.

After spending most of the money Bob had given them on liquor, Bert and Tonnie had staggered home and passed out on their bed. In the morning, Bert woke up with a sodden blouse and very sore and swollen breasts. In order to ease her discomfort, she reached over the side of the bed to pick up Gladys from the box where she slept, but was shocked to find it empty. "Tonnie! Tonnie! Wake up Tonnie! The baby's gone!"

Tonnie mumbled, "What baby's gone?"

"Our baby! Our Gladdy! Somebody's took 'er! Oh, Tonnie, someone's took our Gladdy! Go and find 'er." When Tonnie didn't move, Bert reached under the bed for the chamber pot and hit him over the head with it. "Go find our Gladdy. Now!"

Tonnie was on his way out the door rubbing the bump on his head when Bob came running down the street calling, "Mrs Tunner, Mrs Tunner!"

Some ladies were outside talking and stopped him before he reached the Tunners' door. "What's all the ta-do about, Bob?"

"She's left her babe in the cart all night in the rain," Bob answered. Then noticing Tonnie he called out, "Here, Tonnie, you'd better get that woman of yours up to my place, and she'd better hope her baby is still alive when she gets there, or I'll be having the constabulary after you."

Tonnie started to tell Bob to go to hell, but the word "constabulary" softened his anger. He went back into the house, grabbed a sobbing Bert by the arm, and tried to explain what had happened as he pushed her toward the door.

Gladys survived, thanks to Sally, who threatened to call the law—although she knew it would do little good—if Bert ever did such a thing again. In spite of what had happened, Bert did love Gladys, and she was relieved to find her alive. However, she resented Sally's threat and that, along with feelings of guilt, shame, and envy, would forever embitter her towards the woman who had saved her daughter's life, for as long as she lived.

Chapter Two

By the time Gladys was five, her parents were settled deeply into their addiction, and they often showed more affection for a drink of gin than they did for her. Nevertheless, she adored them both and never tired of watching them dance and sing. Like her mother, Gladys had an uncanny memory for songs, and nothing pleased her more than the odd times when Bert would encourage her to join in on a song or two. Those were the only times Gladys felt she was truly loved.

When she was old enough to wander around on her own, Bert and Tonnie seldom took notice of Gladys's whereabouts. Fortunately, she had made friends with a small group of other waifs and strays, who spent their days darting in and out of alleys like a group of foraging monkeys, looking for food or whatever they could find to sell for a penny. Her best friend and protector was a boy of eight who, because of his ingenuity, had earned the role of leader. He went by the name of "Toughie," a nickname his father had given him. It proved to be a name well-suited, as he had survived on his own since the age of five.

❦

Toughie's father, Hugh Matthews, was regarded as a hero when he, his wife, Maria, and his young son, Angelo, lived on Nichol Street. Hugh had saved the life of a young child from the third floor of a burning building, then had returned to the raging inferno to save another. Unfortunately, by the time they exited the building, the child had died of smoke inhalation, and the smoke had damaged Hugh's lungs beyond repair.

A year after the rescue, his shortness of breath had become so acute that he was unable to continue with his job in a blacksmith shop. Hugh could no longer pay his rent, and eventually he was forced to move his family to the poorest part of the slums, where he and Maria had to beg in order to pay rent for a ten-by-ten foot room in the basement of a house of ill repute.

Hugh's condition gradually worsened and he passed away. When Maria could no longer pay the rent and buy food, she was forced into a life of prostitution. The madam who ran the brothel was more than happy to hire her since, in spite of her emaciated condition, she was still strikingly beautiful with a generous head of coal-black, curly hair and dark, almond-shaped eyes.

Toughie was left on his own most of the time and would have gone hungry if the madam and the other girls hadn't felt sorry for him and kept him busy running errands for them. For his troubles, they sometimes gave him a penny or two, but more often they provided him with food.

Toughie, like other children in the slums, had seen more ugliness by the time he was four years old than most people see in a lifetime. His home was a damp, dark, and windowless basement room, but since his parents had lived most of their lives outside of Old Nichol, and were both literate, they made life tolerable for him by reading him stories and teaching him his letters. Hugh, knowing his days were numbered and that there would be times when Toughie would have to defend himself, had taught the boy to use a hidden weapon that he had made when he worked as a blacksmith.

He had fashioned the weapon out of a small horseshoe bent to go around his fist and small enough to be hidden in his woollen gloves. Toughie never left home without wearing his fortified glove. The first bully that grabbed him by his coat collar and demanded to see what he had in his pocket received more than he bargained for, ending up with a bloody nose. When Maria started working, and Toughie was left alone at night, he began wearing the glove to bed.

The only times that he felt safe, and almost happy, were the times when his mother returned home early in the morning. Although she would still be semi-drunk, she would scrub herself down before putting on her nightdress and crawling into bed to snuggle with him before falling asleep.

On the streets, Toughie soon learned the value of money, and on the days when there were no errands to run and he was hungry, he would help himself to his mother's cache hidden in one of his father's old boots. He used the money to buy bread and sausage, or a meat pie for him and his mother to eat when she woke up in the afternoon.

Maria had lost her appetite and for over a month had been living on a diet of mostly alcohol. The madam, who normally would have ordered any of her girls to leave if they couldn't earn enough, realized that Maria didn't have long to live, and allowed her and her son to stay for a time without charge.

When she realized she was dying, Marie managed to find the strength to take Toughie as far as the beginning of Nichol Street and back. This she did three days in a row, insisting he memorize the route so he could find his way there on his own. Then she explained to him that she, like his daddy, was going to die very soon, and when that happened, he was to leave her and go to Nichol Street to find a place to stay.

Although he was only five, Toughie was no stranger to death, having witnessed his father's demise. He'd also seen other bodies that had been left lying on the street to be picked up by the wagon that came once a week to collect the dead. But when he awoke one morning and found his mother had died during the night, his bravado deserted him, and he put his head down on her chest and cried like the little boy that he was. When there were no more tears left, he tried to control the sobs that wracked his little body, and he did his best to make her look nice. Pulling the covers up to her neck, he brushed the curls gently off her face, then kissed her cold lips, and saying, "Goodbye, Mama," he left.

Toughie pulled his cap down over his forehead and ran as fast as he could until he reached Nichol Street. By the time he arrived, it was past noon, and he felt so lightheaded, he had to sit on the street and lean against a building, or he would have fallen down. After a few minutes, he realized that he was very hungry, and, looking around to see if anyone was watching, he reached up under his jumper and into a pouch he had tied around his waist. Maria had made it for him to hold the few coins she gave him along with a faded portrait of her and Hugh, with their names, the date of their marriage, and Toughie's birthday written on the back.

He took one of the coins, and, trying to be as inconspicuous as he could, walked along, looking for a baker's shop. The people he passed were similar to those in his old neighbourhood—just as dirty and shabbily dressed. Still, there was something different about the way they went about their business that Toughie felt, but couldn't identify. It was a good feeling, and he began to believe his mother was right about the place.

When he came to a bakery, he went in, and pointing to some scones on a shelf, he asked for two. The proprietor, whose generous size gave credence to his wares, threw back his head and laughed.

"I've no doubt you would, lad, you and all them other beggin' buggers out there."

Toughie held out his hand and showed him the coin.

"Well now, me boy, why didn't you say you 'ad the price?"

Toughie just shrugged.

"'Ere, I'll wrap them up in this paper so no one will see them and pinch them off you." He took two scones and wrapped them in newspaper then handed them to Toughie. When the lad made no move to go, the baker said, "Go on now, boy, off you go." Toughie shook his head and pointed to the sign under the scones on the shelf.

"Excuse me, sir, but you owe me three pence."

The baker was taken aback. This lad spoke like a young gentleman, and damned if the lad couldn't read and count as well.

"By gore, if you're not right! And what a clever little lad you are." He counted out three pence into Toughie's hand, and added, "What's your name, boy? I don't think I've seen you round 'ere afore."

"Toughie," was the only answer he received, as the boy hurried out the door.

After leaving the shop, Toughie walked until he found a place behind a couple of rain barrels where he wouldn't be noticed, sat down, and greedily gulped down the scones. They were very filling but made him thirsty, so he helped himself to a drink out of one of the barrels before resuming his search for a home. By the afternoon the task seemed hopeless, so he began looking in the alley beside the sewer and the outhouses for a place to rest.

Finally, he lifted up the lid on an old coal bin and discovered that it was empty except for a couple of old blankets. He decided he would sleep there for the night and in the morning start looking for a nice family like his mother had told him. He curled up on top of one of the blankets while covering himself with the other one, and was sleeping soundly in a few seconds.

"Oi, Mick, look what we got 'ere!"

"It's a bloody squatter, Billy boy," Mick said as he picked up a stick and began poking Toughie with it. "Come on now. Get out of it!"

Toughie woke with a start and a pain in his ribs. Still half asleep and forgetting where he was, he cried out, "Mama!"

"'E wants 'is mama. Ya 'ear that, Billy boy? 'E wants 'is mama. Come along now get your dirty arse out of my bin."

Toughie crawled out and apologized, "I am sorry; I didn't know it was yours."

"Coo, ain't 'e the fancy boy? Just moved ere 'ave you, your lord-shit?" This started Billy laughing, and, in between bursts of laughter he kept repeating "your lord-shit" until Mick ordered, "Shut your gob."

By the sharp tone of Mick's voice, Toughie was beginning to feel wary and was glad he had kept his gloves on before he fell asleep.

His fist tightened around his weapon as he said contritely, "I was just looking for a place to stay."

"You an orphan boy?" Mick asked. Toughie nodded. "What's your name?"

"Toughie."

This brought on another fit of laughter from the boy called Billy, but Mick's lips only formed a smirk. "You don't look tough enough to whip a baby. Let's see just how tough you are," he said. Then, taking Toughie by surprise, he punched him in the stomach. Toughie cried out, but as he bent over in pain, he made sure he had a good grip on his horseshoe. "That'll teach you to stay 'way from my bin!"

Toughie was hoping he could go on his way without any further trouble, but Billy had other plans and came at him shouting, "It's my turn now, your lord-shit!"

"Leave 'im alone," Mick ordered, but it was too late.

Billy took a swing at Toughie's face, but Toughie was ready for him and knocked Billy on the ground before his fist reached its target. "Ow, that 'urt like 'ell. 'E's broke my jaw, Mick," Billy cried.

Mick ignored him as he looked at Toughie with sudden respect and, holding out his hand, he said, "My name's Mick, and this 'ere's Billy."

Making sure to use the hand without the weapon, Toughie shook hands, and suddenly, he didn't feel quite as lonely.

There wasn't room in the coal bin for another boy, but Mick said that maybe one of the outhouses would be empty. Then he warned Toughie that if there was one, it would be "the one that stunk the worst." There were so many orphaned children looking for a dry place to sleep every night that almost all the doorways and outhouses were taken.

After Toughie left the two boys, he managed to find a vacant outhouse, but Mick was right; he could only stay in it for a few minutes before the sickening stench forced him to leave. As the evening turned into night, it grew chilly, and the strange noises coming from the black shapes leaning against the buildings frightened him. Some sounded like moans and others like growls. Toughie desperately wanted to run home to his mother, but he could still picture her lifeless body and knew he could never return.

Tears began running down his cheeks, as he noticed a man shovelling something out of a building. A lantern hanging in the doorway gave off such a warm and welcoming glow that he was drawn to like a moth. He startled the man when he timidly, said, "Pardon me, sir."

"Saints alive! Where in God's name did you come from?"

Toughie wasn't exactly sure, but he remembered his father saying that they lived in hell, so he answered, "Hell, sir."

This rendered the man speechless, and he stared at the boy as though he was the devil himself.

"I'm looking for work, sir, and a place to stay."

The man shook his head, then, half afraid of what the boy's answer would be, he asked, "What's your name, lad?"

"Toughie, sir."

"Be you an orphan then?"

In spite of Toughie's brave efforts, his voice broke and a tear ran down his cheek as he answered, "Yes, sir. My father's dead, and Mama died last night."

"Well if I'm about to let you sleep in my barn, I'll have to know their names."

Toughie wanted to stay in the barn so badly, he didn't hesitate to answer.

At first the man appeared shocked, then he smiled and said, "Why, I remember your daddy well. That was when you lived just down the street a mite. Sure an' your daddy was a proper hero, he was."

Toughie's mother had told him all about his father's bravery, but he was too tired to talk about it. "Can I stay, please, sir?"

Mr O'Brian had allowed orphans to stay in his barn before, but they always stole whatever they could lay their hands on, so he had stopped doing it, but he recalled how Hugh Matthews had risked his life to save a little girl and what tragic results had come from it. He smiled at the boy, and said, "Well now, there's no room for more upstairs, but let's see what we can fix up down here, shall

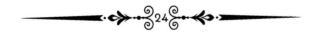

we? How about if we use this little space between old Knicker's stall and the hay bin? I can put some nice hay down here for a bed, and I wouldn't be surprised if the missus can find something to use for a blanket. How's that suit you, Toughie?"

Looking up into the man's eyes, Toughie knew that he had found a home.

Mr O'Brian didn't regret his act of kindness. Toughie was no trouble, and he even lent a hand when it was needed. Most days he earned enough on the street to feed himself, and on the days when he had no food, Mrs O'Brian always managed to have enough stew in the pot for one more bowl.

The barn was not an actual barn, but the gutted-out bottom floor of a building that Mr O'Brian rented to house his animals. He and his family lived on the floor above. The O'Brian's animals consisted of "Knickers," a very old horse that earned his keep by pulling a wagon used to deliver manure to the houses on the outside of the slums, a scrawny sow with a litter of piglets, a boar, and the family's dog: a black and white bitch of mixed breeds called Sheba.

Not long after Toughie moved in, Sheba gave birth to a litter of pups, which was quite a surprise, since she was very old, and no one had noticed any male dogs sniffing around her for a few years. Mr O'Brian couldn't afford to keep the puppies and intended to give them to the poorest families he knew—families who were forced to eat rat meat in order to survive and would consider dog meat a treat.

He was in the process of gathering them up for disposal one afternoon when Toughie reached over, grabbed the scrawniest of the litter, and ran. O'Brian didn't give chase, but that evening he hid and was waiting when Toughie tiptoed into the barn and gently placed the little pup beside its mother. O'Brian was all set to jump out and seize the dog, but the look on the little lad's face as he laid the puppy down beside Sheba to be fed was so moving, he couldn't do it.

Quietly, he approached the boy, and said, "Easy now, Toughie, sure I'm not about to take him. You can keep the little mutt. There's too little meat on his bones anyways. You'll have to look after him now." Toughie merely nodded his head, but the look in his eyes portrayed his gratitude. "An' now, me lad, what would you be naming him?"

"My Dog!" was his answer. My Dog grew to be as protective of Toughie as Toughie was towards the dog, and the two became inseparable. By the time he was six, Toughie had learned to be as proficient at begging and scrounging as any beggar on the street. All the street venders admired his fortitude, and because he never stole anything he didn't need, they seldom complained when he did.

Toughie had never known what it was like to have friends until he met Mick and Billy, and it wasn't long before he befriended a few more orphans. They seemed more like siblings to him since they all looked out for one another. Although they found it necessary to filch whenever they could get away with it, they had made a pact never to steal from each other.

Some, like Toughie, enjoyed working when they had the chance and soon learned how to pool their meagre earnings. One or two would use the money to demand a clerk's attention, while others did the pilfering. Except for Toughie, none had been taught to read or write, but they all had street smarts and were most adept at running and hiding when they had to. They were also clever at picking pockets, though most pockets in the neighbourhood weren't worth picking.

One day, they managed to make off with three large sausages from a butcher shop, making their way to the nearest café where they ordered a pot of tea and sat down to a feast. As Toughie was eating his share of the sausage, he noticed a little girl standing outside, looking in the window.

Gladys was so very hungry that she couldn't help but stare at the boys as they ate. Bert and Tonnie had been drinking heavily all during the previous day and evening and hadn't bothered to feed her or give her money for food. Every time Toughie took a bite and swallowed, she would swallow too.

He couldn't help but smile. Holding a piece of his sausage up, he offered it to her. When she nodded her head enthusiastically, he motioned for her to come and get it. Seeing how she devoured it, he knew that she hadn't eaten for a while and generously gave her the rest of his share. He didn't see her again for two days, until she showed up with a bundle of fresh buns for him and his friends.

There were times, albeit very few, when Bert and Tonnie were sober and feeling guilty for neglecting Gladys, that they would give her a few pence if they had it to spare. Since she always shared it with Toughie and his friends, he began to look out for her and taught her how to survive on the street. Gladys thought he was the most wonderful person she had ever met, with coal-black eyes framed by thick, long eyelashes. And not only could he count, but read as well. She adored him.

Having friends made life for the orphans who lived in the ghetto a little easier, but they still had to struggle just to stay alive, and there were many days when they went hungry. The filth and lack of nutrition caused a lot of them to become very ill. Gladys and Toughie were two of the most fortunate, in that they had a roof over their heads. Some of their friends, especially the youngest ones, suffered with open sores, weak lungs, and nameless other ailments. Many died during the cold nights. Often the friends would take turns guarding the body until the wagon came and took it away.

Tragedy was taken for granted, and they seldom shed tears. Like little soldiers, they accepted their fate, and seldom complained.

One day, Toughie and Gladys were together in Scott's butcher shop, hoping the butcher would take pity on them and spare a sausage or two. Jude, the butcher's son, was filling a jar with pickled cucumbers when the jar slipped from his wet hands, fell to the floor, and broke into pieces. Before anyone realized what was happening, Toughie and Gladys scooped up as many of the pickles as they could carry from the rough wooden floor and ran out the door.

Once out of sight of the butcher shop, they stopped to enjoy their loot. Suddenly, Toughie, noticing that the brine dripping down Gladys's chin was red instead of yellow said, "What in bloody hell are you eating?" Gladys looked down at her hand and became mesmerized by the bright red blood that was oozing from a deep gash in her palm and running down her wrist.

"Bloody hell! We have to get you to Missus Tweedhope's fast." Toughie declared. Then he took a dirty rag out of his pocket and wrapped it around her hand. "Here, close your fist tight on this until we get there."

Sally heard the boy calling, "Missus Tweedhope! Missus Tweedhope!" and had the door open, waiting for them when they arrived. After she examined Gladys's hand to see if there was any glass in the cut, she cleaned it with soap and water before applying a bandage. The cut was rather large, and she would have liked to see it stitched together, but the only doctor in the neighbourhood was a drunken sot who had been a disgrace to his profession and wasn't allowed to practice anywhere but Old Nichol, where, it was thought, he caused more deaths than he prevented.

"I'm afraid you shall have quite a scar there when that heals, my dear," she said to Gladys. To her surprise, the girl seemed more pleased than upset. Most of the children Gladys knew boasted about their scars as though they were medals. Now she would have one to boast about too. If she only knew the trouble that scar would bring to her in years to come, she might have felt differently.

Sally was very impressed with both children; Toughie for his astuteness in getting the girl to her so quickly, and the poor little girl for being so brave. It was only when Gladys said her name that Sally realized she was the beautiful little baby she had helped deliver and saved on that rainy night six years earlier. She couldn't help think that it must be fate that had brought them together again. The fact that the little twin daughter she had lost was also named Gladys made her assumption that much more poignant.

Sally had heard gossip about the Tunners' alcohol addiction and should have been keeping an eye out for the girl, but didn't want to interfere, but now she realized that if she didn't help the girl, no one would. With renewed interest, she looked Gladys over more carefully. Like every other child in the ghetto, she was far too thin, but she wasn't as filthy as most of the children. Sally recalled Bert's promise to try to be a good mother and wondered if perhaps the rumours were exaggerated, and the poor woman was trying to keep her word.

The intense way that Mrs Tweedhope was looking at her made Gladys uneasy, but she didn't offer to leave. Never had she seen such a wonderful room, and she wanted to remember every little detail. Toughie too, seemed impressed. Although the Tweedhope's only had the one room, it was a large one. The entire floor was scrubbed spotless, and an assortment of well worn, but clean, floral rugs added warmth to the worn wood.

The room's only window had been cleaned and polished so well that if it wasn't for a large taped crack, Gladys would have thought it was open. Clean white curtains with appliquéd yellow daisies were pulled back on both sides of the window and tied with a ribbon. A large oval table was covered by a damask table cloth with exotic designs made with threads of gold and red. The holes in the table cloth were so cleverly darned that it was difficult to see them. In the middle of the table was a beautiful cut-glass swan, and it sat in such a position that Gladys didn't notice one of its wings was missing.

The bed was covered with a clean comforter and looked so inviting that Gladys wanted to crawl under the covers and go to sleep. Even the bricks around the fireplace were scrubbed clean. Never had Gladys been in such a dirt free room, and it smelled nicer than anywhere else in the neighbourhood. She gulped the fresh air in.

Meanwhile, thoughts of how she could help the girl were racing through Sally's mind. She appeared to be a bright child, but Sally knew that if she didn't have some guidance soon, Gladys, like all the other unfortunate children in Old Nichol, would lose the desire to learn. She didn't intend to allow that to happen, and unable to control her emotions, she threw her arms around the child, giving her a squeeze.

Gladys had no idea what was happening. She almost kicked the lady in the shins and bolted for the door. One thing Bert and Tonnie had drilled into her was that she should never allow grownups to touch her, but this lady had been so gentle when she bandaged her hand that she didn't know what to think. She didn't know what she was supposed to do, so she just stood perfectly still.

Sally sensed her uneasiness and apologized, "Oh, I didn't mean to startle you, my dear. You see, I once had a little girl whose name was Gladys. I loved her very dearly, and you remind me of her."

"Where'd she go?" Gladys blurted out.

"She became very ill and she died."

"I'm sorry, missus, but we 'as to go 'ome now," Gladys answered, but before she and Toughie could make their exit, Sally's husband, Bob, arrived. He put them at ease with a big smile when Sally introduced them.

Although Sally had hoped to make the boiled meat and potatoes she was cooking last for two nights, she invited the children to stay for dinner. Toughie shook his head in refusal as he looked down at My Dog, who was lying at his feet, but he changed his mind when Sally assured him that she would be able to spare a little gravy and bread for his dog as well.

Not wanting to hurt the boy's feelings, but noticing how filthy his hands were, Bob smiled and said, "Now, how about if us men nab a little of that hot water Sally has boilin' fer tea, and take it outside to wash our hands? A man gets his paws pretty dirty after a day's work, right?" Toughie had never been talked to like a grown up before and was flattered beyond belief. He grinned and nodded his head enthusiastically. When Sally handed Gladys the cutlery and asked her to put it on the table, Gladys didn't know what to do. "What is the trouble, dear?" Sally asked when she saw the perplexed look on the young girl's face.

"What about that pretty cloth?"

"Why that is just an old table cloth. Don't worry, we eat there all the time."

Gladys was amazed. She had never eaten at a table with a cloth on it before, but the whole idea of eating in a home as fine as this one was beginning to worry her. What if she or Toughie were to spill something? She put the cutlery on the table then announced, "We'd better go, missus. Ma'll be looking for me."

"Oh, I think she will understand when you tell her what happened, and after that ordeal you just went through, I think both you and Toughie must be very hungry."

The delicious aroma coming from the stove was more than

Gladys could bear, and for the first time, she rewarded Sally with a smile.

There were only three chairs, but Bob insisted on sitting on a box covered with a heavy wool cloth that was used as a bedside table. Once they were seated, Sally filled each plate with some meat, potatoes, and cabbage that had all been cooked in the same pot. After she took the vegetables and meat out of the pot, she thickened the juice with flour to make gravy, which she put on the table in a gravy boat, so they could help themselves.

Toughie and Gladys watched every move their hosts made so as to mimic them. Toughie hadn't forgotten how to use a fork, but he had a little difficulty using a fork and knife together and felt very embarrassed when he tried to cut a piece of meat, and it slithered off his plate and onto the floor. Before he could retrieve it, My Dog had gulped it down. Sally and Bob did their best to let on they hadn't seen what happened, and after a few minutes Sally offered him another piece of meat, but Toughie, afraid he would make the same mistake, refused.

Sally had made enough corn starch pudding for her and Bob, but she managed to divide it up between the four of them. Toughie had never tasted pudding before, and he enjoyed it so much he had his finished before Sally had begun eating hers. "I'm much too full to eat my dessert," she said. "Would you care for it, Toughie?" This time he didn't say no.

As soon as they were out of sight of the Tweedhopes, Gladys threw her arms in the air and squealed with delight. "Oh, Toughie, wasn't that wonderful! I'm so glad I cut my 'and." Then she danced around him chattering away about all the wonderful things they had seen. She didn't notice his lack of enthusiasm until he gave her a small push aside, mumbling something about having to get back to the barn.

Gladys, not understanding what was wrong, ran after him and grabbed hold of his sleeve. "Hi! Wait for me."

Once more he pushed her aside then snapped, "You had better go home now."

"Didn't you like them?"

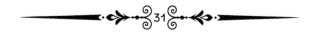

"No! An' I shall not be going there again. You can go by yourself!"

Gladys didn't know what she had done to make Toughie speak to her so crossly, but she thought it must have been something terribly bad, so she hung her head and mumbled an apology.

Toughie's coldness toward her melted like ice in an oven. "Here now, don't go pouting, I shall still take you there next week, but I shan't go in."

"Why are you mad at me, Toughie? Did I do something bad?"

"I'm not mad at you, Gladdy. It's just them."

"What did they do?"

"They think I can't even eat properly. I know they do. Who needs a knife and fork anyway? I've managed just fine with my fingers, and I've not starved yet."

"But she was just being nice, and she gave you 'er pudding. It's not their fault they aren't like us. I 'eard Missus Prescott telling Missus Murray that Sally warn't even born 'ere so 'ow can you blame 'er for being the way she is? And you even talk just like 'er, cause your folks weren't born 'ere either."

"Aw, I guess you're right, and that was the best food I ever ate. But I won't eat there again until I learn to use a knife like they do."

"I'll teach you, Toughie! We got knives at 'ome, and when ma and pa aren't there, we'll practice." Toughie agreed, so the next day they found some stale bread and began lessons.

Chapter Three

A few days after Gladys cut her hand, she awoke in the morning to find her mother standing over her with her hands on her hips and a scowl on her face. "What's all this, ay? When was you going to tell me about this 'ere?" she snapped as she took hold of Gladys bandaged hand.

"It's just a cut, Mama. It 'appened two days ago, and Missus Tweedhope bandaged it for me."

"Why did you go runnin' to 'er? Ain't I your ma?"

"You and Pa were away with the cart, so Toughie took me to 'er."

Bert longed to say something derogatory about Sally, but realizing that it shouldn't have taken three days to notice the bandage, all she said was, "Well this 'ere don't look very clean to me. I woulda thought her ladyship woulda put a clean rag on it." Then, in a softer tone, she added, "Set up to the table, and I'll put a clean one on."

Gladys was amazed at how gently her mother wrapped her hand with a fairly clean piece of cloth. It wasn't as neat a bandage as

Sally had done, but she was so pleased that her mother cared enough to do it that she didn't mind.

Toughie and Gladys had promised to return to Sally's in a week's time, so she could apply more salve to Gladys's injury. Now that Toughie had mastered the proper use of a knife and fork, he was as anxious to visit the Tweedhopes as Gladys.

They arrived just before noon one day and were happy when Sally seemed genuinely pleased to see them. Sally was relieved to see that Gladys's wound was healing nicely, which was remarkable considering the bandage Bert had applied was so loose it did little to keep out the dirt. She had been right though; the injury would certainly leave an ugly scar.

Although they were delighted to be invited to stay for tea and a sandwich, Toughie would have much rather been invited for a meal in order to show off his new cutlery skills. When they finished their tea, Sally asked them to stay a little longer. Then she opened the floral-carved, wooden trunk that they had both admired on their first visit and took out a big book in a dark blue cover with gold lettering.

"Oh!" Toughie exclaimed. "We had a book just like that. Mother used to read it to me before she . . ."

Sally had a good idea what he was going to say and hoping to spare his feelings, asked, "Was there one story you enjoyed more than the others, Toughie?"

"Well, I really liked them all, but I guess the one with Hansel and Gretel was my favourite."

"That is one of my favourites, too. Do you know the story, Gladys?"

"No, mum. Was they from 'ere abouts?"

"No, Gladys. You see, Hansel and Gretel are not real. They are make-believe children. Jacob and Wilhelm Grimm, two brothers who live in Germany, wrote the story, and it is all about two young people about your ages, their parents, and a wicked, wicked witch who lived deep in the forest."

"What's a forest?" Gladys asked.

"Well, do you know what a tree is?"

Gladys nodded her head. "I see them every time I go outside

with Da on the cart."

"Well, a forest is made up of thousands of trees all growing close to each other. Sometimes it can be very dark and scary, but when the sun filters down through the branches and lights up patches of all the pretty mosses, it is like walking on a magical carpet in fairyland. You can just imagine seeing little fairies and wood nymphs running and hiding behind mushrooms or ferns, and you have to be careful not to stand on them." Gladys wasn't quite sure if she was imagining the same thing Sally was describing, but it was fun.

"Now, this is the first book the brothers have ever published," Sally continued, "and there are many more wonderful stories in it. There is one about a girl named Cinderella, and one about a funny little man named Rumpelstiltskin. I know you would especially enjoy the one about a girl named Snow White. Would you like me to read them to you sometime, Gladys?"

"Oh yes, mum, I ain't never 'ad anything read to me before!"

"Well then, I have an idea. How would it be if you two were to visit me every afternoon, and we shall have story time?" When they both nodded their heads enthusiastically, she added, "I may also be able to teach you how to read it yourself. What do you think about that?"

"I can read already! I know lots of words," Toughie boasted.

"That is wonderful, Toughie, then you can help me teach Gladys."

Every morning after she returned from pushing the cart with her father, Gladys would spend the afternoon visiting Sally, but she never told her parents, knowing her mother would forbid it. They were always in such a hurry to get to the pubs that they seldom took the time to wonder where she went.

Before Sally began reading to her, Gladys could only imagine what it would be like to have all the food she could eat and parents sober enough to provide it. Now the wonderful stories Sally read to her filled her head with images of another world—a world of magic and adventure. She and Toughie sometimes argued about what it would be like to live on the "Outside." She was convinced it would be wonderful, but Toughie, who was a little older and wiser, knew that if you didn't have a job, life in other parts of London could be almost as bad as it was in Old Nichol. He also realized that there would be no one out there who cared about you, like Mr O, Sally, and Bob. He told Gladys that if she had lived in the "hell" he and his parents lived in, she would be content to stay where she was.

Sally was amazed at how quickly Gladys and Toughie learned to read and write. Toughie wasn't as keen about spending time indoors as Gladys. He preferred to help Bob out in the junk yard. Sally and Gladys soon became very fond of one another. Sally was the most intelligent person Gladys had ever known, and she never seemed to tire of all the questions Gladys asked her. Sally was amazed at the astuteness of the questions. The girl was particularly curious about life outside Old Nichol and what it was like to go to school. Sally explained that education was one of the most rewarding things a person could have, and that if she had enough money, she would send Gladys to a school just for young ladies. Gladys also wanted to know why Sally only drank water if it was boiled or made into tea.

"I do drink plain rainwater sometimes," Sally answered, "but the water we get from the pump smells so terribly foul, it makes me bilious. If I boil it, it has a far less repugnant odour, and if I add a little tea, it tastes even better. I know you won't understand this, but my father told me that he had read a paper written by a man named Agostino Bassi, a scientist. Mr Bassi had discovered that some common diseases are caused by living organisms, or what you might call bugs. He said that these bugs are so very small no one can see them. You know, I think someday someone is going to discover that there are bugs we can't see in our water, and that may be why it smells and tastes so terrible."

A few days later, Gladys told Bert and Tonnie that Sally knew a "scientific" man who said that there are bugs everywhere, and they are so small no one can see them. Bert, standing with her hands on her hips and her chin thrust forward gave a sarcastic laugh, then added, "If 'e can't see them, 'ow's 'e know they's there?" When Gladys had no answer, Bert looked at Tonnie and said, "See, I told you that Sally was crazy in the 'ead, didn't I?"

Tonnie, on his way out the door, stopped and offered, "Might be they's that small where 'e lives, Gladdy love, but down 'ere, they's as big as elephants!"

Gladys and Tonnie broke out laughing. For some reason even she couldn't explain, Bert took their laughter as a personal affront and tried her best to think of a reply. Failing to come up with one, she vented her frustration with a sharp slap to Gladys's head.

"I don't like you spendin' your time with that lazy cow!" she shouted, "She don't ever get 'er 'ands dirty, she don't. And if she thinks she's better'n your ma and da 'cause she's educated, she's balmier than that idiot kid of the O'Brian's."

Gladys, unable to control herself, shouted back, "Johnnie O'Brian can't talk plain cause 'e can't 'ear, and 'e's still a lot smarter than you!"

This outburst brought on another blow to Gladys's head, knocking her to the floor. Bert was just about to add a kick when Tonnie grabbed her, scolding, "'Old on there now. That's enough." He helped Gladys to her feet then reached into his pocket and gave her sixpence. "'Ere you goes, Gladdy luv, go fetch yourself a sweet, and take that there jug with you and bring us back some ale while you're at it."

After she left, Tonnie said, "You know, Bert luv, she wouldn't a sassed you if you didn't 'it 'er."

Surprisingly, Bert didn't argue. "Damn me, anyways, Tonnie! I know it ain't 'er fault; it's all that garbage she's being told by that crazy Sally woman. I don't know what right she 'as meddling with our little girl. God, I 'opes she comes back soon; I don't 'alf need a drink."

Proper diction was another thing Sally tried to teach Gladys, by making up sayings. Gladys enjoyed practicing them and would go about in the daytime singing, "Take the haitch from your ear and put it over here," or "An haitch on 'ers and one on 'is—is the proper way to say hers and his." Then, one day, without thinking, she made the mistake of correcting her mother, "It's not ''ere,' Ma, it's, 'here.'"

Bert slapped her across the face and added a warning, "Don't you ever, ever, tell me 'ow to talk. It's that stuck-up cow that's putting these fancy idears in your 'ead. Well, Miss Knows-it-all, you can talks anyways you likes, but that ain't going to make you any better than your da or me."

The next day Gladys was helping her father unload the cart when her mother called out, "Gladdy, I wants you 'ere for a minute."

Gladys, wondering what she had done wrong, approached her mother with trepidation. "What do you want, Ma?"

"Gladdy, I don't mind if you learns 'ow to talk proper, but I 'opes you don't get your 'eart broke with any fancy ideas. Fancy talkin's not going to do you any good where you lives, and it's 'ere you'll be living for the rest of your days."

Gladys was so stunned by Bert's atypical concern that she didn't know how to respond. Bert saved her the trouble, "Well, don't just stand there with your gob 'angin' open; get on back, and 'elp your da."

Chapter Four

Bert and Tonnie spent most of their days collecting and sorting junk and their nights drinking in the pubs. Except for the mornings when they ate their porridge together, Gladys hardly saw them, but Toughie and Sally kept her from being lonely.

She was a pretty child with large hazel eyes, a sunny disposition, and a generous mouth that showed off a perfectly even set of white teeth when she smiled, an unusual feature in the slum. Her mother could claim credit for that since she taught Gladys how to use wood ash to clean them. She would have had a lovely full head of curly, chestnut-coloured hair if her mother didn't hack away at it every few months with the excuse that now her head wasn't such an attractive home for nits.

As she grew older, Gladys became more acquainted with many of her neighbours, people of all races and occupations. The streets were crowded and noisy with countless shops, stalls, and even barns that housed all types of fowl and animals. This would have made a cheery and colourful combination if it wasn't for the fusion of vermin-infested rubbish, open sewers, and the unwashed and half-starved residents who lived there. The odours that emanated from all the rot and decay that lay about were so disgusting that only a person born in the Rookery could ignore them.

Gladys was especially fond of the O'Brian family—the same family that allowed Toughie to live in their barn. The O'Brians lived in a two-storied building that was so in need of repairs that Mr O, as Gladys called him, used the ground floor as a stable where he kept his cart and animals. He removed enough bricks from the back and front of the building so that he could drive his horse and wagon right through from the street to the alley.

The stable doors were fashioned out of odd pieces of scrap wood. An open stairway supplied an entrance from the barn to the second floor where the O'Brians slept and ate, and the heat from the animals added much needed warmth in the winter.

The pig pen was divided into two parts: one half housed the old boar, and the other a very large and skinny sow whose litters usually numbered ten to fifteen. Sometimes Mr O would pick up one of the piglets and allow Gladys to cuddle it, but he didn't allow any of the children inside either pen.

"That old boar's so blind he'd mistake you for a bucket o' slops an' there'd be nothing left of you but your noses. And you know why he wouldn't eat them?" he would habitually ask.

They all knew the answer, but were polite enough to ask, "No, Da, why?"

"'Cause they's full o' snot, that's why!" And then he would laugh even harder and louder than the little ones.

Knickers, the O'Brian's horse, was old and sway-backed, but Mr O still used him to haul manure. There were nine O'Brian children with ages ranging one to twenty. Gladys heard that there was an O'Brian born every year for the last twenty-one years and that only nine had survived, which, according to most families living in Old Nichol, was very good odds. Mrs O was a plump lady and showed no difference in her profile when she was with child or without. She was unique amongst her compatriots in that her cheeks were always rosy. She often wore a baby tied around her middle while she went about her daily chores.

Mr O's features, from his head to his toes, were long and bony, and his temperament as complacent as that of his patient old horse. All the O'Brian children had to work as soon as they were old enough to follow orders, and Gladys often lent a hand. She loved brushing old Knickers and putting her face to his neck to inhale his unique and pleasant odour. There were times when Mr O would lift her and one or two of his smallest children up on top of the animal's back and let them have a short ride when he was hauling manure nearby. Three little ones could fit very snugly in the sway of Knickers's back, and the gentle old nag didn't seem to mind.

Never having known any other kind of life, Gladys was accustomed to the scourges of bug bites, head lice, and hunger, but she was far more fortunate than the rest of the children in Old Nichol since she slept by herself, albeit on a worn out divan. Most families were forced to live in a crowded, one-room flat and had to sleep side by side on the floor with nothing but pallets made out of straw for mattresses. Having once spent a night with a friend, Gladys was privy to more sex education than she desired, and even though she often received a slap or two from her mother when Bert came home drunk, she didn't want to ever spend another night away from home.

Bert and Tonnie were not the best parents, but to their credit, Gladys wasn't put to work as young as most slum children. She was nine when she began pulling the cart alongside her father while her mother looked after the yard. It was hard work, but she enjoyed it, except when they went up and down the streets on the outskirts of their neighbourhood. It wasn't the ladies with their fur-trimmed cloaks and their fancy bonnets who crossed over to the other side whenever they saw the cart approaching that she minded; it was the look of pity on the faces of those who didn't. "Someday I'm going to be a proper lady, Da, and when I am, I'll always be kind to those who aren't. Not like those snotty cows out there with their noses stuck up in the air."

"Right you are, Gladdy; you are a good girl, you are!"

"Would you like to get out of Old Nichol, Da?"

"Can't say I would, Gladdy. We don't 'ave to answer to nobody 'ere. If I 'ad to live out there, I'd be spending 'af my time saying 'No, sir. Yes, sir. Can I kiss your arse, sir?' An' I've 'eard that there's just as many what's starving out there as there is in 'ere."

There were a few times when her father was sober that Gladys had a glimpse of the decent man he once was. They would laugh and joke as they pulled the cart along. One of their standing jokes was, "What are we going to do, Dad?"

Tonnie would grin, and answer, "Don't call me a Doo-dad."

After Gladys began working, she didn't have as much time to visit with Sally as she would have liked, but when she did, she continued with her lessons. Toughie had begun helping Bob push his cart to Warehouse Corner and back, which meant competing against Gladys and her father for the most advantageous parking spot. However, Gladys was having more and more trouble waking her father in the mornings, so they seldom arrived at the corner until most of the junk was gone. Toughie felt bad that he wasn't helping them, but he felt obligated to Bob for supplying him with food that he often shared with Gladys.

Now that Toughie was helping him, Bob made enough profit to give the lad a selection of second hand clothes after convincing the boy it was time to change his attire. The change came none too soon since the lad had grown so tall that his overcoat no longer came down past his knees. Sally had a harder time talking him into bathing and allowing her to cut his hair in order to comb out the knots and tangles.

The change in Toughie's appearance was so amazing that at first Gladys didn't recognize him. His black, curly hair was cut so short that Gladys was surprised to see that he actually had ears—and very nice ones too. He wore a shirt tucked into a patched, but clean, pair of woollen britches and a man's suit coat with the sleeves turned

up. He wore a pair of boots that, although well-worn, fit him well. His skin had been scrubbed clean and had the warm hue of polished mahogany. Gladys had never seen such a handsome creature before and mentally pledged him her troth.

By the time Gladys was eleven, she was adept at reading and writing, and her grammar had improved to such an extent that she sounded as out of place in Old Nichol as Sally. One afternoon when she came to visit, she was shocked to find both Sally and Bob packing up their belongings. When they told her they were moving out of Old Nichol, she was devastated.

Sally explained that her aunt's husband had passed away, and now, finally able to make amends, her aunt had offered to share her house with them. During the last ten months Sally's health had been on the decline, and Bob had warned Gladys that they might lose her before long. Even though Gladys understood that the move was for the best, she couldn't help but cry. Sally couldn't hold back her tears either. She loved Gladys as though she were her own, but she knew she didn't have long to live if she remained in Old Nichol.

They held each other until they stopped crying; then Sally pinned a little cameo onto Gladys's bodice, and said, "Gladys darling, I want you to always remember that I love you, even if we are apart. My father gave me this little shell cameo when I was eleven, the same age you are now, and it is the only piece of jewellery that I refused to sell. I want you to have it as a keepsake."

Gladys was overwhelmed. She had never owned anything so lovely. And what made the gift even more memorable was the resemblance of the lady in the cameo to Sally. "I will treasure it forever," she promised and hugged her dearest friend so tightly that Sally had to push her away in order to get her breath. Gladys was overwhelmed with grief, and their tearful goodbye counted as one of the most heart-wrenching acts of her life.

When Gladys arrived home, she was afraid to wear the broach, knowing that her mother would take it and sell it for booze money.

So she wrapped it in a rag, climbed up on a ladder, and hid it on top of a timber in the junk yard. Toughie was also very sad to see Bob and Sally leave, but his sorrow was alleviated by Bob's generosity. Bob, knowing that he would gain little by selling his junk yard, had seen the only legal official in Old Nichol, and signed it over to Toughie.

As a rule, puberty was late in coming to the children in the slums due to undernourishment, but by the time Gladys was twelve, she could no longer hide her femininity. Men began making lewd remarks when she walked by, and one of the store owners she knew groped her one day, offering her some food if she would come into the back of the shop with him. She refused and was so upset over the incident that she longed to talk to someone about it. Her parents had become so reliant on liquor that she hardly saw them, and now that Sally was gone, she decided to confide in Toughie. Reading fairy tales had enhanced Gladys's imagination, so when she told Toughie about the incident, she thought he would react like a brave, bold knight, and smite the blighter to defend her honour.

However, the brave knight merely shrugged his shoulders, and remarked, "I can hardly blame him."

It wasn't what she expected, or wanted, to hear. She couldn't have felt more betrayed if he had slapped her face. Stammering, she asked, "How can you be so mean? I thought you liked me!"

"I do like you, Gladdy; you know that. In fact, I love you."

"Then how could you not be angry at anyone who did that to me?"

"Gladdy, don't you know how beautiful you are? All the men want to kiss you—and do it to you."

She knew what he meant, and it gave her an unusual feeling of power. "Do you want to do it to me too, Toughie?"

Toughie's face turned red, and he hung his head and confessed. "Every bloody time I see you!"

There were times when she had noticed him looking at her

in a funny way, and now she realized that it was the same look her father often gave her mother before they became so addicted. She smiled, and said, "I'll let you, Toughie, but no one else."

Toughie, being four years older than Gladys, was beginning to have manly needs, but he knew that when one bedded a girl, she would indubitably have a baby. Therefore, he did his best to ignore his desires, and replied, "Maybe in a year or two, Gladdy, if you still want me. By then I'll have finished the shed I'm building for me and My Dog in the junk yard, and we'll have a place to live. I shan't take a wife to live in O'Brian's barn."

The thought of having a house of their own was more than Gladys could wish for. She threw her arms around him and kissed him on the mouth. It was their first kiss and, although Toughie would have liked more, he pushed her away, before giving her a stern lecture about the dangers of being too friendly with men.

After Toughie had inherited Bob's junk yard, he had been kept so busy collecting junk that he had little time to find material to build his shed and even less time to spend with Gladys. In the meantime, Bert and Tonnie's addiction had progressed to the point where they could barely look after their business. Every penny they earned went to buy booze. They would have gone without eating if it wasn't for Gladys's begging and stealing in order to put food on the table. Gladys could hardly wait until Toughie had their shed built. When she turned twelve, and he still hadn't been able to find enough material to put a roof over their head, despondency overtook her.

For the first time since she was a little girl, her mother began to take note of Gladys's whereabouts, not out of affection, but to serve her own self-interest. Years of alcoholism had taken its toll on both Bert's beauty and her voice, and she could no longer earn money singing in the pubs. Subsequently, she began to scheme how best to use Gladys's beauty to her own advantage. She insisted Gladys take occasional baths in an old, battered galvanized tub they seldom used, and she encouraged her to keep her hair clean and lice-free. Sally had also taught Gladys on the importance of cleanliness, so Bert met with little resistance.

One day, when Gladys was still twelve, Bert surprised Gladys with a shocking proposition. "There's this 'ere gentleman what wants to 'ave 'is way with you, Gladdy luv, and 'e'll give us thirty quid for just a few minutes of your time. If we was to give our business to Toughie, and then take the money you gets to build another room on 'is shed, we'd 'ave no rent to pay and Toughie'd 'ave twice the business."

Gladys was growing tired of waiting for Toughie to build a place for them to live, and although she looked sceptical, she didn't turn away, so Bert continued, "It's just one time, luv, an' it only takes a few minutes. Then we'll be set for life. Just think how 'appy Toughie'd be to 'ave our junk alongside is. An' after the gentleman leaves, we can go and gets those pork pies you and your da loves."

"But what would Toughie say?"

"'E never needs to know."

Gladys knew he wouldn't agree, but how many more years would she have to wait before he could afford to build their home? How was she going to continue to look after her parents if she couldn't keep the junk yard going? Perhaps this would solve all their problems. She convinced herself that it wouldn't hurt if she were to make up a small fib to tell Toughie about how she got the money. She made up her mind to do it, but told her mother how terribly afraid she was.

Bert assured her, "It won't 'urt more than a mosquito bite—and if you closes your eyes, it'll be over before you knows it."

Late the next evening, Bert came home with a tall man wearing a long, black cloak with a large collar pulled up to hide his identity. Anxious to get back to the pub and spend some of the money the man had given her, Bert wasted no time with introductions. She gave Gladys a smile and a wink then quickly left. As soon as they were alone, the man removed his cloak and hat then turned to face Gladys before sitting down. Gladys had begun shaking as soon as her mother brought the man into the room, but when she saw the stranger's face, she gasped with fear.

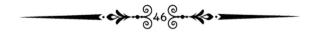

It was Mr Gaylord, their landlord. He was the most repulsive-looking creature she had ever met. He had sagging jowls, large wet lips that allowed slobber to dribble down his chin, and a fat belly that hung down almost to his knees. She had always been sickened with the way he ogled her whenever he came to collect the rent, and she knew she would rather die than let him touch her. Her eyes began scanning the room for a way out.

Gaylord could sense his prey was ready to bolt, and he positioned his chair so that his back was to the bedroom door in order to block her path to both exits. "Now, now, my little mouse, don't be frightened. If you are a good little girlie, I shall be very gentle with you, and we shall spend a pleasant night together, but if you are naughty—well, I shan't go into that, my dear. Suffice to say that I paid well for a night with you, and I intend to make good use of it, so I would recommend that you treat me with respect."

When Gaylord said he paid for an entire night's pleasure, Gladys knew her mother had betrayed her, and there would be no money for Toughie or her. Determined to avoid being raped, she looked frantically around the room for a suitable weapon while feigning interest in the landlord's attempts to seduce her with false promises. She spotted the only large knife they owned. Unfortunately, it was also in Gaylord's sight causing her to abandon that idea. She thought of making a run for it, but gauging the brute's strength by his enormity, she knew she had little chance to reach a door before he could grab her. Finding a weapon would be her only chance of freedom, but there was nothing she could see that would do.

She was ready to run when he moved his bulk slightly, and she spied the big, grease-filled cast-iron skillet sitting on the stove behind him. Quickly, she devised a plan. Smiling invitingly at the landlord, who licked his fat lips in expectation, she walked closer and closer to him. When he reached out and grabbed her arm, she sat down on his knee. Suppressing a scream, she gave him a teasing smile and asked if he would like her to remove her frock.

"Oh, yes, yes indeed," he hissed.

"First let me make you a little more comfortable," she said as she rose and walked behind him. She began taking off his cravat and undoing his vest. He was just about to protest when she slid her hands down inside his shirt, and swallowing the sour bile that rose in her throat, she ran her hands over his chest. The obese landlord was moaning with such desire that Gladys knew she had to act fast or it would be too late. Suddenly she pulled her hand from his body, stepping back as she turned, grabbing hold of the skillet's handle and swinging the grease-filled weapon with all her might.

The skillet hit the side of Gaylord's head with a heavy, wet-sounding thud, knocking him off the chair and onto the floor. The blow jarred Gladys's arms so painfully she lost her hold on the skillet, and it landed upside down on the top of the culprit's bald head. The mixture of dirty brown grease and bright red blood oozed from under the pan, over his head and onto the floor.

At first, Gladys was in shock and could do nothing but stare down at the bizarre scene with amazement. Then, as she regained her senses, the bile she had stifled earlier returned, and without warning, vomit spewed out of her mouth on top of the skillet and the victim.

Her legs were shaking so much that she was forced to sit down for a few seconds as she managed to collect her thoughts. She knew she had to do something and do it before her parents returned. Her thoughts flew to Toughie, but she knew he would be sent to prison too if they were caught, and not wanting to cause him trouble, she decided she would make a run for it by herself.

In spite of her fears, Gladys managed to plan her escape with the shrewdness of a thief. She went into the junk yard and donned a ladies' fur-trimmed cloak and bonnet that her father had collected from Warehouse Corner the week before and the only pair of ladies boots she could find. Returning to the kitchen, she forced herself to look down at the landlord and was relieved to see that he was still unconscious—or dead. She didn't know which, but it no longer mattered.

Taking a soft leather purse from his cloak, she threw a handful of the bills on the table, uttering, "There you are, Ma. That's enough for a whole year of bloody pork pies, and I hope you choke on them."

She was rushing up the alley, trying not to tread in any of the filth in the street, when two young ruffians who were urinating against a wall, caught sight of her. Although it was a moonless night, they could see that the lady approaching was well dressed. "Hi, Rob, I bets she's got a shilling or two for us."

Gladys tried to run past them, but they were too quick. Pushing her against a building, one of the boys said, "Now let's just see what ya got in your 'and."

Afraid she would be found out if she called for help, she tried her best to hold on to the purse, but one of the boys twisted her arm as the other snatched it from her grasp.

"Ha! I got it Rob!" The words were hardly out of the boy's mouth when he was struck over the head and the purse dropped to the ground. Both boys took off on the run when they saw their attacker was a man.

Mr O had been working late shovelling pig manure out of his barn when he saw the boys attack the lady, and he ran to the rescue armed with his shovel. He picked up the purse, but when he handed it to the lady, he realized that she was shaking with fright.

"Now, now, me lady, don't you go a fretting. Sure and I've got your purse right here." As he held the purse out to her, he bent down to see her face. "Jaysus! Gladys! What the devil are you up to?"

Gladys's knees began to buckle, and she threw her arms around Mr O's waist for support. The Irishman held the shaking girl tight as he tried to calm her down.

"Shush, shush now, me girl. Shush now!"

When Gladys regained her composure, Mr O suggested they go into his house so his wife could help sort it out, but Gladys began crying again and pleaded with him to let her go on her way. He was adamant in his refusal, so she had no choice but to make a full confession. When she was finished her story, Mr O didn't answer for a moment, and her hopes for a rapid escape were diminishing. Shocked and disgusted with the Tunners' heartless actions, he felt no sympathy for them. He also knew that Gladys would be incarcerated if found out.

"Well, Gladdy, I agree you have to leave Old Nichol. Have you enough money in that purse to get you anywheres? I've only got a few shillings, and that wouldn't get you far." When Gladys showed him the contents of the purse, he realized her chances were much brighter. "But I'll not be letting you start out on your own. I've driven many a wagonload o' manure past a coach-house not far from here, an' I'll walk with you that far at least."

As they were walking, Mr O wished he had some sagacious advice to help the poor girl in the days ahead, but he had no idea what to say. Finally, he offered, "I think you'll be fine, me girl, as long as you says your prayers every night." Then he couldn't help but think to himself, *Maybe it'll do her more good than it's ever done us.*

It took them a half hour's walk, and they didn't arrive at the coach-house until midnight.

Gladys had a hard time keeping up with Mr O's long strides because the boots she was wearing were two sizes too large. Although the inn where the coach station was located was closed, there was a waiting room adjoined to the building, and a schedule was tacked to the door.

"There's one leaving for somewhere called Dover at four in the morning. That's not long, Mr O, so don't you worry about me; I can wait alone. You had better go home, or Mrs O will be worried."

He was reluctant to leave, but he knew she was right. Giving her a hug, he promised to tell no one of her whereabouts. "An' don't you worry about that landlord feller. Sure an' if he's dead, your folks'll have him stripped down and be selling his togs in less than an hour. And if he's still alive, they'll do 'im in so as to avoid dealin' with the law."

Gladys pulled his head down and kissed him on the cheek. "I'll never forget you, Mr O."

Taking hold of one of her hands, he placed an old coin in it. She tried to protest but he insisted, "'Tis only a piece o' 'Gunmoney,' Gladdy. That's an Irish half crown. Old King James had a lot of them made, but they're not worth a twig now. This one, and one other I has, been in my family for a couple o' hundred years, an' I wants you to have it so you won't forget us."

With that, he turned and walked away. As she watched him disappear down the road, she realized that he was probably the last person from Old Nichol she would ever see. She didn't even try to stop her tears.

Chapter Five

The wait seemed endless as Gladys paced back and forth in front of the inn. The building, in total darkness, appeared devoid of life and offered little comfort. Intermittent clouds obstructed the moon's light and cast ominous shadows causing her to jump at every little sound. Then, just before four o'clock, she breathed a sigh of relief when an elderly gentleman carrying a lantern appeared from the back of the building and opened the door of the waiting room.

It was as cold inside the building as it was outside, but the light from the lantern the old man placed on a small desk seemed to add warmth. Gladys felt a little more relaxed as she sat down to rest on one of the benches. Surprised to find such a pretty young lady waiting outside by herself, the watchman couldn't curb his curiosity. As he busied himself with the lighting of a pot-bellied stove, he began asking questions. Gladys kept her head down and only answered with small nods and shrugs. After a time, he decided that the poor soul must be thick-headed and let her be.

Even with the growing warmth of the heater, she soon found

the wait almost unbearable. Every minute she expected someone to arrive, grab her by the scruff of her neck and haul her off to prison. She had almost decided that it might be far safer to escape on foot than risk waiting any longer, when she heard the coach approaching.

She hurried outside to watch it pull in, but as it drew nearer, she could see that instead of the coach, it was just a small chaise. Returning to the waiting room, she peered out the grease-coated window and watched as the driver hopped down from the seat. *Oh, no,* she thought, putting her hand over her mouth to stifle a moan of despair. The man was a constable.

She lost all hope and hung her head submissively, thinking the police must have caught Mr O and made him tell. Although she knew it was senseless, she kept her head down to hide her face and failed to notice that the constable wasn't alone. When she heard him enter the waiting room and say, "There you are," she looked up ready to beg for mercy. The relief she felt on discovering that his words were directed to an elderly lady and not at her was so physical as well as emotional that she couldn't stop her hands from shaking, and had to hide them inside her coat.

The constable put the lady's valise down on the floor and with a tone of affection said, "Thank you so much, Mother. I don't think Iris could have managed the baby and Simon without your help. You must be tired out."

"Don't you worry about me; I shall sleep all the way home. I usually do, you know. Now you had better be off down to the station. I shall be just fine," she replied. They embraced and he left. Gladys felt too emotionally drained to fully appreciate the reprieve. The stage coach arrived shortly after.

Two gentlemen who were already aboard were sitting across from one another, but when one of them realized that the two oncoming passengers were women, he thoughtfully gave up his seat and sat beside the other man. Gladys stared at the driver in shock when he told her the price of the fare then quickly tried to cover her surprise with a smile as he looked at her suspiciously and hesitated before taking her money. *I must contain my emotions from now on,* she thought, *no matter how costly things are.*

As she followed the elderly lady into the coach, she noted that the accepted greeting seemed to be a mere nod which suited her just fine. She had never been inside a coach before and found it far more luxurious than she had imagined. There was a sweet smelling essence that she couldn't identify, and it appeared to be coming from one of the gentlemen. For a second she didn't know why the odour disturbed her because it wasn't terribly unpleasant, but then she remembered that most of the men who came to Old Nichol to collect rent had smelled the same. It was said that they doused themselves in perfume before entering the slums to overpower the smell of the open sewers and garbage.

Gaylord was wearing a strong scent when he had arrived at her house the previous night, and although the gentleman sitting across from her emitted a far subtler essence, it still made her feel a bit ill. But not long after they left the station, she noticed another familiar odour. This one came from the leather upholstering that lined the coach, and it smelled enough like Knickers's old harness to make her surroundings seem less formidable. Her thoughts surged and as they left London, the joy she should have felt over her escape was overshadowed by the thought that she would never see her beloved Toughie again.

The constable's mother, true to her word, was soon nodding off. Both men seemed to be enjoying a nap as well since their heads hung down and swayed from side to side along with the motion of the coach. For two hours they rode in darkness and silence, except for the rhythmic clomping of the horses' hooves. Although she was exhausted, thoughts of her unknown destiny kept Gladys wide awake.

She had no idea what the place called "Dover" would be like, but hoped it was nothing like Old Nichol. Sally had said that all you needed to get along outside of Old Nichol were good manners and proper diction, but she could tell by observing the obvious confidence and refinement of the lady who was sleeping beside her, that her friend was mistaken.

Even in her sleep, the woman had her small gloved hands folded neatly on her lap and her ankles daintily crossed, as though posing for a portrait. Wearing no stockings, Gladys felt naked in comparison, and her gloveless hands felt as though they were as big and rough as Mr O's. Mile after mile, her feelings oscillated between trepidation, excitement, loneliness and depression. Then, as the morning dawned, she became so enchanted with the passing scenery that her fears and doubts were forgotten.

The sky became clearer and more blue the farther they travelled away from London, and the scenery exceedingly more beautiful. They passed mile after mile of lush green fields scattered with fat cows and shiny-coated horses, and all the pastures had tidy, clipped privet-hedges defining one from another. She saw one or two buildings that were so grand she thought they must belong to either the Queen or some other royalty. But the ones that looked the most inviting were the picturesque, little thatched-roofed cottages. Some had stone paths adorned with colourful flower borders leading to the door and resembled the pictures of the houses she had seen in the Grimm brothers' book.

The children she saw playing in the yards were all rosy-cheeked, and the dogs playing with them appeared far fatter and happier than the half-starved dogs in the ghetto, including My Dog, and she knew Toughie made sure he didn't starve. Thinking of Toughie and My Dog almost set her mood back on a glum road, but the passing countryside was so breathtaking that she couldn't be sad. She felt as though she were travelling through a surreal, but glorious, dream world. Never could she have imagined that such places existed, and she found herself thinking how fantastic it would be to grow up in such a place and how wonderful it would be if old Knickers could spend even one day in those green, grassy fields. She thought that he just might eat so much he would burst.

Around midday they came to a little hamlet with a scattering of small cottages. Stopping at an inn that also served as the station, they were allowed to stretch their legs, buy refreshments, and make use of the outhouse. Gladys had never been to a proper eating establishment, so was relieved when the elderly lady offered to share a table. The woman must have been as thirsty as she was because she asked the barmaid if they could have two tankards of water instead of ale. Although it was an unusual request, the girl obliged.

Remembering the fetid water in Old Nichol, Gladys just intended to wet her dry lips, but the water the barmaid brought had such a sweet and delectable taste that she didn't put the tankard down until it was empty. Then she suddenly realized that the manner in which she had gulped the liquid was anything but ladylike. Glancing around the room, she was relieved to see that no one seemed to have noticed except her companion, who politely, remarked, "It is so nice to have sweet water again, isn't it?" Not waiting for an answer, she added, "That is the only thing I dislike about visiting my son. The water in London is simply undrinkable. Shall we ask the girl for another glass?"

Gladys said yes, determined to sip the second one as daintily as did her companion.

Sitting across from the woman instead of beside her, Gladys now had a better opportunity to study her face. She decided that the lady looked exactly like a grandmother should look. Her wrinkles were all in the right places to show that she laughed a lot. But it was her eyes that Gladys liked best. They reminded her of Sally's even though they were different in colour. Gladys felt she could trust the woman since she hadn't asked too many questions or looked at her accusingly. Gladys had never thought what it would be like to have a grandmother since she had never met one. Few women in Old Nichol lived long enough to have such a title. But if she could have one, she'd want her to be as kind and thoughtful as the constable's mother.

The lady had also taken note of the young girl's appearance, and her perceptive appraisal would have sent shivers up Gladys's spine. Not only was the lady's son an officer of the law, but her husband had been one as well, and throughout the years, she had become almost as astute as they were at sizing up people; therefore, she had little trouble deducing that Gladys was a runaway, especially when the station of her departure had been so near Old Nichol. She also noticed the girl's bare legs when they got off the coach. She felt sorry for the child since her son often talked about how horrible life was in such places. A wave of compassion overcame her and she smiled warmly and held out her hand. "We haven't been properly introduced, young lady, so I shall do the honours. I am Mrs Rutledge."

Gladys, embarrassed over the poor state of her hand, blushed as she offered it; then, managing a weak smile, she answered, "My name is Gladys, ah, Gladys Tweedhope. Pleased to meet you, mum."

"Gladys is such a pretty name. It has a ring of gaiety to it."

"Thank you, mum."

"You are very welcome, my dear. Now, what do you suppose they have for us to eat?"

Shrugging her shoulders, Gladys waited for Mrs Rutledge to order then said she would have the same. She spent more money for the meal than she intended, but the meat pie was so delicious and the large glass of warm milk so comforting, that she had no regrets. Mrs Rutledge could tell by the manner in which the girl devoured her meal that she was still hungry, so she only ate half her pie and said, "I simply cannot finish this, Gladys, and I do so hate to see good food go to waste. Do you suppose you could eat a little more, dear?"

Gladys wasn't sure if accepting the pie was the proper thing to do, but the temptation was too great to refuse. She did her best to sound nonchalant as she replied,

"Well, if you are sure. I didn't take the time to eat breakfast this morning, and I am rather hungry."

When Mrs Rutledge finished her tea, she excused herself and went to the outhouse while Gladys walked a little way down the road to stretch her legs. It was a lovely summer's day, and the oats in one of the fields beside the road had just been cut. The smell was so unbelievably sweet that Gladys threw back her head, closed her eyes, and breathed deeply. She never dreamt there were such wonderful places and made a silent wish that Dover would be as pretty and smell as nice. This last thought made her wonder if the other passengers could smell offensive odours on her or her clothes. She put the sleeve of her cloak up to her nose and sniffed. There was a rather unpleasant smell, but she couldn't tell if it was her or the fur trimming. Just to be safe, she decided to sit over as far as she could to her side of the coach for the rest of the journey.

She was just about to go to the outhouse when she saw a young lady who was dressed in a pretty blue frock walking toward her smiling. Gladys returned the smile, but when she noticed a brooch pinned to the lady's bodice, her smile faded. Her face paled, and she looked so upset that the lady inquired, "Are you alright? May I be of help?"

Recovering a little and sounding more like a child than she had intended, Gladys replied, "It's that shell cameo you're wearing; I had one almost the same, but I lost it."

"Oh, I am sorry. This was a gift from my husband, and I know how upset I would be if I lost it. Well I must give this parcel to the driver. I hope someone finds your pin and returns it to you."

Gladys had forgotten to bring Sally's brooch. The realization that she would never be able to retrieve the precious gift was so upsetting that she almost broke out in tears. She had promised Sally she would keep it forever, and now she would never see it again. The day was no longer so magical, and after making use of the outhouse, she returned to the coach in a sombre mood.

Mrs Rutledge, noting the sad look on Gladys's face, was about to inquire as to the reason, but the girl seemed so intent on keeping as much distance between them as possible that she took it as a plea for privacy, and settled down to enjoy another nap.

As they continued on with their journey, the food, and perhaps a few tankards of ale, appeared to have loosened the tongues of the two gentlemen, and they began to chat about a variety of subjects. Their discussions were amiable until the topics of the Queen's politics and her marriage to Prince Albert arose. On both subjects their opinions differed greatly, resulting in a loud dispute. Gladys was intrigued with the conversation, and both men, who had seemed uninteresting to her before, now took on personalities.

She surmised that both were middle-aged, but that was where the resemblance ended. The gentleman, who wore the scent which thankfully had dispersed, was tall, fair, and had an open and friendly countenance. Although she knew nothing of the latest styles in men's attire, she noticed that his clothes appeared new and were made from expensive material. The other fellow, who talked with a decidedly Scottish accent, was small of stature and had short-cropped, iron-grey, bushy hair with matching brows. He had ruddy cheeks, a tight upper lip, and small, but bright, brown eyes. His clothes were neat and tidy, but they showed a good amount of wear. His voice had a short, clipped, decisive tone, and he appeared to be a man of set opinions.

It seemed that the tall man was in agreement with the Queen's choice of parties and declared, "She supports the Whigs, and that, sir, is proof enough for any man that she has compassion for all her subjects and not just those of a higher echelon."

The Scotsman, a dedicated Tory, sat upright in his seat and the ruddiness on his countenance spread up to his temples and down his neck. He emitted a sputter that sounded like a drop of cold water on a hot skillet, before he was able to respond, "Ye've nae a brain in your head, mon! Di ye ken, the lassie has been hoodwinked by that unco, Melbourne? He and that foreigner she married. Neither hae worked a day in their lives an' they want tae take money from us tae put food in the mouths o' laggards too lazy to earn a shilling."

The tall gentleman calmly replied, "Nonsense you say! There are those who are too sick to work and are forced to beg. Have you no pity, man?"

"Dinna talk to me aboot pity. I've been as poor as the lot o' them but I dinna ask for pity. I went to work shovelling coal wi' a crooked leg, and I kept working and saving until I had my ain business." Gladys had noticed the man had a limp.

The tall man still appeared unruffled by the Scotsman's outburst and continued the conversation in such a condescending tone that it hinted of smugness, "I commend you, sir, on your success, but my opinion remains the same, so we shall have to leave that subject in disagreement. As to Prince Albert, he certainly seems like a good chap to me. He's well educated, and they say he has a keen interest in the sciences, so I expect he may bring about some modern changes, which God knows we could use."

The Scotsman's reply was delivered in such a loud tone that it woke Mrs Rutledge. "Och! A fancy education ye say! He does na ken what the working man needs if all he has done is read books? Dinna ye ken he's a foreigner and has no business muddling in our—"

His dialogue was suddenly interrupted by Mrs Rutledge who, although softly spoken, used her voice with authority, "Sirs, would you mind controlling your voices? If you two gentlemen are not in agreement, then may I suggest that you leave Miss Gladys and me in peace and spend the rest of your trip enjoying the scenery?"

Both men, taken aback by the woman's astute advice, emitted small, undecipherable noises to cover their embarrassment, then settled back in their seats and were quiet for the rest of the journey. Gladys gave Mrs Rutledge an appreciative smile, but in truth she was disappointed. The men had spoken of the Queen and Prince Albert as though they knew them personally. Conversations such as theirs were never heard in Old Nichol. The Queen and Prince Albert might as well live in another country for all the difference their politics made to the populace born in the slums.

The concerns there were far more practical, such as where one could find the most lucrative corner to apply one's talents for begging and pickpocketing. The daily news of a death or two, and who could lay hands on the poor beggar's belongings before he was taken away by the dead cart, always merited a lengthy discussion. This was usually followed by the topic of who would inherit the deceased's living space. Gladys knew now that she was in another world and must adapt to her new environment. One of the things she intended to find out was what on earth was a wig party?

It was early evening when the coach arrived at a small, red brick station with the sign that read "Dover" painted in big black letters over the entrance. A few people were standing outside, and as the tall gentleman exited and turned to assist Gladys and Mrs Rutledge down from the coach, the driver announced, "The convenience building be out back. We leave for Hastings in ten minutes."

Once on the ground, Gladys couldn't help but remark, "Oh my, what is that nice smell?"

The tall man laughed and replied, "That, young lady, is good salt air!"

Mrs Rutledge, who was met by her husband, a man obviously delighted with his wife's return, gave Gladys a hug and then surprised her and slipped her gloves into Gladys's hand, whispering, "You may need these, dear. Good bye and good luck." Before Gladys could thank her, her husband whisked her off. Gladys didn't have a chance to ask her if she knew of an inn nearby.

The tall man, who was continuing on to Hastings, hadn't taken his luggage from the coach and was sitting on a bench nearby, so Gladys walked over to him and shyly inquired if he knew of a place where she might find lodgings. He looked pensive for a second, then shook his head, "I am sorry, my dear, but I live in Hastings and am not acquainted with the establishments here. Perhaps you can ask Scotty over there when he has his bags down from the rack. I trust his manners will be more courteous towards such a pretty young lady than they were toward me."

Gladys waited for the Scotsman to collect his luggage before she approached him. "Pardon me, sir, could you tell me where I could find lodgings for the night?"

"Aye," he replied, then turned abruptly, and walked away.

Gladys, not knowing what else to do, ran after him. "Sir, please wait!"

The Scotsman stopped and with a look of annoyance, asked, "What is it ye want now?"

"Could you please tell me where I can find the place?"

Once again she received an abrupt, "Aye" before he continued on down the road. Gladys had no recourse but to follow. Although the man walked with a limp, she was amazed at the rapid pace he set. They walked in silence for about a quarter of a mile, passing tidy, little shops that were nestled under tiers of identical looking apartments. Finally, they stopped at one of the taller buildings. A sign above the entrance door was decorated with painted sprigs of heather in each corner and the name "Scots Inn" in the centre. Underneath the title were the words, "Whiskey and Freedom Gang Thegither" and, below those colourful words of Robbie Burns, "Proprietor, Neil Watt."

The man unlocked the door and entered. When Gladys hesitated to follow, he called out, "Weel, Lass, do ye want a room or no?"

Gladys, unsure of what she was getting into, decided to throw caution to the wind, and nodded, "Yes."

"Weel it's two shillings a night, and ye'll have to pay now."

When Gladys entered the room, it took her a few minutes to realize that she was in a public house unlike any she had seen in Old Nichol. Behind a shining slate bar with a curved trim of unblemished oak was a huge mirror that reflected the polished leather on the chairs around a number of tables. Even the sculptured copper ceiling was brightly polished, and the windows were beautifully etched with scenes of Scottish landscapes. She was taking it all in when she suddenly realized that the Scotsman had disappeared, and she was alone. Feeling somewhat nervous, she was just about to call out when she heard voices coming from the back of the building. As they came nearer, she could make out, not only the Scotsman's brogue, but a woman's as well, although her accent was nowhere as broad.

They seemed to be arguing over something to do with the gas lamps, and as they entered the room, the woman declared, "I'll no do my cleaning by candlelight!"

The man had calmed down by this time, and he merely uttered a weak "Shush yer tongue, woman," before addressing Gladys. "Now, lass, ye want a room. How long will ye be staying?"

Gladys, who was going to look for work and unsure of the length of her stay, decided to book it for three nights. After giving her name as Gladys Tweedhope, the man identified himself and his wife as Neil and Laura Watt, the owners of the inn. Then he left the woman to take Gladys's money and settle her into a room while he busied himself turning out lamps.

Laura Watt was built much like her husband, only chubbier. Their facial features were also similar, even and rounded. Laura wore her generous head of white hair up in a bun on the top of her head, while her brows, although grey, were thick like her mate's.

Before Neil had extinguished all the lights, Laura bade Gladys follow and led her down a hallway for a short distance until they came to a stairway on their left. The room was on the third floor, and Gladys was amazed at how easily the older woman took the stairs and how agile both she and her husband were for their ages.

For the average traveller, the room would probably seem adequate, but far from elegant; Gladys, however, considered it luxurious, but managed to hide her delight. In a very mature and casual tone, she remarked, "I suppose it will do," as though she was accustomed to far better accommodation.

When Laura Watt wasn't cleaning, cooking, or doing the washing, she spent her time prying into other people's affairs. Gladys's lack of luggage was enough to fuel her suspicious mind, and she began making inquisitions worthy of a seasoned detective. Instead of avoiding the personal inquiry, Gladys, giddy with hunger and lack of sleep, was experiencing a false sense of overconfidence, and happily supplied the landlady with an imaginary history. She said that she came from London and had recently lost her mother, her only living relative. Then she remarked that she had come to Dover to find employment.

Such commonplace information rendered no basis for gossip, so having no further excuse to remain in the room, the landlady began to leave. As she was going out the door, she informed Gladys that theirs was the only inn in Dover that had a hip-bath and that if she desired to use it, there was a fee of six pence. When Gladys asked if there was somewhere nearby where she could buy a sandwich, Mrs Watt kindly offered to send one up along with a nice hot cup of tea.

After Laura left, Gladys studied each piece of furniture as though it were a work of art. There was a jug of clean drinking water sitting on a dainty, little, round-topped table and a clean towel hung on a rod on the side of a commode. On top of the commode, there was a lovely flowered china jug and basin and a small piece of manufactured soap in a little china dish. She had never seen a fancy bar of soap before, and thinking it might be something to eat, almost bit into it. When she opened the doors of the commode, she was amazed to find a china chamber pot with the same flowered pattern as the jug and basin. She thought it far too pretty to use and looked around the room for one more suitable. When she couldn't find one, she giggled, and said out loud, "Coo, won't my bottom think it belongs to the Queen herself when I squat on that."

She hadn't taken her cloak off when she heard a knock on the door. She opened it to find both of the Watts, one with hot water for her toilet and the other with her tea and sandwich. When Laura Watt didn't leave with her husband, Gladys was afraid the woman had become suspicious. Then, after a few awkward moments of silence, Laura asked for two pence for the tea and sandwich. Gladys was so relieved that she was happy to oblige.

The sandwich was made with fresh bread and delicious brawn, and the tea was sugared and creamed to perfection. After she ate, she took off all her clothes and scrubbed her skin until it was red. Then she took a damp cloth and wiped it over her clothes hoping to eliminate a little of the ghetto's essence. The only thing that dulled the excitement she felt was that she had no one with whom to share the amazing experience. She found it hard to believe that she was in such a magical place. It felt to her as though she had been swept up by an angel and dropped into heaven. Looking around the room, she noticed that there was a good-sized dresser to put her clothes in, if she had any, and a lovely big window adorned with pretty draped curtains. The pink and red roses on the wallpaper added more warmth and beauty to the room.

When she went to bed, she pulled back the eiderdown quilt and was astounded to discover two bed sheets. She had never seen such finery, and got in between them naked in order to enjoy the feel of the clean, fresh-smelling material against every inch of her body. She wanted to enjoy the soft down pillow and the rest of the bedding, so she tried her utmost to stay awake, but fell asleep in seconds.

Chapter Six

It seemed like a wonderful dream when Gladys awoke in the morning. She stretched out under the sheets and had to fight an urge to scream for joy. The bed was so comfortable that she would have stayed in it all day if her empty stomach would have stopped its grumbling. Getting up, she wrapped herself in the quilt, went over to the window, and pulled back the curtains. It was a bright, sunny morning, and as she looked down at the tidy buildings in the street, they appeared so inviting that she wasted no time getting dressed. As she tied her hair back, she decided that one of the first things she would buy would be a hairbrush.

After attempting to arrange the bedding the way she had found it, she left the room, remembering to lock the door with the key that Laura had left on the dresser. Having no idea of the time, she made her way down the stairs as quietly as possible in order not to wake any of the other guests. A curtain-less window at each end of the hallway allowed her enough light to find her way to the stairway, but Mrs Watt must have extinguished the wall lamps the night before, so she had to hold onto the banister as she made her way down in the darkness.

It was a relief when she came to the last set of stairs, and someone opened the door at the bottom landing, letting in enough light to make out each step, but just as suddenly, the light disappeared. At first she thought someone had closed the door, but as her eyes adjusted to the darkness, she could make out the form of a very stout woman who appeared to be clad in an array of ruffles, flounces, and furs. Although the lady could clearly see that Gladys was more than halfway to the bottom, she began her ascent. A tall, thin gentleman, mostly hidden behind her bulk, placed his hand gingerly on the lady's shoulder and in a timid voice, said, "Shall we wait for the young lady, my dear?"

The woman, a seasoned busybody, had acquired a talent for sizing a person's social standing in a glance, and Gladys's bare legs and worn boots gave her away. She shrugged the man's hand from her shoulder, and, unmindful of Gladys, who could hear every word, answered, "She is no lady, Roger. She is obviously one of the servants here and should know enough to make way for a guest."

When Gladys didn't move, the woman stuck out a few of her chins, and added, "You, girl, get back up those stairs and wait until we have made our way to the top!" Gladys was so shocked by the woman's rudeness that she stood staring down at her with her mouth hanging open.

"Are you a dimwit then?" the woman continued; "Roger, fetch the proprietor. We shall soon put an end to this nonsense. It is disgraceful the way some of these servants don't know their place."

The thought of having to answer more questions was enough to frighten Gladys, so smiling sweetly, she said, "Oh dear, I am so sorry, but I was so taken with your beautiful outfit that I found myself spellbound. I was just on my way to purchase some stockings. I tore mine yesterday while walking through some tall grasses. I don't work here, but I can see you are a lady of a high echelon," she remembered the word from the gentlemen's conversation in the coach, "please forgive me for making you wait." Then, without waiting for an answer, she turned and ran back up the stairs hoping the woman had believed her.

The ruse worked, and the woman swelled up like a balloon with the praise. To be mistaken for a lady of quality had always been her utmost ambition, even though she was merely the wife of a salesman. It took a fair time and a good deal of huffing and puffing, along with a few boosts on her backside from her husband, for her to reach the landing. As Gladys stood and waited, she congratulated herself for her cleverness in using flattery as a weapon. It had worked so well, she vowed to remember it from then on.

This was her first encounter with class distinction, but Sally had explained it to her, saying that not having it in Old Nichol was the only good thing she could say about the place. Gladys knew she wasn't going to like it any more than Sally did, but when the woman walked past her with her nose in the air, she managed a sweet smile while at the same time recalling her father's words, *Yes, ma'am, no, ma'am, kiss my arse, ma'am!* and she realized that he was right.

Once outside, all negative thoughts vanished, and taking note of all the buildings and scenery, she could hardly believe her eyes. Looking up and seeing a castle sitting on top of a nearby hill, she forgot where she was and exclaimed aloud, "Oh, look! It's a real castle."

A jolly looking man who was passing by stopped and looked where she was looking. Smiling, he said, "That it is, young lady, and she's the oldest castle in all the country." Realizing she had spoken out loud, Gladys's face turned crimson and she just responded with a shy nod, so tipped his hat and walked on. Gladys stared at the castle for a little longer. Promising herself she would climb up and have a closer look someday, she began to walk down the road.

The salt air was so invigorating, that she took too many deep breaths and, becoming quite lightheaded, she took hold of a lamppost to prevent falling down. Not that she would have minded falling down; the streets were so clean. Walking along, she took in all the sights and enjoyed looking at all manner of interesting things in the shop windows.

A shoemaker's window displayed an assortment of shiny and soft leather shoes for both men and ladies. In a candle maker's window, she not only saw a variety of different candles, but ornate gold and copper candle holders as well. There was a life sized, cleverly carved wooden pig, sitting amongst piles of sausages in a butcher's shop window, and a milliner's shop had a showy display of men's beaver hats, some tall and flared at the top and others in styles less ostentatious.

They were nothing in comparison to the ladies' bonnets. Flowers, feathers, ribbons, and lace, all used in abundance, glorified every hat, and Gladys tipped her head from one side to the other as she pictured herself walking down the street in such finery. The display in the store window next to the milliners was Gladys's favourite. It had everything from china thimbles to china dolls, all arranged prettily on blue velvet. She couldn't imagine covering such pretty plates with food when she noticed a setting of dinnerware that had a border of dainty purple violets on each plate.

She was so excited that she hadn't realized how hungry she was until she smelled the tantalizing odours coming from a baker's shop. It took less than a minute for her to find the place, but when she went in, there were so many tempting things to eat that she wanted to buy one of each. Finally, she settled on a large raisin scone, and then walked to the little town square just a block from her room and sat on a bench to enjoy it.

After savouring every morsel, she continued her walk until she came to a store that had the title, "Millie McIver—Dressmaking and Alterations" painted on the door. Since she was in need of a proper frock, she decided to go in, hoping she had enough money in the leather purse to buy a dress and enough left over for three weeks rent. A bell on the door made a pleasant sounding tinkle as she entered. As there was no sign of the owner, it gave her a chance to look around. A variety of stylish dresses hung on a rack, and some very attractive accessories were lying on shelves under the counter. As she looked closely at the dresses, she was dismayed at their grandness.

Certain she could never afford one of them, she was about to leave when a youthful voice called out, "I shall be there in a minute; please have a seat."

Although the voice was that of a young person, the woman who came from a back room was quite elderly. Millie McIver was an immaculately dressed woman with an hourglass figure. Her hair was pinned up neatly but had an unnatural red hue and tell-tale roots of grey. She wore a good amount of rouge on her cheeks on top of a generous layer of powder. However, instead of appearing garish, the composition added youthfulness to her appearance. Gladys thought her very attractive, unaware that Queen Victoria had recently made a statement saying that make-up was only worn by prostitutes and actresses.

Millie welcomed Gladys with a cheery greeting and a smile. "I am sorry to keep you waiting, my dear."

"Oh, I don't mind, missus—er, I mean, mum. I was enjoying looking at all the pretty dresses."

"Well, I am pleased that you approve of them. Now what can I do for you?"

Gladys's answer sounded more like an apology than a request, "Well, you see, mum, I was hoping I could buy a new dress, er, a, not as fancy as these—maybe just a plain one if it's not too costly."

While Gladys was talking, Millie took notice of her attire. The girl wore no stockings. Her shoes were well worn and appeared too large for her feet, and although her coat was stylish, it was far more suitable for an older person and much too large for the girl. Millie's ability to tell a person's background by her attire, and her posture, left no doubt in her mind that this young girl had come from a poor neighbourhood. However, what intrigued her most about the child was her speech. It lacked refinement but showed fairly good articulation.

By the time Gladys had finished talking, Millie had made up her mind to befriend the girl and said, "Well now, I was just about to put my sewing aside and make a cup of tea. How would you like to join me? We can discuss a frock while we drink our tea."

Gladys's face lit up. "Oh, I shouldn't say no to that, mum."

Millie lived in the back of the store in one large room. She had curtained off a small space to use as a fitting room between her living area and the store. This allowed her some privacy. Although she only had one room, her furniture was arranged so cleverly that, with the help of a screen, a person could be sitting at the kitchen table and be unaware of the bedroom furnishings.

While they were drinking their tea, Millie asked the girl her name, and Gladys told her it was Gladys Tweedhope. Then she inquired if Gladys was new in town. The morning had been so exciting that Gladys couldn't contain her enthusiasm and spit a few cookie crumbs from her mouth as she exclaimed, "Yes, mum—oh dear, I beg your pardon, mum; you see, I just arrived here last night, and I've been walking about this morning, and I even saw the castle!"

Millie laughed and said, "That's Dover Castle, the oldest castle in all of England."

"Are you allowed to go up there?"

"Certainly, but you are not allowed to go in."

"I guess the Queen doesn't allow it."

"Oh, no, my dear, the Queen doesn't live there. There are just soldiers there from time to time." Gladys's lack of knowledge regarding the Royal family only added to Millie's suspicions. Then, when Millie asked her where she was from and Gladys hesitated to answer, Millie decided to be frank. "Now, Gladys, I shan't pry into your lineage, but I sense you have seen difficult times, and I understand your desire for privacy. I too have a past that I do not wish to recall, so shall we build our friendship on the present and not the past?"

Gladys, overwhelmed with the idea of making a friend so soon, jumped up, and hugged the dressmaker. Startled, but not displeased, Millie gently pushed her aside. She suspected the poor girl was a runaway, homeless, or perhaps both. Although she knew she might be making a mistake inviting a stranger into her home, there was something about this girl that she liked. She perceived there was a certain amount of both vulnerability and strength to Gladys's character, and made an impulsive vow to help her.

As soon as they finished their tea, Millie rose, pulled Gladys to her feet, and insisted she take off her coat and bonnet. Gladys hesitated. The frock she wore under the coat resembled a child's dress more than a young lady's. It was clean—her mother had seen to that—but it just reached halfway between her knees and her ankles, and her underpinnings were not much more than rags.

Somehow, Millie seemed to understand the young girl's dilemma and said, "Perhaps you would like to take off your coat in my little dressing room." Gladys nodded thankfully. "Now just sit there for a minute, and I shall see what I have. You are so slim, my dear, that almost any dress I have should fit you. Yes, I think I have two that will do nicely." Then she hurried into the shop and returned with two of the dresses Gladys had seen earlier. Holding them up, she said, "This is one that I made for Mrs Grey. It only took me three weeks, but by the time it was ready, she had gained ten pounds." Then with a little laugh, she added. "Fortunately, she paid for the material."

The frock was a lovely green colour, adorned with fine lace lappets, brown piping, and brown nodes—a dress like none other Gladys had ever seen. "Oh, I could never afford a dress like that, Mum."

"Well, we shall see, we shall see, my dear. I am certain you can afford this one." Millie said holding out the other dress. "I made this for a dear lady who, unfortunately, passed away before she had a chance to even try it on. I am sure it will fit you perfectly with a few tucks here and there." It was a high-necked, practical brown frock complete with a white linen tucker. Although it wasn't nearly as fancy as the first one, Gladys thought it grand.

Gladys took the plainest dress and went into the dressing room. Just as she had taken off her old dress, Millie pulled back the curtain to ask her if she wanted to try on both the frocks. Gladys's face went red with embarrassment, but Millie didn't appear to notice as she hung the fancy dress on a coat peg and left.

Millie had noticed the state of her underpinnings, but had managed to hide her shock. She wondered how long Gladys had been out on her own and what the poor child had done to earn enough money to buy a dress. One thing that she did know was that Gladys was not leaving her store until she was decently attired, especially since the girl intended to spend the day looking for employment.

Gladys said she would take the plain dress, and it didn't take long for Millie to make the alterations. Millie insisted on adding a Holland pinafore, black woollen stockings, gloves that were the right size (Mrs Rutledge's were far too small), two complete sets of lady's underpinnings, and a blouse and skirt that she insisted were too small for her. Millie knew Gladys couldn't afford it all, so she gave it to her at a third of the cost. What she didn't know was that after Gladys paid for the clothes she only had enough left for two more night's lodging and a few bowls of soup.

"I shall put aside the fancier frock until you have earned enough money to buy it," Millie announced when Gladys was ready to leave. "Then we shall have to get you into a corset. It will do wonders for your posture."

Gladys was feeling a little sick with worry by this time, but the thought of wearing a corset struck her as funny, and she giggled.

"Now what is so funny about that, young lady?" Millie asked.

Gladys didn't dare tell her that she was recalling her mother's words on the subject of corsets, "They's 'arnesses, an' only 'orses n' oxes wears 'arnesses," so she just smiled and said, "I was just thinking about how pleased my mother would have been to know that I've found such a wonderful friend."

"What a lovely thing to say! I think your mother must have been a most loving and thoughtful woman to raise such a sweet young lady."

"Oh, she was, mum, she really was. She was a governess you know, and when I earn enough money to pay for my training, I think I'll be one too."

Millie smiled and replied, "I think you would make a wonderful governess, Gladys."

The dressmaker's acceptance of her story was so unexpected it gave Gladys an unfamiliar feeling of confidence, so much so that she began to think that someday she could actually become a governess like Sally had been, before she came to Old Nichol. It seemed to Gladys that she was blessed with one miracle after another. Dover was the greatest place in the world to live; she had just made a friend who seemed as kind as Sally, and now she had a career to work toward. The dressmaker could see the joy in Gladys's eyes. She knew she should warn her of the everyday drudgery in the life of a house-maid, but she couldn't bring herself to spoil the little time she had left before she went to work.

As Gladys was leaving, Millie offered her some wise advice, "Don't ask for a position as a scullery maid, my dear. Scullery maids are no better off than slaves and are often forced to work from morning until night without a day off. A housemaid works long hours as well, but can demand a day off now and again. And, Gladys, since we are going to be good friends, I would prefer you call me, Millie; 'mum' makes me feel so old." After promising to visit whenever she could, Gladys hugged her new friend goodbye.

She soon learned that anyone applying for a menial job was obliged to knock on the back door of a residence because it was up to the housekeeper to do the hiring. She did have one offer, but when she couldn't produce a reference, it was withdrawn. By evening she had knocked on countless doors to no avail and returned to the inn down-hearted. She sat down at a table, and when Laura Watt came to ask what she would like, she ordered a cup of tea and a bowl of soup. Laura noticed the bundle Gladys was carrying when she entered the inn, and when she took off her cloak, Laura also saw the new frock.

"I see you have a new frock, and it looks like a good one. How did you manage to find one that was already made?" Gladys gave her a brief account of her meeting with Millie and hoped that would suffice, but Laura wasn't about to give up that easily. "You must have found a good job to be buying such a fine frock."

Gladys confessed that she hadn't found work, but since she had left her belongings in London, she needed a change of clothes. Then she added that since there was no work to be had, she would be leaving the next day.

"What sort of job were you looking for?" Laura asked.

"I was hoping to find work as a housemaid, mum."

Noticing the roughness of Gladys's hands, Laura nodded and said, "You look to be a good strong lass."

"Oh yes, mum, and I don't mind hard work."

"Well, I'd best fetch your soup an' tea." With that, Laura hurried away.

Gladys had finished her soup and was enjoying her tea when the landlady surprised her by bringing a cup of her own to the table. "Do you mind if I sit with you?"

Gladys didn't care for the woman, but she smiled and nodded politely. There were a few men standing at the bar and one at another table, so Laura leaned towards her, and in a low voice, said, "You can see it's not very busy these days, so we canna afford to pay muckle, but if you want to work here, you can." Gladys was so pleased and excited that she could do no more than nod her head in agreement. "There's a room in the attic where you can sleep, an' we'll give you three meals a day and your work togs. Do you ken I expect a good ten hours work from you each day?"

Gladys said she understood, then, trying not to sound too forthright, she asked, "May I ask what my wages will be, mum?"

"We canna pay more than ten pound a year." When Gladys didn't argue, Laura felt quite pleased with herself, aware that a chambermaid was usually paid twelve. "I'll show you to your room and give you your work clothes."

"But I already have a room."

"Oh, lass, we canna allow our maids ta stay in the guest rooms. You can hae your money back along wi' your first pay.

Gladys was dismayed to find that her room, although half the attic, had only a very tiny window and was so dark and ominous that it reminded her a little of Old Nichol. A lamp helped brighten the room and add a little warmth, but Laura cautioned her to use it sparingly because she would only be given a small amount of fuel every month. Gladys wondered if she would be allotted more in the winter but hadn't the courage to ask. "You'll begin in the morn at five," Laura informed her as she left.

Gladys went back to Millie's shop to tell her the good news, but her friend wasn't as pleased for her as she thought she would be.

"I've heard that every girl who has worked there couldn't work hard enough to satisfy that woman and was let go. Oh, I do wish I could afford to keep you here as an apprentice, but the landlord wouldn't hear of it."

"Don't you worry, Millie; I'm not afraid of hard work, and as long as I can visit you now and then, I'll be just fine. Er, a, you wouldn't have an extra candle or two that I could borrow until I can find where to buy some, would you?" Then she told Millie how dark the attic was and how she had to be careful not to use too much lamp fuel, which caused the seamstress to be even more upset. She found two candles complete with holders then said, "Goodnight," as Gladys returned to the inn.

With the added light from the two candles, Gladys was able to find some pegs in the wall to hang her clothes, cheering her up somewhat. To Laura's credit, the bedding was fresh and clean, and when she snuggled in for the night, she thought how lucky she was to have found a good friend, a place to stay, and a job, all on her first day in Dover. She had heard talk of "God's Blessings" and although she had never seen evidence of anything you could call a blessing in Old Nichol, she now felt she had truly been blessed. Before falling asleep, she looked up at the blackened rafters, and, remembering Mr O's advice, said, "If it was you, God, thank you ever so much!"

She arose early the next morning, anxious to begin work, donned the clean work clothes Laura had given her, and found her way to the kitchen. She was greeted warmly by the cook, a large and pleasant woman named Hilda; Becky, the scullery maid, and Lily, another chambermaid. Hilda dished Gladys out a generous bowl of porridge and poured her a cup of hot tea. "You can add cream and treacle to suit your taste, luv."

The kitchen, like the rest of the establishment, was immaculate, and the porridge was excellent. Gladys scraped her bowl clean in such record time that Hilda offered her another. "Oh, thank you, Hilda. This is the best porridge I've ever eaten. I think I am going to like working here."

Both girls stopped eating and looked at her with amazement. Hilda stopped what she was doing and went over and put an arm around her. Instead of a smile, she wore a foreboding frown as she said, "Now, luv, I have to warn you—" She stopped in mid-sentence when she saw Laura Watt coming and quickly returned to her duties.

No one could have worked harder than Neil and Laura Watt

in order to acquire their small, but lucrative business, but they expected the same dedication from their employees, while begrudging them a decent wage. Laura was only too happy to offer Gladys a job, and the fact that she appeared to be strong and unaware of a chambermaid's chores, let alone the rate of pay, made her that much more appealing. Tied down with cleaning and housekeeping, Laura had little time to spend tending the bar, a job where she could enjoy all the local gossip as she worked. She also wanted to visit her ailing mother in Scotland, and Neil wanted to open the bar earlier in the day, all impossible without hiring more help.

Gladys greeted Laura with a cheery, "Good morning, mum," and received nothing more than a nod in return. Nevertheless, she remained in an amiable mood as she was informed of her duties, not knowing they included many of the chores usually allotted to the scullery maid and chambermaid. She was expected to empty and scrub out the chamber pots, clean out the fireplaces, fill and carry the coal scuttles to every room, and clean the outhouses. She was also expected to sweep or scrub every floor, beat the carpets, do the dusting, and iron the linen.

The building had four stories and an attic. The basement was used for storage. The pub, the kitchen, the scullery, the pantry, and a large unused room were all located on the main floor. The Watts resided on the second floor. The third floor, below the attic, consisted of six small rental rooms, including the one Gladys had rented.

Becky and Lily shared the other half of the attic which was a much better room because their entrance was at the top of an outside stairway at the back of the building, and allowed a refreshing breeze during the summers.

The first day Laura followed Gladys everywhere to see she did her chores properly. Except for a half hour at noon and a half hour for dinner, Gladys didn't stop working until nine in the evening. Every muscle and joint cried out in pain as she slowly climbed the stairs to the attic, and she felt like she had been run over by something as big as Mr O's manure wagon. As she fell on top of her cot, she could still hear Laura's voice giving her yet another chore, "When you get done wi' that, you can do the dusting." Oh how she would have loved to tell the old bat to go to hell. Somehow she managed to get her clothes off and climb between the sheets, but she was sure she wouldn't have the strength to rise at five the next morning. Her last thought before she fell asleep was that she would be lucky enough to die before then.

Chapter Seven

Gladys didn't see her new friend Millie for more than two months after she began working at the inn. Except for the brief times allotted for meals, she did nothing but work and sleep. After the first month, the sores on her hands and knees became calluses and her overall appearance dishevelled. There were moments when she was tempted to deliver a swift kick to her employer's backside, but she knew she couldn't survive without a job. Besides, Laura had such a smug look on her face every time she added to Gladys's workload that it was obvious she expected her to admit defeat and quit. Gladys was not going to do so.

Hilda felt sorry for her, and tried her best to convince her not to work so hard. Referring to Becky and Lily, she advised, "You don't sees them working themselves to death do you? Her ladyship tried the same thing with them, but they just couldn't keep up, so she let them be. That's what you've to do, luv, then she'll give over."

But Gladys knew that Laura Watt had taken a dislike to her and would welcome the chance to fire her over the slightest provocation. The woman seemed to derive some sort of sadistic pleasure from watching her newly-hired girls falter under the heavy workload she gave them. Whenever they couldn't handle the chores, she would brag to her husband, "They're not as bonnie as the Scottish lassies!" But if they could still manage to handle what she considered a fair day's work, she, as Hilda put it, "let them be."

However, Gladys was not like the other girls and had accomplished every task Laura had given her without complaining. Laura knew she was being unfair to continue adding to her burden, but after the first two weeks, stubbornness took the place of good sense, turning the situation into a test of wills.

Finally, even Neil began to notice what was going on. He warned Laura that she had better let up. "She's a good lass an' will no have trouble finding another position." Laura had never had a housemaid to compare with Gladys, and the thought of losing her to another inn made her realize that he was right. Even if she disliked the girl, she valued her worth, so she begrudgingly began giving some of Gladys's chores to Lily.

With a lighter workload and the aid of three good meals a day, Gladys's strength and endurance improved, and before long she was able to finish her chores in time to take care of her personal needs. Having clean water with which to bathe and wash her hair added to her enjoyment, and she even found time to visit with Millie on her half day off. The dressmaker had been worried about her and was delighted to see that she had not only managed to survive Laura Watt's harsh demands, but had gained weight while doing it.

Gladys was much happier now that she had a little free time, but she also suffered bouts of melancholy. While she was working from morning till night, she had been too tired to feel anything. Now she had time to think about the loved ones she left behind. Whenever she saw two young people walking hand in hand, she longed for Toughie. Every horse and dog she saw brought back images of Old Knickers and My Dog. Much to her surprise, she even missed her parents. Having Millie for a friend helped to ease her loneliness.

After being apart for such a long time, Gladys and Millie had plenty to talk about. When they finished discussing the Watts and their cantankerous ways, they began talking about Millie's persnickety customers. The dressmaker related how some of them actually expected her to make them a frock that would magically transform them from plain, dumpy, middle-aged women, into beautiful maidens.

One afternoon, Millie showed Gladys some new material with a colourful pattern that she had ordered from India. "It is called Tabby, and I have heard that it was named after a tabby cat with similar markings. It would look marvellous with your hair," she said, as she held it up to Gladys's head.

"Yes, I expect it would, Millie, but I don't think I shall even be able to buy that other dress you put aside for me. I won't receive any wages for a whole year, and when I do get paid, I've decided to save the money to go to school and learn how to be a governess."

"How much do you think that will cost?"

"I have no idea."

"Well, I just might be able to find out for you. One of my customers sends her children's governess to pick up her dresses, and I could ask her. I imagine you would have to learn a language or two though."

"Do you think I could, Millie?"

"I think you could. That is, if you can find a good teacher."

During their time together, Millie taught Gladys how to sew and how to alter the appearance of a plain dress—two very important talents because most ladies only owned two dresses, one for every day and one for Sundays and social events. Millie was an expert at remodelling old clothes, and she showed Gladys how to alter sleeves, waistlines, and hem heights. She also showed her how to replace pleats with gathers, or vice versa, change ribbons and trims, and add new collars.

"Cloth is far too costly to discard, and you have to spend far too many hours sewing an outfit just to throw it aside when the styles change," Millie explained. "Why I can remodel a gown at least six

times before I tear it apart. Then when I do, I put the material to good use making children's clothing."

Eventually, Gladys was able to help with some of the sewing. When Millie protested, she insisted that she found the work relaxing.

Millie laughed, "You continue helping me, young lady, and you are going to earn that dress."

As time went on, Gladys had more and more amusing stories to relate, and having a talent for mimicry, she often had Millie in stitches with her imitation of Neil Watt and his colourful vocabulary, especially when he and Laura were arguing. She also told stories about Hilda the cook, who was in the habit of smuggling out food to the coal delivery man, Pete.

Gladys thought that Pete was one of the dirtiest and scrawniest looking men she had ever laid eyes on, but, evidently, Hilda thought otherwise. After taking fresh baked goodies out to him when he was shovelling coal into the coal shed, she would invariably return to the kitchen with black fingerprints all over the pinafore that covered her generous bosom and frequently a few on her backside as well.

Millie thought that the funniest story Gladys had to tell was about the morning when she went to clean out the men's outhouse and found that one of the guests had died while sitting on the seat with his trousers down around his ankles. "His bald head had fallen down on his chest, and forgive me, Millie, but at first glance, I thought his face was in the hole and I was looking at his bare arse!"

After Millie stopped laughing, she asked, "What did you do?"

"I just screamed."

"How long had he been there?"

"Well, near as the doctor could tell, he'd been there all night. Believe it or not, Millie, when Laura Watt came running out to see what I was screaming about, the first thing she did was go through his pockets so as to get her money for a night's lodging."

Millie laughed, and said, "I wonder what she charges for a night in one of her outhouses?"

"I don't know. I guess it depends if it has one hole or two." This brought the two women once more to the point of hysterics.

Millie was always interested in how the guests were dressed, and what they were like. Gladys told her that most were businessmen, salesmen, or seamen, but seldom women.

"You'd be surprised, Millie, but it's usually the sailors who are the nicest. They even smile and say thank you when I bring them hot water, or get a nice fire going to warm their room. Some guests don't even let on that they see me. You'd think they'd at least answer when I smile and say good day, but they act like I'm invisible." She appeared so upset when she said this that Millie noted the change in her mood, and although she felt sorry for the girl, she was also concerned about her overly friendly nature and felt obliged to give her advice.

"I'm afraid your naivety will lead you astray, Gladys. Sometimes it's the friendly ones you have to be wary of. Did your mother ever talk to you about men and their desires?"

"Oh, I've seen, ah, I mean, she told me all about it, and don't you worry, Millie, I don't intend to be too friendly with any of them, at least not until I'm married."

"Sometimes that can be easier said than done. Most women have no trouble warding off advances, but blood runs hotter in some than others, and when that is the case, it can be difficult not to yield to temptation."

"Well, I know I will never have trouble saying 'No.'"

"Be especially careful of the wealthy ones—the ones who offer you gifts."

"I can take care of myself, and besides, all rich men aren't that way. There's one salesman, a Mr Pidcock, who stays a few days at the inn every month. I think he sells spices because he smells like cinnamon."

When Millie started to laugh, Gladys said, "No, he really does! His clothes and even his luggage too. The last time he came he brought his wife and little girl with him. When they were invited to spend the evening with one of his clients, they asked if I would mind putting the little girl to bed and staying with her until they returned. They were gone ever so long, but I really didn't mind. And the little girl seemed to enjoy my company, especially when I sang to her."

"I had no idea you could sing! What songs do you know?"

"Well, I sang three lullabies, but the one she liked the most was the 'Riddle Song.' Do you know it, Millie?"

"I don't think so, dear. Sing it for me."

"Right now?"

"Of course! There is no one here but us, so you need not be embarrassed."

"Oh, I wouldn't be embarrassed, Millie. I love to sing more than anything else in the world. But you must promise that if you know the song, you'll join in."

Mille nodded and Gladys began, "I gave my love a cherry that had no stone. I gave my love a chicken that had no bone."

Millie was amazed by the richness of Gladys's voice and felt a bit embarrassed by her own weak efforts as she joined in with the last verse. After they had finished, Gladys clapped her hands, and said, "Oh, Millie, that was such fun, we should sing together more often."

Millie shook her head, "I don't think so. You have such a beautiful voice that I just want to sit back and enjoy it. Now, my dear, I shall expect at least one song from you on every visit. Do you know many more?"

Without thinking, Gladys blurted out, "Oh yes, I do. Ma was always singing." Then a look of melancholy spread across her face, and she changed the topic. "But I didn't finish telling you what happened when the man and his wife returned, did I?"

"No indeed, you did not. Did they appreciate your kindness, and apologize for keeping you up so late?"

"They certainly did! And they gave me a whole pound note. Can you believe that, Millie? A whole pound. That's more than a month's wages."

That wasn't the last perquisite Gladys was to receive. Her cheeriness and adeptness at little things such as sewing on buttons, shining shoes, or removing spots from un-washable garments, earned her many gratuities, especially from the bachelors who stayed at the inn. She kept every penny she received under her mattress in the soft leather purse she had stolen from old Gaylord, until the night she returned home a little earlier than usual from visiting Millie and found Laura Watt in the attic snooping through her belongings.

When Gladys surprised her, Laura's face turned red, and she stammered a weak excuse about looking for a footstool before making a quick retreat. From that time on, Gladys left the purse with Millie for safe keeping.

The friendly manner in which the guests treated Gladys hadn't escaped Laura's attention. She began to suspect that the girl was receiving money. Not only did she think all profits from the guests should rightfully belong to her and Neil, but she also worried that Gladys might eventually save enough money to be able to leave, and they might lose the most efficient housemaid they ever had. So she informed Gladys that any gratuities she received must be handed over to either her or Neil.

Gladys, fearful of being caught, tried to refuse any gifts or money, saying that Mrs Watt didn't allow it. Nevertheless, most guests insisted she accept a token of their appreciation, promising they wouldn't mention it to anyone, and, in order to quell Laura's suspicions, they made sure to leave her a small gratuity as well.

The first Christmas Gladys spent at the inn, she not only received more gratuities than usual from the guests, but small gifts, such as fruit and candy. Then, when she visited Millie a few days before Christmas, she was amazed to find that the seamstress had decorated her little shop with boughs of spruce and sprigs of bright, red-berried holly. It looked so festive, and smelled so wonderful, that she clapped her hands, and exclaimed, "Oh, Millie, it looks so pretty in here! There are no decorations at the inn, and if it weren't for the guests wishing me a merry Christmas, I would never know there was such a thing."

"That is because the Watts are Scottish, Gladys, and Christmas has been banned in their country for over three hundred years."

"What's wrong with Christmas?"

"Well, it goes back a long way, and I'm not entirely certain, but I think church officials there deemed the celebration a Catholic one, so they considered it pagan. One of my Scottish customers told me that working folks in that country are even forced to work on Christmas Day."

"Oh! That explains why Laura Watt complained so much about closing the inn then too."

"Don't judge her too harshly on that. One week after Christmas she will put us all to shame with her celebrating."

"Why would she celebrate Christmas then?"

"Not Christmas, dear, Hogmanay, or what we call, New Year's. Most Scots celebrate this holiday, and the party often lasts for two days or more. During those two days, you never saw such hospitality! They exchange gifts as well. Speaking of gifts, I have a little one for you, but you shan't have it until Christmas day."

"But I haven't anything for you."

"I do not expect anything. Your friendship is all I need, and, Gladys, if that old witch gives you Christmas Day off, I want you to join me for Christmas dinner. I shall buy a big, lovely goose and even make a plum pudding. How does that sound?"

The lump in Gladys throat prevented her from answering, so she just smiled and nodded her head.

Although the night was cold and there was frost on the ground, Gladys walked home warmed by the spirit of Christmas—a new experience for her. Children in the slums had no way of discerning Christmas Day from any other except for the odd times when some benevolent church group would show up with some apples and nuts, most likely resulting from an overabundant harvest.

Before Gladys left Millie, she took a little of her savings from the purse Millie was keeping for her, hoping to buy something nice for her friend on Christmas Eve, but Laura Watt was so annoyed over having to give the girls a day off that she insisted they all work overtime to make up for the holiday. By the time Gladys finished her chores, the stores were closed.

She couldn't bear the thought of going to her friend's on Christmas day empty-handed, so decided to spend the day in her room and maybe go for a walk in the afternoon. It was past ten when she finally finished with her chores. Feeling very tired and sorry for

herself, she made her way to the attic. She had just walked past an open door of one of the guest rooms when a hand reached out and grabbed her by the arm. She managed to break loose and was about to call for help when she recognized her assailant. It was a young sailor who had been staying at the inn for four days.

"Please don't call, miss, I won't harm you. I just wanted to show you something," he pleaded.

He had always been very polite and thankful whenever she brought him an extra scuttle of coal during the coldest days. He had told her that he was shipping out on Christmas Day, and planned to ask his girlfriend to marry him as soon as he returned, so she found it hard to believe that he would harm her. Still shaking, she said, "My goodness, you scared the daylights out of me! What is it you want to show me?"

He nodded his head toward the inside of his room, and answered, "It's in here, miss."

Remembering Millie's warning, she decided to remain in the hallway. "You shall have to bring it out here. I am not allowed in any of the guests' rooms at night."

After a quick glance up and down the hall to make sure no one was about, he looked toward the bed, and quietly called, "Here, boy, come." A light-brown and white spotted terrier obediently jumped off the bed and came to the sailor. The dog's face was all brown except for around one eye where he wore a patch of white that looked so much like a monocle it added a look of aristocracy to his appearance.

His short tail was wagging so vigorously that Gladys thought it may fly off at any minute. He was making little, excited, whiny noises that, although not loud enough to wake any of the other guests, were loud enough to worry Gladys.

"Oh, he is lovely!" she cried before shooing them both into the room and going with them, closing the door behind her. "You mustn't let Mrs Watt find him. She would never allow an animal in any of the rooms."

"I know, miss, but you see, I had no choice. I got him for that girl I told you about, so she wouldn't be lonely while I'm gone." Then his voice broke as he added, "She gave me the boot, miss. Said she wasn't about to wait for anyone, and especially not a sailor. Pardon me, miss, but that made me so bloody angry that I refused to give her the dog. I guess that was pretty dumb of me because now I'm shipping out in the morning, and I haven't time to find anyone to give him to. I hate to leave the poor thing on the street to fend for itself." "Oh, no, you mustn't!" Gladys cried as she bent down to pat the dog. It licked her hand, then surprised her and licked her face. Instead of being annoyed, Gladys was delighted.

"I don't suppose you could take him, miss? Or maybe you know of someone who could give him a good home?"

"I could never keep him here. The Watts wouldn't allow that, and besides he would have to spend all day alone in the attic." She sat down on the bed without taking her hand away from the dog's head. She had never seen a dog like it. It even smelled nice. "Oh, I would just love to keep you. We'd have such fun together," she said. The dog's tail wagged in agreement. "But I'm sorry, it's just not possible."

She was almost in tears when suddenly she had a brilliant idea. Her eyes lit up; she held the dog's head in both hands, and said, "What a perfect present you would make for my best friend, Millie! You would have the best home you could ever wish for. Millie is such a kind person, and I shall be able to visit you every week."

The sailor grinned, and said, "I hope this Millie person is as nice as you, miss. He's already taken to you."

"Has he got a name?"

"He certainly has. It's Taffy, and you knows, miss, he's no cur. He comes right from Lord Huntley's kennels. He's been done and had his tail docked an' ears cropped as well."

Gladys had no idea what the sailor was talking about, and her confused expression must have given him the wrong idea because he gave a mischievous wink, nudged her with his shoulder, and said, "I mean the pup, miss, not his lordship." When she didn't laugh, his face turned crimson. Afraid that he had been too brazen, he tried to look as serious as he could as he added, "Of course he'd be worth a mite more if he was all white, miss."

"But why? I love his colour! I am sure he is much handsomer

than any old plain white dog."

"You think that, and so do I. You see, miss, it's the white terriers they like the best for hunting. I suppose it's because they can tell them from the foxes. When this one came out spotted, they gave him to a friend of mine who works for his lordship. He's had him about a year now, but he has two others so when I asked if I could have Taffy, he was only too happy to give him to me."

"I have a leash here for him too, so you can take him out for nice walks, and if you come to a field, you can let him loose to have a good run. He'll come directly back when he's called; you'll see. My friend said he was a good ratter as well, so your friend won't be bothered with those bug—err, I mean, pests any more. Now you had best wait here, and I'll hide him under my coat, and take him outside so he can do his business. You'll not have any puddles to wipe up in the morning; he's well trained, he is. Oh, and I've some bread and roast beef that I saved from my dinner, so you can feed him that if he's hungry."

Taffy spent the night curled up beside Gladys on her bed. She hadn't been so warm since she moved into the attic. When she woke in the morning, she kissed him on the nose and said, "Merry Christmas, Taffy, I love you so much. Someday I will be rich enough to have a dog of my own, and I'll find one just like you. Now we'd better get up and see how we are going to get you to Millie's without being seen."

That would have been a difficult task without the aid of Hilda, Becky, and Lily, who were kind enough to delay their departures in order to keep watch as Gladys and Taffy escaped out the back door of the inn and ran quickly down the alley until they were out of sight.

Once they were safely away, they slowed down to enjoy the walk. At first Taffy wanted to keep running, but Gladys held him back, and it didn't take long before he was walking along quietly, looking up at her now and again for approval. "That sailor was right; you certainly are a well-trained little doggie," she said. As though Taffy understood, he held his head a little higher, and walked with a more dignified gait.

As she was walking, Gladys thought about how kind Becky

and Lily were to stay and help them escape without being seen—especially since she hadn't gone out of her way to be friendly. She could tell by the way they avoided eye contact whenever they met her that they thought she came from a higher station in life than they did.

Maybe it was because of her proper diction, but whatever the reason, she found it quite pleasing. Although it was done with a hint of condescension, she vowed to be much friendlier towards them in the future. Gladys had taken her first step up the social class ladder, and although the step was minuscule, it kindled a resolve to climb higher.

Just before arriving at Millie's, she took the red satin ribbon she had in her hair and tied it to Taffy's collar. "There, now you look lovely. Millie is just going to love you!" When she knocked at Millie's back door, she picked the dog up and held him in her arms.

Millie wasn't expecting anyone except Gladys, so she called out, "The door is not locked, Gladys. Come on in, dear."

When no one entered, Millie went to the door and started to open it, but was almost knocked down as Gladys pushed it open and thrust Taffy into her arms, saying, "Merry Christmas, Millie."

Millie let out a scream, threw her arms in the air, and dropped poor Taffy. Luckily, he landed on his feet. "What is that?" she cried.

"It's a dog, silly! It's your Christmas present. Isn't he beautiful? His name is Taffy, and he is such a good little dog." Millie's mouth hung open, and she remained staring at the dog as though she had been struck dumb. Gladys put a hand on Millie's arm, and asked, "Millie, what's wrong? You do like dogs, don't you?"

Millie shook her head to clear it, then swiped Gladys hand away. "You foolish, silly girl! What on earth have you gone and done?"

Gladys's face fell, "Don't you like him, Millie?"

"It matters not whether I like him or not. I cannot have a dog here any more than you can have one at the inn. You know I do not own the premises, and if my landlord were to find out I have a dog, he would not hesitate to evict me."

"But, Millie, if I hadn't saved him, he would have ended up on the street starving. The sailor who owned him was shipping out today, and he was just going to leave Taffy on the dock."

"What do you think I shall have to do with him then?"

"Oh, Millie, you wouldn't just leave him, would you?" Her bottom lip started to quiver.

"Don't you dare cry," Millie said crossly, as she stamped her foot. "It is I who should be crying. You should have thought of all that before you took the dog. Now you expect me to do something that may cause me to be thrown out on the street. Oh, damn you, Gladys!" Gladys had never heard her friend use profanity before, and she backed away, fearful that Millie might even strike her. "I shall have no choice but to get rid of him. Can you not see that?" the dressmaker added as she dropped down onto a chair, and put her hands over her face.

Taffy seemed to sense her sadness. He sat down at her feet, looked up at her, and whined. Millie broke out in tears.

"Please don't cry, Millie. I am so sorry. You are right, I am a stupid dolt. I shall take him back right now, and keep him in my room until Hilda comes back in the morning."

Millie wiped her eyes on her pinny, "What good will that do? She can't keep a dog there either."

Gladys's voice was nothing more than a nervous whisper as she pleaded, "Could you keep him just for two days, Millie? Just until I find someone to take him. Maybe Hilda could give him to Pete, the coal man. He's such a friendly dog, and he's a very special one too. He comes from Lord Huntley's kennels."

"I guess I have no choice. I just hope to heavens the landlord doesn't come around in the meantime." She stood up, giving Taffy an unconscious pat on his head, and went toward the oven. "Now help me get our Christmas dinner on the table before it is ruined."

In spite of their argument, Millie and Gladys had an enjoyable Christmas day. Before they sat down to dinner, Millie sent Gladys

up to the flat above hers with two plates of dinner for Ed and Myrna Harper, an elderly couple. Although the Harpers weren't much older than Millie, she always referred to them as "the old folks upstairs." Through the years, Myrna Harper's eyesight had failed so drastically that she was now considered blind. Ed managed to care for her even though he was severely crippled himself with rheumatism and had to use two canes to get around.

Millie would have changed apartments with them if it wasn't for her shop. When Gladys asked if they had any family, Millie explained that they only had one son, Jeffrey, who had done very well for himself when he married a wealthy lady. She went on to say that although he didn't invite his parents to his wedding, they still thought the world of him. "I only met him once," Millie said, "and although I was all set to give him a piece of my mind, I found him most likeable.

"Although he is small of stature, he is well built, and I would even say he is quite handsome. Unfortunately, he is a meek fellow, and that makes me think he would be easy to take advantage of. In fact, I have come to the conclusion that his wife is the culprit and not poor Jeffrey. I may be mistaken, but I think because they are disabled, she considers his parents not presentable enough to associate with her kind. I only hope that if they have children, she will be kind enough to allow him to bring them to visit Myrna. I don't think she could bear it if he didn't."

"But how do they manage without someone to take care of them?"

"Oh, Jeffrey does that. He pays a lady to come every week for two hours to cook and clean for them, and he comes himself at least once a week for a good long visit.

When they finished their dinner, Gladys and Millie took Taffy for a little walk, and although Millie didn't say anything, Gladys could tell that she was impressed with the dog's behaviour. After they returned, Millie gave Gladys the gift she had promised her. It was the fancy dress she had put aside for her on the first day they had met. Pinned to the bodice was a pretty silver brooch with blue painted violets on it. Except for the cameo Sally had given her, they were the only gifts she had ever received.

With tears of gratitude, she said, "Oh, Millie, I don't know what to say. I never ever thought I would own a dress as beautiful as this one, and I think this is the most beautiful brooch in the whole world! I shall treasure it forever and ever." Then she remembered promising the same thing to Sally, and she cried even harder.

Just before she left to return to the inn, Taffy jumped up and curled up on Millie's bed. Gladys started to scold him, but Mille stopped her, saying, "Oh leave him alone. He is in a strange house and is probably feeling very lonely. I shall make up a pallet for him on the floor tomorrow." Gladys smiled. She didn't think Taffy was one bit lonely, and she doubted there would be a pallet made the next day.

Chapter Eight

Millie proved to be right, as the Hogmanay celebrations continued for two days at the inn. Both the Watts' personalities changed so completely that they seemed like strangers. Gladys was surprised at the many superstitions they and their guests insisted on following. All debts had to be settled before midnight. The first visitor to arrive after the clock struck twelve must be a dark-haired male bearing a lump of coal, some shortbread, a little salt, a black bun, and whisky. Then once he had been made welcome, the other visitors were met with a warm hug, a kiss, and often a gift. But what Gladys enjoyed the most was the boisterous and wholehearted way that everyone sang Robert Burns's song, "For Auld Lang Syne." Laura even encouraged her and the other girls to join in.

An added amount of cleaning and preparations during the week before Hogmanay meant more work for the help, and Gladys didn't have a chance to visit Millie until nine days after Christmas. Because she was so busy, she had forgotten to ask Hilda if Pete would take Taffy, the dog. She knew Millie's landlord might have paid her a visit, and she could already be evicted. If so, Gladys was sure the seamstress would never forgive her.

Her fears were augmented when she finally had an evening off and found the dressmaker's house in darkness. When Millie failed to answer her knock, Gladys felt sick with guilt. She was about to climb the stairs to inquire if Ed or Myrna knew where the seamstress had gone when she heard a familiar bark. She turned, looked down the alley, and called out, "Here, Taffy! Here, boy."

Taffy came running up and danced around her on his hind legs. She reached down and picked him up. "Oh Taffy, you are still here! Millie, is that you?"

"Of course it's me." Millie answered as she came up the alley huffing and puffing like a steam engine. "Who else would it be with our Taffy?"

"Oh, Millie, you weren't evicted! The landlord didn't throw you out on the street."

"I have not seen him, but if he does come, I know what I shall tell him," Millie answered as she unlocked her door, went in, and lit the lamp. Gladys followed and waited patiently for her to stoke the fire and put the kettle on to boil. It seemed as though Millie was deliberately moving in slow motion, and finally Gladys could stand it no longer.

"For heaven's sake, Millie, tell me what you are going to tell him, or I shall have a fit!"

"Have as many fits as you like; I shall not tell you anything until I have a cup of tea in my hand."

Gladys took the hint and quickly took off her cloak, brewed the tea, and poured them each a cup. "Now, will you please tell me what you intend to say if the landlord discovers you have a dog?"

"Well, I shall just tell him that Taffy deserves to have a home with me because he kills all the rats—he does you know—and I know of no one who would agree to pay rent for a rat-infested flat. If he does not appreciate that, he can go right ahead and evict me. Taffy and I shall find another home, don't you worry." She called the dog to her and gave him a big hug and a biscuit.

As time progressed, Gladys accomplished more in ten hours than Laura could in twelve, and although it allowed the landlady more time to spend in the bar listening to the local gossip, there was still something about Gladys she didn't like. She could tell by her speech that she was no guttersnipe. She had even seen her reading a newspaper. None of her other employees had ever shown signs of being educated, and Laura liked it that way. It gave her a feeling of both superiority and dominance over them.

Laura had also heard about Gladys's friendship with the seamstress, and she'd seen the two fancy dresses hanging in the girl's attic room. One of the frocks was fancier than even she could afford. It just didn't make sense why someone like Gladys would have to work as a housemaid. She finally consoled herself with the thought that it didn't really matter why Gladys came to work at the inn, so long as she did her job.

To make sure that Gladys knew her place, Laura gave her the most difficult and undesirable jobs like cleaning the dirty outhouses—a job so objectionable it made Gladys bilious even though the outhouses in Old Nichol had been far more disgusting. She often thought that if she hadn't killed old Gaylord, she would tell Mrs Watt to clean the outhouses herself and go back home.

Things were much easier when Laura visited her mother in Scotland. Neil was content to give all his attention to the running of the pub and leave Gladys and the rest of the maids on their own. During one of the times when Laura was in Scotland, Gladys left work early, and went to the shoemakers to order a pair of soft leather slippers. The only shoes she owned, except for the oversized shoes she had taken from her parents' junk yard, were the ugly, black working boots that Laura had given her.

Finding a shoemaker to make a pair she could afford took more time than she had anticipated, so she had to complete her chores in the evening. She was down on her knees scrubbing the passageway that led from the kitchen to the pub when she heard someone playing a tune called "Jones' Ale" on a concertina. Knowing the song well, she unconsciously began singing the lyrics as she worked.

A customer who happened to be sitting at a table near the hallway overheard and motioned to the musician to play a little quieter. Then he signalled the rest of the customers to come closer in order to hear the sweet-sounding lyrics as Gladys sang. They couldn't resist joining in on the chorus—

> "When the landlord's daughter, she came in,
>
> And we kissed those rosy cheeks again.
>
> We all sat down and then we'd sing,
>
> When Jones' Ale was new, me boys, when Jones'
> Ale was new."

When Gladys realized there were others singing, she looked up and was surprised to see a huddle of five ruddy-faced characters all grinning down at her. Her face went crimson with embarrassment, and she tried to hide it behind her wet soapy hands. Then, when no one spoke, she felt obliged to mumble a weak, "I'm sorry."

"Aye, and ye should be!" was the reply.

She had no alternative but to drop her hands and apologize again, "I didn't think you could hear me. I really am sorry."

One of the men gruffly replied, "You will be a lot sorrier, my girl, if you don't finish the song."

A hand reached down along with a demand, "Give me your hand now, and let's get you over by the bar where we can hear some more of that sweet-sounding voice."

Gladys was ashamed to put her rough and reddened hand into the stranger's, but even more afraid to refuse. The music began again, and she had no recourse but to finish the song. After the applause died down, she was cajoled into singing more songs, in spite of Neil Watt's frown of disapproval. However, as the night wore on, even he couldn't help but be impressed, especially when she sang "Lovely Willie," which was one of his favourites. He even joined in on the chorus.

The next evening after Gladys had left to visit Millie, the same men returned to the inn, bringing along a half dozen new customers, women included, to hear the young songstress. Neil was all smiles until they began to complain and demand to know when the lassie with the voice like an angel was going to sing. Some had walked a fair distance to enjoy a musical evening and felt cheated when she didn't appear. Neil tried to explain that she was just a housemaid and not an entertainer, but it did little good. When they threatened to leave and never return, he offered them all a free round—something he had never done before, and in all probability, would never do again. He also promised Gladys would be there to entertain them if they returned the following evening.

A free drink was something none could refuse, but when they finished the drink most of them left. One fellow Scot hit Neil on the shoulder on his way out, and said, "You dinna ken what a fortune you have with that lassie, Neil," and another added, "Sure an' she's a voice that's as captivating as a revivalist's spiel."

Neil repeated his promise to have Gladys there the following night and was happy when they said they would be there and bring more friends. However, they also warned him that if Gladys didn't sing, they would no longer patronize his establishment. Neil, feeling certain she wouldn't refuse, took the warning lightly. The following morning, he was waiting in the kitchen to tell her that he expected her to sing that night. Although she thought he should have had the decency to *ask* her, she agreed. She had enjoyed singing with the men, finding it a pleasant departure from her tedious routine.

The first time Gladys sang in the pub, she was clad in her drab and dirty housemaid's uniform and dust cap. This time she took special care with her grooming and, although the dress she chose to wear was the plain one she had purchased from Millie, she knew it was

still very pretty and decided it would be perfect for the occasion. By the time she left her room, she was very pleased with her appearance. Except for a few ringlets hanging saucily down her neck, her hair was pinned up neatly and adorned with a pretty yellow ribbon. However, her confidence soon faded when she entered the pub and saw the large crowd of customers waiting to hear her sing.

She was about to make a swift retreat, when one of the men she had sung with two nights before took hold of her arm and escorted her to a table. It took a lot of persuasion, plus two hearty drinks of whiskey, before she found enough courage to render a note. Nonetheless, before long she began to relax and enjoy herself. For the first time in her life she began to understand why her mother loved performing in the pubs of Old Nichol. All the customers looked at her, not only with admiration, but with envy as well, despite her nervousness. It was her first taste of fame, and she loved it.

Because most of the customers knew the songs, they joined in on the choruses, which added gaiety and harmony to the occasion. No one wanted the evening to end, but Gladys had to bid them goodnight in order to get a little sleep before morning. After everyone left, Neil, eager to count the night's take, hurried to lock up. Twice during the evening, it was necessary to leave Gladys serving the customers while he went to the basement for more ale, something he had never had to do before. When he found that his earnings had more than doubled, he began to see the possibilities of Gladys's presence in the bar.

But when he asked her to sing again the following evening, she refused, saying she had far too much work to do as it was. Neil was surprised and annoyed that she would have the nerve to say no. Afraid of losing all his new customers, he grudgingly offered to take over some of her chores. Perhaps if a hint of friendship had accompanied his offer, Gladys might have agreed, but even though she enjoyed the singing and would have appreciated his help, it was far more gratifying to see him squirm. Furious, Neil did all he could to stifle his anger before leaving her with the suggestion that she think it over during the night.

Gladys did think it over—very carefully. She knew how desperate Neil was to have her sing, and, smiling decisively, she reasoned that it might be to her advantage to refuse him, and to see how far he would go with his offers. The idea that it could be the start of a new life appealed to her, and she decided to make the most of the opportunity.

When Neil approached her the next day and found that she was still adamant in her refusal to perform, he was left with no alternative but to resort to obsequious pleas while following her around the pub as she worked. Finally, she lay down her dusting clout, went into the inn's pub with Neil at her heels, sat on a chair, and declared, "Mr Watt, if you would be kind enough to fetch me a drink, perhaps we can come to an agreement."

Neil's blood rose to the boiling point and his face turned crimson. "Just who do you think you're ordering aboot?" he shouted.

Gladys would tell Millie later that he was so angry, she could almost see smoke coming from both of his ears, and she prayed he wouldn't notice how terrified she was as she got up and started to walk away. Her heart was beating rapidly as she heard Neil deflating his anger with a volley of curse words. But then she relaxed as he called her back.

"Och, dinna get your back up, lassie. Sit down and I'll bring you a drink."

Gladys accepted the offer, and, after taking a sip of the refreshing brew, she wiped her mouth on her sleeve, and said, "I am very sorry, Mr Watt, but it is far too difficult to be both a housemaid and an entertainer."

"I canna see why," he answered sharply.

Gladys almost lost her nerve, but she knew that it was now or, more than likely, never. She straightened her back, and, looking much more complacent than she felt, replied, "Well, one of your customers said that I could more than likely find employment as a barmaid and singer in any of the other pubs in Dover."

Neil was so taken aback by her brazen announcement that he sat with his mouth hanging open for a time before mustering breath enough to shout, "You are out of your head, lass! Now you've gone too far. Ye can pack up your belongings and git. Go and find another job if you can." With that he rudely grabbed the mug of ale out of her hand and stomped out of the room.

Gladys knew she should run after him and apologize but her obstinacy was stronger than her sensibility. Suddenly, the realization of what she had done caused her to panic, and she almost gave in until she remembered that she had a year's wages along with her gratuities saved. With a weak shrug of her shoulders, she picked up her dust clout, and loudly announced to the empty room, "And I'll make bloody certain that they can't say I left without finishing my chores."

When her work was done, she ate a hearty dinner, hugged and bid Hilda a sad farewell, packed up her few belongings, then offered a fallaciously, cheery goodbye to Neil on her way out the door.

Neil's answer to her farewell was a loud and churlish, "Good riddance!" Had he known how gruelling and disconcerting the next few days would be without her, he would have realized what a mistake he had made.

Neil thought he'd have no trouble coping. All he had to do was divide Gladys's chores between Becky and Lily, but it only took a few hours for him to realize that they could hardly keep up with their own work let alone Gladys's, so he had to take over the tasks himself. No matter how rigorously he attempted to complete even the easiest chore, he was unsuccessful, and his lack of diplomacy did nothing to soothe the complaining guests.

To add to this dilemma, he didn't have time to open the pub until evening, which angered his regular daytime customers. They would bang boisterously at the door, annoying both him and his guests. When he opened that evening, his regular customers were so disappointed to find that Gladys no longer worked for him that many of them left without buying a drink.

Things were in dire shape when Laura returned from Scotland, and when Neil welcomed her with unexpected enthusiasm, she knew there was something amiss. When he filled her in on the events that had taken place while she was away, he expected a tongue-lashing, but was pleasantly surprised to find her sympathetic. Although she was impressed with the amount of profit Neil had taken in on the two evenings that Gladys had entertained, she wasn't sorry to be rid of her.

She changed her mind after weeks of hard work and listening to the constant complaints from the few customers they still had. Laura became tired enough to admit she had been wrong and not canny enough to realize that the girl's talent could prove to be an enormous asset. She began to think that if the lass were to attract enough customers, she and Neil could even enlarge the pub.

Visions of grandeur overtook her, and she pictured the inn as the most patronized drinking establishment in all of Dover. In no time they would be able to sell the inn and buy a grand one in Scotland. When she began belittling Neil for being so near-sighted, he put up with her nagging for two weeks. Then his patience gave out.

"Shush your gob, woman. You've said enough. If you want the lassie back, go and find her, an' see if you can come to an agreement."

As soon as the door of the inn closed behind her, Gladys had realized she was homeless. Millie was her only friend and would take her in, but Gladys knew that she wasn't allowed guests. For a time, she stood outside the inn, not knowing what to do, before she decided that Millie might know of a place where she could afford to rent a room for a few days while looking for work. She only hoped Millie wasn't going to be too angry with her for quitting her job.

Millie was more concerned than angry. "What are you going to do now?" she asked.

"I don't know. I've nowhere to go, Millie. Do you know any place where I could find a few nights lodging while I look for work?"

"You are not going anywhere. We shall fashion a pallet—that is if you don't mind sleeping on the floor?"

"Of course I don't mind, but what about your landlord? I don't want to get you into trouble."

"We shall just have to be discreet and not let him know you are here. It shan't be easy, my dear, but as far as I can see, we have no choice."

"Oh, Millie, I don't know how I will ever repay you."

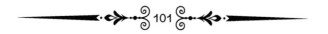

Millie was an excellent seamstress, but not very astute as a housekeeper, so both the shop and her living quarters were in a state of disarray. In a few days, Gladys had the entire place scrubbed and shining and still managed to cook their meals and help Millie with her sewing in the evenings.

Millie's landlord lived in a nearby town and came by once a month, not only to collect the rent and to inspect his buildings, but to keep his tenants on their toes. He preferred to catch them unaware and often dropped in unannounced. This happened two weeks after Gladys moved in. Gladys was in the back when he arrived and fortunately overheard Millie talking to him.

After, a few questions about the state of her affairs, he announced, "Now I shall just go and have a look in the back, if you don't mind."

"Oh, no, you mustn't," Millie answered without thinking. Her attitude caused him to become suspicious, and he pushed her aside and entered the fitting room.

Gladys was ready for him; she had shed her frock and was clad only in her underpinnings when he came in. She screamed, "How dare you, sir! Mrs McIver, what is this man doing in here? Get out, I say! Get out!"

The landlord's face turned crimson as he apologized and stumbled back into the shop. "Excuse me, miss, I didn't, ah, I didn't know."

Gladys continued the gambit by calling out to Millie in what she thought to be an aristocratic pitch, "Really, Mrs McIver, you must take more care with your clients, or I shall be purchasing my frocks elsewhere."

Millie, suppressing a giggle, joined in the charade, "I am so sorry, my dear Mrs Peabody; it shan't happen again, I assure you."

"I should hope not! Now do come and finish this fitting, I must have this frock ready for the mayor's garden party."

The landlord, a prudish bachelor, had never seen a woman so scantily dressed. He wiped the sweat from his brow, offered Millie a mumbled apology, and hurriedly took his leave. Millie watched out the window until he was safely out of sight before she ran into the other room. "He's gone—probably never to return," she announced, and they laughed until their sides ached, Millie's makeup was ruined, and she was forced to make a quick trip to the outhouse.

Gladys didn't mind sleeping on the floor, especially since her surroundings were much cosier than a dreary, dark attic, and Millie seemed to be enjoying her company. Although they both knew the arrangement had to terminate before long, they continued to defer the subject. One sunny afternoon when Millie had a full day of appointments, Gladys took Taffy for a walk alone and was just returning home when she noticed a man sitting on the bottom stairs leading up to the Harpers' flat.

"Hello there! You must be the girl Mother has told me about. It is Gladys, is it not?"

Gladys nodded her reply, then said, "You must be Jeffrey," as she reached out her hand.

Her action both surprised and amused him. He had never met a young lady who had the audacity to instigate a handshake instead of curtsey before, and he couldn't help but chuckle as he took her hand in his. Then he noticed the hurt look on her face, and his smile quickly faded as he apologized. "I am terribly sorry; please don't think me rude. I've heard such nice things about you from my parents. It is so refreshing to meet a young lady who doesn't put on airs."

Gladys wasn't sure if she should be flattered by his words or insulted, but he had such a cordial look to his countenance that she decided he meant it as a compliment. It was quite brisk out, and when he told her he was waiting for the woman he had hired to finish with his mother's toilette, she took the liberty of inviting him in for a cup of tea.

In spite of Jeffrey's rank in society, they found quite a few topics of common interest to talk about as they drank their tea. Jeffrey enjoyed singing, and Gladys was surprised that they knew many of the same songs, but she wasn't surprised when he said his wife and her friends didn't appreciate them at all. In between customers, Millie joined them, and she could see that Jeffrey was enjoying himself. He and Gladys were chatting away as though they were old friends, but when Gladys asked him if he and his wife had any children, Millie thought she was being too familiar. She was relieved, however, when Jeffrey's face lit up, and he told her that they were expecting their first child in about a month.

"How wonderful!" Gladys exclaimed. "Won't your mother be delighted to have a grandchild."

His smiled faded as he shook his head and addressed both ladies in an almost pleading voice, "I would rather you didn't tell her. I don't know if I can explain it so you shan't think I am heartless, but you see, my wife and her family are of a totally different class than my parents. Mother and Father understand, and believe me, they would not be comfortable in my wife's or her parents' company. God knows there are times when I'm not either, so I think it is better for all concerned to keep things as they are. If Mother knew about the baby, she would want to spend more time with it than my wife would allow, and I cannot bear to hurt her. She is such a wonderful person. Do you understand?"

Forgetting for a moment that she had denied her own heritage when she took the name of Tweedhope, Gladys answered as she often did, without thinking, and said, "I think you should stand up to your wife, and tell her you will take the child to visit your parents as often as you please."

Millie choked on her tea, and after a few pats on the back to help regain her breath, she exclaimed, "Gladys! What a rude thing to say. You apologize to Jeffrey right this minute."

"But, Millie, did you hear? Myrna and Ed are going to be grandparents, and Jeffrey isn't going to tell them."

"I heard perfectly well, but that is Jeffrey's decision and has nothing to do with you. Now apologize."

Gladys's face turned red, and she began to say she was sorry when Jeffrey held up his hand and stopped her. "No, Mrs McIver, she only said what I needed to hear. Gladys, you are right. I have allowed my wife and her parents to push me around far too long. I put up with it because I was grateful to my father-in-law for helping me achieve my political position, but now that I am going to be a father, I think it's time I practiced being a man."

After he left to visit his parents, Gladys looked at Millie sheepishly, expecting a scolding, but Millie just shook her head and said, "One of these times your thoughtless remarks are going to land you in deep trouble, and when that happens, I hope I shall be there to say that I told you so."

Four weeks after Gladys left the inn, Laura Watt was outside Millie's shop door early one morning, waiting for her to open in order to inquire about Gladys's whereabouts. Gladys had left the premises early to purchase fresh vegetables at the market.

Worried that her friend might be in trouble, Millie demanded to know why Laura was interested in Gladys's whereabouts. Unaccustomed to sounding contrite, Laura grimaced when she answered, "It seems that my man was a wee bit stern with the lassie, so if you can give her a message, will you tell the lass he dinna mean to dismiss her?"

Millie enjoyed seeing the woman grovel and replied, "Oh, I don't think Gladys needs to work as a maid now, Mrs Watt, since other establishments have heard of her talents and offered her work at a decent wage. In fact, I do believe she has an interview tomorrow."

"Och! Could you tell me where that might be?"

"Sorry, but I'm not at liberty to say."

"Then, will you be seeing the lassie this day, Mrs McIver?"

"I think so. She usually drops in to see me every day."

"Good! Good! If it's not too much trouble, will you ask her to drop in at the inn this day?"

Millie shrugged her shoulders and answered indifferently, "I suppose I could."

Millie's blasé attitude irritated Laura, but she had no choice other than to thank the seamstress and leave with hopes that Gladys would receive the message. Not long after, Gladys returned to the shop.

"Look, Millie, I found these nice small beetroots and new potatoes to go with the leg of mutton I shall cook for us tonight."

"That's lovely, dear, and I have something interesting to tell you. Believe it or not, our illustrious Mrs Watt came looking for you this morning."

"Oh my heavens! I hope she isn't after me for leaving. If she is, I shall just tell her the truth; I didn't leave of my own accord. Her husband let me go."

"Well, I do not think you have to worry; she actually came to apologize for her husband's behaviour."

"I can't believe she would say such a thing. Honestly, did she really?"

"She did, and she wants to see you today. I suspect to offer you a barmaid's job."

Gladys squealed with delight. "I shall go there right away. I can't wait to find out what she wants."

"Don't you dare! You must not appear too anxious. Moreover, I informed Mrs Watt that you are going to have an interview tomorrow for a more suitable position and will no longer consider taking such a menial job as a housemaid."

"Millie, you are simply wonderful! Do you know that?"

"I do know that I am becoming far too accustomed to telling falsehoods."

"Isn't it fun, Millie?"

"Not if you are caught, my dear; not if you are caught."

Gladys's reception at the Scots Inn was far more pleasant than her first encounter with the owners, albeit it insincere. She was offered tea and biscuits, which she nonchalantly accepted. After a few moments of awkward silence, Laura gave Neil a sharp dig in his ribs to loosen his tongue. He coughed a little and then began, "You'll recall, lass, we had a wee squabble a few weeks past?" Gladys merely

nodded, so he continued, "Well, that's neither here nor there. Now, we talked it over, and we just may have another job for you, if you'll take it."

"It depends, Mr Watt, on what the job is and what my wage shall be."

"What would you think of being our barmaid in the evening and doing a wee bit of maid's work in the day? Of course, we would'na mind if you sing a song or two while you serve the customers."

The thought of being a barmaid pleased Gladys, but since she intended to be hired on her own terms this time, she kept the couple in negotiation for over an hour before arriving at a mutual accord. She agreed to move back into the attic the next morning after receiving a promise that if, and when, the Watts hired another girl, the girl would be housed in the attic, and she would be given a small room with a good sized window on the third floor.

On her way back to Millie's shop, Gladys visited the baker's shop and bought two large Eccles cakes to celebrate. Millie was busy with a customer on her return, so she was unable to share the good news until they were seated at the dinner table.

Proudly, Gladys told Millie how she had outwitted the Watts, "I will have a few chores in the mornings, but they are all clean chores, like making beds, ironing, hanging out the washing and maybe do the mending, now and then—"

Millie interrupted, "Oh, ho! Now that the woman thinks that you know how to sew, she shall have you altering her dresses and, more than likely, making her husband's shirts."

"Don't worry, I shall simply tell her I do not know how to sew. I shall be able to have a little time off in the afternoon before dinner. Then I am to be the barmaid. I don't even have to pay to have a bath, and, best of all, I shall have most Sundays free. Of course that means a little less pay, but won't it be wonderful to have a whole day with nothing to do? I'll take long walks in the woods and along the shore. Oh, Millie, I'm so happy!"

Millie, knowing how much she would miss the girl's company, wasn't so elated, and explained, "Although you have only been with me for a short time, I feel as though we are family, and I shall miss you dearly."

Putting her arms around the seamstress, Gladys hugged her tightly and promised, "Don't worry, Millie, I will visit you often."

Chapter Nine

Gladys's musical talent and lively personality brought so many customers to the inn that both Neil and his wife were kept busy serving drinks and food. Everything was working satisfactorily until Lily, the chambermaid, left to look after her sick mother, and Laura had to take over her chores. The extra work proved too demanding for a woman her age, and one night after the last customer had departed, she complained to Neil, "I canna keep up with it all. You have to hire another lass."

Neil, overjoyed with their success, surprised her with his cheery retort, "Laura, me love, you can have two lassies, or even three."

"What did you say?"

"I said you can hire as many lassies as need be."

"You're either off your head or you're fou wi' whiskey."

"I'm no fou, woman! Do you mind the fellow Lyle, who comes for a meat pie an' a pint every Tuesday?"

"The cobbler?"

"Aye, that's the one. Well, do you ken he has a wee laddie working in his shop, and two lassies cooking an' cleaning for him?"

"Good for him, but what's that to do with us?"

"Well, he dinna pay them as muckle as a farthing. Lyle said there are those in London so poor they'll give up their lassies for just a wee stipend. Now, if we have a mind to, he can arrange for us to have one or more. All we have to do is go to London to fetch them."

"Och! I'll no take part in such an act. It's as sinful as buying slaves. I dinna belong to the 'Anti-Slavery Society' for naught."

"But, do you ken, woman? The lassies will starve if you leave them where they be. If we give them some good food, a decent frock, and a warm bed to lie in, they'll be far better off. And we can give them a wee bit o' a wage as well."

Laura's aching back did more to convince her than Neil's words, but her consent came with one condition, "I'll not take a lass under the age of twelve."

One month later the arrangements were made for Laura to travel to London and bring home two young girls if they met with her approval. However, two nights before she was to leave, she suffered a severe bout of ague and felt too ill to travel. Since Neil had no idea how to judge the girls, Laura decided to send Gladys in her place.

The thought of returning to London terrified Gladys, but when she learned that the stage coach would be going directly to Victoria Station, she began to look forward to the trip, feeling confident that no one from Old Nichol would be in that part of town. She hurried over to tell Millie, who made it her business to see that Gladys was not going to London dressed like a servant.

"You must wear that frock I gave you for Christmas, my dear, now that you have the chance to show it off."

"But, Millie, I was saving it for something special!" Gladys insisted.

"Nonsense. What could be more special than a trip to London? If you intend to be a governess someday, this is the ideal time for you to dress up and practice being a proper lady. And you had better behave like one. Hold your head high, and talk quietly with a certain tone of authority."

"I don't think I can."

"Then I advise you to say as little as possible; then no one will know the difference." Millie laughed as she went into the store and returned carrying some interesting looking items. "Now to compliment your pretty green dress, you shall wear this brown velvet cape. See, it has a dark green satin lining, and here is a pair of brown, soft leather gloves to match the brown piping and nodes that are on your dress. I do have a lovely hat that matches the cape, but I think this pretty little straw bonnet will be far more comfortable for travelling. There! Now your ensemble is complete."

Gladys put on the cape and the hat then twirled around in front of a mirror trying to see herself from every angle. She wished Sally and Toughie could see how ladylike she looked.

When she came into the kitchen wearing her outfit on the morning of her departure, Laura had just taken a mouthful of tea and would have choked to death if Hilda, the cook, hadn't been there to give her a few slaps on her back. Perhaps Hilda used more force than necessary, but as she told the scullery maid when they laughed about it later, "It didn't half feel good."

Although Laura had seen Gladys's good dress hanging in the attic, she hadn't seen the cape or the other pretty accessories to go with it. Now the sight of her employee dressed in such grandeur shocked her so that when she stopped choking, she demanded to know how a barmaid could afford such finery. Gladys was tempted to tell her that it was none of her business where she got her clothes, but knowing what a temper Laura had, she was afraid of ending up out on the street without a job instead of on her way to London. She confessed that the cape, bonnet, and gloves were all borrowed from her friend, Millie McIver.

Laura wasn't sure she believed her, but because Gladys was such an asset to their business, she couldn't afford to make accusations. She shrugged her shoulders, handed her three envelopes containing money, then explained that one was for travelling and lodging expenses, one for the man who would take her from her hotel to meet the girls, and one to give to the person who would fetch them.

Then she gave Gladys orders about what to do on her arrival at Victoria Station. "You have to find a cabriolet or an omnibus that will take you to number five Laurel Street where there's a room reserved for you at the Grover Hotel. On the morn after you get to the hotel, a lad by the name of Sandy will come and take you to meet with the lassies. Now you must give them a good once over to make sure they're fit, do you ken?" Gladys promised to do her best, and after enjoying a hearty breakfast that the cook insisted she eat, she left for the station.

The journey to London proved to be far less enjoyable than she had anticipated, mostly because she had promised Millie to act as sophisticated as she appeared. The coach, much larger than the one she had arrived in, held eight passengers who all treated her with respect. If it wasn't for Millie's advice, she would have laughed and chatted away merrily with them all; but she played her role well, smiling sedately and saying little. By the time they arrived in London, she was thoroughly fed up with the charade and wished she had worn an outfit that allowed her to be herself.

As soon as she got off the coach and saw all the vendors' stalls, Millie's advice was forgotten. She went from one stall to another, greeting the vendors with friendly smiles and admiring their wares. They in turn were surprised and flattered that such an obviously wealthy and beautiful young lady would treat them so.

Some of the items in the stalls had exotic titles such as French lace, Moroccan slippers, and West Indies' spices, making them that much more appealing.

Food vendors were selling all types of fish. There were shellfish and eels, alive or cooked, and stalls with an assortment of fowl and cuts of meat that Gladys couldn't identify. The stalls she liked the best were the ones selling beautiful, hand-tooled leather goods, and delightful toys and figurines carved from a variety of exotic woods. Their pleasant fragrance dulled the odious smell of the city.

Suddenly realizing how late it was, she began searching for a

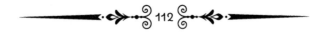

conveyance when she spotted a group of people gathered around one of the vendors. She couldn't see what they were looking at, but there was a column of steam rising over their heads and a smell so tantalizing that it compelled her to inch her way through the crowd to have a better look.

A thickset, elderly woman with a faded green bandana tied around her head sat on a beer keg behind a rough wooden table cutting potatoes into small pieces and placing them into one of the two large wooden buckets in front of her. She seemed to be oblivious of her audience and continued her work without looking up. Near the table stood an apparatus Gladys recognized as a blacksmith's forge.

The forge was alive with red-hot coals on top of which sat a huge kettle of boiling fat. This was watched over by a rotund man wearing a leather apron, whom Gladys took to be a blacksmith. She was just about to take her leave when the man lifted a large wire butterfly net-like basket out of the kettle. It was filled with pieces of potatoes similar to those that the old lady was cutting up, but the ones in the basket were a glistening golden-brown colour.

The man emptied the basket into the empty bucket, refilled it with the cut up potatoes from the other bucket, and carefully lowered it back into the boiling fat. Meanwhile, the old woman began doling out the hot, cooked potato chunks onto pieces of newspaper for the waiting customers. Gladys would have liked to stay and wait for the next batch, but it was getting late, and she didn't know how long it would take to get to the hotel.

She had turned to leave when she heard the old woman say, "'Ere, m'lady, there be one chip left. 'Ere, try it." She couldn't resist the temptation and reached out to take the piece of potato, but the old woman pulled her hand back. "You'd best take off your glove, m'lady. You might soil it!" Gladys blushed with embarrassment. The old woman had been more careful to save Millie's lovely gloves from being grease-stained than she had. The piece of fried potato proved to be one of the tastiest morsels of food Gladys had ever eaten. She thanked the kind woman and would have stayed to have more, but time was running out.

She had brought along a little of her savings, hoping to purchase a small gift for Millie, but since it was so late, she decided to wait and look for something on the way back. As she went to look for a ride, the taste of the cooked potato was still in her mouth, and she thought how nice it would be if there was a way she could take some home for Hilda, so she could try making them.

When she saw a constable coming toward her, her fear rendered her immobile, which was probably a good thing, or she might have run away and been mistaken for a thief. "I say, are you all right? Is there anything I can help you with?" he asked in a very kind and concerned voice.

Gladys sighed with relief then told him that she had never been to London before, was on her way to visit a relative, and didn't know where to find a cabriolet or an omnibus. By her attire, he was certain she would choose to hire a hackney, but felt obliged to mention that to hire a two passenger hackney or cabriolet would be twice as costly as taking an omnibus, since the omnibuses were much larger and carried up to fifteen passengers. Then he warned her that during the day, more people were allowed aboard the vehicle than there was room for, and incidents of pickpocketing were frequent.

Gladys said she didn't have far to go and would take the least expensive conveyance. Then she asked him where she could find an omnibus that went to Laurel Street. The constable offered to walk with her to the station, which was just around the corner from where they were standing. He repeated his warning about the thieves as they were walking, and she assured him she would be extremely careful.

His concern never lessened, so he stayed with her until she got on board, and, with a puzzled expression, watched as the omnibus pulled away from the station. He couldn't understand how someone so obviously well off would choose to travel on such a common conveyance if she could afford to ride in comfort and safety in a cabriolet.

After Gladys thanked the constable and boarded the omnibus, she was delighted to find that it had an open top deck. For a few blocks she had a seat to herself, but then someone sat down beside her and said, "'Opes you don't mind if I sits 'ere, yer ladyship?" At first glance, Gladys took him for a young boy, but then saw that he was a man with a very slight build. It didn't take her long to take in his attire and decide that he was a slum dweller. Instead of being repulsed by him, she experienced a feeling of compassion and surprised him with a smile and a nod of her head.

The fellow, who went by the name of "Slick," a name well suited, was one of the most talented pickpockets in all of London. He had barely sat down before the money Gladys had brought along to buy a gift for Millie had gone from her purse into his pocket. Luckily, the envelopes Laura had given her were safely hidden in the lining of her cape. Normally, Slick would have pocketed the money and made a quick getaway, but there was something about this beautiful lady that fascinated him.

He had never seen a woman so elegant on an omnibus before, and it was the first time someone of her rank had ever smiled at him. All of the high-society ladies he came near to screwed up their noses in disgust and moved quickly away, which made his job that much easier. But this pretty lady was different. She seemed so nice that he decided to ride with her, thinking it would be fun to pretend they were friends.

When he found out that she was a visitor to London and had never ridden on an omnibus before, he began pointing out places of interest.

"There's Gumby's 'aberdashery. 'E's that little far—er, feller—settin' on that water bucket outside 'is shop. 'E come 'ere from Haustralya, 'e did," Slick said, pointing to a swarthy complexioned man who looked to be no more than three feet tall. "An' there's Fa Ling's rest raunt. 'E's a right good Chink, 'e is. Gives 'is leftovers to the poor instead of sellin' 'em to tha piggeries."

The six-horse team pulling the omnibus wound its way through some very narrow and busy streets, and Slick noticed how Gladys's face lit up with excitement as they passed the multitude of vendors, hawkers, and bargain hunters. She loved the kaleidoscope of colours among the fusion of different races, many clad in their tribal outfits. The lively symphony orchestrated by their raucous banter seemed to be in perfect harmony with the beat of the horse's hooves clattering on the cobblestones.

Slick suddenly became aware that it was now Gladys who was pointing things out to him, and he felt as though he had never really seen London before, even though he had lived there all his life. Then when she laughed and pointed toward a little girl who was stealing some apples from the back of a wagon while her friends kept the vendor's attention, he suddenly remembered his daughter's birthday. "I 'as to go now, miss. You sees it's me Hanna's birthday! She be six."

Gladys found that she'd be sorry to see him leave and made a quick decision, saying, "I was going to buy a dear friend of mine a present, but I'm sure she would much rather I give you the money so you can buy something nice for your Hanna." As she went to open her purse, he grabbed it out of her hands.

"'Ere, miss! You don't oughter 'ave yer purse 'angin' on a cord like that. A thief could take 'is knife an' cut it, an' you'd never know it were gone 'til 'e was miles away." In a split second he managed to replace the money he had stolen without being seen—so he thought. Although Gladys was unaware that he had taken her money, she saw him return it. He used the same technique that some of her friends had used in Old Nichol, and instead of feeling angry, she felt a sense of kinship toward him. Although he tried to refuse it, she insisted he take half of the money she had for Millie's present.

"Much obliged, miss. Yer an angel, right enough." Then he gave her a saucy wink and disappeared so quickly, she wondered if he was ever there.

The ride didn't seem as exhilarating without the pickpocket's company, and as twilight descended and the streets became vacant, a melancholic mood overtook her. She was relieved when the omnibus came to a stop outside her hotel. Once she registered, a pleasant woman saw her settled into a drab, but clean, room, then brought her a very welcome meat sandwich along with a hot mug of tea.

After a peaceful night, Gladys had washed, dressed, and was sitting in the dining room having breakfast when an unkempt, but smiling, young man approached her. Saying his name was Sandy, he explained he had come to take her to meet the girls. When he saw she hadn't finished her tea, he politely offered to wait for her outside. As soon as she exited the hotel, Gladys looked around for her carriage, but the only vehicle on the street was a dilapidated, open wagon with nothing but a bench seat at the front. There was a man wearing a large, ragged straw hat sitting on the seat whom Gladys didn't recognize until he turned around and called out, "Up here, miss; up here."

Although she was shocked when she saw it was Sandy, she was even more shocked when she saw the worn-out condition of the animal that was hitched to his wagon. She couldn't help but chuckle as she thought that the straw hat was on the wrong head.

Sandy, aware of the inappropriateness of his rig for such an eloquent passenger, apologized as he helped her up onto the seat, and, pointing to his elderly, sway-backed horse, he said, "Sorry, miss, she aren't no German bay, but old Nellie's reliable and will get us safely there and back in good time—if it don't rain. Nellie's old legs aren't too steady on wet cobblestones. If it does rain, miss, you'll find a piece of canvas under your seat to put over your head. It'll keep you nice and dry."

They had gone about a mile when Gladys cried out, "Stop!" causing the old nag to bolt and Sandy to jump so high in the air that he almost fell off the wagon.

After he calmed the animal, he asked, "What is it, miss, did you get stung by a wasp?"

Gladys's face turned ashen. She has gotten a whiff of an odour that was far too familiar. Her voice shook as she asked, "Where on earth are you taking me?"

"Why, to pick up the girls, miss."

Fearful that the girls they were picking up were from Old Nichol, she jumped up, grabbed hold of Sandy by the shoulders, and demanded, "I want to know where the girls are coming from!" When he didn't answer immediately, she began shaking him while insisting, "You must tell me—right now! For God's sake, boy, tell me."

Sandy, afraid the lady had become unbalanced and at any moment might decide to jump off the wagon and hurt herself, decided that the only thing to do was to throw his arms around her and hold her tight until she regained her senses. Gladys, on the other hand, was beyond thinking straight and treated his actions as an attack. She began pummelling him with a series of wild blows, forcing him to take his arms from around her waist and hold them in front of his face for protection. That's when the oncoming blows knocked him off his feet and into the back of the wagon.

The noise from Sandy's fall startled Old Nellie. Her front feet went up in the air and she came down running, sending Gladys flying backward where she landed on top of poor Sandy, knocking the wind out of him. With no one at the reins to hold her back, Nellie went careening and zigzagging down the road with Gladys and Sandy rolling over each other as they were tossed from side to side. After running over a curb, through a number of flower beds, and knocking over a little picket fence, Nellie finally brought the wagon to a stop amid a lush garden of vegetables.

The old horse had helped herself to a generous helping of carrots by the time Gladys and Sandy managed to untangle themselves and get back up on the wagon seat.

"What a spectacle we must have made of ourselves," Gladys exclaimed, as she attempted to brush the dust from her clothes.

"When you landed on top of me, I thought it was a load of bricks," Sandy replied. Then, realizing what he had said, he was about to apologize when Gladys began to laugh. Relieved, he joined in.

"It's lucky the gardener is nowhere about," Sandy said, after their laughter had subsided. "We'd better get this old girl back on the road before we're found out."

When they were back on the street and out of sight of the ruined garden, Gladys collected her thoughts. On examining Millie's cape, she was dismayed to find two small dark spots and tried to brush them away, but couldn't. She prayed they would come off with a damp cloth when she got home. Amazingly, her bonnet had managed to remain on her head and didn't seem to be damaged.

She stopped worrying about her attire when she suddenly realized that the smell was even fouler than it had been before the accident. Her fear of returning to her old neighbourhood returned. She didn't want to cause another accident, but she knew she would have to do something, and do it quickly, or it would be too late.

Taking hold of Sandy's arm, she suppressed a feeling of panic and calmly asked him to stop the wagon. Then she put forth the same question.

"Well, miss, the girls are from a terrible poor place near here that they calls 'Old Nichol,' but you needn't worry, we don't have to go in there. They'll bring the girls out to a place they calls 'Warehouse Corner.' I wouldn't take a young lady such as yerself into Old Nichol for all the taters in Ireland. No, siree."

Sandy's answer was tantamount to receiving a death warrant, and Gladys was tempted to ask if she could get off the wagon and wait while he went alone to pick up the girls, but she had a duty to perform and couldn't deny it. Mustering up all her courage and praying that there would be no one she knew at Warehouse Corner, she ordered him to continue on.

It wasn't only the sickening stench that told her they were getting close to Old Nichol, she remembered the street they were on, the same street down which she and her da had pushed their cart. A longing to see Toughie seeped into her thoughts, but her mixed emotions of repulsion and fear were stronger. Even though she wanted to see him again, she knew she daren't take the risk. They were a half block from Warehouse Corner when Sandy pulled the wagon to a stop. Five minutes later, Gladys spotted a man leading an old horse with two girls on its back approaching the corner.

She almost cried out when she saw that the horse was Knickers. Then, to make matters worse, she noticed that the man leading the horse was Rod, one of the O'Brian boys. She was paralyzed with the fear of being recognized. Sandy startled her out of her daze when he shook her arm, and said, "Miss, miss, did you hear me? I said there's someone there now with the girls." He pulled the wagon a little closer.

Rod hadn't been a boy for some time. He was twenty-two and the father of three. Tall, with even features, he would have been a handsome man if there was more substance between his bones and his skin. Gladys, numb with fear, could do nothing but sit and watch as he helped the girls down from the horse's back and brought them towards her. As he came closer, she could see there were white streaks down both of his grimy cheeks, making his sorrow obvious. When he reached the wagon, one of the girls hid behind him, and he had to reach around to pull her into view.

"I'm Rod O'Brian, ma'am, and this 'ere's my little sister, Ellie. She's only just twelve, but she's a hard worker an' a good girl, so I hopes you'll be kind to 'er." When he received no answer, he pointed to the other girl, who appeared more curious than shy, and said, "An' this here's Pinky Davis. She's a year older, an' I think she's a good girl too."

Relieved that Rod had shown no sign of recognition, Gladys allowed him to help her down from the wagon. As she gave the girls a quick inspection, she noticed Ellie's puffy, red eyes, and her heart ached with sympathy. Both girls smelled a little of kerosene, so she knew they had been deloused and scrubbed as clean as Mrs O could manage. She had also scrubbed their threadbare garments, removing most of the grease stains along with the unpleasant odours that just might have caused the driver of the coach in Victoria Station to refuse their passage.

Both girls were very thin and much in need of food and warmer apparel, but it didn't take long to satisfy Gladys that they were fairly bright, since they answered the questions she put to them with a passable amount of sensibility. Gladys found it difficult to ignore Ellie's pleading glances, knowing the girl was hoping for a reprieve that would allow her to return home with her brother. She also knew that Mr O would not have sent her without a very good reason.

When she finished with the girls, she directed her questions to Rod, hoping to find out as much as she could about his parents without giving away her identity. "May I ask if you have permission to leave these girls with me?"

"Yes, miss, I do. You see, Pinky's ma died last year an' her pa don't want her, so he gave her to Ma an' Da. Then Da went and broke his leg an' can't git 'round good no more. I'm doin' good as I can, but it just ain't enough, so Pa thought Ellie an' Pinky would be better off where you're takin' 'em. They will, won't they?"

"Yes, I think they will. And is your mother not well?"

Ron looked surprised then puzzled, not understanding why

this proper lady would bother to ask about someone she didn't even know. "I guess she's not sick, but she can't have babies no longer an' that makes her awful sad. She was too broke up to come an' watch Ellie go, so I had to do it."

"I can understand how she would feel. I wonder if you would tell your parents something for me?"

"Yes, miss."

"I want you to tell them that I will be living in the same building as Ellie and Pinky and will watch over them until they are better acquainted with their new surroundings."

"Thank you, miss, I know that'll make 'em feel a whole lot better."

Gladys tried her best to think of a way to let Mr O know that it was she who would be watching over his daughter, and then she remembered the coin he had given her. Luckily, she always kept it with her. Deciding to allow the two siblings a little more time together before saying goodbye, and wanting to think of a way to get the coin to Mr O, Gladys nodded toward Knickers and said, "You know, I once had a horse that same colour. Do you mind if I walk over and pet him for a minute?"

Rod wanted to get away before he changed his mind and refused to let his sister go, although he knew it was the only way to save the rest of his family from starvation. One more person to feed wouldn't inconvenience a middle class family, but for those living in the slums it could be a death sentence. He couldn't understand why such a proper young lady would want to pet an old horse like Knickers, but he didn't dare refuse.

At first the horse ignored her, but when Gladys put her hand on his forehead and talked to him, he rubbed his muzzle against her shoulder. Gladys didn't have the heart to push his head away, and hoping Millie wouldn't mind a few horse hairs on her cape, she laid her face alongside his neck. "How are you, old friend?" she asked, and then noticing the dried mud all over his coat, she added, "Oh, Knickers, I am so sorry; it looks like no one brushes you anymore."

She gave him a goodbye kiss on his muzzle and turned to leave when someone said, "Hoy! Wot cha think yer doin' parkin' that 'orse in my spot, heh?"

The voice was so familiar, Gladys almost fainted. Slowly she turned to see who had spoken. Relieved, and yet oddly disappointed, she realized the man was nothing like her father, who was much taller and half as old. Then he removed his dirty wool cap, exposing a full head of grey and black, roughly cropped, curly hair that she couldn't help but recognize. As he came closer, he squinted up at her.

"Beggin' yer pardon, miss, but I thought you was O'Brian. Me eyes ain't what they used ta be." Then putting his face right up to Gladys's, he added, "Yer a fine lookin' lady, you are. We 'ad a girl what was almost as purty as yerself. That were our Gladdy, that were. We lost 'er aways back an' we still misses 'er, we do."

Realizing that the man was indeed her pa, Gladys suffered a diversity of agonizing and moving emotions: fear, sadness, pity, and most of all, love. In fact, it was all she could do not to throw her arms around him and kiss his wrinkled cheeks in spite of his foul body odour. Being unable to reveal her identity was such torment that she was unable to stifle a low and grievous moan.

Tonnie, afraid he had upset the lady and she might call for help, quickly backed away while offering an apology, "I'm sorry, miss, I didn't mean to frighten you."

Gladys, tears welling up in her eyes, was unable to answer. She quickly took the rest of the money she had for Millie's gift and a little of the amount Laura had given her for food, and handed it to him, but in her haste, she released the coins before he had them in his grasp, and they fell to the ground.

He bent down to retrieve the money, and by the time he stood up, Gladys had walked away. Carefully, he examined the coins to make sure they were real. When satisfied, he called out in a voice that, unlike the rest of his being, had retained its fortitude. "God bless you, miss; God bless you!"

Gladys forced herself not to look back. Her knees were shaking, and she would have collapsed if she hadn't managed to reach Sandy's wagon and lean on it for support. It took a few minutes to gain control over her emotions. Then she took the coin that Mr O had given her and slipped it into the envelope that Rod would be taking to his father; it was an act that did little to lessen her misery.

Tears, including Sandy's, were shed as they bid their goodbyes. On the way to the nearest omnibus station, it began to rain. Ordering Sandy to stop, Gladys took the canvas, climbed over the seat, sat between the two girls, and shared the cover.

Pinky appeared to have no regrets over leaving Old Nichol and didn't hide her excitement at viewing the wonderful world that she had only visited in her dreams. Once they boarded the Dover coach, her frequent bursts of "ohs" and "aahs" brought smiles to the faces of all the passengers. Ellie hung her head and made no effort to look at the scenery. As she watched the poor girl, Gladys appeared to be sympathetic, but her thoughts were of a more selfish nature.

When she saw how decrepit her father had become, her feelings toward him were so different from those she had on the night she left Old Nichol, that they stirred up a sundry of muddled sentiments. As she went over and over the words he had said, the most poignant and startling were, "We still misses 'er." She found it hard to believe that her mother had feelings for anything but a bottle of booze.

Memories she had suppressed for the last three years came flooding back, and although most were better forgotten, others triggered nostalgia. She began to realize that although Sally had left her a legacy of knowledge, her ma had taught her how to dance and sing, skills she had found to be of equal value. In revisiting her past, Gladys could visualize the gradual degeneration of her mother and father, and, in doing so, began to understand that liquor was the culprit.

When the coach pulled into the rest station, Gladys felt more at peace with her state of affairs than she had since leaving the ghetto. The abhorrence she had for both her parents had faded with the knowledge that they missed her.

She helped the girls down from the coach and led them into the dining area, then ordered them each a bowl of soup and a hot meat pie. This left her with just enough money for a cup of tea and

a scone. Although Ellie insisted she wouldn't be able to eat, there wasn't so much as a crumb left on her plate when they rose to leave, and she even began taking notice of the lush scenery when they were back on the road.

Hilda had made a hearty lamb stew and set it aside on the stove for Gladys and the girls to enjoy when they arrived, but delicious as it was, the girls were too tired to eat more than a few bites. Two more cots were set up and ready in Gladys's portion of the attic, and although she intended to hold Laura to her promise of a room of her own, Gladys decided to stay with the girls for a few nights until they were a little more settled.

To Laura's credit, she allowed the girls to sleep until seven the next morning and to spend the next day getting acquainted with their new home. She also saw that they were scrubbed clean and outfitted. The following day after a hearty breakfast, she and Gladys began instructing them in their duties. Oddly enough, it was Laura who suggested that the girls' workload not be too heavy until they had gained a bit more strength. Both girls, familiar with drudgery, had little trouble coping with their tasks. Pinky was delighted with her new uniform and all the good food, but Ellie remained sullen and discontent. Gladys told Millie how surprised she was by the difference in Laura's attitude toward the young girls compared to the treatment she received when she first began working at the Inn.

Two months later, she had more to say about it. "You know, Millie, I promised Ellie's brother I would watch out for her, but I don't think I need to bother. For some reason, Laura has taken a real shine to the girl, and what's more, I think Ellie is becoming very fond of her too. If I have to watch out for anyone, it may have to be Pinky. Laura allots too many of Ellie's chores to the poor girl."

Gladys was right about Laura's feelings toward Ellie. When Laura, who was an only child herself, wed, she looked forward to having a large family and planned to show them the longed for affection that she never received from her own parents. Unfortunately,

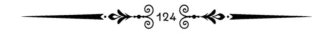

after being married for a few years with no pregnancies, she had to concede that she was barren. The only way she managed to cope with such a depressing truth was to lose herself in her work as a housemaid. Her earnings were added to her husband's, and by living frugally, they eventually had enough to put a down payment on the inn in Dover.

What happened a few weeks after Gladys had moved into her own room was to change Laura's personality for the better. One night, as she was walking past the stairway that led to the attic, she heard someone crying and decided to investigate. When she saw that Pinky was sound asleep, she quietly made her way to Ellie's cot. The poor girl had the blankets pulled over her head and was doing her best to feign sleep, but her uncontrollable sobs gave her away. Not sure what her actions would accomplish, Laura sat on the edge of the bed and gently patted the girl's back.

"There, there, lassie, dinna take on so." The sudden reaction to her sympathetic words took the landlady by surprise. The girl sat up, wrapped her arms around Laura's neck, and proceeded to shed a torrent of tears down the front of Laura's best tucker. Instead of irritating her, the warm tears wakened Laura's maternal instincts—instincts she thought were gone forever.

From that night on, Laura and Ellie's fondness for one another continued to grow until their relationship was similar to that of a mother and daughter. Laura realized how hungry she had been for a loving touch. Neither her parents, nor her husband, thought it proper to display affection, and gradually, during the past fifteen years, her tender thoughts and sentiments were slowly drying up like fruit left on a tree to shrivel and fall to the ground. Therefore, Ellie's hugs caused an awakening of her spirit, and she returned them with such gusto that, on occasions, she came close to breaking the young girl's ribs. Because love can be infectious, her relationship with Neil and the rest of the household benefitted as well.

As for Pinky, she was so grateful to have three meals a day in addition to warm clothes and a bed of her own, that it never occurred to her to be jealous of Ellie's good fortune. Although she was shy, she had an honesty and openness to her character that allowed her to easily make friends with both Hilda, the cook, and Becky, the scullery maid.

It wasn't long before another girl was hired. Ellie was relieved of her duties and moved downstairs to a room in the Watts' flat. Once she settled in, Laura saw that she had her own private tutor plus all the privileges of a girl born into a middle-class family. Ellie never mentioned missing her parents, and because defects are frequently easier to detect in others than in oneself, Gladys considered her disrespectful. The two never became friends.

Chapter Ten

Laura became so involved nurturing her newly found protégé that Gladys was left to train the new girl, Mary, along with her other jobs. This left very little time for the long walks and more frequent visits with Millie that she had looked forward to. She would have complained, but her esteemed title of supervisor boosted her ego, along with the attention she received as a barmaid and singer. Having been brought up in a place of little hope, she found such an expeditious rise in rank went a bit to her head.

Although Pinky and Mary were both hard workers, Gladys, who had become as fastidious a housekeeper as was Laura, took advantage of her authority and reprimanded them over the slightest mistake. Mary, an extremely subservient twelve-year-old with very little sense of worth, did her utmost to follow all the rules required of a chambermaid, but she often neglected to empty and refill her scrub bucket as often as she should.

Mary thought it made no sense to throw out good water after

only dipping a scrub brush into it a few times. Gladys had scolded her so often with the phrase, "You cannot make anything clean with something dirty," that she heard it in her sleep, but still had trouble discerning how dark the water had to be before it was considered "dirty." One day, Gladys lost her patience and angrily accused the poor girl of being lazy, even though she knew it was far from the truth.

Mary was heartbroken and hung her head so Gladys wouldn't see her tears. When she told Pinky about it later, she said, "I think she don't like me, Pinky. I couldn't bear it if she sent me back 'ome. There's nobody left what can look after me."

Pinky tried her best to comfort the girl and to explain that with so much water at their disposal it wasn't a sin to waste it, but Mary just shook her head and said, "Well, it seems awful sinful to me. The water we always drunk was a lot dirtier than what we throws out 'ere."

Pinky could see there was no good talking to her, so offered to let her know when to change the water in her bucket, at least until she learned to judge it herself.

In spite of the rigid rules she set for them, Mary and Pinky were both in awe of Gladys, and whenever they had the opportunity, they would peek around the corner of the hallway in the evenings to watch as she sang to the customers in the bar. They thought she was the most beautiful lady they had ever seen.

One day, Gladys noticed that Mary was walking with a limp, and inquired if she had injured herself. Mary replied that she just had a cramp in her leg, but a few days later her limp was even more noticeable. Gladys took her into the kitchen, sat her down on a stool and insisted she take off her boots and stockings. It was fortunate that she did. The poor girl had been wearing boots a size too small and had a number of nasty sores to show for it. Because of her timidity, she had been afraid to complain for fear of being sent back to the slums.

The sight of Mary's broken and infected blisters was enough to cause Gladys to regret the way she had treated her. She gently bathed the abrasions in a bucket of warm water before applying salve and bandages. The realization that Mary was so afraid that she would put up with the pain without complaining brought back memories of how she had felt during the first few months she worked at the inn. Gladys suddenly realized that she had become almost as mean as Laura Watt. She also knew how much she would have appreciated a kind word from the landlady during that time.

When she had finished bandaging the sores, she said, "Now, Mary, don't you fret; I will see you have a pair of boots that fit you, and I am sure I shall be able to find some chores you can do sitting down until those sores are healed. I have a pair of slippers that you can wear in the meantime." Then, smiling up at Pinky, who had been anxiously watching the whole process, she added, "Will you please run up to my room and bring me my slippers? And, Pinky, when you come back, I think it's time we three had a nice cup of tea and a chat, don't you?"

Both girls, sensing that things were about to change for the better, nodded their heads in agreement. From then on Gladys used her authority with a much gentler approach, and even Laura had to agree that the girls worked harder than ever and were happier as well. Surprisingly, Laura had begun to realize that Gladys had a lot of admirable talents, and even though she still thought the girl didn't show enough humility, she lost some of the animosity she felt toward her.

A chambermaid's uniform was not suitable for Gladys's new job as barmaid, but when she mentioned it to Laura, she was told that it was up to her to supply her own, so Millie helped her fashion two inexpensive, but pretty, new frocks. From what Mille told her, it seemed that men appreciated the sight of a bare arm and a good show of bosom with their tankards of ale. She also explained that the style of dress worn by most barmaids was far less confining than those worn by ladies of the middle and upper echelon of society, which suited Gladys just fine, although Millie had convinced her to wear a corset.

Gladys caused quite a stir when she first wore one of her new dresses, and during the next few months, she was the recipient of many advances from the male customers. Although she was tempted to accept some of the invitations, she always refused, being determined not to enter into a relationship that might jeopardize her plans to have an education.

When she was a girl in Old Nichol, Gladys often dreamt of being as well-educated as her friend Sally, but such opportunities were unheard of. Then the day she lied to Millie and said she planned to go to school, Millie didn't seem surprised, and even went as far as to say she thought Gladys would make a very good student. It was then she realized her dream could actually come true.

Fortunately, Gladys had the good sense to use tact when refusing invitations, therefore remaining friends with all the customers. By the end of the following year, she had more than her wages in tips— money she kept from Laura by using a hidden pocket sewn inside each of her dresses.

Millie hadn't been able to find out where Gladys could get enough schooling to be a governess, but Mr Schneider, a retired teacher and one of the inn's regular customers, said he did. He was acquainted with a Professor Morris in London who had suffered an accident and was confined to a wheelchair. Because the man could no longer work, he couldn't afford a housemaid. Mr Schneider reported that the professor would be able to teach Gladys the subjects she needed if she would do the household chores. She would be supplied with her room and board, but was expected to provide her own personal needs. Gladys was thrilled with the prospect even though it meant moving back to London.

Millie and Gladys had figured out approximately how much money she would need, and one day she said, "I just need another five pounds. Can you imagine—me a governess! Sal—er, I mean, Ma and Da would be so proud."

Millie asked, "Da? You mean your father?"

Gladys nodded, "I've always called him 'Da.'"

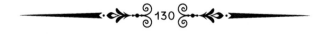

"You've mentioned your mother before, but not your father. Is he still living?"

The memory of her father when she last saw him at Warehouse Corner came back to her, and she answered honestly in a quiet voice, "I don't know, but I hope so."

Millie patted her on the shoulder, "You don't have to talk about it, dear, if it's too painful."

After Gladys began working as a barmaid, she met men who were successful in various occupations, and she often imagined what it would have been like if her father had been something other than a junkman in Old Nichol. She could picture him as a constable, he was big and strong enough; or an innkeeper, he had a much nicer personality than Neil Watt; or even the town crier. Goodness knows he had a loud enough voice! But the one she could picture the most was a ship's captain.

She had noticed the respect the sailors showed to their captains when they talked about them at the inn and could picture her father and his crew sailing to places with exotic names she had never heard of. Since no one in Dover had any idea what her father did, or if he was alive or dead, she didn't see what harm it would do if she pretended he really was the father she daydreamed about; a ship's captain who travelled all over the world.

One evening, she was in the middle of a song when a noisy disturbance began just inside the pub entrance. Neil was shouting at a patron, "Did ye no hear me, mon? I said ye canna come in here. This is no a gin palace in Drury Lane. You are not fit to be among respectable folk. Now, gie away wi ye."

Gladys couldn't see the intruder, but when he shouted, "By all the saints, you'll not stop me from seeing me dear little Ellie; I've come too far, and I'll bloody well stay until I sees me darlin' girl," she knew it had to be Mr O.

"We'll see aboot that," answered Neil as he motioned for two of his burliest patrons to assist him in throwing the man out on the street, after which he bolted the door.

Gladys knew she should go to her friend's aid, but she was afraid he would recognize her, so she quickly began a lively song, encouraging everyone to join in. Mr O began pounding on the door, and the louder he pounded, the louder she sang. When the song was finished, and she could still hear the pounding, Gladys could stand it no longer. Approaching Laura, who was twisting her wiping cloth around her hands in obvious agitation, she said, "Mrs Watt, I heard that man say, 'Ellie,' and I think he must be her father. Remember that I told you I had promised her brother that she would be well looked after? Perhaps if I was to tell him how happy she is and hand him enough money to return home, he might go away."

Laura called Neil over and told him of Gladys's plan, but because the banging on the door had become much weaker, Neil said, "Perhaps the man weel give over an' get home without our help."

"And he might just go to the police," Laura answered. "I'll no want to live, Neil, if he takes the lassie from me!"

Neil believed her and gave in, saying, "Here, Gladys, give him this two-pound note." Then, before she could take it, he reached into his apron and added, "You'd best give him five. That should satisfy any beggar."

Laura grabbed hold of Gladys arm and added, "And, Gladys, tell him that Ellie has been taken by good folk to another country."

Mr O had ceased his attacks on the door, and Gladys hoped that he had left, but to her dismay, she found him sitting against the building with his head hanging down. Her heart broke when she saw how thin and ragged he looked. She also noted that he had only one complete leg, the other ending above the knee. His homemade crutch was lying in two pieces on the road where his assailants had thoughtlessly thrown it. His bare elbows were sticking out of his torn shirt and looked as thin as two plucked chicken wings. They were also clotted with blood from dragging himself back to the building after being thrown on the cobblestones.

He moaned pitifully as she laid her hand on his bony shoulder, but he didn't look up. She bent down and was shocked to see the deathly ash tone of his countenance. "You are going to be alright, Mr O. Just stay there; I shan't be long," Gladys assured him. Receiving no response, she went back into the pub and called out, "There's a man outside who might be dying. Will someone please help me take him to the infirmary?"

When no one answered, she couldn't stop the tears from running down her cheeks. Ignoring the Watts' scowls of disapproval, she was on the verge of begging someone to help when a young man rose and came towards her, "My buggy is just down the street, so let's see if we can help the poor chap, shall we?" He followed her out with the best of intentions; but when he saw how dirty Mr O was, and how badly he stank, he might have withdrawn his offer if Gladys hadn't offered to fetch a blanket to wrap around the poor fellow.

The young man had a large frame and was huskily built and had no trouble lifting Mr O into the buggy and laying him down on the seat. The buggy, a handsome model, upholstered with fine-tooled leather, had only one seat, and with Mr O lying across it, there was no room for the two to sit. "It seems we shall have to kneel on the floor, Gladys. You don't mind me calling you that do you?" Before she could answer, he held out his hand and added, "My name is Tom, by the way, Tom Pickwick."

Gladys took his hand, and he didn't let go until he had her in the buggy. There were no side pieces in front of the seat, and when the horse took the first corner rather swiftly, Gladys almost fell out. Tom held the reins in one hand, then put an arm around her waist and pulled her to him. He laughed, and said, "Oh, ho, I can't lose you now. Not so soon after finding you, can I?"

At a loss for words, Gladys answered with a smile. Although she was concerned with Mr O's condition, the feel of Tom's strong arm around her during the short ride to the infirmary was so comforting that she was sorry when it ended. After arriving at the infirmary, Tom lifted the unconscious Mr O out of the carriage and started toward the door while Gladys ran on ahead to announce their arrival. A middle-aged man dressed in a white smock answered the door but refused to allow them to enter, even though Gladys explained how deathly ill Mr O was.

"I'm really very sorry, but I am only allowed to admit charity cases, and even then, they must have a letter of recommendation from a governor or a subscriber," said the man, and although he seemed sincere in his apology, Gladys wasn't going to let Mr O die without a fight. She had no idea what the male nurse was talking about, and she didn't care. The guilt she felt over trying to sing loud enough to deaden the sound of Mr O banging on the inn door was more than she could bear, and damned if she was going to let any man stop her from getting help. Luckily, before she could say a word, Tom came to the rescue.

"My father is Andrew Pickwick, and he is a 'Governor for life.' Now this man may not survive if I were to take the time to find my father and have him draft a recommendation. However, if you were to admit him now, he might live, and I shall bring you a letter before the night is out."

Andrew Pickwick was well known for his frequent donations, and the attendant was not about to endanger that relationship. "I would appreciate it if you would do that, Mr Pickwick. Now let us get this poor fellow attended to."

After Tom laid Mr O on an examining table and helped remove the blanket, the male nurse could tell by the stench that he had developed gangrene in what was left of his leg. In spite of his filthy condition in contrast to the sterile white of the infirmary, he handled him with as much tenderness and concern as he would a man of higher standing. Knowing what he might find when he exposed Mr O's stump would shock and sicken the young couple, he advised them to leave.

"You can do no good if you stay. I will call for assistance, and we will do what we can to ease his discomfort. By the look of the poor soul, he may not survive, so if you have any idea who I should contact in the case of his demise, will you write their name and address down for me? There's a pencil and paper in the hall by the entrance door." Gladys said she didn't know of anyone but would try to find out and return the following afternoon. Then she and Tom left.

Chapter Eleven

On the way back to the inn, Gladys was so engrossed in her troubling thoughts that she sat quietly with her eyes downcast and her hands clasped tightly on her lap. Although she felt sympathy for Mr O, she knew he could be a threat to her future. If he were to regain consciousness and inform the Watts of her true identity, they would likely call the police and have her sent to prison. In all fairness, she couldn't blame them if they did. The situation was so frightening that, for just a second, she wished the poor man would die, but she loved Mr O and really wanted him to live. Therefore, the only solution she could think of was to be at the infirmary early in the morning and try to talk to him before he had a chance to give her secret away.

Tom took her silence as a show of concern, and her unusual benevolence impressed him. Obviously, the man was nothing more than a beggar, but the way she had behaved toward him, he could have been a Lord. He was anxious to tell his father about her, knowing that he would appreciate her unselfish act of kindness more than anyone. Tom's father, although very wealthy, was a true humanitarian whom Tom respected and looked up to more than anyone he had ever known. Surprisingly, Gladys's silence didn't disturb Tom, and he smiled as he turned his head to look at her.

She appeared so vulnerable and sad that he felt the urge to protect her but had no idea what it was that she needed protecting from. He had been attracted to her the first time he heard her sing at the inn, and now studying her, he could understand why. She wasn't the most beautiful young lady he had ever seen, but she was the most attractive. He noticed that even though she was quite tall, she was still much shorter than he, and she had a figure that was too tantalizing to ignore. She had a rather large mouth for a woman, but Tom thought it far more tempting than the lips of most of the ladies he knew who looked as though they spent their time sucking lemons.

Although Gladys was nothing more than a common barmaid, he couldn't keep his eyes off her. He thought her hair was about the same colour as a bay mare he had had when he lived on his father's estate. He couldn't recall if her eyes were blue or brown but felt a nagging need to find out. They were almost back to the inn when he broke the silence with the only excuse he could think of and said, "Gladys, I think I scraped my face on the door of the infirmary. I'll pull over by the next lamp, and perhaps you could see if I'm bleeding."

"Oh dear, I hope not," she replied. After they stopped, she began examining his face, but there was no visible sign of injury. Thinking there may not be enough light, she ran her hand over one of his cheeks and then the other. She had been so worried about Mr O that she hadn't really paid much attention to Tom's appearance. Although there wasn't much light, she could see that he was really quite handsome. His eyes were a little too deep set, but she loved their colour; the same warm shade of brown as her father's. His eyelashes were so thick and black that they reminded her of someone else's, but she couldn't think of whose. Then she remembered and almost called out, "Toughie!"

She was so busy studying Tom's face that she forgot to remove her hand from his cheek. Tom, mistaking her lingering touch as an invitation, leaned over and kissed her on the mouth. Gladys had never been kissed by a man before and had no idea how to reciprocate, but when his tongue came between her lips, she answered it with hers. The kiss was long and caused such an aching desire in her loins that it was almost as painful as it was thrilling. She had no idea such feelings existed between men and women.

His hands began to wander, and although she would have loved to surrender to his touch, the self-preservation she had acquired, both in the slums, and by listening to Millie's astute advice, took precedence and she pushed him away. "No, stop! I am going to be a governess."

Tom, now with a throbbing tool between his legs, couldn't hide his anger. "I don't give a damn if you're going to be a bloody nun, you don't kiss someone like that and expect them to turn away."

"I am very sorry, really I am, but I didn't mean to kiss you any more than you meant to kiss me. Now, please take me home."

"I shall damn well take you home when you finish what you started and not before."

"Very well, I shall walk." And before he could stop her, she jumped down from the carriage and set out at a quick pace for the inn.

The sight of her walking haughtily down the street with her hips swaying from side to side did nothing to lessen Tom's desires, but pride prevented him from running after her. He was on the way to his father's flat when he suddenly exclaimed, "Damned if they're not hazel."

When Gladys returned to the pub, the Watts had finished cleaning up and were sitting at a table waiting for her.

"Did he die?" Laura blurted out hopefully, as soon as Gladys came through the door.

"Not yet, but he may. I'll find out tomorrow," Gladys answered quietly.

"Did you tell him what I told you to?"

"No, he was unconscious."

"Then you dinna give him the money?" Neil asked.

"I will give it to him tomorrow if he survives. If not, perhaps you can find a way to get it to his family." She bid them both goodnight and turned to go to her room when Neil asked about Tom.

"What about the Pickwick laddie? Did he give you a ride back?"

"Yes, yes he did," she lied.

"Ah, he's a good laddie. He's a soldier in the infantry and weel be off to India one of these days."

Gladys just shrugged, not letting on it was of any interest to her, but once she was in her room, she flopped down on the bed and, as though he was still with her, she said aloud, "So you will be here today and gone tomorrow. I'm so glad I didn't give in to you." Nevertheless, the memory of his lips on hers persisted before, and even after, she fell asleep.

The following afternoon Mr O, heavily sedated with laudanum, was only semiconscious and made little sense when Gladys visited him, so she didn't stay long. She slept very little that night, worried that someone might talk to him before she did. She was also afraid that Laura wouldn't allow her to visit him again in the morning before her chores were done. She needn't have worried—Laura was just as upset over Mr O's presence in town as was Gladys, and insisted that Gladys leave her duties and rush to the hospital immediately after she had her breakfast. She even offered to pay for a cab, so Gladys could arrive there as quickly as possible.

When Gladys arrived at the infirmary, one of the attendants met her at the door and, before taking her to see Mr O, asked if she was a relative. When Gladys answered that she had never met him until he collapsed outside the inn, she felt so guilt-laden that she couldn't look him in the eye. Luckily, her discomfiture went unnoticed. The man smiled, commended her for being so compassionate, then said that they had done all they could for Mr O except to am-

putate all that was left of his leg.

"And, I am certain that with the poor state of his health, he would not survive such an operation," the man added. "He knows he has only a limited time left and, although he seems determined to return home to spend his last days with his family, he refuses to leave until he has seen someone he calls, 'Ellie'."

"Hmm," Gladys said as she paused before answering. "You know, I think that is the name of one of the maids who works at the inn. I shall find out if it is her. If it is, I shall bring her to see him tomorrow, or maybe the next day," she promised, while not having the slightest idea how she was going to manage it. The attendant then told her that she could visit with the patient but warned her not to stay too long, as he needed his rest in order to build up enough strength to go home.

Gladys was pleased to find that Mr O had been scrubbed clean, had his hair cut and washed, and was wearing a clean, white gown. Although his features were skeletal and his skin had a sallow hue, his gentle and kind nature showed clearly in his eyes, and as soon as Gladys saw him, her love overtook any concerns she had about being exposed. She threw her arms around him, crying, "Oh, Mr O, it's me, Gladys!"

The tears ran down his cheeks. He patted her on the back until they both gained control of their emotions. Then he pushed her away so as to look at her face, and in a soft and tender voice, said, "Of course 'tis you, Gladdy, me girl. I knowed it was you when you came yesterday, but me tongue wouldn't mind me brain."

"I'm so ashamed of the way I've treated you, Mr O. You see, no one here knows who I really am. I've told them my name is Gladys Tweedhope, and that I came from London. Oh, Mr O, can you ever forgive me for not interfering when Mr Watt threw you out of the pub?"

"Don't you mind, Gladdy. Why I'd a done the same if it were me. You've no need to worry, I'll not give your secret away. You know when me boy fetched that piece o' gunmoney home it didn't half give Mrs O and me a good feelin'. We knew t'was yerself that sent it an' that our little Ellie was in good hands. Now, Gladdy, I've to ask you to do somethin' for me. I wouldn't ask it if I weren't dying." Gladys shook her head and began to cry again, but Mr O continued, "Don't be upset, me girl; I'm not about to go right now. And when I am ready, you needn't cry—I'm quite looking forward to it. It will be that nice not to have any more pain."

Gladys thought he had such a look of peace and contentment as he was talking that perhaps there really was a place like the heaven she had heard people go on about. He gave her hand a squeeze, saying, "You know, I don't have much time left, Gladdy, and I don't want to die without seeing me darlin' little girl once more. Mrs O, and meself, we never did get over feeling bad for sending her away, so if I could jest see for meself that she's happy—well I could tell the missus when I get home. T'would be better'n any present I could give her. Now, me darlin', if you can make that happen, I'll promise to keep an eye out for you from up there, if that is where I'm goin'."

"You are going up there, Mr O; I know you are! And don't you worry; I promise I will have Ellie here tomorrow, or the day after."

"Do you mean that, Gladdy?" When Gladys nodded, he insisted, "You know it will have to be soon. I plans to get home before I passes on, even if I have to crawl there."

"I will bring her, I promise, and maybe Pinky can come too. And, Mr O, you needn't worry about how you will get home. I have some money here for you from the Watts, my employers." When she handed him the five pounds, she explained how they had practically adopted Ellie and were afraid that he might take her away.

"I'd never do that if she's happy. I know she's better off where she is," he answered.

Both fear and guilt had been Gladys's constant companions since Mr O came to town, but when she left the infirmary, she felt lightheaded with relief. She didn't think about the impulsive promise she had made until she was confronted by Laura and Neil a few minutes after her return to the inn. When she told them that Mr O was dying and how much he appreciated the money they gave him, they were relieved, but when she said that he wouldn't leave Dover without seeing Ellie, they became agitated and angry at her for not telling him the girl had left the country.

"But you must understand; he doesn't want to take her away from you. He just wants to see her once more, and then only for a few minutes," Gladys explained. "I feel so sorry for the poor man. I could tell that he really doesn't want to cause trouble. I know he will be happy to see how much you've done for her. I told him I would bring her to say goodbye, so please do not disappoint him," she pleaded.

Gladys's deep concern for what Laura thought to be a beggar was beginning to make her suspicious, and she answered sharply, "I canna see what business 'tis o' yours. What has the beggar to do wi' you?"

The question took Gladys aback, and she had to think quickly so as not to raise the woman's suspicions. Then she said, "Well, Mrs Watt, I realize that he is just a poor old man, but my mother taught me to have compassion for all those who suffer."

The shamefaced reaction of both Laura and Neil was enough to convince Gladys she had come up with the right answer. They offered to think about allowing Ellie to visit her father, but later that night, they called Gladys aside and said they had told Ellie her father was at the infirmary and had not long to live. They also told her that he wished to see her before returning home. Ellie, shocked and angry, didn't hesitate with her refusal. She enjoyed living with the Watts and wanted nothing to do with the life she had left behind in Old Nichol.

The day her brother brought her to meet Gladys at Warehouse Corner, she had no idea of the agony her parents were going through and was thoroughly convinced that the money they received for her was their only motivation. Now, she only felt hatred toward her father and was adamant in her refusal to visit him. The pandering that she received from Laura Watt had managed to erase any memory of how much her father loved her.

Nevertheless, Gladys had given her word to Mr O, and was not about to accept Ellie's refusal so easily. After she devised a plan, she had no trouble convincing Hilda, the cook, to play along with her. Ellie had been quite rude to Hilda lately, and the cook thought that it was time the girl had a little comeuppance. So the next morning they were both waiting for her in the kitchen when she came down for breakfast.

Ellie, still dressed in her dressing gown, didn't even bother to greet either of the ladies, before saying, "I'd like a cup of tea and two pieces of toast with jam brought up to my room, Hilda, and tell Pinky to bring it up as soon as it's made. I hate cold toast." Then she turned to leave.

As she was passing, Gladys reached out and caught her by the arm. "Just a moment, young lady, I want to talk to you about something." Then, hoping the girl was gullible enough to believe her, she added, "You know, Ellie, we haven't become the best of friends, but I truly am sorry that you may have to go back to your family. I know how much you like living with the Watts. But then again, it will be nice for your mother to have you back home. And who knows, maybe Mrs Watt will allow you to take some of your wardrobe with you to share with your sister or others who need it."

The thought of such a thing made Ellie sick to her stomach. "What on earth are you talking about?" she demanded.

"Well, now that you have refused to go and see your father, he will probably take the doctor's advice and go to the police. When he tells them how much you are loved and needed at home, they certainly won't deny him his rights. It's rather sad, seeing as you only had to visit him for just a few minutes to avoid something like this happening."

"You are lying!" Ellie shouted. When Gladys just shrugged her shoulders, Ellie turned to Hilda, "She's lying isn't she, Hilda?"

"Well, I do remember when Bessie—she worked here 'fore your time—well, the same thing 'appened to 'er," Hilda replied. Then, managing to look sad, she just shook her head.

"What happened to her for goodness sake, Hilda? Tell me, did she have to leave?" Ellie asked, her eyes wide with fear.

"Yes, but that may not 'appen to yourself if you go with Miss Gladys 'ere, and if she explains 'ow well you're doing 'ere."

"He can't really make me go with him, can he, Gladys?"

Gladys shrugged her shoulders and answered nonchalantly, "We'll see." Then she started to walk away.

This time it was Ellie who grabbed Gladys's arm. "Did you say I only had to see him for a few minutes and then he would leave me alone?"

"Yes, that's the promise he made to me, and I shall make sure he keeps his word. You know, Ellie, I think you are a very spoiled and selfish young lady, but if you were to show your father a little respect, even if you can't show him any love, I know he will allow you to stay with the Watts."

The ruse worked and arrangements were made for Gladys to take Ellie and Pinky to the infirmary the following afternoon. Gladys suggested Laura dress the girl in her finest, so her father would know she was in good hands. When the three entered Mr O's ward, he was sitting in a chair dressed in second-hand clothes that were patched and clean. Even his one shoe had a good sole on it, and there was a good strong crutch leaning against the wall behind his chair. When Pinky saw him she ran and hugged him, but Ellie just offered a weak nod of her head.

"Ellie, me girl, don't you have a hug for your pa?" Mr O said. Ellie wasn't going to move, but Gladys was standing behind her and delivered a knee to her back, sending her into her father's arms. Luckily, Mr O was so delighted that he didn't seem to notice her cool behaviour. Looking her over, he exclaimed, "By all the saints, if you aren't a sight! Angels would be jealous of you. Are you happy, me love?"

Ellie, determined to convince him she should stay with the Watts, answered with enthusiasm, "Oh, yes, yes, extremely happy!"

Impressed with both her good fortune and her diction, Mr O kept remarking on how beautiful she looked and how happy her ma would be if she could see her. "I wish I had a likeness to take for her," he said.

When her father said he wished he had a picture to take to her mother, Ellie knew Gladys was right, and she could remain with the Watts; so she finally rewarded Mr O with a smile. Gladys saw the look of joy it brought to his face and thought, how ironic it was that just one small smile from such a selfish, little snippet would warm her father's heart until he died. She could stand it no longer and gently pushed Pinky in front of Ellie. "Mr O, we must go now, but Pinky has something she wants to give you."

Pinky had tears in her eyes as she approached him. More out of politeness than interest, Mr O looked at her and said, "Now, me girl, how are they treating you?"

Pinky, bursting with news, answered, "Oh, Mr O, I have nice warm clothes and lots to eat—so much food you can't imagine. And if I do a good job, some of the folks what stays at the inn gives me money. 'Ow's Mrs O and everybody? I wish I 'ad more to give them but I just 'as these 'ere mittens that one of the guests give me, and 'ere's a shilling I managed to save. It's not much, but I wants you to 'ave it for all you done for me. I miss you all so much." With that she threw her arms around him once more.

Mr O patted her on the back and said, "I'm glad you are doing so good, and I hope you looks out for me Ellie if she needs you."

"Oh yes, I will, Mr O, if she needs me."

Before they took their leave, Mr O said his goodbyes to the girls and asked Gladys to stay for a minute after they left.

"Sure, and isn't she grand?"

"If you mean Ellie, yes she is, quite grand, but I'm afraid she is also quite spoiled," Gladys answered. She wanted to add that it was Pinky who was grand, and that he should have thanked her for the gifts, gifts that the poor girl had worked so hard to obtain. But she knew it would serve no purpose.

"You mustn't judge her too harshly, Gladdy; she's just a youngster. I can't wait to tell her ma an' the rest o' the family what a proper lady she is; they'll never believe me. And, Gladdy, me love, you be sure an' tell them Watts that I'll not bother them again. And now, I want to know why you haven't asked about your folks an' your friend, Toughie?"

"I suppose I was afraid to." She told him about the meeting with her da and how badly she felt about not telling him who she was. "He looked so old and tired. I guess they didn't go to jail or he wouldn't have been there that day."

"All I know is that about a week after you left, the police were around lookin' for Mr Gaylord and askin' questions. Nothin' came of it though, so I guess Tonnie did a good job of getting rid of the evidence. When folks noticed you were missing, your ma said you'd run off one night and hadn't come back."

"I should have known they wouldn't look for me."

"But they did love you, Gladdy, and would have showed it if it weren't for their sickness. Whenever I see your da, he talks 'bout you with tears in his eyes."

"And what about Ma?"

"I'm sorry, I forgot you had no way of knowing. Your ma, she passed on a few months ago. Your pa took it real hard and he's not been right in the head since. He's gone and lost his business, but the man that has it now; he's a good sort he is and lets Tonnie sleep in with the junk. He even gives him a bite to eat whenever he can, but I sort of think your da's days are as numbered as mine."

"Oh, Mr O, please try to prevent him from being sent to the workhouse. He used to say there was nothing in this world worse than dying there."

"Don't you worry; if I'm not around to do it, sure an' me boy will see to it that your da dies in Old Nichol."

"I haven't much to give you to show my gratitude, Mr O, but there is something I left back home that I treasured very deeply, and I would like Mrs O. to have it. It's a beautiful cameo that Sally gave me. I felt sick when I realized that I had left it behind, and it would make me feel so much better if I knew someone as nice as Mrs O owned it now," Gladys said, and then explained where she had hidden it.

Mr O thanked her then put out his arms for a hug goodbye, but Gladys wasn't ready to leave. She had been afraid to ask about Toughie, afraid he had met someone else and married. Although she knew that would be a good thing for him, it wasn't what she wanted to hear. Nevertheless, she couldn't leave without finding out. The last thing she expected to hear was that Toughie had left Old Nichol a few months before Mr O came to Dover. This upset her more than she thought it would, and she cried, "Oh no, Mr O."

While Toughie remained in Old Nichol, Gladys felt as though he would always be there if she should ever find a safe way to get to him, but now, unless Mr O knew where he went, they could never be together. She prayed for the right answer when she asked, "Mr O, do you know where Toughie was going?"

"I just know that this gentleman came an' took him an' his dog away."

"Not a policeman?"

"No, it was a well-to-do gent, and a relative by the looks o' him. And you needn't worry, me girl, Rod told me that Toughie didn't half look pleased to be going. He was a saint, that boy. You know, Gladdy, he went an' gave my Rob his junk yard before he left. I don't know what we'd have done if he hadn't. Poor old Knickers dropped dead one week and my faithful old sow the next. I had nothing left to earn a penny with, even if I would have had two legs. I was sick with fever and didn't find out he was going until after he left, or I would have told him where you went. The poor boy nearly went balmy trying to find out, but I knew you didn't want to get him into any trouble, so I never told him, but that time I would have. Especially since he had an uncle to look after you both. But I was too sick with fever to know what was going on. I'm sorry, Gladdy, love."

"It's not your fault, Mr O," she assured him. She gave him a big hug, saying goodbye.

Once out of the ward, the nurse informed her that Mr O'Brian would be picked up the next morning and taken to his home. On the walk back to the inn, Gladys told Pinky that Mr O loved the gifts. "But he said that just seeing you again was gift enough, so he gave me the money to return to you and said he would give the lovely mittens to his girl." She took a shilling out of her purse, and gave it to Pinky.

Chapter Twelve

One evening, while Gladys was helping Millie hem a dress, she confessed that Tom Pickwick had kissed her the night they took Mr O to the infirmary. When she began describing how she felt during the kiss, there was a sudden change in the colour of Millie's complexion. Gladys suddenly realized she was embarrassing the older woman and said, "Oh, Millie, forgive me, but you see, I've never felt like that before, and I wondered if it means that I'm in love?"

Millie laughed and shook her head, "No, I assure you that was not love." Then she patted her chest and added, "You feel true love here, not down there." Seeing Gladys's look of surprise, she continued, "Now, don't look so appalled. I personally believe that such feelings are not in the least shameful. If I appeared flustered, it's just that I have been living under the pretext of being a 'proper lady' for so long now that I blush at almost everything. It's ludicrous, that's what it is."

"What's ludicrous?"

"How ladies nowadays think it fashionable to dislike any form of intimacy. I have no idea why. It is certainly not because we lack deep sentiments; we're passionate about our children and our elders, so why not men? I wager our dear Queen doesn't find her bedroom activities abhorrent, not if you can go by the incessant amount of babies she's birthing. They say men must have their sexual pleasures, but what about our needs? We dare not say that we enjoy such intimacy for fear of being labelled whores."

"Oh, my heavens, do you think that's what Tom thought of me?"

"I haven't the slightest idea."

"Well, he can think whatever he wants. No one is going to spoil my plans."

"I hope you never forget that."

"Oh, I won't. I bet you didn't let any man have his way with you when you were my age, did you, Millie?"

Millie looked pensive for a few seconds before she replied, "As a matter of fact, I did."

Gladys's mouth fell open. She could hardly believe her ears. "Really, Millie?"

"Yes, really."

"Oh my goodness, what was it like? Was it terrible?"

"No, I would say it was just the opposite. It was really quite wonderful—at the beginning that is. But such an act can only end in tragedy."

"Oh, dear, I am sorry, Millie. You don't have to tell me what happened if it makes you sad."

"Not sad, dear, just a little melancholy, but I think it may do me good to talk about it. And it just might prevent you from making the same mistake."

She was set to begin when Taffy, who had been waiting silently and patiently beside the door for a half hour, interrupted her with a demanding yelp. Millie reached for her shawl, then apologized to the dog. "Oh dear I am so sorry, Taffy. How long have you been standing there? My goodness, you are such a patient little boy. We shall have to give you a cookie when we have our tea, shan't we, Gladys?" Then not waiting for an answer, she added, "Put the kettle on, dear;

we shall be back as quickly as possible. I am afraid Taffy is not the only one in need of a tinkle."

Gladys laughed as she recalled how upset Millie had been that Christmas morning when she showed up on her doorstep with the dog. Now she thought that Taffy meant as much to the dressmaker as if he were a real little boy.

By the time they returned, Gladys had the tea made and biscuits set out on a plate. She was anxious to hear all about Millie's "mistake" but didn't want to pry. Fortunately, she didn't have to. As soon as the dressmaker took off her shawl, sat down, and had a few refreshing sips, she began to explain.

"If I am going to tell you my story, I suppose I may as well start with the events that led up to it. You see, dear, my parents were both thespians, so I was brought up in the theatre."

"I don't know what thespians are, but I hope it doesn't mean they weren't nice."

"Thespians are actors, and they were both extremely nice, that is whenever they had time to spend with me. They were always busy learning lines, songs, or dances, while I was spending time being tutored, or what I referred to as tortured. Then when I was thirteen, I began my own acting career. At that time my parents were performing in a small theatre in the country, but I found work in the Sans Pareil, a new little theatre in London. My parents found a flat for me to rent near the theatre and next door to a dear family friend, who promised to keep an eye on me until I was old enough to look after myself.

"Jane Scott was a very kind and talented lady, and her father ran the theatre. Jane was also an actress and performed in many of the plays. She was very kind to me and the other actors. She made sure we all made enough money to pay our rent and buy food and if there wasn't a part for us in one of the plays, we were given other tasks to do such as setting up props and cleaning the theatre after the audience left at night. Jane was the most talented person I have ever met. Besides acting, she wrote most of the melodramas, pantomimes, comedies, and even operas that were featured at the Sans Pareil. Oh, I forgot, you weren't even born when the theatre went by that name.

You probably know it as the Little Adelphi."

Gladys hesitated, then decided to answer truthfully; "I've never been to a theatre Millie. I don't know any of their names."

"We shall certainly have to remedy that. I think the *The Pickwick Papers*, a wonderful play by that young man, Charles Dickens, is still playing at the Adelphi. His plays are always worth seeing, especially when he takes a part. You know, he's a very talented actor as well as a writer. If we are not able to go to a theatre in London, there are plays that come here—not often, but occasionally."

"Do you really think we could?"

"I shall be delighted to take you to the next one that comes to town. Now shall I continue?"

"Oh, yes, please do!"

"Where was I?"

"You had just begun acting."

"Yes. Well as time went on, our little theatre became very popular, especially with the high society crowd. Although I had parts in many of the plays during the next four years, I never had a leading role until I was seventeen and then I played the heroine, a poor little waif by the name of Amelia, in a play titled *A Penny a Posy*. The play was written by an unknown author, not Jane, and unfortunately, was not a very good play. In fact, it only ran for three nights, but those three nights were to shape my destiny."

Gladys began to interrupt, but Millie put her hand up and continued, "The first night of the play, the lack of applause was so depressing that I made my way to the dressing room in a very dejected state of mind, feeling certain that I was to blame. My mood changed when I found a big bouquet of red roses waiting for me."

"How romantic! Who were they from?"

"I had no idea. All that was written on the card was, 'To Amelia, from an admirer.' I took the roses home to my little one-room flat where the scent of the roses, along with my curiosity, kept me awake for most of the night. Before the next performance, I asked everyone who worked in the theatre if they had any idea who gave me the flowers, but no one knew. That night our play received another poor reception, and I was sure that if the person who left the roses was in the audience, he must now regret his actions. Therefore, I was really surprised to find another bouquet of roses waiting for me that evening.

"They came with another note and my hands shook as I opened the envelope, and read, "Tomorrow night, I shall deliver the roses in person." Some of the other actresses, far more talented and beautiful than I, often received gifts, but I never dreamt it could happen to me. I was both fearful and titillated, having no idea if my admirer was tall and handsome or short and ugly.

"The following night, after the final curtain, I was so afraid to come face to face with the stranger that my legs were shaking, and I almost left the theatre without changing out of my costume instead of going with the others to the dressing room. I needn't have worried; there was no bouquet—no admirer, tall, short, handsome, or ugly. Although I tried to convince myself that I should be relieved, I still felt jilted. I also felt very annoyed, more at myself for being so naïve than at the mysterious man who had jilted me.

"In fact I felt so depressed that I had no desire to join the gaiety the other actors were displaying as they changed their clothes, and no matter how much they tried to cheer me up, I just sat feeling sorry myself until they had all left. Finally, I began to see how silly I was behaving, and decided to get changed and join the cast in a nearby inn where we usually gathered after the closing of a play. I was almost ready to leave when someone knocked on the door. Thinking it was one of the cast coming back to get me, I called out rather irritably, 'Keep your britches on, I'm coming.' Then I put on my shawl, opened the door, and there stood the most handsome man I had ever seen.

"I have no idea how long I stood frozen like a statue with my mouth gaping open before the man handed me another bouquet and said, "You are even more beautiful than you appeared on the stage." The next thing I knew I was riding in an elegant, open carriage with a fur rug over my lap."

"Just like a princess."

"That is exactly how I felt. He kissed me that night, and I had all the same sensations you had. Our rendezvous soon became habitual. I fell hopelessly in love, and, even though he confessed to having a wife and family, I continued to see him. Many men of aristocracy had mistresses, and although I never planned on being one myself, I found I hadn't the will to turn him away. As I told you before, most wives of wealthy men think it stylish to be frigid, so I believed him when he said that he no longer shared his wife's bed."

Although Gladys found it very difficult to picture Millie living such an immoral life, she knew what a good person she was and didn't judge her. She had learned all about mistresses the hard way, having made the mistake one night of addressing an elegantly dressed woman as the wife of the man she was with. The man never returned to the inn, and Laura threatened to fire Gladys if she addressed any more of the customers presumptuously. Since then, she vowed never to become anyone's mistress, but she'd never say that to her friend. She did, however, ask Millie for her lover's name.

"His first name was John; his last name I will never divulge, even to you. John wooed me like no other man had, but I held him at bay for many months before succumbing to his charms in spite of the many gifts he gave me: perfume, jewellery, and even furs. We continued to see each other for three years. Then, to my utter delight, I found that I was going to have his child. Until then I thought that I was barren.

"Because we could never marry, John enlisted the aid of a Mr McIver, a man he knew who had dallied away all his fortune, and was now dying of consumption. The man desired a decent burial, but had no money, so John promised to pay for the service and internment if the man would agree to marry me in order to legitimatize my unborn child. Shortly after the ceremony, Mr McIver most obligingly passed on, leaving me only his name as an inheritance.

"John found me a nice flat, and I sent off a letter to my parents with the news of their expected grandchild, but, sadly, it arrived too late. The theatre they were performing in caught fire, and because it was an old building with only one exit, they were among the twenty-six poor souls who perished. It took the joy out of my pregnancy for many months, but then, on the 15th of June, 1821, our precious son Michael was born, and my happiness was restored.

"Unfortunately, when he was just four years old, Michael became very ill, and the doctor informed us that he had a faulty heart and would only live for a year or less. John seemed to be as devastated as I and came to visit us more often. Even though Michael was small for his age, he was an exceptionally bright and happy little boy, and although the slightest exertion tired him, he never complained. He passed away two days before his fifth birthday."

Tears were running down Gladys cheeks as she said, "Oh, Millie, I'm so, so sorry."

Millie also had tears in her eyes, but continued, "My life fell apart that day and not just because of Michael's death. His gradually declining health had prepared me for that. It was John's reaction to his death that I could not bear. Oh, he said all the things I suppose a father should say after losing a child, but I could sense that his grief was coupled with relief.

"It damaged my love for him, and I could no longer submit to his passion. Being a gentleman, he bore my indifference well. Our affair had run its course. Since I had no luck finding work in the theatre, he paid my fee for a seamstress apprenticeship and gave me enough money for my keep until I could manage on my own. No man could have been kinder. We never saw each other again, and when I finished my training, I moved to Dover and have been here ever since."

"That is the most romantic story I have ever heard," Gladys swore, giving Millie a hug.

"Thank you, Gladys. Looking back now, I can understand how you would say that. I suppose I have dwelt on the sad times instead of the good ones. However, with a dashing sea captain for a father, you have also had an exciting life."

By relating her own story, Millie had given Gladys the courage to confess. Taking a deep breath, she blurted out, "I am sorry, Millie, but I didn't quite tell you the truth. Da wasn't really a captain at all. He never even saw an ocean in his whole life."

Millie put an arm around her and, nodding her head, replied, "I suspected as much, my dear."

"You did? But why didn't you throw me out if you knew I was

a liar?"

"I guess I decided that you were more of a dreamer than a liar. Now why don't you tell me the truth? I assure you, I shan't think any less of you."

Gladys was surprised how good it felt to finally have someone she could confide in. She admitted to being born in Old Nichol and confessed not only that she had run away, but her reason for doing so.

Millie had suspected that the poor girl was a runaway, but she never imagined there were actually parents so cruel they would sell their daughter for the want of a drink. She also felt a little like one of the gossiping women who came into her shop as she urged Gladys on, asking, "I have heard terrible things about that place. Is it as dreadful as they say?"

"I don't think anyone can imagine how bad it really is, Millie. Even I had no idea until I discovered what the outside world was like."

"Do you feel like telling me about it? If you would rather not, I shall understand."

"Well, I don't know if I can describe it." After thinking about it for a minute, Gladys began slowly, "The sewers were open and were right alongside the back of the buildings, so you can just imagine the horrible stench. Come to think of it, when a person's never lived anywhere else, they think everywhere is like that. I guess I did too, until I left. And now that I look back, I think the worst thing about the place was the water, or lack of it. You see, there wasn't enough for everyone, and the little we were able to carry from the pump to our house was so putrid, some people, like Ma and Da, drank liquor instead—that is, if they could afford it."

Since leaving Old Nichol, Gladys hadn't spent much time thinking about how sordid her life was back then, and now, as she tried to describe it, she shuddered as the memories came back to her. As she continued, her words were as shocking to her as they were to Millie. "And some folks never ever bathed. Mind you, we were luckier than most because we had a rain barrel, and even after Ma became sick with liquor, she insisted I keep myself as clean as possible."

"Now I know why you drink so much water and bathe so

often."

"You have no idea how wonderful it is to be able to do that. That's what I appreciate the most."

Millie, a little discomfited, found herself making excuses about why she didn't bathe very often; "Another thing that surprises me, Gladys, is your speech. I have heard children from far less impoverished neighbourhoods than you grew up in speak, and it was apparent that they had no schooling. By what you have just told me, it is difficult to believe you had the opportunity to attend a school."

"Oh there were no schools, or if there was, I never have heard of one except the one the nuns called Sunday school. They only had it twice that I can remember, and Da wouldn't let me go. He said he went once when he was a boy and all those "penguins," forgive me, Millie, but that's what he called the nuns, wanted to do was to make him to get down on his knees and thank the Lord. He said he couldn't think of one damned thing he owned that the Lord had given him, so why should he thank him."

"Then how on earth did you come to speak so well? Perhaps your mother was an educated woman?"

Just the thought of that made Gladys laugh, and she assured Millie, "No, not Ma. But I did have a wonderful friend; a woman called Sally. Sally had been a governess before she came to live in Old Nichol, and she taught me a lot of things, like how to act like a lady, and how to talk better."

"You mean, 'how to speak properly.'"

"Now you even sound just like Sally."

"I am sorry, Gladys. I had no right to correct you."

"Oh no, Millie, please correct me every time I say something wrong. I need all the help I can get if I am going to learn how to be a governess."

"I shall do my best. Tell me, did you have friends?"

"I did have friends, but it was very sad when they died. And most of them did."

"How sad that must have been. I only had two friends when I was a girl. Actors seldom brought their children to the theatre when they were working, but I know that I would have been broken-hearted if one of them had died."

"Death is something you get used to at a very young age when you live in the slums, Millie, but I think my very best friend is still alive. At least I hope he is. His name was Toughie, and he was my hero. I don't think I would have survived without him. He had beautiful, shiny dark skin and his teeth were very white. His eyes were a warm brown colour, and his hair was even curlier than mine." Gladys had managed to put Toughie out of her mind, but now as she described him to Millie, tears welled up in her eyes.

"I think that's enough, dear. I know how memories of loved ones that we will never see again can be heart-breaking."

When Gladys was leaving to return to the inn, she gave Millie an extra-long hug and said, "Millie, now we are more than just good friends. From now on, you are my family, and I will, I mean, I shall, never lie to you again."

From that time on, Millie coached Gladys on her diction and proper etiquette. Gladys, an attentive pupil, was determined to be as "ladylike" as any of the upper class women who sometimes came to the inn with their husbands to enjoy a night of music. Unfortunately, the more "ladylike" she became, the more she forgot that she was nothing but a barmaid and was expected to act accordingly. Her illusory self-image suddenly collided with reality one wet and stormy night when two upper class couples dropped in for a drink on their way to a party.

Having to make a dash from their carriage to the pub, their outer garments were a bit wet when they entered. Gladys was on her way back to the bar when one of the women held out a wet cape and ordered, "Here, girl, take this, and be sure to shake the water off before you hang it up." Then pointing to her friend, she added, "And hers as well."

Gladys, displeased with the lady's haughty tone, reached out her hand, but a sudden impulse made her pull it back just as the lady let go of the garment.

"Now look what you've done, you stupid girl! Remove my cape at once from that dirty floor."

"The floor is not dirty, and you can hang up your own cape on one of those pegs." Gladys snapped back and pointed to some pegs on a wall just inside the door, before walking away. Both Neil and Laura were busy and didn't witness the incident, but when Laura went to take the couples' orders, the woman, who had no intention of letting the matter drop, said, in a loud voice, "I demand to speak to the proprietor."

Startled by the woman's tone, Laura stepped back in fear of being attacked, before she admitted, "Aye, that would be me."

To which the woman replied, "Well if you are the management, I should like to know what sort of establishment you are running." Then, not waiting for an answer, she pointed to Gladys and added, "That idiot girl threw my cape on the floor. I have never been treated with such disrespect."

Before Laura could reply the other woman joined in, "She stood there and allowed Mary's cape to drop on the dirty floor, then had the audacity to walk away. Such insolence is intolerable—especially from a barmaid. I usually have sympathy for hardworking servants, but even I would not endure such rudeness."

In the previous months, Laura had noticed the change in Gladys's attitude. She did her best to appease the group with free drinks and a promised apology from the barmaid before making her way over to Gladys. Then, within earshot of most of the customers, she gave Gladys a severe tongue lashing. The tirade came with a broader Scottish accent than usual, but Gladys understood enough to know that she could either apologize to the customers or lose her job.

Her face was burning with embarrassment, and she was on the verge of telling Laura that she would rather die than apologize, but as she looked around the room, expecting support, especially from the customers she had known for a long time, they all kept their eyes downcast and showed no empathy. It was then she realized that although they enjoyed her singing, they considered her nothing more than a mere servant girl. Knowing what a fool she had been, she vowed to show them all someday as she walked over to the customer's table and delivered her apology, but she did it bending over the table lower than necessary, which infuriated the women and pleased the men.

One summer evening in 1844, the pub was packed with guests celebrating the beginning of the direct rail link from Dover to London. Gladys was in the middle of a song when two uniformed men joined the crowd. They were greeted by friends with so much gusto that it drowned out Gladys's voice, and she stopped singing. She was surprised to see that one of the soldiers was Tom Pickwick who called out to her, "My apologies, Gladys, please do continue—your sweet voice is what I've brought my good friend, Keith, to hear."

Gladys was absolutely awestruck. Dressed in their attractive uniforms, both men resembled the pictures of all the princes she had seen in Sally's storybook. They were both handsome and stood over six feet tall with muscular builds. They wore bright scarlet jackets, tight, robin's egg blue trousers and white shakos, similar to one she had seen on the head of a toy soldier somewhere. It was all she could do to be nonchalant as they came toward her.

"Keith, this is the singing angel I've been telling you about. Gladys, this is my friend, Keith Corkish. He's really not a bad sort—for a Welshman."

Keith took Gladys's hand, kissed it, and said, "Now I know why he's talked about nothing else for the past eight months. Miss Gladys, an honour I would deem it, if you would consider me your humble servant from this night on."

Gladys took an immediate liking to the man, not because of his light-hearted flattery, but because of the way he looked into her eyes when he said it. "I may hold you to that, sir!" she replied with a smile.

When Keith heard her sing, he was even more impressed and whispered to Tom, "I don't know what you had to complain about, old boy, she could tease the devil out of me any time, and I'd come back for more. You don't mind if I have a go at her do you?"

"Not bloody likely! She's been on my mind for a long time now, and I intend to have my way with her even if I have to, to—"

"Marry her?"

"My god, I wouldn't go as far as that!"

"If I thought I could take along someone who looks and sings like her to India, I would marry her myself."

When Gladys finished her songs, both Tom and Keith gave her a standing ovation. Tom then approached Neil and asked if he might pay for the pleasure of having Gladys sit with them for the remainder of the evening. Neil, being a patriot of sorts, and knowing there was little time left before closing, said the drinks would be on the house and that Gladys would be free to join them.

Surprisingly, she enjoyed the evening more than she had anticipated, since neither she nor Tom mentioned their past encounter. Both men had spirited personalities and their own unique attractiveness; Tom was suave and confident, while Keith appeared boyish and naïve, perhaps due to his red hair and freckles. They were looking forward to being posted to India and had many interesting stories from fellow soldiers returned from that exotic country to share. Both were due to receive their commission the following year and had been transferred to the castle in Dover for officer's training.

Before they said good night, Tom said that he would be honoured if he could take her for a drive in the country the following Sunday. "Perhaps we could have a picnic," he suggested.

"Will you be joining us?" she asked Keith.

"I'd consider it an honour, my dear," he managed to say with a smile, despite the painful kick to his shins.

"Then, yes, I would love to."

"Shall we pick you up after church?"

Gladys, who had never been inside a church, replied, "That would be lovely."

Chapter Thirteen

The following Sunday, Tom arrived at the inn dressed in civilian clothes. He was driving the same chaise he used to take Mr O to the infirmary. When Gladys asked where Keith was, Tom said he had gone to visit his brother, but sent along his regrets. Although she was flattered when Tom had asked her to go out with him, she feared he intended to begin where he had left off the night they went to the infirmary, and she had counted on Keith's presence to avoid an embarrassing situation. She felt guilty for thinking so badly of Tom, but she could think of no other reason why a handsome and wealthy gentleman would want to spend a day with a lowly barmaid.

Just the touch of Tom's hand on her arm as he helped her into the buggy excited her and made her more determined than ever to refuse any advances he might make, especially if he tried to kiss her.

As they left the inn, Gladys said, "What a lovely little horse you have, Tom. What is his name?"

"I'm not sure if it is his proper name or not, but Dad calls him Tig. He and the buggy belong to my father. Dad keeps a few horses and a buggy or two with an old friend—a blacksmith who has a barn and pasture on the outskirts of town. The only time I'm in need of a buggy is when I want to take a beautiful damsel for a ride," he said with a smile and a cheeky wink.

Gladys blushed and answered, "I imagine you've taken quite a number of damsels for rides."

"Ah, but none as pretty as the one I have with me today!"

"What a flatterer you are. Anyway, I think Tig is the most handsome horse I've ever seen."

"Well, I must say, this is the first time that I've taken a young lady for a drive, and she compliments the horse instead of me."

"I am sorry, but you see I haven't decided if you are the most handsome man I've ever seen. I know for certain that Tig is the handsomest horse."

"Are you a good judge of horses, Gladys?"

"Good heavens, no. I've always lived in the city, so haven't had the opportunity to own one, but I would love to learn to ride someday."

Tom almost offered to give her lessons, but he remembered that a long-term relationship wasn't in his plans.

Luckily, the sun was shining, and it was a perfect day for an outing. As they made their way through the city they passed a row of very elegantly styled homes that Gladys had never seen before. She especially liked one of them and mentioned it to Tom. When he said it belonged to his father, she looked up at him to see if he was joking, but he appeared to be serious.

"Oh, what a lovely home you have, Tom."

"It's not my home," he replied rather sharply. "My stepmother and her two children, Peter and Mildred, live there."

Gladys recalled Tom telling the attendant at the infirmary that his father would sign the papers to admit Mr O, so she said, "And your father too, I suppose."

"Good heavens, no! Dad and Rose, that's my stepmother, separated many years ago. He lives in a flat close to his office on the Government Quay."

As soon as the words were out of Tom's mouth, he regretted

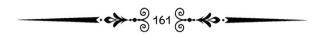

them. He was certain that, being a woman, she would want to know why they separated so she could go home with a bit of gossip. However, Gladys knew by the intonation of Tom's voice when he mentioned his stepfamily that it upset him, and not knowing what to say, she remained silent.

Surprisingly, Tom explained the reason for the separation without being asked. "You see, after mother died, poor old Dad was so very lonely that when he met Rose, she had no trouble convincing him she could take Mother's place. Before he had time to realize what a mistake he was making, they were married, and he had adopted her two children. I suppose Dad thought they would be company for me. I was ten, and at that time we lived on our estate in the country. Except for Joel, the six-year-old son of our head gardener, there were no other children close by."

"It must have been nice to have a brother and a sister to play with."

"No, it was anything but nice. You see, it didn't take long after they moved in before Father and I realized what a selfish and conniving woman Rose was and how utterly pampered Peter and Mildred were. It was too late by then. At the beginning, I did my best to make friends with them, but they were such badly behaved children that I couldn't help but dislike them, especially Peter."

"How old were they?"

"I think Peter was eight and Mildred a year younger. Fortunately, Rose abhorred living in the country and made such a fuss over it that Dad, who was only too happy to be rid of her, moved her and her two little monsters into our town house, and we were left in peace."

Gladys had no idea what an estate was, but said, "I would love to hear all about your estate, Tom. Is it far from here?" Tom said it was only about one mile from town and then told her about the green fields, and how he loved riding out to the river that ran through their property in the summer and swimming his horse across the deepest spots. As he talked about all the animals and the people who looked after them, Gladys was picturing it in her mind, and she thought an estate must just be another name for a farm. "Do you and

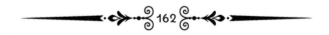

your father still live there?"

"No, when I went away to military academy, Dad leased it out and wanted something to keep him busy, so he found a government job on the quay and moved into a flat nearby." Gladys didn't say anything, but she looked up at him and smiled so sweetly that he couldn't help but remark, "You would like my father, Gladys. He's a kind and generous man, who I admire very much."

"I am sure I would. Perhaps you could bring him to the inn one night."

"We shall see," was the only thing Tom could think of to say. Things were not going at all as he had planned. He hadn't intended to share his life history with Gladys, but once he started, he didn't know where to stop. She seemed so interested in what he had to say that he felt flattered and had to remind himself of his reason for asking her to spend the day with him. On the other hand, she seemed like a nice girl, and he didn't want her to think their relationship could ever be serious.

The tone of Tom's voice when he said "We shall see," bothered Gladys. She suspected that he didn't plan on ever introducing her to his father. It was clear to her that she wasn't the sort of girl he would want to take home. She consoled herself thinking that if he felt that way, he wasn't the sort of man she would want to go home with.

Tom broke the silence. "I didn't intend to spend the day talking about my life, Gladys. From now on, I shall concentrate on nothing but showing you a good time."

"Actually, you needn't worry; I am already having a wonderful time."

Tom was puzzled, he had taken barmaids out before, but they were nothing like Gladys. He couldn't stop thinking how innocent she appeared. It was obvious to him that she wasn't highborn, but she certainly wasn't ill-bred either. He had never met a woman he couldn't classify before. He could tell she was enjoying the ride; almost as though she had never spent a day with a man before. Tom began to wonder if she wasn't as promiscuous as he had thought, and if that kiss they shared might have been her first. It was all too perplexing to think about, so he heaved a sigh and decided to relax and enjoy the day.

They did a quick tour of the town then followed the trail along the Dour River where Tom named the different owners of four flour mills and two paper mills as they drove past. Around noon he stopped the buggy in front of another flour mill. "Have you ever been inside a mill, Gladys?" he asked.

Gladys had seen bags of flour, but had no idea where they came from, so she answered eagerly, "No, but I should like to."

As he helped her from the buggy, a man near the same age as Tom came out of the mill and called out, "Hi there, Tom, I heard you were back in town. Who have you got there?"

"Hello, Will, this is Miss Gladys, ah . . . you know, Gladys, I don't even know your surname."

"Tweedhope," Gladys offered.

"Well, Gladys Tweedhope, this is Will Manson, an old school chum of mine and owner of this thriving business and two more like it."

Will reached out his hand and, with a welcoming smile, said, "You've picked a winner this time, Tom. If I wasn't married to such a treasure myself, I might try to impress her with my all my wealth. You must be hungry, my dear. Come, you're just in time to sample my flour in a loaf of my dear wife's freshly baked bread. I think you'll find it goes down very well with some of our local cheddar and a cup of tea."

Will was short and stocky with a barrel-shaped chest and muscular arms. He had a round, pleasant looking face, and near white hair that proved to be blonde after he brushed away the flour. Instead of going into the mill, he led them into a little, thatched-roof house that sat prettily beside the river nearby. His wife Enid, unlike Will, was tall and slender with rather aristocratic features. Her pregnancy was so obvious that Gladys wasn't surprised when she said the baby was due in a month's time.

In spite of her bulk, she moved about graciously as she sat them down at a table by a window with a splendid view of the river and began making the tea. When Gladys admired the pretty embroidered tablecloth, Enid shared that she'd made it from a flour sack.

"Would you like me to make you one, Gladys?"

Tom looked a little flustered as he tried to figure out how to explain that, more than likely, Gladys and Enid would never meet again. Gladys was enjoying his discomfort and allowed him to stew for a minute before she replied.

"Thank you, Enid, I would love to have such a beautiful cloth, and if you do have a chance to make one for me, I shall treasure it and keep it until I have a home of my own." She then related her plans to become a governess.

After they finished a delicious lunch of tea, bread, cheese, and jam, Will offered to show Gladys through the mill. "Have we time, Tom?" she asked.

"As long as we start back home shortly," he answered.

To his surprise, he enjoyed the tour as much as Gladys. He had never bothered to go into one of his friend's mills before, thinking there would be little of interest to see, but he was surprised at the complexity of the modern machinery Will had installed, and Gladys asked such intelligent questions that he found he was as anxious as she to hear the answers. Will was in his glory and was beaming with pride. His mill was the first one on the river that had been converted to steam power, and he couldn't resist the chance to do a little boasting now that he had such an attentive audience.

As they were returning to town, Tom said, "I don't know if I should allow you to meet any more of my friends." Gladys looked so puzzled that he started to laugh and added, "I think old Willie was quite smitten, and he has a jewel for a wife."

Relieved, she smiled rather smugly and replied, "Oh, that's nonsense; Will is happily married. But thank you so much for taking me there. I had no idea how flour was made, and now every time I eat bread, I shall appreciate it that much more."

The tour of the mill had taken longer than Tom had planned, so by the time they arrived back in town the sun had set, and they were both very hungry. The restaurant he chose was called "The Whale's Tail" and was in one of the buildings along the Custom House Quay on the waterfront. There was only one empty table when they entered, but it was the best table in the place and had a clear view of the ships that were anchored in the harbour.

Gladys thought it odd that no one was sitting there, so she mentioned it to Tom, who explained that the table was reserved for his father's use, because he was in the habit of taking all his meals there.

Although the window gave them a romantic view of the moon shining on the water, the décor of the place was so unadorned, and rather shabby, and the other customers such a motley group, judging by their attire, that Gladys felt depressed. She couldn't help but wonder why Tom would bring her to such a place. He must have sensed her displeasure. "Please don't judge the place by its appearance, Gladys. The service and food here are the best in Dover."

He was right. She had never eaten such a delicious meal, and Tom seemed to take great delight in watching her as she ate. She was so unlike the other women he was acquainted with, who sat stiff-backed and picked at their food as though it was poison. Whatever was brought to the table, Gladys ate as much of as Tom. She told the waiter how much she enjoyed it, and he in turn, told the cook who was so pleased, he came out from the kitchen to see "the beautiful lady who eats like a man."

After they left the restaurant, it was such a lovely evening that Gladys asked if they could take a short stroll along the quay before getting back into the buggy. Tom agreed, but before they began their walk, Gladys went up to Tig and fed him a lump of sugar she had taken from the café, then taking his muzzle in her hands, she kissed him on the nose and said, "We won't be long, Tig, and if you are a good boy, I shall have another treat for you when we return."

The kind gesture touched Tom more than he wanted it to. He knew what he wanted from Gladys and was determined not to allow his sentiments get in the way, but she kept doing little things that he couldn't help but admire. Although the boards they were walking on were worn smooth, some were worn down a bit more than others and Tom put his arm around Gladys's waist to prevent her from tripping.

She had vowed to protest if he made any advances, but the feel of his arm around her waist was so comforting that she convinced herself it meant nothing more to him than an innocent act of chivalry. As they came to an old man sitting on the dock leaning against a post with a bottle in one hand and a fishing rod in the other, Tom stopped and said, "Rather late to be fishing isn't it, Pike?"

"What time be it, Tommy lad?" the man answered with a slight slur to his words.

"It's long past time you were going home. Addie will be waiting at the door with her rolling pin, if you don't hurry."

"Aw, she likes to let on she's the boss, but she ain't got a mean bone in 'er body, she ain't." He finished the liquid in his bottle, held it upside down and added, "Yep, I guess since there ain't no fish an' no more grog, it's time I went 'ome. Give us a 'and up, Tommy lad." Tom took the man's hand and pulled him to his feet, but when he let go Pike teetered on the edge of the wharf and would have fallen in if Tom hadn't grabbed him, leading him across to the other side before aiming him in the right direction.

"He would have fallen in if you hadn't been here," Gladys exclaimed.

"It wouldn't have been the first time if he had, but he always sobers up when he hits the water and manages to splash around until he makes it to a ladder, or keeps shouting until someone hears him and pulls him out with a pike pole. That's how he earned the name 'Pike.'"

Gladys was very impressed with the kindness and respect Tom showed the drunk and was happy when he put his arm around her again as they continued their walk.

The creaking of boats tied up to the wharf and the soothing slaps of the waves against the pier added romance to the setting. Gladys felt so content that even if Tom never took her out again, she planned to remember the night as the most romantic of her life. As they were passing a huge five-story building with large windows and two twelve-foot, hand-carved, doors, Tom said, "This is the Custom House. See that big window on the second floor? That's my father's office."

"What an interesting place to work. Oh, look, Tom, someone's waving, is it him?"

Tom nodded, offered a feeble wave in response, and said, "We must be getting back to the buggy." On seeing his father's face in the window, a feeling of guilt had overtaken him. It was as though his father could tell by one glance how dishonourable his intentions were.

It was dark by the time they arrived back at the Inn, and Gladys was more disappointed than relieved when Tom delivered her to her door without so much as asking for a kiss. Every time she looked at his lips, she could feel them on hers, but she knew it was best this way, so she smiled warmly at him and said, "Thank you, Tom, for a lovely day. I had a wonderful time. Please give my best to Keith, and tell him he missed a magnificent dinner."

Tom merely nodded his reply and left abruptly. Gladys was both hurt and puzzled, wondering what she did wrong.

When Tom arrived back at the barracks, Keith was lying on his cot waiting for him. "Accomplish what you set out to do, did you?" he said, more in the tone of an accusation than a question.

"You needn't have worried, 'Mother,' I was a perfect gentleman," Tom answered jokingly.

"Enjoy the day, did she?"

Unable to resist, Tom explained how much fun she was to be with and what a good time he had. "And you should have seen old Will—she practically had him licking her boots. I think Gladys knows enough about his business now to run it herself. And, my God, Keith, you should see how that girl can eat! Old Cookie, at the Whale's Tail, is now another of her fans. I have to say, she certainly leaves a good impression wherever she goes."

"She's left quite an impression on you, by the sounds of it."

"Yes, I guess she did. You know, Keith, I am not so sure I was right about her. She seems so naïve—perhaps that kiss was her first, and she didn't know how to reciprocate. Do you think that's possible?"

"I just met her that once, but I'm certain she's no whore. I was quite smitten with her myself. Just what are your intentions toward her, Tom?"

Tom knew he wanted to see her again, and he longed to make love to her, but he couldn't honestly say his plans were entirely honourable, so he answered honestly, "I really can't say right now."

"Do you intend to marry her?"

"Court her, perhaps; marry her, no."

"I say, that's not cricket, old boy. To continue courting her just so you can have your way with her is not what a gentleman does."

"Oh, come on, Keith, the girl is just a barmaid! I shan't force her to do anything she doesn't want to do; you have my word."

"Well, you know how I feel. I think she deserves to be treated like a lady, and I don't care what her background is. And if that's how you feel about her, you shouldn't mind if I ask her out as well, right?"

Surprisingly, the thought of Gladys seeing another man bothered Tom, but he was determined to prove that she meant nothing more to him than any other person, so he replied, "It matters little to me."

For the next few months, Gladys was courted by both men. She thoroughly enjoyed the attention. Her fondness for Keith increased, but it was Tom she fell in love with. One evening, she and Tom accidentally arrived at the Whale's Tail the same time as his father, and Tom had no recourse but to introduce them to each other. Andrew Pickwick was favourably impressed with the attractive young woman and insisted on their company for dinner. Gladys immediately felt at ease with the older man, and before they took their leave, she invited him to come to the inn one evening to hear her sing. She didn't notice the look of disapproval on Tom's face. As for Andrew, he did come to hear Gladys sing, and enjoyed the evening so much that he became a steady customer.

There were times when Gladys thought that Keith was on the verge of proposing marriage. He had even suggested it was time she met his brother, who lived in Sandwich. Unfortunately, Tom's intermittent display of affection hinted more of passion than love, and she was finding it harder and harder to refuse his advances. Not wanting to hurt Keith's feelings with a refusal, and afraid her relationship with Tom was headed for disaster, she arrived at Millie's one afternoon with an announcement. "I need my purse, Millie. I am going to see that teacher who told me about Professor Schneider in London. He just lives around the block from here. You remember; I told you about him."

"That's the crippled professor who is going to teach you everything you need to know to be a governess?"

"That's the one, Millie. He said it will probably take two years depending on how quick I am to learn. I just have to do a little housekeeping to pay for my room and board. I've got enough money saved now to take care of my personal needs, so I'm ready to go."

Millie had been worried about Gladys's future because she knew that both Keith and Tom were from wealthy families and unlikely to marry a barmaid. Although it would break her heart to see her friend leave Dover, Millie was pleased for her. "That's wonderful news! You've worked so hard for this. But, oh, how I shall miss you."

When Gladys arrived at the teacher's home, she was excited with the thoughts of setting forth on a new adventure, but sad to be leaving Millie. She was also a little heart-broken over her disappointing relationship with Tom. Standing on the porch, she hesitated before knocking, knowing that once she gave her word to go to London, there would be no turning back. Then she thought about Sally and took hold of the knocker and banged it firmly against the door.

Gladys was in tears when she returned to Millie's shop. The dressmaker was busy with two ladies, but seeing how distressed Gladys appeared, she excused herself and followed her into the back room. Gladys was about to explain what happened between sobs when one of the women in the shop called out, angrily, "Mrs McIver, we have no time to tarry. Are you going to take care of us or not?"

"I shall be right there, Mrs Pickwick."

The name, Pickwick, brought an abrupt end to Gladys's tears and she whispered, "Did you say, Mrs Pickwick?" Millie nodded and

returned to the shop while Gladys put her ear to the curtain.

"Now, Mrs Pickwick, can I show you and your daughter some of my latest patterns?"

By then Rose Pickwick was more interested in gossip than gowns. Feigning concern, she laid her hand on Millie's shoulder and offered, "My dear, Mrs McIver, you must take more care with whom you keep company. Although I take no interest in local gossip, I have heard that girl," she nodded toward the back room, "visits you often. Now you mustn't take offense, but I feel it my duty to warn you that allowing someone of that sort into your home—albeit the back of a dress shop—will do irreparable damage to your reputation. You do know, do you not, that there are now two other dressmakers in town?"

Removing Rose's hand from her shoulder, Mille stood even straighter than usual, and although Rose Pickwick was five inches taller than the seamstress, she shrunk under Millie's glare. "Mrs Pickwick, who I invite into my parlour, albeit the back of my shop, is not any of your, or anyone else's, concern. Now if that bothers you, may I suggest you take your business elsewhere?" Before Rose could reply, Millie continued, "Furthermore, although I have appreciated your business in the past, and will continue to do my best to satisfy you in the future, if you so wish, I shall not tolerate any more slanderous remarks about my niece, Gladys. Do you understand?"

Rose's face turned red, and her mouth closed so tightly that her lips disappeared. If there were a few more hairs on her chin and less under her bonnet, her face would have resembled a dried up beetroot. Nevertheless, as shocked as she was by the dressmaker's effrontery, she knew Millie was the best dressmaker in town and had no idea what to say. Fortunately, her daughter did. "Oh fiddle faddle, Mommy, who cares who she keeps in the back. I want to see the latest styles. Do you think they will flatter my figure, Mrs McIver?" The girl did have a tidy figure and would have been quite pretty if her countenance didn't display her character.

Millie smiled, held up a bolt of dark blue and grey striped voile enhanced with bright gold threads, and said, "There is one style I think you shall like, Miss Mildred, and I just received a shipment of this pretty new material that would look lovely on you."

"Oh. I love it! I think it's simply stunning, don't you, Mother?"

The red hue was slowly fading from Rose's face as she tried to regain her attitude of superiority. "Yes, dear, but I do think the colour would suit me more."

Millie assured the two women that she had enough material to make them each a gown. They left the shop smiling.

As soon as Millie came into the back, Gladys exclaimed, "Did I hear you right, Millie? You did say my 'niece,' did you not?"

"I hope you don't mind, Gladys. I just thought of it on the spur of the moment, but now that I think about it, why shouldn't you be my niece?"

Gladys clapped her hand and danced around the room with delight. "Thank you, Millie, or should I say, Auntie Millie?"

"I think I've become accustomed to just plain Millie, so we shall leave it at that. And if that Pickwick boy does ask you to marry him, as your only living relative, I will give you my blessing, just to see the look on that old cow's face when she finds out.

"I don't think he has any intentions of marrying me, and I really can't blame him. After all, I am nothing but a barmaid."

"Never you mind, dear, in a year or two you shall be a governess, and that will be far more gratifying, I am sure."

This caused Gladys to burst into tears again. Then she shared with Millie the news that poor Professor Schneider had fallen ill and passed away a month ago, so she wouldn't be going to London after all.

Knowing how hard it was for Gladys to save up the money she needed, Millie was empathetic, but had dreaded losing her young friend, so was also relieved. "I am certain there will be other opportunities for you to have someone tutor you, Gladys, and if not you still have two wealthy suitors, and perhaps, one will propose."

"I think Keith might. His parents live in Wales, and they're farmers, so they might not object to him marrying someone like me. But I don't love him. I love Tom. What do you think I should do, Millie, if Keith does ask me?"

"Only you can decide that, my dear, but it would give you security for the rest of your life, and I've often heard it said that love is a luxury only the rich can afford."

A few days later, Keith and Tom had just finished a strenuous exercise, and were sitting on the ground getting their wind back when Keith said, "Look here, Tom, I've decided to ask Gladys to marry me tomorrow night. I suppose you gathered that I've fallen in love with her. I hope you don't mind."

Tom didn't know what to say. Although he had no reason, he felt his friend had betrayed him. He had told Keith that he had no intentions of marrying a barmaid, but now hearing his friend admit to loving Gladys, he suddenly realized that he did too, although he hadn't planned on marrying her. Keith was anxiously waiting for his reaction, so he gave a shrug of his shoulders, got up, and said, "Why should I?"

"No reason, I guess. I just wanted you to be the first to know." Then smiling, he got to his feet, threw an arm around Tom's shoulder, and added, "If I'm lucky and she says yes, I'm counting on you to be my best man."

Tom mumbled an answer, then said he had to rush off to meet his father, leaving Keith wondering just how sincere his friend had been when he said he didn't object to the marriage.

Andrew was surprised when Tom arrived at the café unexpectedly. He was just about to have his dinner, so he ordered another plate. While they were waiting for their food, Tom downed two large whiskies then ordered another after the waiter brought their meals. Andrew knew there was something wrong when Tom hardly touched his meal. He was also drinking far more liquor than he usually did. "Is there a reason for this?" he asked.

"For what?" Tom replied sharply.

"For gulping down four drinks and ignoring your food?"

"I'm just not hungry."

"Come on, son, I don't believe that. You're obviously very upset, and I'll not let up until you tell me why. Has it anything to do with Gladys? I've become very fond of that girl, you know."

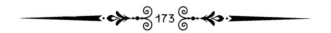

"Keith will be delighted to hear that! He's going to marry her," Tom blurted out with more vehemence than he could suppress.

"I always suspected he was brighter than you."

"She's a barmaid, Father."

"And you think it would be wiser to marry a lady? Perhaps someone like my wife, Rose? Now there's a lady for you, or how about your stepsister, Mildred? Now she's what they call a real lady. Are they the sort of wife you intend to provide me with grandchildren?"

"You mean that you wouldn't object if I were to marry a barmaid?"

"I don't give a damn what she is! Gladys has more character than any of the other girls you've ever courted, and she's by far the prettiest. If I was a few years younger and single, she wouldn't be marrying anyone else; you can bet on that."

"But Keith is my best friend."

"Look here, Tom, if you love her and she loves you, their marriage would be a mistake. Now go on, boy, go and propose before he beats you to it!"

Tom reached over the table to shake his father's hand, and then with a big grin, he said, "Wish me luck!" As Andrew watched Tom leave, he couldn't help but think how he would love to see Rose's face when she found out her stepson was going to marry a lowly barmaid.

When Tom arrived at the inn, Gladys was singing "Home Sweet Home," a popular new song by an American songwriter, John Payne.

One of the Watts' regular customers was leaving the following day for Australia and his wife had asked Gladys to sing it for him. After she sang the chorus the first time, everyone joined and sang along with her.

When she had sung all the verses, they begged her sing it again. As she looked around the room, she was surprised to see Tom since he didn't usually come to the inn during the week. Gladys thought that the only reason he would be there must be because he was going to India. She knew he didn't love her, but she loved him and didn't think she could sing the song again without crying. Then he smiled at her and said he would like her to sing it especially for him. Knowing she might never see him again, she couldn't refuse.

When the song was over, there wasn't a dry eye in the room. Gladys started to leave while the crowd was still applauding, but Tom blocked her path and said that he had one more request. Gladys wiped the tears from her eyes as she informed him she was through singing for the night. Tom shook his head, then put his hands around her waist, lifted her off the floor and sat her up on the bar. The crowd cheered, and when they quieted down, Gladys, more angry than amused, said, "Now you've had your fun, Tom, please lift me down."

"But I have one more request."

One of the patrons called out, "Go on then, Gladys, sing another one for him, that's the girl!"

Tom looked at her and smiled. She couldn't refuse. "Oh very well then, one more. What shall it be?"

Tom's answer took her completely by surprise. "My request is that you, Gladys Tweedhope, consent to be my wife."

Chapter Fourteen

When Gladys accepted Tom's proposal, everyone in the pub, except Laura, gathered around to offer congratulations. Knowing that losing Gladys would harm their business, Laura was too upset to join in and busied herself wiping down the tables. Their profits had tripled since Gladys became their barmaid and songstress. They would have only needed one or two more such lucrative years before they could sell the inn and buy one in Scotland.

They had planned to ask Gladys to go with them, knowing she would be just as popular in Scotland, and they even talked of giving her a healthy raise in pay. But now that she was going to marry Tom Pickwick, it would take twice as long before they could pay off their mortgage and sell the business.

Later, after Tom left along with the rest of the customers, Neil, still in a festive mood, brought out a bottle of his best Scotch whiskey, and suggested that the three of them have a drink of the 'guid' stuff to celebrate. Pleased by his thoughtfulness, Gladys replied, "I think that's a wonderful idea! My heart is still beating so fast I feel lightheaded. I cannot believe that Tom asked me to marry him."

Neil filled the glasses, lifted his in the air, and with spirits accentuating his brogue, he announced, "A wee toast to our ain nightingale, Gladdy!

"May the best ye've e're seen
Be the worst ye'll e're see;
May a moose ne'er leave yer gimal
Wi a teardrop in his e'e.
May ye aye keep hale and hearty
Till ye're auld enough tae dee
May ye aye be just as happy
As I wish ye aye tae be."

Gladys had tears in her eyes as she hugged him, but when she attempted to embrace Laura, the woman moved aside. At first the landlady's rebuff upset her, but then she became angry, and for the first time in all the years she had worked at the inn, she felt free to say whatever she pleased without fear of retribution.

"Mrs Watt, ah, Laura, I know we have never been close friends, but this past year, working side by side, I assumed we had at least come to respect one another. There were many times when I thought you were far too cruel with your demands; nevertheless, I think I shall be a better wife to Tom because of it, and for that I thank you. Now, I don't know why you can't be happy for me, but if it is because you think I would leave you without a replacement—well I promise that will not happen. I have heard Pinky sing and she has a lovely voice. I know she will be a perfect replacement if I teach her some songs and train her to be a barmaid."

The promise did little to ease Laura's concerns. She knew no one would ever be able to take Gladys's place, but she also knew how much she and Neil owed the girl. She really had enjoyed working with her in the pub over the last two years and wanted to remain friends. Although she gave a little cough trying to clear her voice, it still broke when she said, "Tis not that I dinna like you, Gladdy, for I do. 'Tis that I dinna want to see you go." And, for the first time, the two ladies hugged each other.

That night, when Tom returned to barracks, the place was in darkness, and Keith and the other eight men who shared their quarters were sleeping. Tom couldn't wait to share his good news. Shaking Keith's shoulder, he whispered, "Keith, wake up."

Keith woke with a start. Seeing it was Tom, he sat up, rubbed his eyes, and said, "What happened to you? I was worried. Did something happen to your father?"

"No, he's just fine."

"You left in such a hurry, I thought it must be an emergency. You know this was our last practice before we play the officers this weekend. I covered for you by saying you had a family crisis."

"I'm getting married!"

"You're what?"

"I'm getting married!"

"That's nice. Let me know when you find the girl. Now go to bed," Keith said, as he laid down again, pulling the blankets over his head.

Yanking the blankets down, Tom laughed and said, "It's Gladys, you idiot! I'm marrying Gladys."

"What kind of a bloody joke is that?" Keith demanded, sitting up.

"It's no joke, I asked her tonight and she said yes. Can you believe it? I'm actually getting married."

The windows in the old castle allowed little light in, and since Tom didn't see the look of anger on Keith's face as he jumped out of bed, he opened his arms expecting an embrace and was knocked to the floor by a solid right to his chin. Stunned, he looked up to see Keith standing over him shouting, "You bastard! You dirty, backstabbing bastard. Come on, you yellow-livered coward! Stand up so I can knock you down again."

The shouting woke the rest of the men, and they gathered around to see what was going on. They were surprised to find that it was Keith who was the instigator since he was known to be the better natured of the two.

Tom rubbed his jaw, and remaining on the floor, replied, "I'm not fighting you, Keith. I am sorry, but I only realized tonight how much I loved her."

"To hell you say! Just because I told you I was going to propose to her, you went behind my back and got there first. You only want one thing from her, you bounder, and you were afraid if she agreed to marry me you would be out of luck. You don't love her, and I shall bloody well tell her so."

Tom got up from the floor while attempting to explain. "Now look here, old boy, I do love her, and she loves me. I'm sorry if you—" His apology was shortened by another blow aimed at his chin, but due to the darkness landed on his shoulder. "Ouch, damn it, that hurt. That's about enough, Keith. Cool down and let's talk about it."

"This is the only talking I'm going to do," Keith replied, as he took another swing. Tom managed to block the punch with his arm and said, "All right, if that's the way it's going to be, let's go outside and get it over with."

"I'm going to beat the hell out of you," Keith warned as he was pulling on his trousers, and Tom was removing his jacket. It wasn't much lighter outside than it was inside the building, but as soon as they were out the door, both men started circling each other looking for an opening. Tom found one first and landed a punch to Keith's gut, which would have had more effect if his anger matched his opponent's.

"Is that the best you have?" Keith taunted then landed a punch on the side of Tom's head. Tom shook his head, but didn't go down; however, the blow managed to fuel his ire, and he retaliated with two consecutive hits, one to Keith's solar plexus and one to his jaw. Those landed Keith on the ground, where he managed to get hold of one of Tom's legs, toppling him over. As the struggle continued, it became more of a wrestling match than a boxing duel, and because the land sloped toward the stables, the fighters ended up in a pile of manure. Arms, legs, and horse dung were flying when a shrill whistle startled the men, and a lantern lit up the area.

"Break it up now!" the sergeant major shouted. Tom and Keith jumped to their feet and stood at attention. Blood and manure were smeared over their faces and their clothes. The sergeant stood back, fanned his nose then continued in a voice as deep and gruff as a mastiff's bark, "If it's a fight you're wantin', you'll be getting more than your share in a few months. Now, ladies, since you seem to enjoy playing in the shit pile, I'm going to let you spend a couple o' days shovelling it. It's time our stable boys had a day or two in the kip. And I think the rest of you lads will be happy to know that these two ladies will be spending the night in the stables." A loud cheer went up, the crowd dispersed, and the two weary, injured, and foul-smelling warriors were left standing in the cold.

The sergeant major's reprimand had quelled Keith's anger. Having a pacifist nature, he could never stay angry with anyone for long. Such a characteristic would normally be an asset, but for a young man who would soon be fighting a war, it was more of a liability. Nevertheless, he may have still been angry if he hadn't known that Gladys was in love with Tom. Feeling a little embarrassed over his actions, he attempted to hide it by saying, "At least you have boots on," as he looked down at Tom's feet.

"I suppose you expect me to give you one."

"You bet I do. Take it off."

"You're joking."

"No. Take a bloody boot off."

"Don't be ridiculous."

"Take off the damn boot, or I'll take it off myself!"

"If you think—oh, bugger it." Tom sat on the ground, took off one of his boots, and handed it to Keith, who looked at it then threw it back.

"It's a size too small, but I think one of those stockings will fit."

Tom gave Keith a stocking, then said, "There, now can we get out of the cold?"

Keith reached down and gave Tom a hand up. "I was hoping you'd wash some of that shit off your face before you bed down with me."

"Your wish is my command," Tom replied, relieved that Keith

was no longer angry. Then arm in arm, they made their way to the horse trough.

The following day, as they were shovelling dung, Tom said, "Look, I know I've been an ass, but I didn't mean to hurt you. I had no idea you loved her too. I thought you were just threatening to marry her to save her from me. If I could, I'd go back and do it differently. Your friendship means a lot to me. When we go to India, I'd prefer to have all my enemies on the other side."

"As Willie Shakespeare put it," Keith replied, "'By my troth, I'll go with thee to the lane's end . . . I am a kind of burr—I shall stick!' Besides, I guess I always knew it was you she preferred, but I have no idea why. I'm far more handsome and strong."

"Ha, I'd have beaten your sorry ass if old Sarge hadn't come along."

"I guess we shall never know, unless you want to have another go at it."

"No bloody way! I've shovelled enough of this horse shit."

Keith laughed, then in a serious tone said, "She's a very special lady, you know."

"Yes, I know, but then, so are you."

"There you go again, darlin', making me blush," Keith said as he threw a shovel of wet manure at Tom.

Millie was delighted when she heard the news. But when the excitement faded, a feeling of apprehension overtook her. Her life had been far more exciting having Gladys as a friend, and she knew how very lonely she would be without her. Once Gladys was married, things were bound to change. As Mrs Pickwick, she would be living a life in society and a life very different from the one she had shared with Millie.

Gladys could sense there was something bothering the seamstress and insisted on knowing what it was.

"I really am happy for you, my dear, but I am sad too. Now that you are marrying into a wealthy family you shall be making new and influential friends. I doubt you will have time for someone as common as me—not that I fault you for it."

"Millie! You are my family, my only family. Don't you know that? When you told that old cow that I was your niece, I was so proud. Oh, Millie, you will always be my closest and dearest friend. I'm afraid you are stuck with me for the rest of your life."

Tom had no idea when his regiment would be sent to India, but it was rumoured that it wouldn't be until autumn, so he and Gladys had plenty of time to plan their wedding and find a place in which to live. Gladys also had time to teach Pinky some songs. The girl had a lovely voice, but her timidity and lack of confidence prevented her from using it to its advantage. Under her plain and shapeless uniform, she also had a petite, but shapely figure and a head of thick blonde hair that she wore tightly braided and tucked under her dust cap. Her nose and chin were too sharply sculptured, but her large, doe-like, brown eyes were enough to render her pretty, if only she could break the habit of keeping them downcast.

Millie's help was enlisted in making two attractive gowns for the girl, and she also used her theatrical experiences in the art of curling and styling Pinky's hair. Most of the girl's coaching took place in Gladys's room or at Millie's in the evenings; therefore, on the night of her debut, both Laura and Neil were pleasantly surprised with the end result.

The night Gladys introduced her protégé, she waited until she had the audience warmed up with a few lively songs, then she had Pinky join her in a duet. After an enthusiastic round of applause, Pinky's confidence was sufficiently bolstered, and she sang her first solo. Gladys's vivacious personality lent gaiety and naughtiness to her songs, whereas, Pinky's voice rendered such sweetness that it touched the hearts of the audience, and she received a standing ovation. Of course the Watts were relieved, but Gladys found her congratulations undermined with jealousy.

She had been so enthralled over her upcoming marriage and

what it would mean to her socially that she hadn't thought about leaving the inn. Now, seeing the look of pride on Pinky's face, she suddenly realized how much she would miss the exhilarating applause she received every night. Although she had done her best to coach Pinky, she never imagined that the customers she knew so well would welcome the chambermaid with such enthusiasm. It seemed she wouldn't even be missed. Unable to hide her feelings of disappointment, she decided to say she wasn't feeling well and retire. That's when Pete Riley, one of her favourite customers, stood up, held his tankard in the air, and in a loud voice, called for silence.

Then he walked over to Gladys and said, "Gladdy luv, I have a few words to say on behalf of everyone here. We all know that you have the sweetest voice in all of Dover, and how very fortunate we have been to have you share it with us these past years. We shall miss the good times we've spent together more than you will ever know." His eyes were moist as he continued, "But we don't intend to let you go without something to remember us by. Now this is a little token of our appreciation." He handed her a small, beautifully embroidered, cloth bag that was closed at the top with a red ribbon.

"Oh, Mr Riley, it's so lovely. Thank you all very much."

"My Shirley made the bag for you, Gladdy, but it's what's inside the bag that's from us all. Go on now, open it!"

Gladys's hands were shaking as she untied the ribbon. She reached in and pulled out the most exquisite comb she had ever seen. It was made from a tortoise shell and had two rows of pearls that shone like satin, across the top. Tears blurred her vision as she tried to express her gratitude. "I shall wear this when I get married and treasure it forever. Every time I look at it I shall remember each one of you. Oh, how I am going to miss you all!"

"You're not leaving Dover, are you, Gladdy?" One of the men called out.

"I hope not, Jack, although I do intend to go wherever Tom is stationed if I can. As long as we are living here, Tom and I will drop in now and then, and if Pinky does not object, I might even sing a song or two." The applause was long and loud. Then Gladys made the rounds hugging and thanking each one personally.

Because of Andrew Pickwick's status, many of Dover's wealthier residents were expecting to receive an invitation to his son's wedding, certain it would be a prestigious affair. Even Rose was heard to praise Tom's choice of a bride, hoping to secure an invitation. Gladys was invited to a tea party in her honour from Mrs Eloise Dundas, one of the wealthiest ladies in town, who had been a close friend of Tom's mother. She showed the invitation to Millie and said that even though she was pleased to receive such a fancy invitation, she had no intention of going.

Millie was surprised and said, "But you must go, for Tom's sake."

"Why on earth would I go for Tom's sake?"

"Well, to prove that the girl he is going to marry is not just a barmaid, but a beautiful and graceful young lady who knows how to behave herself even among the highest of socialites."

"But that's just it, I'm not any of those things, and I have no idea what one is expected to do at a tea party; so how can I possibly know how to behave? I shall make a fool of myself, and that will be even worse for Tom and his father."

"Nonsense! Just remember that no matter how amazed you are at the grandeur of the house, do not allow it to show. In fact, you may even act a trifle bored as though you have visited many such homes before. And be sure to only take one of the little cakes they offer you and only nibble at it, no matter how delicious it tastes. Anyway, my dear, we do have a week before the party, and by that time I shall have you sipping tea as daintily as though you had done it all your life. I shall also see to it that you are attired in a gown so stylish that all the other ladies will be green with envy."

Millie made it all sound like an adventure, and Gladys began looking forward to the event. She was excited right up to the day of the tea when she was met at the door by Mrs Dundas's butler. When she greeted him with a smile, he returned it with a disparaging look, and her enthusiasm waned. However, his attitude reminded her of

Millie's advice about not appearing too friendly.

The butler showed her into the parlour where her hostess, Eloise Dundas, rose and held out a welcoming hand. Gladys thought the woman to be in her mid-forties, and even though she had a full-bodied figure, her gown was tailored so cleverly and exquisitely, it minimized her excesses. She also had a pleasantness to her countenance that helped put Gladys a little more at ease.

The parlour was so elegant that Gladys wanted to remember every detail so she could describe it all to Millie later. The cream coloured wallpaper was striped with shiny wine coloured strips that Gladys wanted to touch to see if they were real satin. The same rich wine colour was accented in the rose pattern of the large Persian rug on the polished floor. A life-sized portrait of a pretty young girl, who Gladys thought must be the Dundas' daughter, who had died of consumption at the age of ten, hung over the large fireplace. The picture was in a gilded frame that glittered from the light of a huge chandelier that hung from the ceiling and added a heavenly glow to the young girl's face.

Two cherubs stood on each side of the fireplace, but instead of appearing like a shrine, the entire scene was a cheerful one since the sculptor had given each cherub a sweet smile and a dimpled cheek. In spite of Millie's advice, Gladys felt obliged to compliment Mrs Dundas but managed to do it without gushing. Eloise accepted the compliment graciously and asked if she would care to see the rest of the house after they had their tea. Gladys said she would look forward to it.

She was then introduced to six other women in the room, and at first she was pleased to see that two of them, Miss Greta Rowland and Miss Jane Newell, were about her own age; but when they shook her hand, they neither smiled nor spoke, and it left no doubt in Gladys's mind that they were not there to welcome her.

She was right. Greta and Jane had been shocked when they heard that Tom was going to marry a woman who was not only a commoner, but a lowly barmaid, and they came to the tea out of curiosity. Tom was one of the most handsome and eligible young men in town and had a very rich father. He had attended many of the same parties as the girls, and although he had danced with them, he never courted them in spite of their flirtatious gestures. Therefore, they consoled themselves by saying that the only reason he would marry a barmaid was because he had gotten her in the family way. They knew he was a man of honour, and instead of resenting his actions, they felt sorry for him.

What they couldn't understand was why Tom's father hadn't behaved as most fathers would in such a situation, and saved his son's future by arranging another marriage for the tart. Believing that Gladys had deliberately set a trap for Tom, they had no intention of welcoming her into their coveted circle of friends. Then when they saw how stylish and pretty she was, they understood why it had been easy for her to play on Tom's sympathies.

After Gladys was seated and tea was served, the two girls began to belittle her by asking pertinent questions about her past. She did her best to keep calm, but her face felt hot, and she knew it was flushed as she tried to answer their prying questions. In spite of her stylish attire, Gladys felt like an elephant among gazelles and had done all she could not to burst out in tears. Then when they stopped asking questions and started discussing the latest styles in dresses and the different dressmakers in town, she began to relax. That is until Greta remarked how comical Mrs McIver looked with her face made up like a clown, knowing she was a friend of Gladys's. When Jane nodded in agreement and added that Millie must be receiving men customers in the evenings, Gladys couldn't tolerate any more.

"Mrs McIver happens to be my aunt," she said indignantly, while sitting up straight for the first time since entering the house, "and she is the kindest and most caring person I have ever met."

"Well, that may be, but you have to admit she looks as painted up as an actress." Greta snapped back.

"It so happens she was a famous actress. She has even been on the stage with Mr Dickens."

"I have never heard of the man, but then we are not in the habit of associating with that sort. Oh, my, I am afraid I have said the wrong thing, Gladys. Naturally, you have sympathy for the woman. After all, you are a working girl yourself, are you not?"

Before Gladys could answer, Eloise, trying to defuse the awkward situation, said, "I think you have said too much, Greta. I am well acquainted with your aunt, Gladys, and I agree, she is not only a kind person, but a most talented seamstress as well. I have been to her shop and found her to be a most gracious lady and her diction is commendable."

Gladys should have accepted Mrs Dundas's attempt to refute the young ladies' remarks, but she couldn't control her anger. Holding her nose high enough in the air so as to look down it, she addressed the girls, "Of course she has good diction. My aunt is a well-educated person and speaks three languages. Just because she works for a living does not mean she is not as intelligent as any of you, and if you think it does, you must think the same about me.

"Because of circumstances beyond my control, I was forced to go into service in order to live, and I happen to be proud of what I have accomplished. If I had not met and fallen in love with Tom, I would have accomplished even more by becoming a governess, like my mother." Gladys's problem was that when she started making up stories, she didn't know when to stop, so when no one spoke up, she recklessly continued. "In fact I may still seek a career of some sort even after I am married."

This shocked them all, even Eloise. Someone spoke up and insisted that Tom would never allow such a thing. Although Gladys had no intention of being anything other than a wife and mother, she was not about to give them the satisfaction of knowing that. "Oh, I think that if I still desire to have a career after we are married, Tom will be most understanding and not stand in my way."

"Now you are just being silly!" Jane remarked, pleased that Gladys was finally showing her ignorance.

"There is nothing silly about wanting a career. If you think about it, a woman can make a career out of whatever she excels at, be it a seamstress, a governess, or a barmaid. Even raising children or keeping house is a career of sorts."

"Oh my, Gladys, you are joking, are you not?" Eloise broke in.

"Not really, Mrs Dundas, but then I have no idea where I shall be in the future, or what opportunities await me." Gladys was shaking and felt as though she would faint at any minute but she couldn't stop talking. "You see, Tom is waiting to be deployed to India, and if he receives his commission before he goes, I shall be going with him. If that is the case, there are many exciting things I can probably do over there." Ignoring the girls, she looked at Eloise. "Wouldn't you like to do something different someday?"

"I've never thought of it before, but now that you've mentioned it, I probably would."

"Humph! What a lot of nonsense. Keeping a household running smoothly is a duty not a career. Isn't that right, Mother?" Jane replied, but received no answer—her mother more in favour of Gladys's ideas than her daughter's.

"Well, when I am married to Tom, I shall consider looking after our children as a pleasure and more of a career than a duty," Gladys replied.

"I do not think you have any idea what you are talking about," Greta remarked contemptuously. "Besides, now that you are going to marry an aristocrat, you had better start learning how to be a lady. That is if you plan to be accepted into Dover's society. There is a lot more to becoming a proper lady than you can imagine. You have to know how to handle those below you, most of whom are thick in the head or lazy. Then again, being one yourself, you probably don't understand what I am talking about."

"Apologize at once, Greta!" her mother ordered.

Greta may have done so, but she hesitated too long. Gladys stood up, and shaking her finger at Greta, said, "I might be thick in the head, Miss Rowland, but one thing I have managed to learn is how to be polite. And that seems to be more than you have accomplished. Now, Mrs Dundas, I must excuse myself. Tom will be calling for me soon, and I would prefer to wait outside for him. Thank you very much for the tea."

"Oh, Gladys, I am sorry! Please do not judge us all by these silly girls. The rest of us were delighted to meet you, and we would like to be your friends. Isn't that right ladies?" The four older ladies smiled and nodded. Eloise then rang for the butler, and asked him to see the ladies out before she put an arm around Gladys, and said,

"Now, my dear, first I want to show you the conservatory. It is my favourite room."

They were almost finished with the tour when the butler informed Gladys that Tom was waiting for her outside in his chaise. "I mustn't keep him waiting, Mrs Dundas, but I think you have a beautiful home. Thank you for showing it to me."

She held out her hand, but instead of taking it, Eloise embraced her then apologized, "I am so sorry the afternoon turned out so badly, Gladys. The only reason I can think of for such rude behaviour is jealousy. The rest of us enjoyed your visit very much, and I would like you and your aunt to come for tea another time. I can promise you it will be a much more pleasant afternoon." Gladys, seeing that she was sincere, replied, "Thank you, I shall look forward to it."

Tom greeted her with a big smile and said, "Hello, my darling, and how did you enjoy sipping tea with the 'Who's Who' amongst Dover's social butterflies, or should I say social wasps?"

"Oh, Tom, I'm such a fool!" She told him how she had allowed them to upset her so much with their rude questions that she shocked them by saying she might seek a career after she was married. He laughed at first, but then realizing the inappropriateness of her statement, complained, "Now look here, Gladys, you are going to be my wife, and that is all you will ever be. So don't get any silly ideas."

There was something about the severity of Tom's statement that shocked Gladys. He spoke to her as though she was an errant and spoiled child instead of a woman. Besides, his statement sounded more like an order than a suggestion. Gladys was beginning to understand that there was far more equality between the sexes in Old Nichol than in the outside world, and that when she married Tom she would be expected to obey him. With a sigh of resignation, she snuggled up to him and said, "To be your wife, my darling, is all I shall ever want to be."

Chapter Fifteen

When Tom's mother was alive, she insisted he and his father, Andrew, attend St. Mary's Church with her on Sundays. Although Andrew liked the preacher, he didn't enjoy his sermons since they were based on a book he considered mostly fiction, but he dearly loved his wife, so he went to please her. After she passed away, the family pew sat empty except when Andrew and Tom were invited to weddings, funerals, or christenings. However, Andrew's second wife, Rose, and her two children were so taken with having a reserved family pew of their own that they dressed in their finest every Sunday and marched down the aisle with their noses in the air, as though they were members of the royal family.

Most of the congregation knew Rose was a gossip and schemer and usually paid little attention to what she said, but when she began talking about her stepson's upcoming wedding as though she was privy to his plans, they began to wait anxiously for the banns to be read. But that didn't happen.

Tom and Gladys were married on the 18th of February, 1845,

in the Dover Courthouse. Gladys was sixteen. A law allowing marriages to be solemnized by civil contract had been passed on the 1st of December that same year. Gladys, who had never been to a church wedding, had no idea what she was missing and was happy to be married anywhere. Although the courthouse was a small and austere building, Millie insisted Gladys wear a beautiful wedding gown that she had made and had on display in her shop. Along with the gown, Gladys wore the tortoiseshell comb—her gift from the customers at the inn. She not only looked like a princess but felt like one, which she thought was most appropriate since Tom looked like a prince in his uniform.

Keith, Millie, and Tom's father, were the only witnesses to the ceremony, but Neil and Laura Watt generously offered the use of their pub for a reception. No formal invitations were sent out, but the regular customers were surreptitiously informed, and they were delighted and honoured to join the celebration. Andrew hired Sam, the cook from the Whale's Tail restaurant, to prepare the food, allowing Hilda and the rest of the Watts' staff to enjoy the evening too. Besides the regular inn patrons, there were a few well-known dignitaries, who were good friends of Andrew's, and Will and Enid Manson.

It took Sam and three of his kitchen staff three days to prepare the feast, and the results were so delectable that Andrew doubled his pay. Every kind of seafood was perfectly prepared using recipes from Portugal and India—recipes enhanced with herbs and curries that most of the guests had never tasted before. There were also Oriental dishes that Sam had learned to make from cooks who sailed to China and Japan. The Whale's Tail was a favourite place for most of the cooks from the foreign ships to spend their time when they were in port, and it was there they drank, laughed, and traded recipes.

One of Sam's friends, a cook on a French freighter, taught him how to make all the fancy sauces so popular in France. He also gave him the recipe for the newlyweds' wedding cake, which Sam decorated with marzipan and icing. All in all, it was a feast like no other, and as Andrew put it, "I am certain the queen herself has never sat down to a tastier meal!"

When the last piece of cake was gone, the dishes were cleared away and the tables set aside to make room for dancing. It only took a couple of tunes played on two fiddles and a banjo to get everyone on their feet and kicking up their heels. The dancing and drinking went on until early morning.

Tom was ready to leave the reception right after the banquet, but the guests wouldn't hear of it. After a good many drinks and a dance or two, the guests began begging Gladys to sing. She could tell that Tom wanted to leave, but she said, "I'll sing if Pinky, Tom, and Keith sing with me." At first the men refused, but Pinky and Gladys, along with a few boisterous guests, pulled them up from their seats and pushed them to the front of the pub.

Initially, Tom and Keith felt awkward and embarrassed, but when Gladys and Pinky began singing the song, "Waxie's Dargle," they couldn't help but sing along since it was a popular song with their regiment. The rest of the men in the pub joined in with the chorus:

"What'll you have, will you have a pint?
Yes, I'll have pint with you, sir.
And if one of us doesn't order soon,
We'll be thrown out of the boozer."

Once that song was finished, there was no stopping Tom and Keith, and they soon had everyone singing some of the songs they sang in camp. The last one they sang was about a gentleman soldier. The lyrics were a little risqué and sad—a song Gladys remembered her mother singing:

"It's of a gentleman soldier, as a sentry he did stand,
He kindly saluted a fair maid by waving of his hand.
So boldly then he kissed her, and passed it off as a joke.
He drilled her into the sentry box wrapped up in a soldier's cloak.
For the drums did go with a rap-a-tap-tap and the fifes did loudly play,
Saying: fare you well, my Polly dear, I must be

going away."

As they continued singing the rest of the verses there was plenty of sympathetic, "ohs" and "ahs" from the ladies and laughter from the gentlemen. After Tom and Keith finished the song, the newlyweds were finally allowed to leave. Keith delivered them to their house in Andrew's best carriage, hugging them both as he left. He was barely out of sight of the house when he broke down and began to cry.

Andrew had offered to buy the newlyweds a furnished home and hire servants for them, but they refused his generous offer, preferring to live alone. Perhaps if they had planned on staying in Dover, they would have accepted, but Tom knew he would be sent to India, and if he received his commission before he left, Gladys would be allowed to go with him. Only commissioned officers were allowed to take their wives.

They had found a two storied house they could afford to rent a week before the wedding. It was very plain inside and out and hadn't many windows, but Gladys was thrilled with it, even more so when she saw there was a little, overgrown flower garden in the front yard.

She was so elated with the prospect of living in a house of her own that she could hardly hide her enthusiasm, but she managed to convince Tom and his father that she considered it a mediocre dwelling. If they only knew what it meant to her to have all that room for just two people, they wouldn't have been so generous with their praise. She felt like she was the luckiest person in the world. In Old Nichol, five families could live in a house that size and still have room for more.

After Keith dropped them off, Tom grabbed Gladys's hand and ran up the stairs, pulling her after him. He could hardly open the door with the key; he was so anxious to hold her in his arms. They were no sooner across the threshold when he began hugging and kissing her in the darkness of their sitting room. Although Gladys wanted the kisses as much as Tom, she managed to wiggle out of

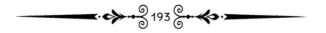

his arms and insist he quell his passion, asking that he light a lamp so she could make her way up the stairs to the bedroom in order to take off Millie's dress so it would be fit to put up on display in the shop again.

Gladys had lived in a tiny space with parents who had openly enjoyed each other's bodies until liquor rendered them incapable of all such sentiments. She had also gone with Sally a few times on her rounds and had seen naked bodies of every shape, so she felt no embarrassment when she took off the rest of her clothing and stood naked in front of Tom. He was shocked but aroused. Her beauty and her brazenness was all it took, and their marriage was quickly consummated.

Granted a weekend leave for his wedding, Tom returned to the castle on Monday morning heavy-eyed but wearing a grin of contentment. Although Gladys had bid him goodbye while vowing how lonely she would be without him, she could hardly wait to be on her own. Having an entire house to herself was more than she had dared dream of. Many of the inn's patrons, along with Millie, Keith, Tom's father, and the Watts, had surprised her and Tom by giving them wedding gifts.

Now, without Tom's demanding attention, she had time to closely examine each of the precious gifts. There was an assortment of linens, dishes, cookware, bottled preserves, and a lovely China ornament of two blue and grey turtle doves, a surprisingly sentimental gift from Laura Watt.

She picked up each gift, fondled it and marvelled at the wealth it represented. Picking up the ornamental doves, she addressed them out loud as she walked about the parlour, "Now, my dears, we must find the perfect place for you to perch. It has to be in a place where everyone can see you and admire you as soon as they come into the parlour. How about on this little table? No, someone could accidently knock you off. How about upon the mantle? Yes, you will look elegant there, and you shall be out of danger. Let me see." She placed the doves on the mantle then left the room and went into the vestibule.

After a few seconds, she returned to the sitting room pretending to be a guest. She glanced around the room then looked at the ornaments. "Oh my, Mrs Pickwick," she exclaimed, "what a beautiful pair of turtle doves you have. I would give anything for a pair of those." Then she flopped down on the divan and burst out laughing. The rest of the day she spent cleaning everything that was already clean and rearranging furniture.

Having little to do the following day, and since Tom's training would keep him away for a few days, Gladys decided to visit Millie and invite her to come and see her house. It was a pleasant spring day when she set out, so she took time to stop and admire the spring flowers in some of the front gardens. A middle-aged man with a friendly face was on his knees working in one of the yards. He looked up at her then smiled and said, "Primroses take over the lot if thee's not careful."

"Is that what those pretty yellow ones are?" Gladys inquired.

The man seemed delighted to have someone admire his work, and with the help of a stout stick, he slowly got to his feet before answering. "Yes, miss, those, an' the red an' pink ones. Does thee have a garden?"

When Gladys lifted her eyes to look at the man, she was unable to answer for a second, having realized that she was standing in front of the Pickwick home. "Does thee have a garden, miss?" the man repeated.

"No, no, but I wish I did. Do you live here?"

The man laughed, shook his head and pointing in the direction of the castle, replied, "No, miss. I live over there at the bottom of the hill, at the beginning of St. Mary's cemetery. My wife and I live in St. Mary's Lodge. I am the Superintendent of the cemetery, but I come here once in a while to clean up Mr Pickwick's flower garden. 'Tis his wife who lives here now. Mr Pickwick, he lives at the quay, and I can't say I blame him, if you'll pardon me, miss." Then with a nod toward the house, he added, "She has no interest in flowers at all. Does thee know her, miss?"

"No. Surprisingly, I don't, even though my husband is her stepson. You see, Tom Pickwick and I were married last Friday."

"Well, if that doesn't beat all! Young Tom has gone and wed.

And if thee will pardon my frankness, I should say he's picked a mighty pretty wife."

"Why, what a nice thing to say. Thank you, Mr . . .?"

"Grimsby, ma'am, Grimsby. Will thee be living here now?"

"Oh dear, no, Mr Grimsby, I don't think Mrs Pickwick would appreciate that!" Gladys answered with a chuckle. "Tom and I have rented a house on Mulberry Lane." Just then the front door of the house opened and Rose Pickwick, dressed in a bright patterned paisley shawl and a large feathered bonnet, stepped out. She was about to descend the stairs when she saw Gladys. After delivering a contemptuous look at both her and the gardener, she made a swift retreat, slamming the door behind her.

"I hope I haven't caused you any trouble, Mr Grimsby," Gladys said.

"Don't thee worry thyself, miss. 'Tis Mr Pickwick himself that hired me. Now if thee would like some of these primroses I am thinning out, I shall bring them over later in the week."

"I would love some, but I have no idea how or where to plant them."

"We shall find a place, don't thee worry. And please feel free to drop in on my wife and me any time. I keep a good show of flowers about the cemetery if I do say so."

"Thank you, Mr Grimsby. I shall look forward to that."

As Gladys was saying goodbye, she could feel she was being watched, so she looked up at the parted curtains, smiled sweetly, then gave Mrs Pickwick a dainty finger wave.

She arrived at Millie's just as the dressmaker was closing for the day.

"You look very pleased with yourself, my dear. I wonder why that is?" Millie joked.

Then, expecting her answer to be about marital bliss, she was surprised when Gladys exclaimed, "I have the whole house all to myself. Imagine having so much room. Pinch me, Millie. It has to be too good to be true."

"That's very nice, dear, but I wanted to know how you like being Mrs Pickwick?"

"Oh, I like it fine." Gladys said offhandedly, then eagerly added, "But you have to come home with me and see the house. If we hurry, we can dine at the inn on the way home, then I shall send you back in a cab later—or you can even stay with me. I have two lovely bedrooms, and each one has a window. Now do hurry, Millie, and put your bonnet on; we should be going."

The weeks that followed were the happiest that Gladys had ever known. She knew how different her background was from that of Tom's, and she had been afraid he would find her too ignorant and unsophisticated once they were married and living together; but both he and Keith treated her with more respect than she had dared hope for. She soon felt as free to express herself with them as she did with Millie, and the more unpretentious she was, the more they seemed to enjoy her company.

The three of them played board games and went walking on the beach after every storm to hunt for treasures that came off the unfortunate ships that were victims of the turbulent sea. They found tins of tea from China, crates of oranges from Spain, and sometimes bowls and figurines carved from the exotic woods from other distant countries. Most of what they found they gave to two local scavengers and acquaintances of Tom and Keith. These men made their living selling whatever they could pick up on the beach.

Mr Grimsby arrived one morning with the primroses in the back of a little cart pulled by an old horse that reminded Gladys of the one the fellow called Sandy owned when he took her to pick up Ellie and Pinky. And judging by the kind tone of Mr Grimsby's voice when he talked to the old mare, he was just as fond of her.

When Mr Grimsby saw the sorry state of Gladys's front garden, he shook his head and remarked, "Thee shall need more than a few primroses to make a show of this plot. Has thee any tools for digging?" Gladys had no idea, but when they went around to the back of the house, they found some in a little shed beside the outhouse, that, according to Mr Grimsby, would do the job.

"Now, miss, er, I mean, missus, I—" Gladys interrupted him by requesting that he call her Gladys. "Very well, Gladys it shall be then," he replied smiling. "Now if thee will fetch a pail of water, we shall dig a little bed for these primroses and give them a drink before they die of thirst."

After the primroses were planted, Mr Grimsby dug around amongst the weeds finding plants that had been neglected for years. "Now if thee rids thyself of these nasty intruders and put some manure on the good plants, thee will be surprised at how quickly they will grow and bloom with gratitude. Look here, see these shoots," he said as he pulled back the weeds. "These are irises, and here are some gladioli. Oh ho, and what have we here? Glory be! 'Tis a delphinium and the poor thing is even showing a few blooms in spite of being squashed by those blighters." He shook his head and added, "'Tis a sad thing when such a pretty plant is being choked to death, is it not?" Gladys wondered if he expected her to cry when she agreed. She was dumbfounded to hear someone talk about plants as though they were human beings.

Before Mr Grimsby left, he did his best to show her the difference between weeds and flowering plants. He also gave her some explicit instructions, "Now thee must be sure to get the roots when thee pulls out a weed. Some shall have to be dug out, but others thee may be able to take out by using the same method the birds use when they pull worms out of the ground. Use gentle, little tugs like this," he said, giving her a demonstration.

Gladys really enjoyed gardening, and once she had room for more plants, Mr Grimsby kept her supplied. Then when she visited him, he showed her the colourful assortment of flowers he grew in the beds that bordered the cemetery. It was such a new and wonderful experience for her that she almost forgave her mother, thinking that if she hadn't had to murder old Gaylord, she would never have known there was so much beauty in the world.

Gladys also spent time helping and learning to sew with Millie and soon became almost as adept with a needle as her teacher. Millie also encouraged her to read, and she soon realized why, after trying to follow the directions on a dress pattern. But in spite of all her gardening, sewing, and housekeeping, Gladys found she still had time on her hands. For years, she was accustomed to working from sunrise until bedtime, and now she found idleness boring.

After the debacle that happened at Eloise Dundas's tea, Gladys was surprised when she received more invitations and even more surprised that they included Millie. She had no idea why they wanted to entertain her or Millie, but it only took a few afternoon teas for her to determine it was because their difference was fodder for gossip. No matter how lovely Millie said Gladys looked, she always felt awkward and ugly when she was among aristocrats, and she said as much to Millie one night on their way home from a dinner party.

"I think they've never even talked to people like us except to order us around. It's as though they had no idea we are capable of having feelings, let alone having ideas of our own, or even preferences. Haven't you noticed the look of surprise on their faces when we say something intelligent? You would think we came from another country."

"Are you sure you are not letting your imagination run away with you, dear? I know Eloise was sincere when she said she wanted us to come to dinner soon," Millie replied.

"Eloise, and maybe one or two of the other ladies are different, Millie, but you must admit most of them will never consider us as equals."

"Nor are we."

"Of course we are. Maybe we don't have as much money as they do, but you just wait and see. When Tom leaves the army and inherits his father's fortune, they will all treat me as though I am one of them. Now, am I right?"

"Yes, I suppose that will be the case."

"Well, I shall still be the same person then as I am now. How silly is that?"

"That is how it is, Gladys, and we are obliged to live with it."

"Well, I am not going to any more of their teas. I might have

Eloise and a few more of the nicer ladies to my place one afternoon—that is if you help me entertain them."

Millie readily agreed, but she was sorry when Gladys said she wouldn't accept any more invitations. Although her background was not as sordid as Gladys's, she had never been in such luxurious homes before, nor had she partaken of such rich food and beverages. Being waited on by servants while listening to all the latest gossip had been a lovely change from the dull routine of her daily life. She was thinking of this when she realized that Gladys was still venting and had to apologize for not paying attention.

"I was just saying, Millie, how odd it is that I wanted to be one of them ever since I came to town, and now I can't imagine why. I don't envy their fancy homes or their money. As far as I can see, they are no freer than their servants. They have to abide by as many rules and dare not do anything that's not considered ladylike. My heavens, I would love to have a good, loud belch in their company just to see the look on their faces." She started laughing and added, "Just imagine what they would do if one were to pass a little wind while having tea. I bet it would shock the pantaloons off them."

Millie didn't laugh. Instead she said, "If you start talking like that, you will never have to worry about ever becoming a lady."

Gladys knew how hard Millie had worked to help her improve her manners and felt ashamed. "I am sorry, Millie. I really do appreciate all you have taught me, and I suppose I want to be respected." Then she grinned and added, "Especially if it means I can learn to ride and have a horse of my own."

Gladys often thought about riding and the next time Tom came home, she mentioned it to him. He said he would be happy to teach her, but insisted she have Millie make her a riding habit. The outfit Millie made, with Gladys's help, was cut from a rich rust-coloured brown material. The skirt was fashioned in an A-line style but was about three inches shorter than usual and had plenty of fullness at the bottom to allow her freedom of movement.

The sleeves, collar, and cuffs of the jacket were made of the same material as the skirt, but the rest of the jacket was made of emerald green velvet and cut to enhance the shape of Gladys's small waist and generous bosom. Tom also insisted she wear a hat, so although she would have preferred to ride bare headed, she took some of the leftover material from her habit to a milliner who made her a smart looking chapeau decorated with green ribbon and three pheasant feathers. It fit neatly to one side of her head and was held firmly there with a shiny gold hat pin. Tom was more than pleased with the results.

Learning to sit side-saddle on a horse was nothing like sitting in the sway of Old Knicker's back, but Gladys soon adapted to it. Of course, Tom had no idea she had been around horses before and was not only amazed by how quickly she learned to ride, but how adept she was at handling Tig, the horse he had chosen for her. After a time, both he and the blacksmith, who boarded the Pickwick horses, began referring to Tig as Gladys's gelding. Although her side-saddle was of the latest design, with a second lower pommel allowing her to ride at a gallop, Gladys couldn't keep up with Tom and Keith if they chose to race, and this continued to irk her.

One day Keith was already mounted and waiting for them at the stable when she and Tom arrived. In their rush to saddle up, Tom wasn't paying any attention to the saddle boy who was supposed to be looking after Gladys's horse. He was outside and mounted when Gladys came out seated on a man's saddle. Under her skirt that she left in the barn, she had worn a pair of men's britches she had found in a second-hand store. She was hatless and her hair was tied back with a bright red scarf. Keith was the first to see her. "I say!" he exclaimed in a complimentary tone of voice.

Tom's reaction wasn't so generous, "What on earth do you think you are doing?" he demanded.

"I am going to beat you both to the fork!" she yelled as she gave Tig a slap across his rump and left them behind with their mouths hanging open. If she had beaten them, Tom would surely have been far angrier, but when the two men came to the fork and reined to a stop, Keith said, "My God, did you see her when we went past? I've never seen anything like it."

"No, and you shan't again."

"Come on, Old Sport, you have to admit, she looked smashing in those britches, and she was handling her horse almost as well as a man. Look, here she comes now. We only beat her by a couple of minutes." Gladys reined in, then dismounted and gave her horse a kiss on his nose.

"Good boy, Tig! We shall beat them next time."

"Well, you will have to do it on foot then," Tom retorted.

"Oh, ho, someone's being a poor sport," Gladys replied.

"Get on your horse now! You're going straight back to the stables. If we are lucky, no one will see you."

It wasn't Tom's angry words that upset Gladys, it was the look of disdain that went with them—it made her feel ugly and stupid. This was a side of Tom's character that she had never seen before. One of the reasons she fell in love with him was because she thought he was impetuous, fearless, and most importantly, rebellious. As she mounted and began riding back to the stable, she wondered if she really knew her husband.

Keith did all he could do not to interfere, and waited until she was out of earshot to voice his disapproval.

"I know it's none of my business, but you were quite hard on her, you know."

"You are right; it is none of your business. However, seeing as you insist on butting in, what in the devil did you expect me to do?"

"I don't know."

"Precisely. Can you imagine what the gossips would have to say if they saw her dressed like that—straddling her horse like a man? My God! She's no longer a barmaid, Keith; she's my bloody wife now."

Keith couldn't help but laugh, "But, by heavens, Tom, no man ever looked that good in a pair of tight britches." Then, after receiving a warning glower, he added, "You know, she's not the first lady to ride that way. Catherine the Great did and even wore a man's uniform when she rode. And then there was Marie Antoinette. I bet no one criticized her."

"They not only criticized her," Tom snapped back, "they cut off her head."

By the time they arrived at the stable, Tom's anger had faded, and he even offered to look after Gladys's horse while she donned her hat and pulled her skirt over her britches. After they arrived home, Gladys, almost in tears, was in a hurry to change her clothes, but Tom caught her hand and pulled her to him. He ran his other hand up under her skirt and over one of her thighs, "There's no need to change yet," he whispered in her ear.

Gladys broke from his embrace, "I don't understand," she said, "I thought you were disgusted with me?"

"Disgusted? Never! I was just worried that someone would see you and start gossiping. Actually, you look rather wicked—so wicked that I wouldn't complain if you decided to spend the rest of the evening in britches."

Gladys smiled, relieved. This was more like the Tom she loved. She posed provocatively with one hand on a hip, her head tilted, and in a husky voice, said, "Well, now, why don't you follow me upstairs, and then we shall see how long you want me to keep my britches on." Later, when they were having dinner, Gladys voiced her opinion.

"It's just so unfair, Tom. You men can wear britches and ride the way a person should ride, but because we are women, we have to wear stupid dresses and sit sideways on a horse. If men were forced to ride that way, the rules would be changed in a day. You know, I think I'll have Millie design a dress for me—one that's split up the middle. What do you think?"

"How about doing what Lady Godiva did instead?"

"What did she do?"

"Well, my love, Lady Godiva is supposed to have ridden her horse through the city of Coventry, naked."

"Why?"

"Well it all took place long ago, during the reign of King Edward the first in the County of Coventry. Godiva, a passionate lady and a devout Christian, thought that her husband, Leofric, was burdening the people with too many taxes so she pleaded with him to remove them. Evidently, Leofric, who was somewhat a prankster, became so tired of Godiva's nagging that he devised a plan that he was sure would put an end to her pleas. Certain she would refuse, he said that if Godiva were to ride through the town naked, he would do away with taxes on everything except horses. To his surprise, she called his bluff and did it."

"Did Leofric remove the taxes?"

"As a man of honour he had no choice. Of course, there are other versions. Perhaps because she was a devout Christian, some stories have her nakedness hidden by her long hair, and some stories say that before she rode, the townspeople agreed to stay in their homes with their curtains pulled while she rode through the town. One story even has it that there was one chap who couldn't resist a peek and was instantly struck blind. His name was Tom, hence, the expression 'Peeping Tom.'"

"I think I would have liked Lady Godiva! Did she ride side-saddle?"

"No, and according to most history books, she even rode the horse bareback."

Gladys thought for a minute then said, "Mm, I can just imagine how delightful that would feel—riding naked with nothing between me and the horse's back." She closed her eyes and smiled.

"I am just beginning to realize what a wicked, wicked woman you are," Tom said before he kissed her.

Chapter Sixteen

Gladys knew she was pregnant two months after the wedding, but didn't tell Tom until a month later, thinking he might be overly protective and exclude her from their outdoor activities. When she finally told him, they had just visited Willard Sawyer, a good friend of Tom's. Willard was starting the world's first Velocipede Works in Dover, and when they arrived, he was busy working on one of his inventions: a new and unique model of a velocipede. Other inventors had tried to make similar machines with poor results, but Willard had been working on his for over two years and was confident he would succeed. Tom had suffered more than a few scrapes and bruises, volunteering to take the invention out for trial runs. He admired Willard greatly and wanted Gladys to meet him.

When they were introduced, Willard merely gave Gladys a quick nod and began talking excitedly about the new changes he had made to his invention. As a gentleman, he did his best to direct his words to both his guests, but they were wasted on Gladys, who had no idea what he meant when he talked about switching something called a crank axle to the front wheels and using a rope and pulley system to the rear ones. Tom, on the other hand, was as enthused over the changes as Willard and couldn't wait to try it out again.

Willard held the machine steady while Tom climbed up on the seat and put his feet on the pedals. When he got it going, Willard ran down the road with him, holding on to the bike and shouting, "Pedal like hell, Tommie, pedal!" until Tom was going fast enough to balance himself. Gladys was afraid he would topple over and break some bones, but he didn't fall and even managed to turn it around and pedal back to where Willard was waiting to stop him.

"I say, that's much better, Willard. By Jove, I think you've done it!" Tom said as he slapped the man on the back.

"Yes, I thought that might be the answer, but there's a lot more alterations to make, and I have to work out a way for the rider to stop. Can't have someone waiting to grab hold of the machine every time they need to get off. I've heard Prince Albert is planning to have his Great Exhibition in six years, and I intend to have a variety of my velocipedes in it. I wager they shall be the first successful velocipedes in the world," he said with pride in his voice. He looked at Gladys and added, "Perhaps you, ah, it's Gladys, right?" Gladys nodded. "Perhaps you would like to try it?"

"Gladys will try anything that doesn't have a side saddle," Tom joked.

"Thank you, Mr Sawyer, but I think I shall decline. Maybe another time though," she said, surprising Tom.

Later, when they were walking home, Tom, thinking Gladys hadn't shown enough interest in Willard's invention, said, "Someday Willard is going to be famous, and his velocipedes will be ridden all over the world, mark my word."

"Then you can tell your grandchildren all about the bruises you suffered helping him invent it."

"And you, my girl, will have to admit that you were too timid to ride one. You really surprised me, Gladdy. I never thought there was anything you wouldn't try."

Gladys put her hand on her stomach and replied, "Well, I don't know about the rest of our children, but I'm sure this one will be thankful I refused." She continued walking, leaving Tom standing with his eyes wide and his mouth hanging open.

"Hold on there!" he called, running to catch up. "What do you mean 'this one?'" Gladys just smiled and continued walking, so he grabbed hold of her arm and spun her around. "Are you sure?"

"I've been sure for two months now," she answered.

"Two months! Why on earth didn't you tell me?" Without waiting for an answer, he continued, "Who else knows? Have you told everyone but me? If you have known for all that time, why didn't you tell me? My God, Gladys, why would you do something like that?" Suddenly Gladys realized how silly and irresponsible she had been. Instead of being overjoyed with the news, Tom felt betrayed.

She rested her hand on his arm and said, "I am really sorry, Tom. I haven't told anyone else, and I didn't mean to hurt you. I've been so stupid. Please don't be angry." Tom shook her hand away and ran off.

When Gladys arrived home, he was sitting in an armchair with a glass of whiskey in his hand. She went to him and kneeled in front of him, "Please say you'll forgive me, Tom. I only did it because I wanted to keep doing the things we do together, and I was afraid you would forbid it if you knew. Please, darling, let's not argue. It's so wonderful! We are going to be parents."

"You may be, but how the hell do I know that I am?"

Gladys felt like she had been slapped across the face. She got up off her knees and cried, "That's a cruel thing to say! You know you are the father. Why would you say such a thing?" When he didn't answer, she burst into tears, ran upstairs and fell onto their bed. An hour later when she came down, Tom had left.

Keith and two of his army buddies dropped into the Scots Inn for a drink that night and were surprised to see Tom sitting by himself in a corner. When he didn't look up, Keith told his friends to go over and join him while he went to order drinks. "What's going on?" he asked Neil Watt, pointing to toward Tom. Neil said he didn't know, but Tom had been there for a few hours and had been drinking all that time.

Thinking that he and Gladys were having their first quarrel, and Tom was drowning his sorrows, Keith wasn't too alarmed. He also knew how quick-tempered Tom could be at times, therefore, his sympathies were with Gladys. Making his way over to the men, he was trying to think of something to say that would encourage Tom to go home and apologize.

Tom hadn't seen the men enter, and didn't know Keith was with them, so when they walked up to his table, he greeted them in a loud and slurred voice. He was laughing and waving his arms about when Keith joined them, followed by Neil with a jug of ale and four mugs. "Here we are, boys," was all Keith said, but he couldn't help showing his disapproval when he glanced at Tom. As inebriated as Tom was, he saw the look, and taking offense, he jumped up just as Neil was putting the jug on the table, knocking it out of his hand. The jug fell to the floor and broke, sending ale and shattered glass across the floor.

Neil began to complain, but Tom interrupted, "Sorry about that. Here, this should cover it," and he threw a handful of notes on the table, almost falling down at the same time. Keith reached out to steady him, but Tom pushed him away. "Get your hands off me, I do not require ashsishtensh." Then he bowed and added, "Good evening, gentlemen," and left.

Keith was going to run after him, but knowing how stubborn Tom could be, decided to stay and offer to help Neil clean up. Neil thanked him but said he could manage, so they moved to another table and ordered more ale. "We'll scout around later and find him," Keith suggested. "By then he should be too drunk to argue."

Gladys spent a restless night on the divan waiting for Tom to return. Every time she nodded off, she woke with a start, thinking she heard the sound of his footsteps. In the morning she not only felt exhausted, but worried. When she saw the time, she knew he wouldn't be home again for at least two days, because he had to report back to barracks that morning. She feared he might have left her for good, and fought back more tears as she made herself a cup of tea and toasted some bread, but the food did little to cheer her up. What she really wanted was a sympathetic ear, and even though it was very early in the morning, she set off to visit Millie.

Because it was Sunday, Millie had slept in and was in her nightgown and robe when Gladys knocked. When she opened the door, Gladys threw her arms around her and wailed, "Oh, Millie, he's gone! Tom has left me, and I shall have to raise the baby all by myself." Millie, accustomed to the girl's emotional outbursts, wasn't too worried as she ushered her in and sat her down on a chair.

"There, there, now whatever is the matter?"

Between sobs Gladys managed to tell Millie what had happened. Then she remembered she hadn't told Millie about the baby. "Oh, Millie, I'm so sorry, I never told you I was going to have a baby."

"Well I knew you would tell me sooner or later."

"You knew?"

"I suspected it about a month ago. Now did you get any sleep last night?"

"No, not really, and I don't think I'll ever be able to sleep again."

"Well, you just lie down on the bed there and rest, while I attend to my toilette, and then we shall talk some more over breakfast." Gladys was asleep before Millie had even applied her makeup.

Keith's predictions had been spot on; he and his companions found Tom later that evening, out cold and lying in front of a seamy drinking establishment, probably tossed there by the proprietor. They managed to wake him up enough to get him back to the barracks and into his bunk, but the next morning he had such a hangover, he was unable to attend mess call. Feigning a bout of ague, he remained in his quarters for the rest of the day. Keith didn't have a chance to talk to him until that evening.

"Okay, Tom, tell me what happened," he said.

"Gladys is having a baby."

"Congratulations! But do you not think you should have included her in the celebrating?"

"She has been pregnant for months."

"How come you didn't tell me?"

"I didn't know until yesterday. She did not tell me until then."

"Well, I guess she wanted to wait to make sure."

"Or she was pregnant before I married her."

"Come on! You would surely know if she wasn't a virgin."

"I thought so, but I have heard that there are ways to fake that, and God knows, you could even be the father."

"Now, look here, Tom, I am not going to stand for any more of your nonsense. I am not the father, but I wish to God I was," Keith said, turning away.

Tom's accusation had hurt Keith so badly, he refused to talk to him after that, and even went so far as to change beds with another soldier that same night. Tom regretted his words as soon as he had said them and was about to apologize, but changed his mind when Keith turned away from him. In the following days, he allowed his suspicions to grow and fester, and by the time his next leave was due, a perplexing mixture of pride, guilt, and stubbornness caused him to volunteer for extra duty, thinking it would serve Gladys right.

Hearing that Tom wasn't going to take his leave, Keith knew that Gladys would appreciate a shoulder to cry on, and with not entirely unselfish intentions, he saddled up and left camp.

When Gladys looked out the window and saw a soldier riding up, she was sure it was Tom. As she heard his footsteps approaching, she threw the door open and fell into his arms, tipping her head back for a kiss. By the time she saw it was Keith and not Tom, it was too late. Keith, unable to resist, took advantage of the moment and kissed her back. Embarrassed, Gladys broke away from his embrace and Keith stammered, "Forgive me, Gladys, I . . . I . . . couldn't stop myself."

She acted as though she hadn't heard him and quickly changed the subject, "Is Tom alright? Nothing has happened to him, has it?"

Keith assured her that Tom was well and then related what had happened. Gladys appeared so upset that Keith almost returned to barracks in order to give his friend a good thrashing, but he didn't want to forfeit the opportunity to be alone with her. He accepted a cup of tea and asked what he could do to help. She explained that she would like to visit Tom's father, Andrew, and tell him what had happened. Because Keith didn't have a buggy, he offered to take her to the quay, riding double on his horse.

Many nights, Keith had dreamt of holding Gladys in his arms, and now as they rode toward the quay, his dreams had come true. He couldn't help but fantasize that if Tom and Gladys didn't reconcile, she would turn to him and perhaps learn to love him. Friend or no friend, he figured it would serve Tom right. Gladys was so busy wondering if she should be running to Andrew with her troubles and what she would say to him when she got there, she didn't even notice how tightly Keith held her.

Reality returned to Keith as he and Gladys sat facing Andrew Pickwick in his office. Although Andrew had shaken his hand when they arrived, there was something in the elder man's look that made it perfectly clear he understood how Keith felt toward his daughter-in-law, and it caused Keith to feel guilty and disloyal.

Andrew was thrilled with the prospects of becoming a grandfather, but upset and angry with his son's obstinate behaviour. "That boy's pig-headedness has gone too far this time," he declared. "I shall soon put him right when I see him. Unfortunately, it will have to wait until I return. I leave today—in a few minutes actually—to settle some shipping problems in Ireland. Those poor souls over there are getting the raw end of the stick, and I must try to help if I can. In the meantime, I think you and my unborn grandchild should have some means of transport. Let us see, a shay to go with Tig should do the trick.

"According to Tom and Bob Hennessy, who boards Tig, he is so attached to you that you may as well call him yours. You tell Bob I said you were to have the use of the little shay and Tig any time you want. Bob is a good sort and will look after you." After Gladys thanked him, he added, "You are more than welcome. In fact, I shall write you out a bill of sale. That way my wife and those other two leeches, cannot accuse you of thievery. They would love the chance to have you arrested. And to make it perfectly legal, you can pay me a guinea."

"I don't have one here, Sir. Keith, could you lend me one? I shall pay you back as soon as you take me home."

"Here you are," Keith replied, and laid a guinea on the desk.

Andrew took the money, wrote out a bill of sale, then, as he handed it to her, he asked, "Now what about money? Did that rascal leave you penniless?"

"Oh, I have a little savings; I am sure I can manage."

Andrew rose from his big leather chair and came around the desk. After giving Gladys a strong and reassuring hug, he said, "Don't you worry, he may be a stubborn clout, but he's not completely brainless. He will be back with his tail between his legs, you will see. And Gladys, if you could manage it, I would prefer 'Dad,' or 'Andrew,' to 'Sir.' As for you, Keith, thank you for bringing Gladys to see me, but I think she should take a cab home or tongues will be wagging, if they aren't already. Will you be able to walk to the stable when you need the shay, Gladys?" She assured him it wasn't too far.

Before they took their leave, Andrew insisted she accept a generous amount of money, saying he hoped that would be sufficient until either Tom came to his senses, or he returned from Ireland. As soon as Gladys returned home, she pulled a chair over to the built-in China cupboard in the dining room and put the note of sale from Andrew on the top shelf for safe keeping.

The next afternoon, Keith visited Gladys again and took her to Bob Hennessy's stable so she could have Tig harnessed to the shay, and then he went for a ride with her since she had never handled a rig before. Tom had often handed her the reins when they were together, so, although she was a bit nervous at first, she soon felt at ease. The thought of owning her own horse and buggy was so exhilarating she laughed, and called out, "I feel like a bloomin' Queen!" without

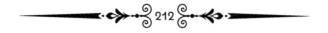

realizing her language had momentarily regressed.

Keith, overjoyed to see her happy once more, answered, "And I'd say you looks like a bloomin' Queen." For a second, she thought he was making fun of her, but then she realized that he didn't know she wasn't joking.

During the days that followed, Gladys was so thrilled with having her own means of conveyance, she seldom stayed home. Her evenings were spent visiting with Millie or Keith. It was the nights she dreaded, laying awake for hours longing for Tom's warm body and his loving caresses. She often thought of sending him a message, begging him to come home, but as time went by, she began to feel less and less culpable and more and more the victim, so decided it was up to Tom to do the begging.

Tom was also having his share of sleepless nights, and he no longer wore his usual carefree, lopsided grin. Also noticeable was the adverse change in his personality. He missed Keith's company almost as much as Gladys's. He tried accompanying some of the other men into town for an evening, but found little enjoyment in it. He spent a good deal of his spare time reading, but nothing he read took his mind off his troubles.

When he heard that his father had returned from Ireland and had requested a meeting, he knew he was in for a tongue-lashing. Surprisingly, he looked forward to it. Andrew wasted no time with greetings when Tom met him at the Whale's Tail. His first words were, "My God, boy, you really are an idiot!" He then went on to say that as much as he liked young Corkish, "I shall not sit by and let him raise my grandchild."

"But, Dad, you don't know what she did."

"I do indeed! Gladys gave me a clear explanation of the event. She admitted she made a silly mistake, now you have to admit to yours, which I may add, was far worse."

Tom knew he was being a fool, but until he heard his father say it, he couldn't admit it. When he left his father's office, he was in high spirits and wearing his familiar, lopsided grin.

On his way home he envisioned how happy Gladys would be to see him, and he gave his horse, Monty, a slap across the rear to speed him up, but when he came in sight of the house his anger returned. Keith's horse was tied to the gate post. "Well, I shall soon get rid of him," he said to his horse. He dismounted, ran up the steps, and entered without knocking, taking Keith and Gladys by surprise. They were in the living room, their heads bent over a game of draughts.

When Gladys saw him, she did all she could do to remain seated. She wanted to jump up and run into his arms, but she was afraid of being turned away again. "Well, Tom, this is a surprise. We are just about finished with this game. I am a poor opponent, so it will not take Keith long to finish me off, then I shall make us a cup of tea. I baked a seed cake today," she said, as though he had never left.

Tom's ire was building as he looked down on the two of them. Touching Keith on the shoulder, he said in a threatening tone of voice, "I would advise you to get on your horse now and leave."

"I will leave when Gladys asks me to and not before," Keith replied.

"Gladys?" Tom said, expecting her to respond accordingly.

"I think you are being very rude, Tom. Keith has been a big help around here since you've been gone. I don't know what I would have done without him."

Her words reinstated Tom's earlier suspicions, and his face turned red. He gave a malicious sounding laugh, and said, "Oh, ho, I imagine he made himself right at home; but now the master of the house has returned, and his services are no longer required, so he can bloody well leave."

Keith rose to go, but Gladys put her hand on his arm. "No, Keith you don't have to. I think we should all sit down and talk."

"There has been enough of that. Either he leaves or I do," Tom snarled.

"Now you are being childish," Gladys replied.

Her words hurt both Tom's feelings and his ego. He not only felt embarrassed, but betrayed. "I guess it is me then," he stammered as he stormed out of the house. Once outside, he quickly mounted Monty, whipped him across his flanks and rode off. Gladys and Keith ran to the open door in time to see him galloping down the road.

"Oh, Keith, go after him, please. You have to bring him back," Gladys pleaded. "I can't go on with this. You have to make him believe that I only love him. Please!"

Heartbroken, Keith left. Gladys's words finally convinced him that she would never be his. Realizing what a fool he had been, he rode towards the castle.

It had been a stormy day and although the rain and wind had subsided, dark clouds made dusk as murky as night. Tom's fury was like a fire in his brain, and he heedlessly spurned his horse on at a dangerous pace. Suddenly he saw a barrier, but it was too late. A large elm tree had been uprooted and fallen across the trail. Monty saw it at the last moment as well and tried his best to scale it, but only made it halfway across. The last thing Tom thought as he went flying through the air was, "Oh, God, I hope that was a branch snapping and not one of Monty's legs."

Keith arrived at the fallen tree about ten minutes later, and would have suffered the same fate if he hadn't been going at a much slower pace. Seeing the road was blocked, he dismounted and began leading his horse around the branches when he heard a faint neigh. Instinctively, he knew what had happened and called out, "Tom! Tom, where are you?" Receiving no answer, he tied his horse to a limb and began climbing over the debris. It didn't take long to find Monty and realize that the animal had broken a leg or two and would have to be put down, but it took another five minutes to locate Tom, who was lying over a branch, his head hanging, his body as limp as a blanket.

Keith reached over to put his hand on Tom's forehead. The sticky wetness he felt was easily identified and sent shivers up his spine. Knowing he couldn't leave his friend in such a state while he went for help, he managed to lift him over the debris and lay him on the ground. Part of Tom's scalp was hanging loose, exposing a portion of his skull and a huge gash ran down one side of his face. Feeling

certain his friend was dead, Keith was both surprised and relieved to find a pulse, albeit a weak one. He took off his jacket and laid it carefully and tenderly under Tom's head, then used his shirt to wrap the wound. "There now, I am going to go and bring some help. Don't you go dying on me now, or I will beat the hell out of you," he said, before riding off.

Night had fallen by the time he returned, accompanied by two medical assistants, a wagon, and a few torch bearers. There were tears of joy on his cheeks when he found that Tom was still alive, and although unconscious, he was breathing without too much difficulty. As the medics looked after Tom, Keith, who had brought along his musket, did what Tom would have wished and put Monty out of his misery.

Keith didn't tell Gladys or Andrew what had happened until the next day, hoping the doctor would be able to patch Tom up so as not to frighten them. He was right. By the time he brought Gladys and Andrew to the garrison's infirmary, Tom had his scalp stitched back in place. The ugly stitches ran about four inches up into the left side of his hairline and down through one eyebrow, stopping just above his cheek bone and were covered in dry, blackened blood. Half his hair and one eyebrow had been shaved off and his face was swollen and blue. Gladys went pale and staggered when she saw him, and Andrew had to steady her with an arm. Luckily, Tom hadn't regained consciousness and didn't see the look of distress on their faces. Once she regained her composure, Gladys sat down, took Tom's hand in hers and held it to her lips. She and Andrew were allowed to remain with him until three in the afternoon, at which time the doctor arrived.

The doctor, a young, dark-skinned, slightly-built fellow with a large nose, thinning hair, and a distinct Indian accent, had been brought to Dover Castle after interning on the battle fields of India.

"I am Doctor Carvalho. Are you his wife?" he asked.

"Yes, Doctor, and this is his father, Andrew Pickwick."

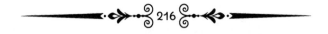

After the two men shook hands, the doctor directed his diagnosis to Andrew, precisely, ostensibly, and seemingly, without empathy. "Your son has had a severe head injury, sir, and, until he regains consciousness, it is impossible to tell the amount of brain damage he might have suffered. I have managed to stitch up his wounds, but that is all I can do for him at present. I can tell you that he is most fortunate not to have lost an eye."

"Thank you, Doctor. I suppose there's nothing we can do now but wait and hope for the best," Andrew replied in a tone more query than statement.

"I would suggest you both talk to him as much as possible; it sometimes helps," the doctor advised.

"Isn't there anything else we can do, Doctor?" Gladys pleaded.

"Try to get some water into him—by little dribbles—we don't want him to choke. I will come by later tonight to see how he is progressing."

Tom didn't regain consciousness until two days later. The doctor, whom Gladys had first thought to be uncaring, had allowed her to sit by his side every day, and on the third day she was bending over him, trying to give him a drink, when he suddenly opened his eyes. She was so startled, she spilled the cup of water, and it ran down his chin.

"Are you trying to drown me?" he asked with a slight grin.

"Tom!" she cried, and then laid her head on his chest and sobbed.

He was so weak, it was all he could do to lift his hand up and put it on her head.

Chapter Seventeen

Aware that he was to blame, Tom was devastated when he heard Monty had to be put down. "All this is my fault," he confessed when Gladys was visiting him along with his father and Keith. "Monty would still be alive if I hadn't been such an idiot."

"It wasn't your fault, darling. I started it all by not telling you about the baby sooner," Gladys insisted.

"If anyone is to blame, it is me," Keith added. "If I had been any kind of a friend, I should have tried harder to set things right between you both instead of keeping you apart."

"Well you shan't get a confession from me," Andrew responded. "I am too old and too wise to get myself in such a state, but I do agree. You are all three responsible. So let's have no more of this nonsense. There is my grandchild to consider. Now, Tom, I have some good news. The doctor said you are strong enough to go home tomorrow."

"How do you feel about that?" Tom asked Gladys, still feeling guilty for his childish behaviour.

"Well now, let me think about it. If you promise to stay there, I just may allow it."

"What was that line from Shakespeare about a burr that you quoted the night when we were rolling around in all the horse dung?" Tom asked Keith.

"By my troth, I'll go with thee to the lane's end . . . I am a kind of burr—I shall stick," Keith answered.

"By my troth, Gladys my love, that is what I shall be from now on—your burr."

Andrew offered to bring Tom home the next day, but Gladys insisted on picking him up in her little shay. When she arrived at the castle, she was delighted to see he was smiling, but sad that his injuries had robbed him of the lopsided grin she loved. Since the accident, someone had carefully shaved Tom's face every day so as not to disturb the stitches, and because he hadn't looked in a mirror since he had his accident, he had no idea how drastically his appearance had changed. On the ride home, they came across two young boys who he recognized that were playing alongside the road. Unfortunately, when he waved and called out to them, they returned his greeting with an unmistakable look of repulsion.

"Do I look that horrible?" he asked Gladys with concern.

"No, darling. It's just that the stitches are sticking out, and you look like a porcupine. When you get them removed and your hair grows back, you will be just as handsome as ever," she lied.

It had been a long time since they had made love, and when they arrived home, they went directly upstairs to their bedroom. "How I've missed you," Tom said as they lay in bed later. Gladys smiled and started to get up, but he pulled her back down, "No, no, don't get up yet. Let's never get up. In fact, I intend to spend the rest of my life right here on this bed with my beautiful wife."

"Have you forgotten that there is someone else here now, and he, or she, is telling me that I need food?"

Tom put his face on her tummy and said to his unborn child, "You are a greedy little fellow aren't you? Well, you are just going to have to go hungry for a little longer, there is something I have here that is just as demanding as you."

It was a good thing he was still in a weakened condition, or Gladys would have gone hungry until morning. After she left their bedroom, Tom stretched out on the bed contentedly and then dozed off until Gladys wakened him by calling out that dinner was ready.

"I shall be right there, my love, as soon as I wash up a little," he replied.

When ten minutes had passed and he hadn't come down, Gladys called to him again, but received no answer. Laughing, she said, "You devil, you've gone back to bed. I'm coming up there, and if you are not up and dressed by the time I get there, you'll be sorry!" When she went into the bedroom, he was standing with his pants on, braces dangling and shirtless, staring out the window.

"Tom?"

"Why didn't you tell me I looked like a monster?" he cried without turning. Gladys went over to him and tried to turn his face toward her, but he pushed her hand down. "No, I cannot bear the thought of you looking at me. I thought it was love I saw in your eyes, but now I know it was nothing but pity."

"You can't do this to me again, Tom. I won't stand for it!" She tried to turn him towards her, but he pushed her hand away again. "Don't you dare push me away," she shouted. "Look at me, Tom. I said, look at me!"

Slowly, he turned to face her. Tears were running down his cheeks as he moaned, "How can you possibly love someone this ugly?"

"You are not ugly, Tom. When your wounds are healed and the stitches gone, you are going to look much better. Please believe me, darling. I love you so very, very much."

Tom tried to believe her, but he couldn't help wondering if she would still feel that way if her predictions proved to be wrong. The following week they were kept busy with visits from Keith, Andrew, and other forewarned friends who tried their best to hide their shock when they first saw Tom's face. They weren't very successful, resulting in Tom seldom leaving the house in the daytime.

One afternoon while Tom was upstairs sleeping, and Gladys was busy in the kitchen baking pies, she heard someone knock at the front door. She tried to pin her hair back as she went to answer the door, but only succeeded in leaving a streak of flour on both her hair and her forehead. When she opened the door, she couldn't have been more shocked if the queen was standing there. Greta Rowland and Jane Newell, dressed in all their finery, both offered a feigned smile and said, "Hello, Gladys."

When Mrs Newell heard about Tom's accident, she felt sorry, not only for him, but for Gladys as well, and recalling how rude Jane and Greta had been to the poor girl, she decided it was time they apologized. She was surprised and pleased when both girls consented without complaining. She wouldn't have been so pleased had she known that the only reason they wanted to visit Gladys and Tom was to see what sort of home the young couple lived in.

They had heard it was a common peasant dwelling, and because they hadn't forgiven Gladys for lecturing them about their bad manners, they hoped their visit would be more of an embarrassment for her than a pleasure. They had also heard that Tom was no longer handsome, and although neither girl would admit it, they both felt his injuries were somewhat justified for not choosing one of them instead of a barmaid.

When Gladys answered the door in the same work clothes she wore when she worked as housemaid for the Watts, Greta had to stifle a wicked laugh of satisfaction. She nudged Jane in the ribs, but Jane was staring at Gladys in amazement and ignored it. She couldn't believe any girl could be clad so drably and still look so beautiful. In fact, she thought Gladys looked even prettier than she did the day when she wore a fancy frock to Mrs Dundas's tea. When Jane didn't speak, Greta grabbed the large basket from her hand, held it out to Gladys and said, "This is for you. We heard about Tom's accident, and we wanted to let him know how sorry we are. How is he? Could we see him?"

Reluctantly, Gladys took the basket and mumbled a thank you. She would have liked to refuse it, but because she had once criticized them over their rudeness, she felt obliged to invite them in. Although she was sorry to be dressed so shabbily, she decided not to give them the satisfaction of an apology. This was difficult to do, however, when Greta didn't even try to hide a smug smile as she looked around at the bareness of the room. Jane was looking around as well, and when she spotted the two doves, she remarked how pretty they were. Gladys, not quite sure if the compliment was sincere or not, didn't thank her. Instead she answered, "Yes, they are lovely, aren't they?"

They sat in awkward silence for a few seconds before Jane pointed to the basket Gladys had placed on a table, and said, "We thought since you have been visiting Tom at the hospital every day, you would not have had time to shop for food, so Greta and I filled a basket with things we hope you might use."

As she explained the reason for the gift, her expression seemed sincere, so this time Gladys smiled when she said thank you. It was the first time they had shared a smile, and Jane was surprised at the unexpected feeling of friendship she felt. She reached over, took the cloth off the basket, held up a currant cake, and said, "This is our favourite cake at home, Gladys, I hope you like it as much as we do."

"I'm sure I shall. Let's all have a piece with our tea then, shall we?"

Greta didn't have any idea what was going on, but she didn't appreciate Jane's change of attitude and glowered at her. Jane glowered back then shocked her even more by standing up and offering to help make the tea.

Gladys was also surprised, but just smiled and said, "That would be nice, Jane, but you will have to excuse the mess in my kitchen. I was just baking pies when you came in."

"My heavens, do not tell me that you have to do your own cooking," Greta said sarcastically.

"No, Greta, I do not have to do my own cooking. I could have a cook if I wished and as many maids I want, but I happen to enjoy baking. I don't suppose you have ever done any cooking."

"I should say not!" Greta exclaimed.

Her haughty attitude didn't have any effect on Gladys or Jane, who said, "I've always wanted to try baking, and when I was little, I even asked our cook if she would show me how, but she just laughed and shooed me out of the kitchen. Perhaps you would teach me some time."

"I would be happy to, but let's wait until Tom is well enough to return to duty."

"Wonderful. Speaking of Tom, how is he?"

"He didn't sustain any brain damage, did he?" Greta inquired in a voice void of sympathy. "No, thank heavens," Gladys replied. "But he is quite sensitive about his appearance, so I would appreciate it if you would try not to appear too shocked when you see him. I shall put the kettle on then wake him up. Jane, you can cut the cake for me and put it on a plate. I will show you where the knives and plates are. Greta, why don't you get out some cups and saucers?" she added, along with a wink at Jane.

Greta could sense they were joking, so put her nose in the air and answered, "I shall leave that up to you. Unlike Jane, I have not the slightest desire to learn how to be a chambermaid."

Gladys laughed, "Forgive me, Greta, of course you don't. It does take a certain talent. You just sit back, and we shall have your tea served in no time."

"And we will even stir it for you, if you like," Jane said, teasingly.

Greta was angry enough to leave, but she was determined to see Tom so she could tell to her other friends how ghastly he looked.

Of all the visitors Tom had, Jane and Greta were the least successful at hiding their shock when they saw his disfigurement. Nevertheless, before they finished their tea, both girls had become accustomed to his appearance, and enjoyed his company. The three had grown up attending the same social functions and had a lot to talk about. Greta did her best to exclude Gladys from their conversation, but Jane and Tom were just as determined to include her. Gladys appreciated their visit, and as they were leaving, she invited them to return whenever they could, although she was sure that Greta would never set foot in their home again.

As they were walking back home, Jane had to almost run to keep up with Greta, who was still angry. Her best friend had humiliated her, bending over backward just to please a common barmaid; as far as she was concerned, that's all Gladys would ever be, no matter who she married.

"For heaven's sake, Greta, slow down," Jane shouted as she grabbed hold of Greta's arm and stopped her. "Why are you in such a hurry?"

"You know perfectly well why," Greta snapped back.

"Are you angry with me?"

"You behaved like a fool!"

"You mean because I helped Gladys serve the tea?"

"Since when have you been a good Samaritan? You seem to have forgotten why we went to visit her in the first place!"

"I know we only wanted to see how she lived, so we could tell the girls, but I never knew what she was like then. Now I really like her, Gret. I think she is so beautiful, and she really doesn't care if Tom's face is a mess. They are so much in love; it gives me gooseflesh."

"A lot of her sort are pretty, Jane, but that does not make them any less common. She can never be like us, and we must never stoop to her level, or heaven knows what the world would be like. People are born different and nothing can change that. We should certainly have sympathy for those less fortunate, and give them what we can, but that does not mean we should treat them as equals. Tom made a mistake when he married Gladys, and mark my words, he will live to regret it." Greta felt as though she was explaining the facts of life to a child, and her anger dissolved, "Come on, let's stop at the Petersons and see if Amanda is home."

Jane didn't argue. She had enjoyed herself in Gladys's company, and she didn't want to spoil the day. After the two girls left, Gladys sat on Tom's knee and said, "If you had told me this morning that I was going to be friends with one of those two girls, I would have thought your accident had rattled your brains."

"There you go then. You see, we of the upper classes can be quite likeable when we take a notion." Then pushing her gently off his knee, he said in a deep voice, "But we can also be demanding. Where is my dinner, wench?"

Gladys bowed and, pointing to the basket, answered, "I shall have it on your plate, master, just as soon as I look into that magic container and see what the cooks have prepared for us." They both made a dash for the basket.

Two weeks later, Tom was able to return to duty. His stitches were gone, but contrary to Gladys predictions, the scars they left were puckered and dark coloured, leaving his appearance little improved. To his amazement and delight, Gladys treated his disfigurement as something to be proud of, and not hidden. In fact, she seemed more enamoured with him than ever, even going so far as to say that the scars made him look more masculine, which added to his sex appeal.

This made him laugh, and he had answered, "You really are my Esmeralda."

"Oh? And who is this Esmeralda? Should I be jealous?"

"Not unless your name is Quasimodo."

"Quasi who?"

"Quasimodo. Have you not read Victor Hugo's book, *The Hunchback of Notre-Dame?*"

"I've never even heard of it. Tell me all about it. Was Esmeralda pretty?"

"She was in fact—almost as pretty as you."

"Tell me about her."

"I shall do better than that, I shall buy you the novel; then if I go to India before I get my commission and have to leave you behind, it will give you something to do until you join me. It may even help remind you of how much your ugly husband loves you."

"You mustn't say that. We all have scars, and some are far uglier than yours. Only they're inside, and you can't see them."

"What would a beautiful and innocent young thing like you know about ugliness?"

"I'll tell you some day."

"Tell me now."

"No, but I promise I shall after we are together in India." And no amount of coaxing could change her mind.

Tom's scars bothered him less and less, and it wasn't long before he was making jokes about them. "I won't even have to draw a sword against the enemy," he declared, "I shall just glare at them, and they will run." What he didn't divulge to anyone was that he had suffered a few short spells of blindness. Keith found out about it one day when they were playing rugby. Tom, who seldom missed a shot on goal, missed the ball all together and fell down.

The other players, thinking he was acting the fool, laughed, but Keith had seen the look of fear on his friend's face. When he confronted him later, Tom confessed, but begged him to keep it a secret, "It may never happen again, and if I go to the doctor now, he may have me discharged. I want that commission, Keith. Then, if I do get discharged, I shan't feel this has all been a waste of time."

Keith, just as anxious to receive his own promotion, understood and agreed to say nothing, but he kept a closer eye on Tom from that day on.

They received their deployment notice early in June, and were given a week's leave before being shipped out. A photographer was hired to take a picture of their squadron, and if anyone could afford it, they could have individual pictures done as well. At first Tom was adamant with his refusal, but when the photographer assured him that his would be a profile, he finally agreed. The photographer was also an artist, and did an expert job of hand painting the photos, so that their bright, scarlet-red jackets, and blue pants could be appreciated.

During that week, Tom hardly let Gladys out of his reach. "I want to be able to close my eyes and see every bit of you."

"I hope we are in India before your memory fades," she said.

"Sergeant Major thinks we will have our commissions early in the New Year, and then it won't be long before we are together again."

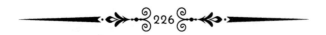

"Maybe you will be able to come home for Christmas?"

Tom laughed, "I might not even get there by then."

"Oh no! How dreadful. How far away is India?"

"Don't you have any idea where it is?"

Gladys lied, "Of course, but I didn't realize how slow the ships were."

"I'm afraid we will just have to wait until you come to India to celebrate Christmas, and perhaps the birth of our child."

They both found it difficult to forget their upcoming separation, which cast a sense of gloom on the days that followed. Sleep was needed, but resented. And the thoughts of leaving his father, who he might never see again, also added to Tom's despondency. Two days before his departure, he and Gladys were in their kitchen. She was making a steak and kidney pie, her hands covered in dough, and Tom was sitting nearby on a stool, polishing his boots when someone knocked on the front door. "I'll get it," Tom announced as he jumped up. Everything turned black, and he began flailing his arms about trying to feel for the nearby wall when Gladys turned and saw him. "Tom, what's wrong?" she asked anxiously, then reached over and took his arm.

"It's nothing. I'm just a little dizzy—probably breathing in too much of this boot blackening. Just help me sit down for a minute, and I shall be fine," he answered.

"Hello there!" Tom's father called from the front hall, after letting himself in.

"We're in here, Andrew," Gladys called back. When he entered the kitchen, Tom's eyesight hadn't returned, and he kept his head in his hands as though he was still suffering giddiness.

"What's the matter with you?" Andrew inquired.

"I must have sniffed too much boot blackening."

"I've heard of that happening. You had better lie down for a minute or two. I've come to ask you both out for a farewell dinner."

"Oh, dear, I've just got a steak and kidney pie ready to go in the oven," Gladys said.

"That's fine, Gladys, the celebration is for tomorrow night. I don't suppose there's enough pie there for me too, is there?"

"Of course there is!"

While they were talking, Tom's vision was slowly returning, and he made his way carefully into the living room to lay down on the sofa. His father and Gladys thought no more about it.

Keith had gone home to Wales for his leave, but returned the day before they were to sail for India, in time for Andrew's farewell dinner at the Whale's Tail. When Andrew said he was taking them out to a farewell dinner, he didn't disclose that he had invited most of Tom's good friends too, so it was a wonderful surprise. Tom was happy to see everyone, but saddened to think that there was a possibility he might never see them again. Many British officers had fallen in love with India and opted to remain there even after they retired, and he knew that may happen to him and Gladys. He looked around the tables as they ate and thought about how much each person meant to him.

He wondered who Willard Sawyer would find to take his place trying out his velocipedes and how many years it would be before his invention would make him rich and famous. Then there was Will and Enid Manson with their little one. Tom hoped that he and Gladys would be as happy as they seemed to be once their own baby was born. Thinking about it, he reached down and put his hand on her stomach. She covered it with hers, and they looked at each other knowingly.

Even Jane came to say goodbye. Tom was disappointed that she hadn't been to visit Gladys again since he thought that Gladys could use another friend other than Millie after he and Keith left. Then he thought that perhaps she had stayed away so he and Gladys could have more time to themselves. Actually, Jane liked Gladys and wanted to know her better, but she was afraid it might jeopardize her friendship with Greta and her other society friends.

Neil and Laura Watt were there as well. Tom felt he owed them a lot since he never would have met Gladys if they hadn't hired her as a barmaid. Surprisingly, they had left Pinky in charge of the

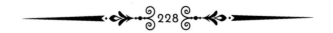

inn for a few hours in order to join in on the farewell dinner.

Sandy did himself proud with his culinary expertise, and there were many jokes made about how it was a shame to waste such fine food on Tom and Keith when they were sure to be heaving it over the rail the next day. Since they had to report back to camp by ten o'clock, Andrew insisted that Tom and Gladys leave the party early so as to spend their last few hours together alone. Before they left, Gladys hugged Keith and whispered in his ear, "Look after him, Keith dear."

Gladys and Andrew were standing in the doorway of Andrew's office building early the following morning waiting for Tom, Keith, and the rest of their battalion to march by and board their ship. When they came into view, Gladys, who had promised Tom she would be brave, couldn't help but cry.

"Look here now, Tom will want to see a smile on that pretty face. It won't do to make him worry about you before he even leaves the dock," Andrew said as he took out his handkerchief and wiped the tears from her cheeks.

By the time the soldiers were close enough to be able to make out Tom and Keith, Gladys had her emotions under control. She was determined to give them a big smile as they marched by, but when she saw that Tom's cheeks were wet, even though he smiled, she let the tears run too. She and Andrew sat on a bench for hours and watched until the ship was out of sight. Then Andrew took her up to his office and made her a hot cup of tea.

Chapter Eighteen

Tom's father said that it now only took one month for a letter to reach India because the mail went by an overland route with the Egyptian Transit Company. He also gave Gladys an address in India where she could send her letters and they would be kept for Tom until he arrived there. Gladys was too embarrassed to tell Andrew that she had no idea how to write a letter, so she asked Millie for help. Millie wrote out a sample for her to follow then showed her how to address an envelope.

"Thank you, Millie, but what should I write about?" Gladys asked.

"You might tell him how much you miss him and love him, and you can even tell him about that old shirt of his that you sleep with every night, but do not tell him if you are sad or ill. I know he would love to hear about everything you are doing and about the people you see every day. Tell him about your garden and about the baby clothes we are making; happy things like that. You must never write about things that will worry him."

She then suggested Gladys purchase a dictionary. From then on, Gladys wrote a little to Tom every day, and sent a letter to him once a week. Sharing her daily activities with him was a little like talking to him, and it helped ease her loneliness. Except for a brief bout of morning sickness, she had never felt healthier, and she refused to rest, which worried both her father-in-law and Millie.

Hard work, along with the generous number of plants Mr Grimsby gave her, made such a difference to Gladys's garden that people came by just to admire it. Mr Grimsby was so pleased with her efforts that he kept her supplied with manure from his own stockpile. One day when she went to look at the border of flowers he had around the cemetery, she remarked that her favourites were the ones in front of his little thatched-roof cottage that sat in one corner of grounds. The tall, pink delphiniums and purple hollyhocks that leaned against the house were accented with a wide hem of deep yellow and maroon wallflowers. They made such a pretty picture that Gladys wished she knew how to paint.

When Mrs Grimsby came out and invited Gladys in for tea, Gladys was thrilled. For a long time, she had wondered what Mrs Grimsby was like and from the time she first saw their cottage, she had wanted a glimpse of the interior. She remembered how taken she was with similar cottages she saw the day she left Old Nichol, and how she had wished she might live in one someday. The large, elaborate houses she and Millie had visited on occasions didn't impress her. As she looked around the Grimsby's parlour, she could understand why. They weren't nearly as cosy.

It only took a few minutes to realize that Mrs Grimsby was every bit as friendly as her husband and kept as tidy a house as he did a garden. All the furniture was thoroughly polished and smelled of citrus oil. The settee and easy chairs were covered in chintz with a white background and green leaves and red roses. The walls, except from the floor up to the plate rail, were whitewashed and made an attractive background for the family pictures.

Gladys felt like she had walked into Hansel and Gretel's house. But the Grimsby's had something in their sitting room that she didn't remember being in the house in Sally's story book. It was a piano. Mrs Grimsby shared with Gladys that her father had been the superintendent at a Polish piano factory and she had begun playing when she was just five years old. "As soon as I was old enough, I went to work in the factory, too. After a few years, I had saved enough to buy my own piano. When I came to live in England, I brought it with me."

Gladys had never seen a piano before and was thrilled when the woman offered to play it, but first she asked if there was a favourite song Gladys would like to hear. Gladys chose "Home Sweet Home," because that was the song she sang just before Tom proposed. Gladys sang along with the music, and Mrs Grimsby was so impressed with her voice that she played more tunes that Gladys knew.

When it was time for Gladys to go home, Mrs Grimsby kindly invited her back and surprised Gladys by asking if she would like to learn to play. Although she wanted to, Gladys said she didn't know if she could afford it. Mrs Grimsby came up with the perfect solution, saying that since she could use a little help with her chores, she would gladly give an hour's lesson for an hour's work. Gladys clapped her hands in delight and gave both the Grimsbys a hug.

As she walked home, she thought about all the things she could tell Tom about her visit. Mrs Grimsby had a delightful Polish accent, and Gladys was amazed how affectionate the two of them were with one another since they said they had been married for twenty years. Mrs Grimsby had a habit of answering every question she asked Mr Grimsby before he could reply, but he didn't seem to mind. When she got home, Gladys filled two pages with writing all about the couple. She told Tom that Mrs Grimsby was going to give her piano lessons, but didn't mention how she was going to pay for them. She didn't tell Tom's father or Millie either.

At the end of every letter, Gladys drew a large X and kissed it so that Tom could put his lips on it and imagine he was kissing her back. She also remembered to send a hug to Keith knowing he would be just as lonesome as Tom. She usually read a little from *The Hunchback of Notre-Dame* every evening then wrote to tell Tom what she thought about it. Taking Millie's advice, she always kept her letters cheerful. One Sunday something happened that she was sure would give Tom a chuckle.

Mrs Grimsby had suggested that Gladys share her talent and join the church choir, but Gladys confessed that she didn't know the words to any of the hymns. From then on most of the songs for her lessons were taken from a hymnal, and a few months later, she was able to join the choir. The first time she sang in the church choir she had a surreal feeling of euphoria. Wearing a regal, purple-coloured choir robe, she felt angelic and holy as she sat down with the other singers behind the pulpit and in front of the congregation.

Then, just before the Reverend Mason came in, Tom's step-mother, Rose, and his stepsister, Mildred, came sashaying down the aisle and into their pew. Gladys could hardly wait to see the look on their faces when they saw her, but they didn't look up until the Reverend announced that he would like to welcome Mrs Gladys Pickwick, a new member of the choir. The Reverend went on to say that he would also like the congregation to remember Gladys's husband, Tom, who was a member of her majesty's army in India, in their prayers, but Rose and Mildred didn't hear more than Gladys's name. Their mouths hung open as they stared up at her and stayed that way while they turned to look at each other for confirmation then back at Gladys again. Nudges quickly went from one chorister to another until the entire choir was shaking with stifled laughter.

Rose and Mildred didn't leave with the rest of the congregation, but stayed to talk to the Reverend. They didn't see James Knowles, the choirmaster, who had stayed to choose hymns for the following Sunday and was out of sight behind the pulpit. When the Reverend asked Rose what he could do for her, she demanded that he ask Gladys to leave the choir, because she had recently been a barmaid in a drinking establishment and therefore not fit to be in church, let alone in the choir. Rose had never forgiven Tom and Gladys for the embarrassment they caused her by not inviting her to their wedding.

The Reverend, who considered the demand offensive, replied, "I believe Mrs Pickwick is no longer working, but even if she were, having to work for a living is certainly no sin."

"That girl is not the sort of person we want in our church. She may have married into my husband's family, but she is no lady," Rose practically shouted.

"I believe she is just the kind of person we need in our congregation, Mrs Pickwick, and as far as I am concerned, she is as much a lady as any woman in this church."

Rose began to see that she would have to be more diplomatic, so in a condescending voice, she put her hand on the Reverend's arm and said, "Forgive me, Reverend, but I think you have been taken in by a pretty face. The girl may dress like a lady and even act like one, but mark my word you cannot make a silk purse out of a sow's ear."

Reverend Mason brushed her hand away. "Mrs Pickwick, if in quoting that old proverb, you mean to imply that Gladys is more like a sow's ear than a silk purse, she could consider it a compliment. I am certain that God thinks much more of sow's ears than he does of silk purses. Perhaps it is time you opened your bible and read Matthew 7:1 and 2. Now I must be going. Good day, Mrs Pickwick." He started to walk away but Rose wasn't about to give up.

She hurried to stand in his way. "Either you ban her from the church or you shall force me and my children to leave." He started to answer, but she cut him off. "Before you say anything, Reverend, I warn you that I am well aware of the generous donation my husband gives to your church each year, and I shall make it my business to see that will no longer be the case if we leave."

To her utter amazement, the Reverend just shrugged his shoulders and said that he very much doubted Andrew would do such a thing, but even if he did, it would have no bearing on who attended his church. With that, he pushed her gently aside, and strode away. Rose knew she had lost. With her nose in the air, and her mouth pinched, she slammed the church door with some force on her way out.

The choirmaster had an excellent memory and related the entire conversation at the next choir practice. Most of the members thought Rose's threat was nothing more than a sham and were convinced that she would never give up her pew. Surprisingly, they were mistaken. Rose and her children didn't come back, and no one minded.

Mrs Grimsby was amazed at how quickly Gladys was learning to play the piano. Gladys looked forward to her lessons. Because they had no idea she was doing chores for Mrs Grimsby, Millie and Andrew thought it was beneficial, because it caused Gladys to sit down for at least an hour or two a day. Andrew often dropped by to see if Gladys needed anything, and most times, she invited him to stay for dinner. Millie was also a frequent guest, and the stories she shared about her various customers, along with Andrew's tales about Ireland and the sailors he knew, resulted in many lively conversations during mealtimes. Tom's father hadn't felt so at home since before his first wife passed away.

When Gladys's pregnancy became obvious, Millie made her a loose fitting cloak, saying she could now go about town without embarrassment. Gladys replied that she thought that was ridiculous. In Old Nichol, women didn't behave any different if they were with child or not. She asked Millie if that could be the reason Andrew stopped taking them out to dine. Millie said it probably was, then explained that proper ladies did not flounce about when they were with child and that they usually remained in the confines of their own home, at least during the last three or four months.

"But I'm not embarrassed, Millie, and I cannot see why I would embarrass anyone else. You don't see people blushing and looking away when a bitch or a cow with a fat tummy walks by, do you?"

"Do not be ridiculous, Gladys. You are not an animal! Why do you always have to find fault with customs and behaviours that have been around for ages?"

"I don't know, Millie. Perhaps it's because they are foreign to me, and I can see how silly they are. Having a baby is something I am proud of and not ashamed of. If my father-in-law is too embarrassed to be seen with me, I shall keep out of his sight, but I do not intend to stay home for the next three months."

The next time Andrew came to call on Gladys, she said she wasn't feeling well and would get in touch with him when she was feeling better. After waiting to hear from her for over a week, Andrew called in to Millie's shop to see how Gladys was. Millie could see he was worried, so she told him what Gladys had said. When he left, he went directly to Gladys's house. She was down on her knees in her garden weeding, and when he offered a cheery hello, she just glanced up for a second, then went right on with her weeding.

"Look here, Gladys, I have just come from Millie's and I think the least you could do is to look at me so I can apologize." Gladys started to rise and he reached out to give her a hand, but she ignored his gesture, and, like Mr Grimsby, she made use of a stout stick to pull herself up. Once she was on her feet, she looked at him but didn't say anything, so he smiled and said, "I would love a cup of tea if you have time, Gladys."

"Are you sure you can stand to look at me for that long?"

"What on earth are you talking about?"

"Millie told me that you were probably too embarrassed to be seen with me." She saw the hurt in his eyes and softened her tone. "I know I should be more understanding. Millie said it's natural for people to behave like that around women in my condition, but personally, I think it is cruel."

"I shan't deny it, my dear. Millie was right. I am so very sorry, but I blame it on my upbringing. Now that I know how you feel, I shall take you and Millie to dinner and then for a walk around town anytime you want, just to show you that I do not give a damn what people say. What do you think of that?"

Gladys laughed and said, "That is very noble of you, but it's not necessary. Now that I know what most people think, I would be embarrassed to go with you. You, Millie, and I will just have to have our dinners here until after your grandchild is born."

"You truly are an angel. And speaking of angels—I have something in my buggy for my soon-to-be grandchild. You go on in and put the kettle on while I fetch it."

The gift was a beautiful cradle with hand-carved flowers and butterflies all delicately painted in pretty pastel colours. "Oh, it is simply wonderful! Wait until I write and tell Tom about it. I have never seen anything so lovely. Where on earth did you find it?"

"I bought it in Ireland," he said, but didn't tell her that the man who made the cradle had made it for his third child. Unfortunately, the baby died before it saw the light of day, along with its mother, leaving the carver with two little girls to bring up on his own. Andrew gave the man three times what he was asking for the cradle, hoping it would keep them in food for a long time. He also tried to help as many poor, unfortunate people in Ireland as he could. Bob Hennessy, the blacksmith, who looked after Tig and Andrew's horses and buggies, once told Gladys that it was Andrew who brought him and his family to Dover and set him up in the blacksmith business. He said they would have starved if they had stayed in Ireland.

Gladys was becoming anxious. She hadn't heard a word from Tom, and she thought by now he would have landed in India and received his commission. She wanted to be over there before she had the baby so Tom could be with her, but time was running out. It was already the middle of November and the baby was due in a month's time. If she could go to India via the overland route, she could be there in a month. As each day passed the journey became less and less probable. When her due date was three weeks away, she had to accept that the baby would be born in England. It was a disappointment, but Tom's father made it less so when he announced that when the time came for her to go to India, not only would he go with her and the baby, but they could even take a nanny with them.

Gladys made fun of her size in Tom's letters saying that she now resembled a lady who used to frequent Scots Inn—a woman who required two chairs to sit on. She said she still managed to sing in the choir because the choir robe was generous enough to hide two babies. She was still able to keep up with her piano lessons, but Mrs Grimsby now refused to allow her to do any chores.

The weather had changed and the winter storms had begun. Gladys loved to visit her father-in-law during the stormy weather.

She always wore the loose cloak that Millie had made for her, and, as she was unwilling to leave Tig outside on the wharf in the rain, she took a cab to the quay. One of the cab drivers drove his buggy past her house once a day, so she waited outside her house under an umbrella and waved for him to stop. The storm was never as fierce in her neighbourhood as it was down at the quay. Gladys would sit by the huge window that overlooked the water and watch the waves as they crashed against the wharf and made the boats bob up and down, but the thing she loved most was listening to the big window moan and groan as the howling winds attacked it. Sometimes she would talk Millie into coming too, and Andrew would serve them tea and cookies.

During the last week of Gladys's pregnancy, her father-in-law insisted that the two midwives he had hired move into Gladys's spare room. She was quite annoyed with him, thinking she would have plenty of time to send for them when they were needed, but she knew he was right as soon as she felt the first labour pain. Gladys gave birth to a baby daughter on the 29th of November. A week later she felt strong enough to write to Tom.

6 December 1845

My Dearest Tom—

Congratulations, darling! We have a darling little daughter. She was born on November the 29th at three in the morning. I have not been up to writing until now. However, there is no cause to worry, my love, I am well. I had a bit of a hard time, but your father was good enough to hire not one, but two excellent midwives, so I was in good hands.

Now, I shall try to describe what our little girl looks like. I think she looks very much like her daddy, but Millie and your father think she resembles both of us. She is not bald like a lot of newborns, but has a fair amount of auburn hair. Did I ever mention that my mother had red hair? She now weighs eight pounds and six ounces and is not the least bit red and wrinkly, like some babies I've seen. And she is such a contented little darling, except when she's hungry. I can just hear you say, "Just like her mother!"

Because we still have not heard from you, we named her Dorothy, after your mother, but we call her Dolly. It was your father who started calling her that. It seems that is what he called your mother. If you do not like it, we can change it, since she will not have time to get used to any name before we are with you.

I am having a harder time waiting for your letters now that Dolly is here. I know I am too blessed to be sad, and besides, everyone has been so understanding and helpful. Reverend Mason even came to visit, and didn't object when I said I didn't want to have Dolly baptized until we were together.

Another bit of wonderful news I have for you is that your father has insisted on paying our passage overland as soon as we get word that you have your commission. Not only that, he has decided to come with us. What a relief! He brought me another pamphlet about the trip, and it advises passengers what to take along. It seems I will need two trunks and plenty of linen. Oh, my darling, I can hardly wait to be in your arms once more. Just think how wonderful it will be for the four of us to be together.

You will love your little girl, I know. Your father is such a proud grandfather and the way he boasts about her is, at times, rather embarrassing. I know it is hard to believe, but I vow, they have a deep understanding of each other already.

Every day until noon, I watch and pray your father will ride up with a letter in his hand but, so far, to no avail. They say absence makes your heart grow fonder, but it is not possible for mine to grow any fonder than it already is.

Hopefully, I will hear from you before I write again. Goodbye for now, my darling. I shall hold this paper to Dolly's lips so you can kiss hers as well.

From your girls,
Gladys and Dolly

My kiss is here:

X

Dolly's is here:

X

Tom wrote his first letter home the same day he and Keith joined their outfit in Ferozeshah, India.

10 December 1845

Dearest Gladys—

Your wonderful letters were waiting for me when we finally arrived here. I don't know how many you have sent, but the three I have were written on the 17th of July, the 19th of August, and the 3rd of October. I've read and reread each one so many times that they are falling apart. I hope you don't mind, but I've allowed Keith to read them as well. Until he finds a wife of his own, I don't mind sharing—as far as letters go that is.

I try to picture you doing all the things you have

talked about in your letters like working in your little garden. I can even imagine the birds singing while you work. You see what you have done—you've turned me into a romantic. Because I am so far away from you, I have learned to use my imagination more than I ever thought possible. I can even imagine you sitting at the piano in that pretty blue dress with the squiggly things on the collar, your beautiful hair pulled back and tied with a red ribbon, all but those few strands of curls that always wiggle free fall over your eyes. How I wish I was there to brush them back for you.

As for answering my questions for me, my dear, I think I shall prefer to do it myself if you don't mind. I guess I am not as agreeable as is Mr Grimsby. But I do promise I shall do everything else for you that I can. I regret all the time we lost together because of my obstinacy. I shall never hurt you again, of that you may be certain. How sweet of you to want to name our child after my mother, if it is a girl. Now if it is a boy, would you like to name him after your father? I don't even know his name. We certainly will have a lot to talk about when we are together once more, won't we? Keith and I really had a laugh over your account of my stepmother's departure from our parish. Good for you and for Reverend Mason. I must admit, I have not attended church since I was a teenager. I am not sure why, but I do have good memories of the Reverend.

Now I suppose you would like to hear of our adventures since we left. It was a very long and tiring trip, to be sure. We had not been out to sea for many weeks when we ran into some very stormy weather and many of our regiment suffered with seasickness, including Keith and our Sgt. Major. I was one of the lucky ones. Well, perhaps not that lucky since I had to attend those who were sick— not a pleasant job.

Poor Keith was so sick that he was sure he was going to die, and even confessed that he thought I'd make a great father. That should give you an idea of how bad off he was. Anyway, it all may have worked to our advantage since the Sgt. Major was so grateful he promised to put in a good word for me as far as hurrying my commission.

You need not concern yourself with the cost of coming here by the overland route as I had a letter from father, and he is determined to pay for the journey. In fact, and do not let him know I told you this because he wants to keep it for a surprise, he is thinking seriously of taking a year off and coming with you.

We took much longer getting to India than we were supposed to because the ship's keel was damaged during one of the storms, and we had to spend time in port waiting for repairs. Then, when we did arrive in India, they did not seem to know what to do with us, and we were sent from camp to camp. Finally, we arrived at our destination, which is a place called Ferozeshah, close to the border of Punjab. We are here as reinforcements for General Littler who is the commander of our garrison. There are quite a few different regiments in the garrison: our regiment, the HM 62nd Foot; two Bengal Light Cavalry regiments, who dress in pale blue uniforms; five Bengal Native Infantry battalions, who, like us, wear red coats, however, instead of the white covered shakos we wear, their shakos are much taller and without peaks; plus two troops of horse artillery and two batteries. If we have to fight the Sikhs, I think we should have a jolly good chance to beat them with such a diversified army, don't you?

I was somewhat disappointed when I learned that we would not be with General Gough since I have been told his men are very fond of him. It is said that he even wears a white jacket into battle in order to draw the enemy's fire away from his men. However, General Littler is popular with his men as well. Anyway, there is talk of something big coming up, all to do with Punjab. We are practically on the border of that territory, so I hope it will not happen here.

The good news is that Sgt. Major has inquired about our commissions and was told that it will probably happen early in the new year, so it should not be long now, my darling, until we are all together, all four of us.

This country is so very different from England that it takes a little getting used to. I have seen many ornate and rich estates on our travels. A lot of marble and beautifully coloured tiles are used in the buildings here, but I have not had the pleasure of being in one, so cannot tell you about that. Sadly, there are many, many poor people here as well. I know you will enjoy the markets that are alive with vendors selling brightly coloured silks and materials of all kinds and all sorts of exotic smelling spices and curries. What one has to get accustomed to is the infernal amount of flies. I think the way they allow their cows to mingle amongst the crowds has a lot to do with it! Most of the people here have that attractive polished oak-coloured skin, and I regret to say, the men are quite handsome, but so are the women, who all wear a good amount of jewellery. Some even have jewels on their foreheads and noses. I have no idea why, but I'm sure you will find out when you are here.

By the time you get this, we may be parents. Please, my darling, do look after yourself, and even if I am not there in person, I shall be with you every minute in my thoughts.

I've kissed the spots you kissed over and over again; now here is one for you.

X

My heart goes with this. Yours forever,
Tom

After the battle of Moodkee on the 18th of December, Lal Singh's force of Sikhs withdrew and set up camp around the village of Ferozeshah. General Gough, Commander of the British/Indian army, sent word requesting General Littler march his battalion out of the town in order to join him for a second battle against Lal Singh's force.

Littler began the assault well in advance of the rest of the army, moving his guns forward to engage the Sikhs at close range. The HM 62nd foot led the assault. They were met with grapeshot (fragmented shot used on troops at close range) from the enemy guns.

Many Sikhs preferred to fight hand to hand using their *Kirpans*, (a curved weapon kept so razor sharp it could sever a limb with one swing) and shields. Tom and Keith soon found themselves face to face with the enemy—so close they were forced to fight with bayonets instead of their Brown Bess muskets.

The sound of the gunfire, clashing metal, and screams of the wounded was deafening. Tom and Keith fought side by side as long as they were able to, but as they challenged their foes, they soon became separated. Suddenly, without knowing why, Keith turned to look for Tom.

"Oh my God, Tom, get down!" he shouted as he saw his friend swinging his bayonet blindly and wildly in the air. "Get down!" he called again as he fought his way frantically toward Tom. Then he saw that one of the Sikhs had also noticed Tom's quandary, and was swiftly moving in his direction. Keith reached Tom a split second after the Sikh swung his kirpan, and, though he ran the fellow through, it was too late. Tom and the Sikh fell to the ground together.

"No!" Keith shouted, as he fell to his knees beside Tom's body. Then, seeing no sign of injury, he was permitted a brief moment of hope before reaching over to put his arm under his friend's shoulders. To his horror, Tom's severed head dropped from his body like a cut of meat from a tipped platter, and hung from his neck by a mere portion of skin—a sight so grotesque that Keith opened his mouth to scream, but all he could utter was a pitiful whimper. In a state of shock, the battle was forgotten; Keith was unaware of his slayer's approach.

When the battle was over, Keith's lacerated body was found with an arm still under his dearest friend.

The battle had lasted only ten minutes before Littler and his army were forced to withdraw, and in that short time, they suffered 160 casualties.

Chapter Nineteen

Tom's long awaited letter arrived the same day as the official notice that he had been killed in the Battle of Ferozeshah.

Gladys felt as though her heart had been torn from her breast and no amount of kindness, love, or sympathy was able to fill its empty chamber. Even the happy gurgles of her baby daughter failed to dispel her depressed state. Perhaps because of her grief, she could no longer lactate and she was forced to hire a wet nurse. The rest of Dolly's care she performed efficiently, in a daze and with an attitude of indifference, her mood as sombre as her mourning apparel.

Because Gladys didn't know that Keith had also been killed, she waited anxiously to hear from him. Although she felt he had let her down by not saving Tom, she longed for his return, knowing that Tom would want them to be together. The thought of having at least one of them home was all that kept her going.

When she finally learned that he too had died on the battlefield while holding Tom in his arms, a complete depression overtook her. She was forced to hire a nursemaid to look after Dolly, while she retired to her bed.

Two weeks later, when her father-in-law was visiting, she came downstairs and caught sight of him bending over the crib looking at his sleeping granddaughter. For the first time since Tom's death, she took note of his appearance and realized how the death of his son had aged him. He had done everything possible to console her in her grief, but she hadn't once considered his feelings. Observing him now, she could see that he was as heart-broken and devastated as she was.

Andrew sensed her presence, looked up, smiled, and said, "She looks so much like Tom when he was that age."

To his surprise, she returned his smile and came and put a hand upon his shoulder. "Yes, I can see him every time I look at her." It had been a long time since Gladys had shown any sentiment towards Andrew, and he couldn't stop the tears. For the longest time, they held each other close and cried. Then Dolly woke up and made a sound that was probably a hiccup, but Andrew insisted it sounded like "Grandpa" while Gladys swore it was more like "Mama." Their tears turned to laughter.

Although Gladys was more thoughtful toward her father-in-law during the following month, she continued to pity herself and complained to Millie, "When I go to choir practice now everyone seems to have forgotten that I'm in mourning, and they laugh and joke as though nothing has happened. You would think they would have more respect. Can they not see how sad I am?"

Millie felt sorry for the girl, but she knew it was time she stopped looking for sympathy and began being thankful for what she had. "You are not the only one to lose a loved one, Gladys. Many of those you are criticizing have lost dear ones too."

"But I am certain they didn't have plans like Tom and I did."

"Everyone has plans of some sort, dear."

"Perhaps, but I'm certain none were as exciting as ours. I was all set to go to India, Millie, and I even had some of our things packed. I was going to be an officer's wife. Can you just imagine what that would have been like over there?"

Millie was shocked. "Oh, is that what has been bothering you?

It is not so much your husband's death that has you feeling sorry for yourself. It is that you are not going to be going to India. Well, I must say, Gladys, I am disappointed in you. I thought you had more depth than that."

"I cannot understand why you think I should not be sad. I have not only lost my husband, but the adventurous life Tom and I had planned. I thought you of all people would understand that."

"I don't know what you mean by that, and I do not care to know, but I will tell you this, young lady. I lost both my man and my son and had to fend for myself, while you have a beautiful daughter and a wonderful father-in-law who provides for you. You are so full of self-pity that you do not even realize how fortunate you are. Honestly, Gladys, I am losing patience with you. Now why don't you start being thankful for the things you have instead of pining over what you don't have?"

"I don't know why I should be thankful. I've worked bloody hard for what I have."

"My Heavens, have you forgotten that it was I who took you under my wing when you arrived here? You have only been out of the slums for a short time, and you seem to think you deserve to be a grand lady by now. Well, as far as I am concerned, you can do whatever you want, just don't include me in your plans. Now, if you don't mind, Mrs Pickwick, I have work to do." With that, Millie left Gladys in the shop and went into her living room. She had never spoken to Gladys so angrily before, not even when Gladys brought her the dog, and she didn't even say goodbye to Dolly who was awake in her pram.

Gladys left the shop with mixed feelings. As she pushed the pram up the street, she consoled herself with the thought that Millie had no right to criticize her. She didn't seem to care that everything Gladys had dreamt about for the past nine months was now gone. There would never be an exotic trip down the Nile, no walking through the Indian markets with a manservant to carry her purchases, and no attending fancy balls just for officers and their wives. Gladys had imagined her life in India with Tom for so long that, at times, she could close her eyes and see every event with clarity. She could feel Tom's arms around her and feel the floor under her feet as they swirled around on the dancefloor. Her images had become so real that she could lick her lips and imagine the taste of champagne.

She was not a selfish person by nature, and, although she tried to continue refuting Millie's point of view, her common sense kept telling her the seamstress was right. She also knew how shocked Millie would be if she knew the aberrant thoughts she had before she knew that Keith had been killed as well. Although she didn't love Keith, she knew he loved her, and would have sent for her and Dolly to join him in India. It wouldn't have been as wonderful as being there with Tom, but she would have gone nevertheless.

All these thoughts were running through her mind as she walked along with her head down pushing the buggy. Looking up, she suddenly realized what a lovely day it was. She began to wonder how many nice, sunny days she had missed by being so miserable. For the first time in months she felt alive. She was just about to turn the buggy around to go back to Millie's shop to apologize when she saw Emily Brooker, another young mother she knew from the church, approaching. Emily was pulling her baby in a wagon while her three-year-old son tried his best to keep up by hanging on to her skirt. Emily was somewhat surprised when Gladys greeted her with a cheery, "Hello."

Emily said hello then bent down and looked in the pram at Dolly. "What a lovely pram! You are such a lucky little girl, just like a real princess. I have heard tell that the queen has a pram or two just like yours for her little ones." As though she understood, Dolly honoured Emily with one of her rare smiles. Gladys smiled and said, "Thank you, Emily. It is a nice pram, isn't it?" Andrew had purchased the pram and it was a beautiful Windsor model made of wicker with bright, shiny brass joints and fittings.

"Yes, it certainly is, but I don't think Eddie cares if he's riding in a fancy pram or his brother's wagon." After a few more exchanged pleasantries, the women went on their ways. Emily's obvious lack of envy over the pram surprised Gladys. Lately, she couldn't help but notice how popular Emily was with all the church ladies, and she remembered that was how they used to be with her. For the rest of that day, she did a great deal of soul-searching. Then, as she lay Dolly down in her crib, she said, "Tomorrow, I shall have to go back and apologize to your Auntie Millie." Dolly, puzzled by the unusual soft tone of affection in her mother's voice, offered a one-sided smile.

"Oh, Dolly, you have the same smile as your daddy!" Gladys exclaimed, and she picked her up again and hugged her. The sudden display of maternal love startled the baby for a second, but then as her mother began singing a lullaby, she snuggled down in her arms and was soon asleep.

Chapter Twenty

By the time Dolly was three, she was almost a head taller than most little girls her age. Her name was somewhat ill-suited since she took after her father and mother in build. Her features were more like Tom's than Gladys's; therefore, even her mother would not describe her as doll-like. However, Dolly did have a beautiful head of naturally curly hair that was a deep and warm auburn—an attractive blend of colours she inherited from both her mother and grandmother Tunner. She also had the most unusual eyes. It wasn't their colour that held one's attention, but the directness of their gaze—a look some found disconcerting.

Her unusually serious nature was often mistaken for simple-mindedness, but Andrew soon learned that his granddaughter not only had an inquisitive mind, but the intelligence to retain whatever it gleaned. The two became very close, so much so that Gladys often felt jealous.

Gladys had become fairly adept on the piano and had also learned to play the church organ, so when Dolly was old enough to attend Sunday school, Gladys often took the place of the church organist at the Sunday morning services. Then in the afternoons, if the weather was favourable, Andrew would take her, along with Dolly and Millie, in his rig for what he referred to as mystery rides.

As soon as he had them all settled in the rig, he would say, "Now, ladies," being included in with the ladies never failed to start Dolly giggling with delight, "where do you suppose we are going today?"

Dolly's answers were amazing for such a young child, but one day she even pleased herself when she announced, "I shall be dee-lighted to go anywhere with you, Gamby!"

One of their favourite Sunday outings was to the beach for picnics, but they also enjoyed rides to nearby villages where they usually dined at an inn before returning home. Some days they went for a ferry ride, but only if Millie wasn't along. Unfortunately, Millie suffered from seasickness so severely it even plagued her while walking along the quay.

The place Dolly liked to visit more than any other was Sorenson Hall, or what she called "the fairy tale farm." Lord Cedric Sorenson and his wife, Lady Madeline, were long-time friends of Andrew's, and since they had little to do but enjoy themselves, they were always delighted to have guests.

Dolly was four when they first visited the Sorensons, who lived in Sorenson Hall. Situated on a large estate in the village of Buckland, the hall had been absorbed into Dover's boundaries in 1830. On their first visit, Gladys and Millie were awestruck and a little intimidated by the grandeur of what seemed more like a castle than a house. However, they were put at ease when his Lordship greeted them dressed in a pair of overalls.

Once he had them seated in the conservatory, he apologized for his costume and then rushed away to notify his wife that they had guests. It only took a few minutes before her Ladyship made her entrance. She was dressed in a very stylish gown, causing Millie and Gladys to surmise that she must dress in such finery every day. They also thought that Lord Cedric must have been wearing overalls over his other clothes since he returned with his wife, clad appropriately in gentleman's attire.

His short and stout figure blended well with his owl-like facial features. His large eyes were shaded by red and grey bushy eyebrows, while the bands of hair on the sides of his bald pate stuck out like feathery horns. Lady Madeline had a tidy little figure, a delicate complexion and agreeable features that portrayed honest delight in greeting the ladies. She was surprised to learn that Dolly was only four, and exclaimed, "My goodness you are such a proper young lady for a girl of your age. Our youngest little lad is the same age as you, my dear, but I doubt he could sit still for five minutes." She then addressed the adults, "We have three little ones who will want to meet you, especially if we are having tea. I fear you will find them extremely lively. Did Andrew warn you?" When Andrew just laughed and shook his head, she put her hand up to her cheek and cried, "Oh, dear!"

Lord Cedric chuckled and added, "I say, old girl, you shall have these dear ladies running out the door if you're not careful, telling them such nonsense. Actually, they are a jolly good lot, and great fun to have around. I shall send for them, since I know they shall be delighted to meet our young guest." He pulled on a bell cord, and when the butler appeared, he inquired where the children were.

"I think they took George down to the pond for a swim, your lordship. Would you like me to send for them?"

"Yes, please do, and tell them not to dawdle, or they shall miss tea."

The maid brought the tea shortly after, and Lady Madeline was just about to pour when three youngsters dressed all alike in coveralls, along with a duck, a goat, and a large, barking, tail-wagging, wet dog burst into the room.

Luckily Lord Cedric and Lady Madeline were so busy trying to bring order to the noisy menagerie that they didn't notice the gaping mouths of their two lady guests. Millie and Gladys were aghast to witness so many muddy feet trampling all over what appeared to be an exquisite rug. Their hosts, on the other hand, appeared completely oblivious of any wrongdoing, even though the wet dog shook himself while standing by her ladyship and splattered her lovely gown with drops of dirty water.

Lord Cedric finally managed to hush the lot sufficiently enough to make the introductions, which the guests anxiously waited to hear, since all three wore their fiery red hair long, and in ringlets. Their faces were equally masked in freckles, making it nearly impossible to discern their sexes.

It was indeed a splendid tea, with Devonshire cream served on the finest china. And the children insisted their animals join them and have their tea served on the same dishes. When a maid brought in a gold-trimmed, flowered bowl of cream for Peter the dog, a similar patterned plate of carrots for Sally the goat, and a daintily sculpted cup and saucer of well-sugared tea for George the duck, Millie almost choked. In spite of, or maybe because of, their eccentricities, all the Sorensons were delightful hosts. Dolly was thrilled to be invited to go down to the pond with the other children to watch George swim, but since she was in her Sunday best, Gladys said she had better remain behind.

"Nonsense!" proclaimed Lady Madeline, "A pair of coveralls shall do very well over that pretty frock." Then she directed Dolly to Nanny to be outfitted. If Dolly had a fault, it was that she was far too serious, and it did them all good to see her run happily off with the other children.

After the little ones had departed, Lady Madeline remarked on the style and quality of Millie's outfit. When Millie replied that she was a dressmaker, and had sewn it herself, her ladyship remarked that she needed a new gown or two and she asked if Millie would be kind enough to make them. Millie was both thrilled and flattered.

Chapter Twenty-One

When Gladys worked for the Watts, she had often helped Hilda cook when business at the inn was brisk. She remembered the recipes for many of Hilda's favourite dishes and often made them for Andrew. Andrew appreciated every meal she made and seldom refused an invitation. His favourite dish was Welsh rabbit with onions, and his favourite dessert was suet pudding made with plenty of raisins. Most called the pudding "Spotted Dick," but Andrew called it "Spotted Dog," which always brought a giggle or two from Dolly.

Although Andrew had offered to move his daughter-in-law and granddaughter into a much larger house with a staff of servants, he thought he understood why Gladys refused to move. He preferred living alone as well and didn't hire live-in help. He often marvelled over how much he and Gladys seemed to have in common. Whenever he came for a meal, he would stay to play with Dolly and read her a bedtime story. He also loved to sing to her, and if she knew the lyrics, Gladys often joined in. One evening he sang a ballad titled "The Little Turtle Dove." The first verse impressed Dolly more than

Andrew knew:

> "Oh can't you see yon little turtle dove, sitting
> under the mulberry tree?
> See how she doth mourn for her true love;
> And shall I mourn for thee, my dear, and shall I
> mourn for thee.
> O fare thee well, my little turtle dove, and fare thee
> well for a-while;
> But though I go I'll surely come back again."

Andrew sang all the verses and when he was finished, Dolly jumped up and down and clapped her hands.

"So you like my little song do you?" Andrew asked.

"Oh yes, Gamby, I do!" After her grandfather left that evening, Dolly, looked very serious, and announced, "Mama, I am Gamby's little turtle dove."

The following day, Dolly was upstairs in the bedroom when Andrew arrived, so Gladys told him what she had said. Grinning, he winked, then called out, "Where is my little turtle dove?"

Dolly came running down stairs and into his arms, "Here I am, Gamby! See, Mama, I told you so." From then on, Andrew often addressed her by that title.

After she turned five, Dolly wearied of nursery rhymes and begged her grandfather to read something more exciting, so he began reading the books he had read to Tom when he was a little boy. Two of Dolly's favourites were, *Aladdin's Lamp*, and *Ali Baba and the Forty Thieves*, from Antoine Galland's translation of *The Book of the Thousand Nights*.

Some of the stories were far too mature for such a young person, but Dolly listened to every word with utter delight—even words she had never heard before. Andrew had a deep, rich voice that deserved, but didn't demand, attention. He could read a nursery rhyme as quietly and softly as a loving mother, then recite a robust verse with drum-like resonance. Gladys, who often missed the times Sally read to her and Toughie, listened to the stories and poems with as much pleasure as her daughter, even though she had become an avid reader herself. In fact, like many Englishmen, Andrew enjoyed listening to his own voice as well and was delighted to have a reason to exercise it.

On one of his visits, he mentioned to Gladys that the Watts had sold the inn and were moving to Scotland in a month's time.

"I must try to visit them before they leave," she said. "I never thought I'd say this, but I shall be sorry to see them go. Are they taking Pinky with them?"

"I really have no idea. Why don't we see if Millie will look after Dolly one evening, and I shall take you there for dinner, then you can ask them yourself?"

"I would really like that!"

"Shall I drop in on Millie on my way home and ask her if we could impose on her good nature?"

Gladys answered with a sly grin, "Are you sure you don't mind?"

"Look here! I don't know if that grin you have on that pretty face is meant as an implication or not, but you are a way off course if you think Millie and I are anything more than good friends."

"I didn't say a word," Gladys answered with a cheeky look of innocence.

A few nights later, Andrew and Gladys visited Scots Inn. Gladys was pleased with the warm welcome she received, and throughout the evening Laura and Neil took turns visiting with her. They had purchased a little inn near Laura's mother's house in Scotland and planned on taking Pinky with them. "I've heard that there are those who are trying to do away with barmaids," Laura said. "There are already a few places where it's not allowed."

While they were talking, Pinky began singing, and when she finished, Neil, who preferred the sound of Gladys's warm, throaty voice to the sweet tone of Pinky's, asked her to sing one of his favourites. Now that she was living the life of a lady, Gladys wasn't sure if it would be appropriate, but when Andrew said he would also love to hear her, she agreed. Having learned the lyrics to the song "Twa Corbies" from one of the inn's Scottish regulars, she sang it with a Scotch brogue.

There were tears in Neil's eyes when the song ended. Time

went by far too quickly, and by the time they bid their final farewells and arrived back at Millie's, Dolly had been bathed, fed, and was sound asleep. "Why don't you just leave her with me for the night?" Millie suggested. "Tomorrow is Sunday; I shall bring her home in the morning."

There was a cab just a block from Millie's, but as Gladys and Andrew approached it, they could see that both the horse and the driver, who was lying on the seat inside the cab, were sleeping. Gladys whispered to Andrew, "Let's not disturb them; it's lovely out tonight, and I'd much rather walk home."

"A splendid idea, but I think I should wake the poor chap and have him pick me up at your place in about an hour—one way is enough for this old codger."

"Ha, you know as well as I do, you are not the least bit codger-like."

Andrew just grinned as he held out his arm for her to take. There was an added spring to his step as they made their way home.

Andrew provided Gladys with a generous monthly stipend, and as the years passed, she gradually slipped into a life of near contentment. However, she often longed for Tom and the good times they had with Keith. There were also times when she became bored with the stability of her life. Luckily, she had her own horse and rig, so she could take Dolly and explore the countryside in order to rid herself of the doldrums.

On one of these occasions, she and Dolly came across a small caravan of gypsies who were camped in an open area beside a stream on the outskirts of the town. Gladys had never seen a gypsy before, and she would have liked to stop and talk to them, but having heard that some of them were thieves, she thought it wiser to continue on. As she drove by, she saw three colourfully painted, wooden wagons partially hidden amongst the trees. Two large horses that resembled old Knickers and a smaller one were hobbled in a nearby patch of grass. A large kettle of something steaming over a fire gave off a scent

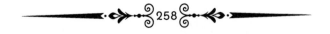

so tantalizing it made her mouth water and caused Dolly to remark, "Mama, that smell makes me very hungry."

"We will be turning around and going home for dinner soon, dear," Gladys replied. Then she laughed and added, "It's making me hungry as well!"

As they were nearing the gypsies on their way home, Gladys had a twinge of trepidation when she saw one of the women standing in the middle of the road waving for her to stop. She knew that there were parents who frightened their children into obedience by threatening to give them up to the nomads if they didn't behave, but as she reined to a stop, she could see that the woman appeared to be friendly. Coming alongside the buggy, the young woman held out some colourful cloths, and in a deep and lyrical voice with an attractive accent, she asked if Gladys would care to buy a pretty shawl.

There was nothing unusual about the woman's plain garb, but the large amount of bangles and other jewellery she wore added an ambience of gaiety and beauty to her costume. She had a full head of black, curly hair that glistened as though recently anointed with oil, and her long, dark lashes added mystery to her smoky, black eyes. Gladys thought she was the most beautiful creature she had ever seen, and as she studied her, she was reminded of someone, but could not think of who it was.

"See, lady, you look," the gypsy said and held up a lovely paisley shawl. "Thees one very pretty for you. You buy? I sell cheap."

"It is very beautiful, but I'm afraid I cannot afford it."

"How much you have? I sell pretty damn cheap."

Just as Gladys was about to answer, Dolly, who was beginning to wiggle about, interrupted, "Mama, I have to widdle."

"You will just have to wait, dear. We will be home soon."

"I can't, Mama!"

"Here, lady, you hold. I take," the woman said as she thrust the shawls at Gladys, and without giving her time to protest, lifted Dolly down from the buggy and ran with her into the woods.

Surprisingly, Gladys wasn't alarmed. In some ways the gypsies reminded her of the residents in Old Nichol who earned a living in much the same manner. It gave her a feeling of kinship toward them, a feeling Andrew or Millie would never be able to understand. She didn't feel the same way a few minutes later when she noticed the woman motioning for her to come; she couldn't see Dolly. Panic was beginning to overtake her as she gave Tig a shake on the reins and drove the buggy into the field. "Where is my daughter?" she demanded in a shaky voice.

"Oh ho, no worry, lady, see, she very hungry!" the woman pointed to a group of five children, one of whom was Dolly, sitting in a circle on the ground eating off tin plates. "You come eat. Ees good," the woman said as she reached up and pulled Gladys by the arm.

Since Gladys's other arm held the shawls, she almost fell out of the buggy. "Oh no, no, I don't want to bother you," she stammered, although the food smelled delicious, and she was very hungry. Then, before she could protest, an older woman took hold of her and pulled her over to a bench beside a table where a plate of hot, sweet smelling stew, a clean wooden spoon, a large bun, and a steaming hot cup of tea was plunked down in front of her.

"Ees rabbeet. Veree good. You try!" the woman insisted.

Afraid of angering the woman, Gladys forced herself to take a mouthful. It tasted as good as it smelled, and she couldn't resist eating it all. Dolly, now well fed and content, came and sat on the grass at her mother's feet as she drank the unusual, but not unpleasant tasting, tea. As Gladys sipped her tea, she looked around and counted thirteen gypsies. One was a very old and shrivelled up woman who was sitting in a wicker armchair by the fire. She appeared to be no bigger than a six-year-old and was wrapped in a faded patchwork quilt. Her only visible feature was her face, which appeared more mummified than alive.

In comparison, the other adults looked exceptionally hearty. There were two middle-aged men, two middle-aged woman, two young men, two young women, one of whom was the beautiful girl who had stopped her on the road, and four children between the ages of twelve and six. Most of the men were dressed in full-sleeved shirts, leather vests, and wore sashes around their waists. The women wore dark skirts layered with other pieces of dark material, and dark blouses and shawls. All but the pretty girl wore kerchiefs on their heads.

The children were dressed similarly to most children from lower class families. The girls were blissfully free of corsets, unlike the young ladies from the upper echelon of society, who began wearing them by the young age of six in order to ensure an hourglass figure. Gladys found herself envious of these people for their lack of conformity.

Once she had finished her tea, she felt obliged to buy a shawl. She chose a lovely paisley one, paid for it, and was just about to leave when a tall, dark-skinned man wearing earrings and a brightly coloured kerchief around his neck, approached her, and in a deep and threatening sounding voice, ordered her to sit. She had no option but to obey. Holding Dolly close to her, she tried not to tremble. The man grinned, showing a huge set of snow white teeth that made Dolly think of the words, "The better to eat you with, my dear," and then he abruptly turned and called out, "Maria, Fernando, 'Algreas de Cadiz' for the lady!"

One of the young men picked up a guitar and started strumming as the pretty woman began to dance, twirling around gracefully while keeping in time to the music with a tambourine. Soon, one of the men joined her and the other gypsies began clapping their hands loudly and calling out, "Ole!" Someone called out, "Uaa," and everyone laughed. When the dance was over, the performers bowed, and Gladys and Dolly replied by clapping enthusiastically.

When she finished her dance, the young woman walked toward Gladys and it was then that Gladys figured out who she resembled. Without thinking, she blurted out, "Esmeralda."

"Eh?" the girl asked.

"Oh, I am sorry. It's just that you remind me so much of a beautiful lady in a story I once read."

"Esmeralda?"

"Yes. And she had a very smart pet goat."

"My name ees Maria, and you see, I 'ave no goat, but I 'ave monkey."

Dolly's eyes widened and she asked, "Really? A real live monkey?"

"Yes, yes, a real monkey. You want to see heem?" Without waiting for Dolly's answer she called out, "Fernando, bring Topio."

The young guitarist waved, then went into one of the wagons and came out with a monkey on his shoulder. Fernando had the monkey perform a few tricks, which delighted Dolly, and she clapped her hands with approval. Topio, a seasoned performer, showed his appreciation by taking off his tasselled, cone-shaped fez and bowing.

It was dusk by the time Gladys left her rig at Bob Hennessy's stable, and she and Dolly walked the short distance home. Before they left the camp, they learned that the gypsies would be putting on a show in three days' time and they wanted Gladys and Dolly to be sure to come and see it. The next day when they went to visit Millie, they were barely inside her door when Dolly exclaimed, "Auntie Millie, Auntie Millie, the gypsies have a monkey! His name is Topio, and he sat right up here on my shoulder."

"Gypsies?" Millie cried.

"Oh yes, Auntie! They were frightfully nice, and even gave us food. I sat on the grass and ate mine with the other children."

"My goodness! Gladys, what is this about gypsies?"

As Gladys explained, Millie uttered small gasps after each detail. Then she began shaking her head and saying, "Oh my, oh my," until Dolly shook her arm.

"Aunt Millie, are you angry with us?"

"No, darling, I was just thinking. I wonder if you would like to look through these lovely buttons that just came in with my last shipment while your mother and I go in the back and make a cup of tea?"

"But, Auntie, I want to tell you what Topio did. It was oh so clever, Auntie."

"Perhaps later, dear, but now I want to make your mommy a cup of tea. I want you to look after the shop for me, and if someone comes in, I want you to be very grown up and ask them to have a seat, then come and fetch me. Do you think you could do that?"

"Of course, Auntie, I shall be most capea—cape aba."

"Capable, darling, and I know you shall be."

As soon as they were in the back of the shop, Millie started

scolding Gladys, "What on earth were you thinking about, taking Dolly into a gypsy camp?"

"They were kind to us, Millie. I don't see why you're so upset with me."

"And what if they weren't nice to you? What could you have done about it then, all alone out there?"

"I suppose you are right, but I really had no choice, Millie. The girl took Dolly away before I could stop her."

"Well it is over with now, thank goodness. You had better not mention this to Andrew when he returns."

"They're putting on a show the day after tomorrow, Millie, and Dolly and I want you to come with us to see it. Will you come?"

"Certainly not, and you had better not go either if you value your status in this town."

"But it's just entertainment. Actually, Millie, it is just show business. Don't tell me you object to that."

"That's not fair!"

Just then the bell sounded and a minute later, Dolly called out, "Auntie Millie, Lady Sorenson is here." Millie hurried into the shop, but before she had a chance to greet Lady Sorenson, Dolly asked her ladyship if she was taking her children to the gypsy show.

Millie, hoping to change the subject before Lady Sorenson realized what Dolly was talking about, said, "I have your suit ready for a fitting, Lady Sorenson; shall we try it on?"

Dolly thought Millie mustn't have heard her asking Lady Sorenson a question, and she spoke up and said, "But Auntie, I was just asking—"

Millie cut her off, "Not now, Dolly, Lady Sorenson wants to see if her new suit fits her. Besides, you haven't finished going through those buttons."

"I am certain a few minutes will not make my suit fit any better, Mildred, and I do want to hear all about these gypsies," Lady Sorenson insisted. "Now, Dolly love, what show is this you are talking about?" By this time Gladys had joined them and gave a full report. When she was finished, Lady Madeline surprised them all by declaring, "Oh how exciting! I have a friend in London who told me that if the gypsies ever came to Dover to be sure to visit them. They have the best medicine for quite a few ailments, especially those to do with the stomach.

"And I should think you would enjoy seeing their wares, Millie. They sell lovely beaded purses and jewellery that would enhance the beautiful evening gowns you create. We must all go together. Cedric will escort us. Now, when did you say they are performing, Gladys?" Gladys grinned smugly at Millie before answering.

Two mornings later, the five Sorensons arrived in one of their biggest buggies to pick up Gladys, Dolly, and Millie and take them to the show. Word that Lord Sorenson and his family intended to be at the gypsy camp had quickly spread around town, deeming it an appropriate act.

The camp was so transformed in the three days since Gladys and Dolly's first visit, that they hardly recognized it. The three wagons, two stalls, and a small tent were set out in a semicircle and bordered a cleared area about fifty feet in diameter. Placed in the middle of the circle was a square wooden platform along with two small wooden benches. In one of the stalls, a woman was selling a variety of items: jewellery, shawls, handwoven table covers, cloth dolls, wooden toys, and pretty embroidered blouses. The man in the other stall was selling herbal remedies guaranteed to cure every sort of human or animal ailment along with a selection of creams and potions that were assured to bring roses to the cheeks and elevate sagging jowls.

A sign on the outside of the small tent advertised fortune telling. Heavy velvet curtains hung over the entrance and separated the fortune teller from a line-up of hopeful young ladies all waiting to hear if their dreams of finding a rich and handsome husband would come true. As the curtains parted and a smiling young lady exited the tent, Gladys was amazed to see that the fortune teller was none other than the little mummy-like gypsy she had seen sitting in the wicker chair by the fire.

Days later, she tried to explain to Andrew how the old lady had looked at her in the few seconds the curtains were open. "I couldn't even tell you what she was wearing since I was unable to look at anything but her eyes. I could feel those beady little eyes piercing through mine and looking deep into my soul; eyes so all-knowing that I could tell she could see into my past and knew what awaits me in the future. I didn't have a chance to hear her predictions though, since the dancing began soon after. I don't think I would have been brave enough to hear what she had to say anyway."

The dancers and the guitar player were dressed in beautiful costumes, and as the music and dancing began, Lady Sorenson, who had once visited Spain and knew the names of many of the songs and dances, shared her knowledge with Gladys and Millie. When Maria and a partner danced the tango, her Ladyship explained that the music originated in the city of Granada and was a flamenco song. As the dances continued, it became more and more difficult to believe that such talented artists could belong to a tribe that most Brits considered unfit to live in their civilized part of the world.

As they danced the various flamencos, stamping their feet, clapping their hands, and moving their bodies to the beat of the guitar, one could see that it was done with both dignity and pride. When the dancing was finished, Fernando, with Topio on his shoulder, went around the spectators with a tin cup, to collect gratuities. When he finished his rounds, he went over and put his big floppy hat down on the stage along with Topio. Then he dumped the coins out of the cup and put them back in one by one as he counted them aloud. Satisfied with the amount, he walked around and bowed to all the spectators.

While Fernando's back was turned, Topio reached into the cup, took out a coin, held it up for everyone to see before putting it into a pocket in his little red vest. Then he hid underneath Fernando's hat. When the adults and the children began giggling, Fernando pretended to be puzzled and scratching his head, he asked a little boy why he was laughing. The boy pointed toward the stage.

Fernando went over and held up the cup and when the little lad shook his head, he dumped out the money once more and counted it again ending with one less. "Thief! Thief!" he shouted. "Who has stolen my money?" He then went from child to child asking, "Was it you? Are you a thief?" All the children shook their heads and pointed toward the stage where the hat had begun sliding across the stage. But when Fernando turned around, the hat was still. Every time he turned and asked another member of the audience if they took the coin, the hat moved farther and farther across the stage, causing loud bouts of laughter.

Finally, Fernando noticed that the hat was sitting on the other side of the stage and shook his head knowingly. "Ah ha, Topio!" he cried. He slowly tiptoed up to the hat, and with a smile of satisfaction, he called out, "I 'ave you now, you leetle thief!" He grabbed the hat and lifted it up high. Both he and his audience were amazed when they saw that Topio was gone. Putting the hat back down, Fernando once more walked around the crowd asking if anyone knew where the monkey went, and when no one answered, he shrugged his shoulders, picked up his hat, put it on his head, and with a sad expression, announced, "My Topio, he 'as stolen my money and run away."

As he walked away, Topio tipped the back of the hat up and waved at the audience. The applause lasted until Fernando came back to the stage and lifted his hat so Topio could bow.

The next day, Gladys couldn't resist going back to the camp to say goodbye to the gypsies, who she now considered her friends. They were just about to hitch the horses to the wagons when she and Dolly arrived. There were no fancy costumes to be seen, but Gladys thought they looked just as appealing in their drab clothes as they did in their finery. Not only Maria, but the rest of the band greeted them warmly and with gratitude. It seemed that they had never put on a more lucrative show, which they credited to Gladys for bringing such a wealthy family to see it. Her ladyship had purchased a good deal of medicines and jewellery without a single complaint over the prices, and his lordship had been more than generous with a donation after the entertainment.

Dolly was given a lovely handmade doll dressed in a colourful skirt and an embroidered blouse. Then she and Gladys stood on the road and waved goodbye to the gypsies until the wagons were out of sight. "I wish they didn't have to leave," Dolly said wistfully.

"So do I, dear, but that's the way they like to live."

"Why?"

"I don't really know why, darling." This wasn't quite true. Gladys thought she knew exactly why. A yearning to join them had come over her as she had watched them pack up their belongings. Their life seemed so much more romantic than the one she was living. She tried to imagine what it would have been like for her and Tom to live like gypsies, but she knew that would have been impossible. Although Tom enjoyed his freedom, he took pride in behaving like a proper gentleman and would be as out of place in a gypsy camp as they would in his world. She remembered when one of the gypsy men had said something to his wife and smiled as he helped her up onto the wagon. His generous set of teeth looked like white pearls in contrast to his dark skin and made her think of Toughie.

It was very easy to imagine him beside her as they packed up their wagon and broke camp. How she wished it could be true. She appreciated all Andrew did for her and Dolly, but she also thought that being totally dependent on him for their living robbed her of the freedom she longed for—freedom to stop pretending she was a lady and be herself, even if she wasn't quite sure who that was anymore.

Chapter Twenty Two

A few days after the gypsies left, Andrew returned from London where he had taken part in a fundraising rally to aid the starving families in Ireland. Unfortunately, all his efforts, along with those of his fellow sympathizers, had only resulted in a fraction of the money they had hoped to raise, so he came home in a slightly depressed state of mind.

Thousands of Irish families were so destitute that they considered themselves lucky to be taken into one of over a hundred Irish workhouses, even though it meant they would be separated and never reunited. Once a person entered into such an establishment, he or she was forbidden to leave, and remained there for the rest of their life. But, as harsh as it sounds, such places did save lives, since two meals a day of oatmeal, potatoes, and buttermilk were provided. To earn the meals, the women knitted, the men broke stones, and the children worked in factories under the pretence of being in training.

Andrew felt ashamed to be an Englishman when he learned of the lack of compassion most of his wealthy friends had for these unfortunate people. An astronomical two million deaths had already happened in Ireland due to starvation and the outbreak of cholera. Cholera had also caused the deaths of some fifty to seventy thousand in England, but Andrew hadn't seen, or heard, any rumours of neglect or starvation.

As a Custom House official, he visited Ireland from time to time on business and had seen the devastation, but what upset him the most was the vast amount of starving children. The sights were so horrific, he often suffered nightmares after each visit. He had vowed to do what he could to help, but in order to save his job he had to do it with discretion. It wasn't that he needed employment—he came from a wealthy family and had received a large inheritance—but the job allowed him the opportunity to do whatever he could to ensure that the Irish merchants were treated fairly. It also enabled him to take provisions and money to Ireland from time to time, to aid the starving.

Twistleton, the Irish Poor Law Commissioner, had resigned in protest against the lack of aid the Irish received from Britain. The Earl of Clarendon, acting as Lord Lieutenant of Ireland, informed the British Prime Minister, Lord John Russel, that Twistleton resigned because he thought the destitution in Ireland was so horrible, and the indifference of the House of Commons so manifest, that he was an unfit agent for a policy that must be one of extermination.

James Wilson, the Editor of the British Publication, *The Economist*, responded to the Irish pleas for assistance by stating in an editorial, "It's no man's business to provide for another." That editorial is what spurred Andrew, an admirer of Twistleton's and an adversary of Wilson's, to join the rallies, even though he expected to receive notice that his prestigious government position would be terminated. Ironically, if he was to lose his job, it would have been over something that proved to be of little help.

The day after returning to Dover, Andrew went to visit Gladys and Dolly. It was a lovely day, so he decided to walk. He was just about to their gate when he saw them working in their front garden. Gladys was kneeling, and Dolly was handing her what appeared to be bulbs. They both wore straw hats with wide brims that hid their faces. Dolly had pretty blue ribbon bows on the ends of her two braids, but Gladys's hair hung loose, and with the sun shining on her curls, they looked like shiny coils of copper. The sight of them with the colourful reds, oranges, and yellows of Gladys's fall flowers in the background was so charming that after studying it for a time, Andrew closed his eyes and tried to store every little detail in his memory, so it would be there whenever he needed it to lift his spirits.

He was convinced he could never have endured the loss of Tom if he hadn't had Gladys and Dolly to take his place. Now as he stood gazing at them, the scene was so peaceful, in contrast to what he had seen during the past few days, that he silently thanked Tom for giving him such a wonderful family.

Gladys's garden also brought back memories of the flower garden his mother-in-law had at her little cottage in Dublin. He and Dorothy took Tom there to visit his grandmother every year, until the old lady died. The picture Gladys and Dolly made in their garden was so similar to the one Andrew had of Tom and his mother-in-law, that it rendered an odd, but welcome, feeling of fulfilment.

As though Dolly could sense his presence, she looked up and saw him standing there. "Gamby! Oh, Mommy, look. It's my Gamby." She ran out through the gate and into his arms.

Andrew scooped her up in a big bear hug; then he put her on his shoulders and jumped up and down while making noises like a horse. She hung onto his big ears, feeling very special, and very, very loved. Then, with Dolly still perched on his shoulders, he reached down to help Gladys up and give her a hug.

"If you only knew how much I needed that," he said a little later as they sat by the fireplace drinking hot chocolate.

Gladys could tell by the sound of his voice that he had been depressed before he arrived, and she commented on it.

"It's just that things didn't turn out as well as I had hoped with the rally, but seeing you both has cheered me up more than you can imagine. What on earth would I do without you?" he said as he leaned over and kissed the top of Dolly's head.

"I love you so much, Gamby," Dolly answered, then she began telling him about the gypsies and Topio, the monkey. Contrary to Millie's warning, Andrew showed no sign of being upset over their visit to the nomads' camp. In fact, he wanted to know all about them.

"I have never seen them," he said. "They don't usually come down this way. I have always been curious about the size and shape of their wagons and I am disappointed that I had to be away while they were here. You know they only started using wagons about eight years ago, and I have heard they paint them quite brightly and artistically. How big were they?"

Dolly and Gladys were kept busy answering Andrew's questions until it was time for him to read Dolly a story and tuck her into bed. When he was ready to leave, Gladys insisted he stay a little longer and have a cup of tea. While they were drinking, Andrew told her about some of the trials and tribulations the gypsies had to contend with.

"Twenty years ago in Germany, the authorities went so far as to take their children away and give them to non-Roma families." He then explained that Roma was another name for gypsies and went on to say, "Even today, there are still places where people keep gypsies as slaves. About twenty-five years ago, there was a law introduced in this country called the "Turnpike Act" decreeing that gypsies would be fined if they camped on the side of the road. I don't know if that is still the case, but if it is, that may be the reason they don't stay in one place very long.

"As you know, Gladys, I'm not a religious man, but if anyone could change my mind, it would be the Quakers. Theirs is the most humanitarian organization I know of. Around 1816, a Quaker by the name of Hoyland wrote a book calling for better treatment for the gypsies in our country. It did a lot of good for a short while. Then, with very little warning, a large number of them were rounded up and transported to Australia as criminals."

Gladys thought about Old Nichol and how most of the people living there would welcome being sent to Australia if they were given food during the trip. As far as she was concerned, Andrew should have as much sympathy for them as he had for the gypsies, who seemed to live a very good life with plenty to eat and the freedom to come and go as they pleased.

Although she thought Andrew was the kindest man she had ever met, she couldn't help but think his priorities were not where they should be. She knew all about people starving to death, and you didn't have to go across the ocean to find them. Forgetting her manners, there was a note of disparagement to her tone as she said, "The gypsies and the Irish are not the only people who are treated unfairly you know. There are hundreds of English people who are starving, and no one is raising money to help them."

Andrew could see he had upset her and apologized. Then he tried to explain why he was putting so much effort into helping the Irish. "You see, Gladys, unlike them, people in this country can find help if they take the trouble to look for it."

"That's not the least bit true!" she declared, then blushed as she realized how impertinent she sounded. "Forgive me, Andrew, I have no right talking to you like that, but you really have no idea what you are talking about."

"And I suppose you do?" Andrew's asked.

"Yes, I do. I had to go near one of those slum areas where people are living like rats when I went to pick up two girls to work for the Watts. Even on the outskirts of that place, the smell of filth and death was so horrific it almost made me sick. You talk about starving to death, why do you think those girls' parents gave them away?"

"But I am sure we have many benevolent organizations to help those poor souls."

"Are you?"

"I thought I was, but perhaps I should do a little investigating the next time I'm in London. If you are right, I promise I shall do what I can for them as well. Now shall we talk about something more pleasant?"

"Oh yes, let's do. You have been away for so long, and what do I do but start an argument the day you come home. Millie is always telling me that I say things without thinking, and she is right."

"Perhaps she is, but you and I are much alike in that respect,

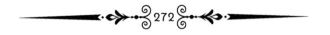

and I doubt we will ever change. I admire your spunk, Gladys. I think you must take after your mother. Tom said she was a governess, and I know that can be a thankless job at times. She must have been someone very special."

"She was the kindest person I have ever known—except for you." Gladys said, thinking of Sally. Then when she saw tears come to Andrew's eyes, she added, "There, now I've upset you and spoiled things again."

Andrew laughed and answered. "No, no, you haven't done any such a thing. What you have done is make me the happiest father-in-law in the world. Gladys, I shall never forget you for saying what you did just now, and I promise that you and Dolly will never have to want for a thing while I am around to look after you." This time it was Gladys who had tears in her eyes.

After he left, Gladys pondered what they had discussed. She couldn't understand why she felt she had to defend the people in Old Nichol. Her parents were both dead—at least according to Mr O's reckoning, Sally and Bob had moved away years ago, and although she had no idea where Toughie was, she knew he was no longer living in Old Nichol. So why did she feel such a strong allegiance to a place she wanted to forget?

Every time she admitted having knowledge of life in the slums, it could end in disaster. She had married into a wealthy family, and she knew that if she intended to remain in her father-in-law's good graces, her past had to be kept a secret. Millie was the only one who knew what she had done, and Gladys knew she would never tell. But the memories from her childhood of her and Toughie foraging for food, along with everything else, were memories she could not erase, no matter how hard she tried. Before she went to bed, she vowed to stop and think of the consequences before speaking.

For two weeks Gladys was kept so busy she didn't have a chance to visit Millie. The regular organist at the church had sprained her wrist, and Gladys was asked to take her place, which meant learning many new hymns. She missed being with Dolly all the time and felt guilty for neglecting her. Fortunately, Millie was always ready to look after her. As soon as the organist returned, Gladys didn't see

Millie for a week; then on the following Monday, she and Dolly went to visit her and invite her to dinner. When they arrived at the shop, Gladys was stunned by her friend's appearance. Millie had always taken great pride in her attire and her personal grooming, but this day she was wearing a soiled blouse and her hair was poorly pinned up in an off-centred bun.

Millie seemed unaware of her condition and welcomed them both with a big smile and a hug. She was delighted to receive the invitation to dinner and even suggested she close the shop and go with them right then. Gladys agreed, but thought it odd that Millie would leave the shop at one in the afternoon, especially since she could see a great deal of unfinished work lying about. Then when Millie put on her coat without offering to change her clothes or tidy her hair, it added to Gladys's concern.

Later, when they had finished their dinner, Millie suddenly remarked, "Oh dear, I must have spilled something on my blouse." Turning to Dolly, she laughed and added, "What a sloppy auntie you have, my darling." Gladys was a little relieved that Millie finally noticed the stain, and tried to convince herself that the reason she hadn't changed her clothes was because she was so excited about going out to dinner.

The next time they saw Millie was on one of their mystery trips with Andrew, and she looked as neat and self-contained as ever. That mystery trip turned out to be the most exciting one they had ever had. At first they all thought that Andrew was taking them to visit the Sorensons, but he drove right past their driveway until he came to a field that bordered their estate.

"Well, here we are," he announced as he drove the buggy into the field and jumped down. Seeing the puzzled look on their faces, he laughed then lifted Dolly down, adding, "What do you think of this place, my little turtle dove?"

"I should say it is a proper place to have a picnic, Gamby. May I pick some of those pretty flowers to take home?"

"You mean those daisies? Of course, you may pick all you want. Now, ladies, let me help you down; I've something I want you to see." When Andrew had them seated on a blanket he had placed on a flat piece of ground, he went back to the buggy and returned with some rolled up pieces of heavy paper and spread them out in front of them.

After they had looked at all the drawings, he asked, "What do you think, Gladys?" Although she had never seen anything like them before, she thought she might know what they were.

"Are they plans for a house, Andrew?"

"Not just any house, this is a special house. See, these are all the rooms," he said as he pointed to them all on each floor.

"But all those rooms? That has to be a mansion, not a house. Why it has as many rooms as Lord Sorenson's manor."

"Not quite, but almost. Well, what do you think?"

"First, explain some of these measurements and symbols to me, so I can try to imagine what it will look like when it is built."

Andrew could tell she was fascinated with all the details as he explained them, and he was amazed how quickly she understood what the architect had in mind.

"It looks like it is going to be simply beautiful. And just as charming as Lord and Lady Sorenson's, but far more modern and stylish."

"Yes, I agree," Millie added. "It also appears like the rooms are more spacious than in most of the older homes."

"I really like those large bay windows, especially since they are not cluttered up with little squares," Gladys said.

"I'm happy someone appreciates that. My architect was determined to have twelve panes to the square yard, but I refused to give in. What on earth is the good of having large windows in a house then blocking the view with leaded panes and draperies?"

Gladys was just about to answer when Dolly ran up with a hand full of daisies, "Gamby, I picked these for you under that big tree over there." She pointed to a large oak tree not far from where they were seated. "I like that tree, Gamby, it looks just like a friendly giant with his arms stretched out."

"So it does. I think he must be welcoming us with open arms," Andrew exclaimed.

Gladys smiled and added, "But instead of open arms it should

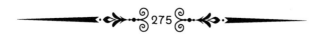

be, oaken arms."

"By Jove, Gladys, I think you have just given our estate a name. Oaken Arms! Is that not a hospitable sounding title?"

Dolly and Millie agreed wholeheartedly, but Gladys didn't answer. She was still shocked by the words, our estate. She was afraid to hope he was including her and Dolly when he said "our."

Andrew interrupted her thoughts. "Gladys, don't you like the name?"

"What name?"

"Haven't you been listening? Your mind seems to be elsewhere. I must say, I am disappointed, I thought you would be as excited about the plans for our house as I."

"There, you said it again."

"Said what?"

"'Our.' What exactly do you mean by our?"

"Whatever would I mean? Ours, of course—mine, yours, and Dolly's. Or do you object to living under the same roof as your old father-in-law?" Then, not allowing her to answer, he added, "If you have another look at these plans, you will see that there are a number of good sized apartments in the building so as to allow everyone plenty of privacy."

"You actually mean it will be ours?" Gladys asked, wide-eyed.

"Of course I do, you silly goose! I am having this house built for the three of us. I shall even put it in yours and Dolly's name, so after I am gone no one can take it from you. I intend to sign the house in town over to my stepson and give him, Rose, and his sister, a generous allowance. They shall not get their hands on this place, by jove. How does that sound?"

Instead of an answer, Gladys jumped up and hugged him so enthusiastically that he fell over backwards, and they all had to laugh.

"There is one thing you will have to put up with, Gladys, when we move into Oaken Arms, and that is having a few servants about."

"A few? Why I was thinking it would take a few dozen at least, that is if I am to play the part of a proper lady."

"Nonsense, you are a proper lady, and I know you will make a superb mistress of Oaken Arms. You must never change, must she,

Millie?"

Millie looked a little sceptical when she agreed. She loved Gladys dearly and was proud of her accomplishments, but the girl had a restlessness about her that worried Millie. Although Gladys appeared thrilled over the prospect of becoming a lady of high standing, Millie knew the disdain she felt for that class of people, and because Millie knew her background, she understood her sentiments.

"I suppose I shall have to have a personal maid to dress me, do my hair, and bathe me?" Gladys said to Millie, scrunching up her nose.

"You will have so many things to do managing a house that large, you will be thankful for all the pampering you can have," Millie replied.

"And when you retire, there will be a place at Oaken Arms for you too, Millie, if you like," Andrew announced.

This caused Millie to shed a volley of tears.

As they were riding back to Dover, Andrew explained how he came to buy the property. "I was most fortunate in selling my other estate a few days after hearing about this place. There are not many pieces of land left anymore, what with the amount of newcomers arriving in and around our town these past few years. I suppose that's why I sold it so quickly."

"It must have been hard to part with though," Gladys replied.

"I do have some wonderful memories of the good times Dorothy, Tom, and I had there, but the place is very old and in a sorry state of disrepair—so much so that I fear the entire house would have had to be remodelled, and then it would still be old. It will be far more exciting to build a new modern manor; don't you think?"

"Oh yes!" Gladys replied. "My head is buzzing with ideas. There is so much to think about that I don't think I shall ever be able to sleep again." Thoughts were racing around in Gladys's mind. She could picture herself and Dolly playing croquet on the lawn and riding their horses across the fields. She even had romantic thoughts of falling in love again and having more children. She could picture Dolly looking like a princess with suitors begging for her hand. All these thoughts in a matter of seconds. She even thought that once she moved into the manor, perhaps she would at last be able to cast aside Gladys Tunner and become the lady Andrew thought she was.

The disappointment she had harboured over not being the wife of an officer vanished that day, and during the following weeks, she and Andrew were kept busy going over the plans and choosing the best place to build the house. A good-sized stream ran through the back of the property, and Lord Sorenson said that because it continued to flow throughout the summer, there was always a good catch of trout to be had. And because they had plenty of water, he even suggested they plant a field of hops since they grew so well in that part of the country. Andrew added to Gladys's excitement by advising her to think about the different styles of furnishings and window dressings she would prefer.

There were no more mystery trips because all they wanted to do was spend time roaming around the property and having picnics under the oak tree. Andrew had hired a carpenter to build a round table and some stools so they could sit under the oak and have their sandwiches. He also contracted an ironmonger to build a fence, made of iron rails and an ornate gate with Tom's regimental coat-of-arms on each side, across the front of the property. Gladys suggested they have an expansive lawn from the gate to the house with flowers planted all along a winding driveway. When the decision was made regarding the placement of the coach house and stable, Andrew promised Dolly a pony of her own as soon as they were able to move in.

Chapter Twenty-Three

When Gladys began looking for furnishings for the manor, she asked for Millie's advice. At first she was delighted with the dressmaker's suggestions, but gradually, Millie's choices began to make less and less sense. Then one day when they were looking at a lovely Persian carpet in one of the shops, Millie shocked her by saying, "There will be children and filthy, dirty animals running all about. They will destroy everything. Second hand furnishings would suit you far better, my dear." This was so unlike her friend that Gladys realized she was confused and must have thought the Sorenson children and their animals were going to live in Oaken Arms. Not wanting to upset her, Gladys suggested they stop shopping and have a cup of tea in a little tea shop. An hour later, Millie was herself again.

Although Millie suffered brief losses of memory from then on, Gladys thought it was just a normal ageing problem and did her best to ignore it. One Monday morning when she and Dolly were sitting at the kitchen table finishing their breakfast, Millie surprised them by arriving dressed in her best suit and wearing her favourite large-brimmed ostrich-feathered bonnet. It was difficult to tell if her face was flushed with fever, or she had applied too much colour to her cheeks.

"Millie, what are you doing here?"

"Am I early?" Millie asked.

"Early? Early for what, Millie?"

"Why, the theatre of course! I walked all the way here so it would be more convenient for Andrew when he comes to pick us up. My goodness, Gladys, you are not even dressed." She continued talking in an agitated tone as she walked past Gladys into the kitchen, "Give me Dolly's clothes and I shall have her ready by the time you are dressed, and, Gladys, wear that pretty blue frock I made for you, I want to introduce you to some of my theatre friends."

Stunned, Gladys had no idea how to respond, so she decided to play along, "You are far too early, Millie. We still have two hours until Andrew comes, why don't you take off your hat and jacket and have a nice hot cup of tea and some toast and jam?"

"It's strawberry, Auntie, and it's very good!" Dolly added, unaware that anything was amiss.

"Now how on earth did I manage to get the time wrong? Never mind, a cup of tea sounds fine," Millie responded. Then with a vacant look, she mumbled, "Odd, but I don't recall if I have eaten today."

Gladys buttered and added a generous portion of jam to two large pieces of toast she had cooked on the stove. Millie gulped the food down quickly and after she finished some of the colour faded from her cheeks, and she appeared calmer.

"Come and rest on the divan, Millie, while we get ready. You must be tired from your walk," Gladys suggested.

"I do feel a bit weary. Perhaps a few minutes of rest will do me good."

Gladys covered her friend with an afghan before she and Dolly left her to go upstairs where they could talk without disturbing her. "Where is Gamby taking us, Mama?" Dolly wanted to know.

"Nowhere, darling. Your Aunt Millie is having a little trouble remembering things now."

"Why?"

"Well, sometimes when people get older they forget things and become very confused. That is what is happening to Aunt Millie, but if we pretend she is acting normal, it won't hurt her feelings. Do you think you can remember to do that?"

"I think so, Mama. Are you and Gamby going to be like that when you are older?"

"I hope not, but one can never tell. That is why it is so important to learn how to look after yourself. I had to look after myself when I was just your age."

"Did your mother get mixed up too?"

"No, but my father was lost at sea, so my mother had to leave me alone and go to work; but now I think we should work on your letters," Gladys said, anxious to change the subject. Dolly took her mother's advice seriously and from then on, she did her utmost to be self-sufficient.

They worked for an hour then went downstairs to peek in on Millie. She was snoring softly, so they left the front door open and went out to do a little gardening.

"Gladys! Gladys! Where are you?" Millie shouted when she woke and found herself on the divan. Gladys came running in. "Gladys, what am I doing here? What has happened?"

"You are fine, Millie. You were tired and just had a little nap."

"What time is it?"

"It's eleven o'clock."

"Then why on earth am I here instead of in my shop? Mrs Prescott will be there in a half an hour for a fitting. What is the matter with me, Gladys?" Millie asked in obvious despair. "Why can I not remember?"

Gladys sent Dolly upstairs to play. Then she sat down beside Millie, and gently tried to explain what had happened.

"Oh, Gladys, whatever shall I do?" Millie sobbed. "I shall go stark raving mad!"

"No you won't, Millie. It's just that your memory is not what it used to be. The same thing happens to a lot of people, but I think you should see the doctor. We are not living in the olden days anymore, thank goodness, and I'm sure there is something he can prescribe to help you." Millie didn't argue; she knew she needed help. She couldn't recall having such a thing happen to her before and didn't want it to happen again.

They visited the doctor the next afternoon, and when he was through with the examination, he took Gladys aside to tell her that Millie was suffering from senility. "There has been a lot of research done, Mrs Pickwick, and some drastic experiments too, but from all I have heard nothing positive has come of it. I can, however, give her medication that may be of help, especially when she becomes cranky or aggressive," he said.

"Millie will never be like that. She's the gentlest person I know. And she never complains, even though she often suffers with toothaches," Gladys assured him.

"But you must understand, Mrs Pickwick, she will become progressively worse and often, in cases similar to hers, their personality alters drastically. Now when that happens, this will help to calm her," he said as he handed Gladys a pint-sized bottle of liquid. "And it will also give her relief when she has a toothache."

Gladys and Millie had always been honest with one another, so when they arrived home, Gladys related what the doctor had said. At first Millie cried out, saying that the doctor must be wrong, but when she calmed down, she had to admit that he was probably right. She hadn't told Gladys, but for a long time she had been forgetting things. One day she had almost burnt the house down by forgetting to close the door on her little stove.

A piece of the red-hot coals had fallen out and burnt a good size hole in her carpet before she came in from the shop and found it smouldering. She cut out a piece of the same carpet from under her bed and covered it over so no one would see it. Now she looked up at Gladys with an expression so sad that Gladys almost lied when she was asked a volley of pertinent questions: "How long have I before I lose my mind completely? How long will it be before I am unable to do my work? Where will I live when I can no longer pay my rent?"

The only answer Gladys could provide was to the last question. "You shall come and live with us, of course. We should be moved into Oaken Arms in about a year, and I'm sure you will be fine until then." But as it happened, Millie's mental disability was not the only adversity she had to contend with. Two months later, she suffered a slight stroke and for a short time, was left with partial paralysis. Until she regained her mobility, she found it necessary to send her customers to other seamstresses.

Unfortunately, Millie didn't fully recover and was not as adept at sewing as she had been, and some of her regular customers began taking their business elsewhere. The worry over the loss of income brought on the anxiety attacks the doctor had predicted, and she was forced to take the medicine he had given her. Although the elixir did little to enhance her proficiencies, or slow down the escalation of her senility, it did provide her with a pleasant sense of euphoria. Gladys, kept so busy with choir practice and working on plans with Andrew for Oaken Arms, didn't fully realize how significantly Millie's life had changed for the worse.

Two Sundays in a row, Millie gave flimsy excuses why she couldn't accompany them on their picnics at Oaken Arms. The following Sunday it rained, so Gladys cooked a large joint of beef and made Yorkshire pudding. Andrew was supposed to pick up Millie, but when he knocked at her door, there was no answer. Assuming she had gone on ahead, he was surprised she wasn't at Gladys's when he arrived. "That's odd," Gladys said when he told her what had happened. "She's not in the habit of going out on her own, at least not that I know of. Do you mind going back to see if she is home now, before we have our dinner?"

Andrew was about to leave when Mr Grimsby arrived with some very upsetting news. "I am sorry to interrupt thee at meal time, Gladys," he said, "but I know thee are a good friend of the seamstress. You see she won't leave the cemetery. I gave her a brella but she were

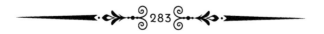

already wet through. I didn't know what else to do."

"What on earth would she be doing there?" Gladys asked.

"She keeps saying her little boy is buried there alongside her parents. I inquired for their names, and she said, Huddleston, and the boy's name be Michael McIver. Now I know every name on every last stone in my yard, and there be no Huddleston. I do have a McIver mind, but he were eighty when he passed, so it could not have been her young one. She thinks I am not telling her the truth, and she won't leave. I am afraid she is likely to catch her death, along with her dog. He won't leave her side."

Andrew offered to take his rig and follow Mr Grimsby to the graveyard in order to bring Millie back. About a half hour later he returned with a very wet, tired, and confused dressmaker. He told Gladys that when he found Millie, she was staggering from one tombstone to another mumbling, "Where are you, my precious? Where are you?" He put his arms around her and told her she was in the wrong graveyard and by that time she was too weak to argue.

Gladys had a warm tub of water ready in the kitchen and quickly stripped off Millie's sopping wet clothes and bathed her. She gave Dolly and Andrew a big towel to dry poor little Taffy, but they had to let him run into the kitchen every so often to make sure his mistress was still there. Gladys was shocked when she discovered an angry looking sore the size of a farthing under one of Millie's breasts and one about the same size under a shoulder blade where the metal stays had worked through the material of her corset and rubbed the flesh raw. Her other undergarments were soiled causing Gladys to realize that she hadn't taken them off for days, and she wondered how anyone could stand to sleep in corsets.

Gladys did all she could do not to cry, and she made up her mind not to allow her dear friend to return home for a long time. After Millie was dried and dressed in one of Gladys's nightdresses and dressing gowns, she appeared to be tired but calm, so they all sat down to an overcooked dinner.

The next day, Andrew put a notice in Millie's shop window saying that it would be closed for an undetermined time due to illness, and Millie and Taffy moved in with Gladys and Dolly. Although Millie behaved strangely at times, Dolly was happy to have her there and enjoyed playing nursemaid. For ten days Millie was content to lie around the house without showing any concern over the unfinished work she had left behind. Then one day, her lethargic attitude left and she seemed to regain most of her senses. It was all Gladys could do to keep her for another three days until her sores were completely healed and her clothes washed and mended.

Andrew went along with Gladys when she took Millie home in order to help get her settled, but when they saw the rundown condition of her living quarters, they were hesitant to leave her on her own.

Millie explained that she had run out of her medicine but would be able to manage if Gladys wouldn't mind fetching some more from the alchemist. "And perhaps you could ask for two bottles? It would save me the trouble of going for another when I need it. I have a few teeth that have been troubling me lately," she said.

There were a number of empty bottles on Millie's drain board causing both Gladys and Andrew to suspect that when she was alone she was overdosing on her medication. Although they knew Millie should pay a visit to her doctor before taking more, they feared the doctor would insist on committing her to an asylum, so Gladys finished cleaning the premises while Andrew went to the alchemist to have the prescription refilled.

They knew before they took Millie home that she would need someone to stay with her, and Andrew insisted on paying for the service. Luckily, Gladys knew of a sixteen-year-old girl who could use the money. Her name was Priscilla Mulberry, and she lived with her parents in one of the thirty houses attached to the Phoenix Brewery, only a block or two from Millie's shop. Priscilla attended the same church as Gladys and was also a member of the choir. She was a small, plain looking girl, with a shy, timid, and unpretentious personality. Both her parents worked in the brewery that employed a good percentage of Dover's workforce since it was one of the largest breweries in the country. Priscilla stayed home and did the housework and the cooking.

Gladys left Andrew with Millie and went to see the girl and

was pleased when both she and her parents were happy with the prospects of having another wage to add to their income. Priscilla began working for Millie the following day and soon proved she was very competent and reliable. Having someone in charge of her medication also did a great deal to help Millie function, and she seemed more like her old self, but her increasing loss of memory was hurting her business. She had trouble remembering the names of her customers and which gown they ordered. As a result, she lost more clients, and it wasn't long before she barely made enough money to pay her rent. In fact, if it wasn't for Priscilla, she couldn't have stayed in business. The young girl had become very fond of Millie, and although her knowledge of stitchery was rudimentary, she proved to be a big help with the basting and cutting out.

Aware of Millie's situation, Gladys invited her to dinner at least three times a week, which not only saved the seamstress money, but allowed Priscilla to spend more time at home. Since someone had to bring Millie to dinner and take her home later, Andrew was more than happy to oblige, being as fond of Gladys's cooking as Millie. The frequent visits to his daughter-in-law did not go unnoticed by his estranged wife and other gossips around town. Andrew had always enjoyed a spotless reputation, so although he had no reason to feel blameworthy, his conscience didn't always agree.

It had been seven years since Andrew left his second wife Rose and her two spoiled children and moved into a flat near his office on the quay. He was saying as much to a sailor friend one night after they had downed numerous drinks at a local pub. Drinking to excess was not a regular habit of Andrew's. Perhaps if it was, he would have been more accustomed to it and not so anxious to share his personal thoughts, but he had consumed enough liquor that night to dull his senses.

"You know, there are advantages to being poor, Pete," He said to his one-eyed drinking companion.

"I can't say I believes that!" Pete answered, his head bobbing

side to side as though mounted on a spring.

"Well, you see," Andrew attempted to explain while trying his best to focus on his friend's only eye, "if I was to be down and out, then I could sell my wife, right?"

According to the law, what Andrew said was in fact true, but only if a man was impoverished, and then it was necessary for both the husband and his wife to agree to the sale. This seldom caused a problem since most wives preferred being sold to starving to death.

"Aye, that you could, that you could," answered Pete, his head changing directions to the affirmative. When it stopped moving, he chuckled and added, "Do ye recall that there feller called, Densie? He sold his ol' woman—Sadie, I think her name were—fer a bottle o' gin."

"I do. I do, I do," Andrew replied, beginning to feel better. Pete's moving head had begun to make him queasy, but now that it had stopped bobbing about, he was able to take another drink and continue with their conversation. "And, if I recall correctly, damned if he didn't buy her back a week later for a bottle of wine."

"Aye, that he did, an' then, by Jaysus, if she didn't talk 'im into selling her again." Then he gave Andrew a poke in the ribs and a wink of his eye and added, "An' I heard tell she enjoyed having a change o' bed partners so much she managed to be sold three more times." Andrew called for another round as soon as they stopped laughing.

Andrew would have divorced Rose without hesitation, but unfortunately divorces were only granted through an act of parliament and that seldom happened, so he had to settle with a separation. This suited Rose and her family very well because Andrew provided her with a generous allowance enabling her, and her daughter Mildred, to dress in the latest styles and to keep her son Peter in one of the finest private schools.

Andrew only visited Rose when he wanted to collect some belongings that he kept in a locked room in the house along with a trunk full of Tom's books and toys. One day he decided that it was time he gave the trunk to Dolly, so he went to pick them up in his buggy, but was disappointed to find that Rose was home when he arrived.

"I have heard you are building a new home in the country, Mr Pickwick," Rose said accusingly. "There are also rumours about, that you and that woman are seeing a great deal of each other."

"I am building a house, which is no concern of yours, and I intend to see a great deal more of my daughter-in-law and my grand-daughter as well, which is also no concern of yours."

"Your conduct, Mr Pickwick, is downright shameful. I should think you would have more respect for me and my children. It tarnishes our reputation when you are seen cavorting about with a barmaid half your age."

In a quiet but threatening voice, Andrew replied, "Madam, watch what you say. Tom's widow is an honourable woman, and I shall not have you going about blabbing derogatory remarks about her." Rose started to protest but Andrew cut her off, "Beware. I have never laid a hand on you, even though there is no law to prevent me from doing so, but if you say one more word about my family, and understand this, I consider Gladys and Dolly my only true family, then I shall be forced to strike you down. And not only will I hit you, but if you ignore my warning, I shall decrease your monthly allowance."

The thought of having less money to squander upset Rose to such an extent that she gave a weak laugh and said, "Do forgive me, Mr Pickwick. Let us not come to grips over something so trivial, shall we?"

"Trivial? Such remarks as those you made are more slanderous than trivial."

"Oh, dear, I have such a habit of uttering inappropriate words when I am flustered. You must forgive me. I do not believe we could manage on any less of an allowance. You see, Peter's school has raised its fees, and Mildred has so many social functions to attend—she is a very popular young lady now."

"Very well, but you have been warned."

After Andrew left with the trunk, Rose uttered curses that would shock a seasoned sailor, then solemnly vowed to get even with Gladys and her daughter.

Dolly was elated when Andrew presented her with her father's trunk filled with books and toys. She hugged him so hard that he had to pry her arms loose from around his neck. The three of them spent the evening looking at the contents, and they all shed a few tears when Andrew told them little stories about each of Tom's favourites.

The Sunday picnics at Oaken Arms came to an end when Gladys volunteered to pick up Millie on her way home from church every Sunday and keep her for the day. This allowed Priscilla to spend an entire day with her parents. Millie was gradually becoming more and more confused and Gladys's home was the only place, other than her own, where she felt secure. Fortunately, there were other days in the week when Andrew was able to take time off work, and then he would pick up Gladys and Dolly and visit the site to see how the building was progressing. Every bit of sod turned and every brick laid added to their joy. Andrew figured it would probably take two years to finish the house and the outbuildings, which seemed like eons to Gladys and Dolly.

One Sunday the four of them were sitting around the dinner table when Millie leaned over and pointing to Andrew, whispered in Gladys's ear, "Who is that man, dear?"

Gladys, a little taken aback, whispered, "That's Andrew, Millie, you know him."

Millie smiled brightly and replied, "Of course, how silly of me! He is your young man." Gladys couldn't help but burst out laughing.

"What is going on between you two?" Andrew asked.

"Millie thinks you are my young man," Gladys said with a grin.

Andrew almost said he wished it were true, but then he felt ashamed to even think of such a thing. "You flatter me, Millie, but I am a little too old for such a young lady."

Gladys laughed again and said, "He's not really so old, Millie. Andrew is a good friend of yours, and he is my father-in-law and Dolly's grandfather, remember?"

"Of course I know that; why on earth wouldn't I?" Millie re-

plied accusingly, as though it was Gladys who was confused. Surprisingly, Gladys enjoyed Millie's company during the following months more than ever. She knew her friend only had a limited amount of time left before her memory would be completely gone, so that made their time together that much more precious. They all had become accustomed to her periodic memory failures, and even Dolly learned not to mention it in her presence so as not to alarm her. When Millie was clear-headed, she maintained a positive attitude, even though she was aware of her bleak future.

She was sitting in the kitchen with Gladys one evening, while Andrew was in the parlour reading to Dolly, and speaking quietly so as not to be overheard, she said, "Gladys my dear, I know that I am losing my senses." Gladys started to protest, but Millie stopped her, "No, dear, I have seen it happen to others, and because there are still times like now when I am thinking clearly, I must tell you what I want you to do for me. You know that I consider you and Dolly my family, and that I love you both dearly, so it may be difficult for you to understand what I am about to say. When I can no longer stay where I am, I do not wish to move in with you."

"Oh, Millie, of course you will. We want to look after you."

"Please listen to me, Gladys. You must do what I ask. When I don't know who I am or who you are, I want you to have me committed. This is what I wish. And I do not want you, or Dolly, to come and visit me. I am a foolish and vain old woman I know, but that is how I feel, so please, if you truly are my best friend then do what I ask. I do not want anyone I know to see me when I can no longer take care of my hair and makeup. I would rather be dead than have anyone, especially you, see me in such a state. I prefer you to remember me the way I am now."

"But, Millie, we love who you are, not how you look. Even Priscilla thinks you are a wonderful person."

"When you begin to age and lose some of your senses, everybody wants to make you feel better by telling you how wonderful you are. But don't you see, Gladys, this time it's not what you want. It is what I want. I want you to swear that you will do as I ask. Swear it, Gladys, for my sake."

Gladys took hold of Millie's hands in hers—the small, capable hands she loved to watch as they made masterpieces out of plain yards of cloth, and she reluctantly made the promise. When Andrew took Millie home that night, she gave him an envelope and instructed him to keep it until she was no longer with them.

It was as though Millie had known it would be the last evening she would spend with them all. The following week she suffered another stroke, far more severe than the previous one. Gladys was able to have her admitted to the Dover infirmary, because Andrew, one of the establishment's Governors for life, recommended her. The infirmary was only for charity patients since it was funded solely by donations from individuals, organizations, legacies, and memorial gifts.

Poor Millie was almost completely paralyzed. For sanitary reasons, her hair was cut short and, without its usual treatment of henna, was now a dreadful orange colour. She appeared to have aged twenty years in two days and was almost unrecognizable, but the cruellest consequence of the stroke was her inability to speak. She could only manage the sound "na," which she repeated over and over again when she became agitated, or was in pain.

When Gladys first visited her, there were tears running down her cheeks and Gladys said, "I know, Millie, I promised, but you might be much better in a few days. You still look great," she lied. "I won't let Dolly and Andrew come until you have your hair done, I promise." Millie closed her eyes, and Gladys knew she understood. She visited Millie a few times during the next week, but they were short visits because Andrew was away and she didn't want to take advantage of Mrs Grimsby, who was kind enough to look after Dolly.

One of the nursing attendants met her on Monday afternoon of the following week and said that the doctor would like a word with her in his office. Doctor Thornsbury, a large, portly man with a handlebar moustache and a ruddy complexion, was seated behind his desk. He smiled warmly and offered her a seat, then inquired about her relationship to the patient. Gladys told him Millie wasn't a relative, but her closest friend.

"Well, Mrs Pickwick, Millie has had a rough time these last two days. Her teeth are in terrible condition and are causing her a great deal of pain. Now I've taken the liberty of calling in Dr Freedman, a dentist I consider very competent. He thinks it will be necessary to pull all her teeth. Fortunately, she only has six on the bottom and eight on the top. Her gums are in a poor state as well."

"Oh no, Doctor, could she stand such a thing?"

"To be honest, Mrs Pickwick, I don't know, but I think we have no choice, since she will die of poison if those teeth are not pulled. I can assure you though, that nowadays, extractions can be painless with the use of anaesthetics. Chloroform is the one Dr Freedman prefers, and I recommend it as well. Now, in her condition, I would not recommend dentures. They take a great deal of getting accustomed to, and I think that the poor woman has enough to contend with."

"Doctor, is there any hope Millie will recover from the stroke, or will she always be paralyzed?"

"One can never say for certain, but I have yet to witness a patient in her condition make a recovery. I am very sorry."

"When will the dentist pull her teeth?"

"He intends to do it tomorrow morning."

Gladys thanked the doctor, and after promising to give his regards to Andrew, she left to visit Millie, who had been sedated and was unaware she had company.

Gladys was advised not to visit her again for at least two days after the operation, since she would probably be heavily sedated. The next time she went to visit her, Gladys was shocked by Millie's appearance. Her face was black and blue and swollen so badly that she couldn't open her eyes. Gladys took her hand and gave it a little squeeze, but Millie didn't respond. Gladys talked to her about Dolly and how they all missed her, but Millie only moaned and turned her head from side to side. Finally, Gladys decided that she was upsetting her more than comforting her, so she left.

It was a few days before she returned to the infirmary. This time she left Dolly with Andrew and went in the evening. When she arrived, there was a woman nurse with Millie. Gladys had heard of Mrs Fry's nurses and by the looks of this woman's clean uniform, Gladys thought she might be one. She was trying to coax Millie to eat a little pudding, but she kept turning her head to avoid the spoon. Although her face was not as swollen as the last time Gladys saw her, it was still covered with black and yellow bruises, and Gladys hardly recognized her. When Millie saw Gladys she cried out, "Na, Na, Na, Na!"

Gladys smiled at the nurse, then said, "I will try to feed her if you like."

Pleased, the nurse smiled and replied, "Perhaps she might take a little from you," and then left.

Gladys sat down and took hold of Millie's hand. "Don't cry, Millie dear; I won't make you eat it." The only response Millie gave her was an intense and pleading look. She continued staring at Gladys that way for such a long time that Gladys couldn't ignore the message it conveyed. She recalled Millie's words when she said she would rather be dead than be seen in such a state. There was no doubt in Gladys mind what her dear friend wanted her to do, but she shook her head in refusal. Tears began running down Millie's sunken cheeks, and her lips kept opening and closing in little short movements that were unmistakably pleas for mercy.

Millie was the best friend Gladys ever had, and she loved her even more than she had loved Sally. She also knew what she would want Millie to do if she were the one laying there with no hope of recovery. Taking hold of Millie's hand, she whispered, "Oh, Millie, I don't think I can." Somehow, Millie managed to find the strength to squeeze her hand, and she knew she had no choice.

Squeezing her hand back, she said, "It's alright, Millie, my dearest; it's alright." Millie's eyes closed, and her face relaxed.

Then Gladys kissed her on the forehead and said, "Good-bye, my darling. I love you so much." Millie smiled, but because she couldn't move her lips, it didn't show.

Ever so gently, Gladys raised Millie's head and slid the pillow out from beneath it. Then she put it over her friend's face and held it down. The seconds seemed like hours, until the feeble struggling ceased. Gladys hands were trembling as she placed the pillow back under Millie's head and smoothed her hair. She forced herself to eat some of the pudding before turning down the lamp and leaving the room; her entire body aching and her legs shaking. She managed to take the half empty bowl to the nurse and report that Millie had eaten a little, and was now sleeping peacefully. She left the infirmary and only managed to get around the corner and out of sight before throwing up the pudding and bursting into tears of anguish.

Chapter Twenty Four

When Gladys arrived home, Andrew had put Dolly to bed and was sitting in the parlour reading. As soon as he saw her, he knew Millie's condition had worsened. He put his arms around her, and the comfort of his embrace was all it took for Gladys to begin crying again. When she finally stopped, he asked about Millie, and although she longed to confess, she just shook her head and didn't object when he suggested she lie down on the divan while he made tea.

They drank their tea in silence until Gladys said, "I don't think she's going to make it through the night, Andrew." He always appreciated it when Gladys used his first name, but if she could read his thoughts, she would have never stopped calling him Dad.

Unwilling to leave her alone, Andrew offered to stay the night, but she refused and as soon as he left, she went upstairs and crawled into bed, hoping sleep would erase the horror of what she had done. She wasn't that fortunate. For hours she lay looking up at the ceiling and massaging her hands that were aching as though they were still gripping Millie's pillow. She knew she'd done what Millie wanted, and she would have wanted Millie to do the same for her if their roles had been reversed, but the ugly word, "murderer" kept coming over and over into her mind. Suddenly, she was very frightened.

If any of the infirmary staff had gone in to see Millie after she left, they might have already discovered she was dead. If that happened, Gladys was certain they would know she was to blame since she was the last one to see her. As such thoughts ran through her mind, she began to realize how foolish her act of compassion had been. It could result in her spending the rest of her life in a prison, instead of in luxury as the mistress of Oaken Arms. She wasn't even sure that Dolly would be spared. The authorities were sure to investigate her past and when Andrew found out who she really was, he might not want to look after his granddaughter, regardless of their fondness for each other.

She thought about getting Dolly out of bed and running away, but there was nowhere they could to go. She would just have to wait until morning, then return to the infirmary as though nothing had happened. Having made that decision, she finally dropped off into a fitful sleep.

Gladys woke up early, and as soon as she had given Dolly her breakfast, she took her to the Grimsbys' before going directly to the infirmary. On her arrival, she thought it odd that the main door was open, and when she entered the building and found there was no one about, she was even more apprehensive. Trying to appear calm, she went directly to Millie's bedside. It was a relief to find her friend exactly as she left her. She appeared so peaceful that Gladys felt a deep sense of gratification. She smiled and gently reached out to touch Millie's cheek. Her hand had barely made contact when suddenly Millie's hand shot up and grabbed hold of Gladys's wrist in an iron grip, then she sat up, opened her eyes, and with a diabolical look, spat blood from her toothless mouth and cried, "Murderer!"

Gladys couldn't stop screaming until she realized that the

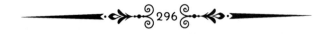

hand gripping her wrist was Dolly's and not Millie's. "Mama, Mama, what's the matter?"

Gladys was shaking, but more with relief than fear. "It's alright, my darling, Mama just had a bad dream."

"I'm sorry, Mama. Maybe I should come to bed with you."

"I think that's a splendid idea."

Cuddling up to Dolly's warm, little body proved to be the comfort Gladys needed, and she slept through the rest of the night.

She wasn't feeling very brave the next morning and dreaded going to the infirmary, but she had no alternative. She was ready to leave as soon as Dolly finished her breakfast. They were putting on their coats when they heard knocking at the door. Certain it was the police, Gladys's heart began to pound and her hand shook when she opened the door. When she saw it was only Andrew, her knees buckled. Andrew caught her before she hit the floor and he helped her into the parlour then sat her down on a chair.

"You must have guessed what I've come to tell you," Andrew said. "Millie's doctor sent me a message this morning asking me to drop by the infirmary where he told me that our dear Millie passed away peacefully sometime during the night."

Gladys, pretending the news came as a shock, uttered a moan. They had both forgotten Dolly until she pulled on Gladys's sleeve and asked, "What does 'passed away' mean, Mama?"

"It means your Aunt Millie has died, dear," Gladys answered. Dolly began to cry, so Andrew sat down, took her on his knee and did his best to comfort her.

"We shall all miss her, my little turtle dove, but we shall just have to try our best to be happy for her as well. You see, Dolly, Auntie was very, very sick and in a great deal of pain, but now she is at peace and her suffering is over."

His words helped Gladys as much, or more, than they did Dolly.

"Is she in heaven with her little boy, Michael, and my daddy?" Dolly asked.

"Yes, I'm sure she is," Andrew answered, for Dolly's benefit.

"Couldn't the doctor make her all better?"

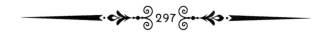

"I am afraid not, sweetheart."

"Gamby, what if you get sick? Will you die too?"

"Well, that would depend on the seriousness of my illness. But death is inevitable, and no one can live forever."

"Why?"

"Well you see, every living thing has a time to live and a time to die. It was Millie's time to die, and if she could talk to you right now, I am certain she would tell you that she wanted to go. Now you, my dear, have many, many more years ahead of you so let us put an end to all this talk of death and just think about the good times we shared with your Auntie Millie, shall we?"

"I shall try, Gamby," Dolly replied, sticking out her chin bravely, and wiping the tears away on her sleeve.

Since the weather was favourable, Andrew suggested they take a ride out to Oaken Arms, hoping to cheer them up, and Gladys offered to make a few sandwiches to take with them. She was relieved when Andrew stayed in the living room with Dolly and didn't see how her hands shook when she sliced the bread. A feeling of weakness and nausea had come over her, and she prayed she could get through the day without breaking down.

On their ride to Oaken Arms, the fresh air helped steady her nerves, and she even joined Andrew and Dolly in singing a happy song. After they had eaten their sandwiches, Dolly ran off to look for grasshoppers. Andrew could tell that his daughter-in-law was taking her friend's death very hard, so he reached out and took her hands in his. "Gladys, you mustn't feel guilty; you could not have been kinder to Millie. The nurse told me how you managed to get her to eat when no one else could. She also said—"

Gladys couldn't bear to hear any more and she interrupted him, "Please, Andrew, I know you are only trying to help, but let's not talk about it anymore today. I think I shall call Dolly and we will walk down to the creek to see if we can spot any trout. Do you want to come with us, or do we have time?"

"Yes, that is a jolly good idea, but I must give you this envelope Millie left in my care."

Gladys took the envelope but hesitated before opening it. She didn't really want to share its contents with anyone but couldn't think of an excuse to avoid it. She needn't have worried. The only thing in the envelope was Millie's will. Gladys had hoped that her friend had written a letter expressing how much their friendship had meant to her, or any other personal sentiment that could be kept as a memento to help ease her conscience. However, the only thing it contained in Millie's own handwriting was her signature at the bottom of the will.

She had Andrew read it aloud, and although she wasn't surprised to find that Millie had left everything to her, hearing it made her realize just how much the dressmaker loved her. "I think that if there is any money left over after I settle Millie's accounts; I should like to use it to see that the she is buried alongside her son. Do you think that would be possible?"

"I cannot see why not. Where is he buried?"

"In London, but I have no idea which cemetery."

Andrew suggested that they forego their stroll and return to town so as to go through Millie's papers and look for a burial receipt. If Gladys hadn't interrupted him when he was telling her what the nurse had to say about Millie's demise, she would have learned that she wasn't responsible for the seamstress's death after all, although her actions may have hurried it along. Gladys was so sure that Millie was dead before she left her, that she had neglected to feel for a pulse. The nurse told Andrew that she was making her rounds about two in the morning and found Millie's breathing to be very weak. She was going to call the doctor, but knowing there was nothing he could do, she held one of Millie's hands to comfort her. She added that Millie surprised her by giving her hand a slight squeeze, then without opening her eyes, her mouth formed a little smile and she passed away peacefully. Unfortunately, Andrew never mentioned it again, and Gladys never knew the full truth.

They found what they were looking for in one of Millie's two trunks. This particular trunk was quite unique in that it was made entirely of leather, and all four sides and the lid were beautifully hand-tooled in a floral design. Dolly had always loved to smell the trunk and run her hands over its smooth surface whenever she visited her Auntie Millie. She referred to it as "my bootiful, smelly trunk," and until she was five, she was disappointed every time she smelled real flowers and they didn't smell like leather. Millie was delighted that someone revered the trunk as much as she did, because it had been a gift from her one and only lover. Therefore, she decided to leave it to Dolly in her will. She even attached a note inside the lid saying, "Property of Dolly Pickwick by order of Millie McIver."

Andrew and Gladys were astonished to discover how many papers, mementos, and valuables that Millie had stored inside such a limited space. Many of the articles were only of value to the owner, such as ticket stubs and dried flowers. However, among her memorabilia was a collection of expensive lace shawls and gloves, small, delicate ornaments she must have thought too fine to display in such a humble dwelling, and pieces of exquisite jewellery in velvet-lined cases. At the bottom of one of the trunks, they found a portrait of a distinguished looking gentleman along with newspaper clippings concerning him. "Now why in heavens would Millie save this picture and these articles about Lord Lackery?" Andrew remarked.

"I have no idea," Gladys lied, then quickly gathered them up and threw them in the trash can. There were also a good number of unpaid bills that Andrew said would have to be seen to. Finally, they found a receipt from an undertaker with reference to the burial of Millie's son, Michael McIver, in the High Gate Cemetery in London.

Dolly couldn't hide her excitement when Andrew suggested that the three of them accompany Millie's coffin to London on the train. When Lord Cedric heard of their plans, he generously offered the use of his flat, since he only occupied it when he attended the House of Lords. The trip took most of a day and although they were thrilled with the train ride, they were also very tired when they arrived. After Andrew confirmed that the undertaker he'd previously notified had picked up Millie's coffin, they went to dinner near Lord Cedric's flat and then retired.

They were at the cemetery early next morning to meet the minister that Andrew had contacted. It had taken quite a bit of persuasion and a great deal more money than was left after Millie's estate had been settled to have her buried in the same grave site as her son and her parents, but Andrew paid it without telling Gladys. The minister gave a short, but heartening sermon, and when he was finished, Gladys sang, "Oh, For a Thousand Tongues to Sing," the only hymn Millie liked. The funeral affected both Dolly and Gladys deeply, in a comforting way. They both could imagine how happy Millie would be to be with her beloved son again, which made Dolly happy and somewhat eased Gladys's conscience.

Ironically, Millie's death brought about the most wonderful adventure Gladys and Dolly could ever have imagined. They buried Millie on the 20th of May 1851, and the Great Exhibition in the Crystal Palace in Hyde Park had been officially opened by the Queen herself on the 1st of May, so Andrew insisted they stay for a few more days and see the exhibits. They were most fortunate in having Lord Sorenson's flat because London was swarming with tourists who had come from far and wide to see the very first World Exhibition. The flat was quite roomy with two good sized apartments on the first floor and one on the second, where the caretaker and his wife, the housekeeper, resided.

The next morning, they left the flat as soon as they finished a tasty breakfast the housekeeper was kind enough to prepare. Luckily, they were able to hail a cab without waiting too long, and after a pleasant ride they came in sight of the Crystal Palace. Travelling in an open cab they were awestruck with the splendour of the building—Andrew as much as Gladys and Dolly. "It's unbelievable," he exclaimed. "I was here about a year ago, and there was nothing but park." The driver, hoping for a generous tip, pulled over to the curb and began his well-rehearsed speech concerning the Palace and the exhibits within.

"It were Prince Albert, who made it happen, yer lordship," he

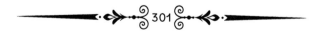

said with pride. "An' the reason you didn't see it afore, was that it only took nine months to build. There's more than a million feet o' glass in that building, and inside there's over thirteen thousand exhibits from around the world. Things the ladies'll like too!" he added for Gladys and Dolly's benefits. "You won't half enjoy it. There's so much to see, you'll want to come back again and again." Andrew stopped him from continuing by suggesting they would like to learn about it inside the building and not out on the street.

Upon entry, they were given a brochure with all the information needed to find their way about, but the doorman, surmising they were well-off by their attire, signalled for one of the official guides to come and assist them. The guide, a small statured, pleasant-faced man dressed immaculately in a scarlet uniform, came running to offer his services, a convenience given only to the wealthy. They soon found out that he had been well trained because he couldn't have been more obliging, even going so far as to secure a comfortable little push cart so Dolly could ride when she wearied.

Joseph Paxton, the man who designed the Crystal Palace, was first and foremost, a gardener. This was easy to believe since the interior of the building was enhanced with full grown trees, colourful gardens, fountains and cascades, which provided shade and pleasing scents, especially on the days when the sun beat down on the glass roof. The cab driver hadn't exaggerated when he told them how many exhibits there were to see. There were 6,861 from England alone, 520 from fifteen of the British colonies and the remaining 6,556 came from other countries. The building was made of cast iron and glass and was 1,851 feet long with a height of 108 feet and had 999,000 feet of exhibition space displaying the latest technology developed during the Industrial Revolution.

Railway engines and mill machinery were among the large machines that were displayed in actual motion, all powered by two large steam boilers. These and the exhibit showing the latest technology in telegraphy were among Andrew's favourites, but with Oaken Arms in mind, Gladys was far more interested in the displays of modern furniture and arts and crafts, especially those from Italy. Then, when they came to the American Exhibits, she couldn't help but exclaim out loud, "Oh, look," causing heads to turn in her direction.

Andrew laughed as her face turned red. "Now what have you found, my dear?" he asked.

"Look at this machine, Andrew. It is simply unbelievable! All you have to do is sit there and turn the handle around with your hand and the machine does the sewing. Can you just imagine how Millie would have loved a machine like this?"

The man in charge of the exhibit stopped sewing, and explained that it was the first successful, manufactured sewing machine. "Would you like to try it?" he asked and held out a small piece of material for Gladys to use. It took a bit of practice before she learned to feed the cloth in while turning the wheel, but she soon managed to sew the material into a pocket-like pouch.

This brought on a loud applause from the rest of the spectators. "That was terrific! Thanks, lovely lady," the man said with a wink and a grin. Then he added, "Ya know, you'd make a great demonstrator."

Gladys didn't take offense over his familiarity. In fact, she liked the casual way he spoke, and smiling, she replied, "Why, thank you, sir, your machine is simply amazing."

Then the man noticed that Gladys's companion was obviously annoyed with his flirtatious manner and, being a seasoned salesman quickly assessed his prospects, and turned his attention to Andrew. Andrew was so interested in the mechanics of the contraption he soon forgot his grievances and told Gladys and Dolly to carry on; he would catch up to them in a minute or two. Gladys would have refused to leave without him, but Dolly was anxious to see more and tugged at her sleeve.

Dolly was mesmerized with the taxidermy exhibits. There were lions and tigers from Africa, shaggy haired bison from America, and many kinds of animals she didn't know existed, all looking so alive that at first, she was a little frightened of them. Next to the shaggy haired bison stood a tepee made from animal skins, and sitting on a bison pelt outside the tepee was a beautiful Indian princess wearing a colourful beaded and fringed buckskin tunic and trousers.

Completing the scene was a handsome, but fierce looking Indian chief, who was standing with his arms crossed in a regal pose beside the Princess. Except for a few streaks of white paint on his chest and his face, he was naked from the waist up, and his skin, like the princess's, had a beautiful mahogany hue. They both had coal-black hair worn in thick braids, but what fascinated Dolly the most was the colourful eagle feathered bonnet the chief wore on his head. When he saw how much she admired it, he walked over to her, bent down, and said, "You feel." When Dolly reached up and touched the feathers, the chief laughed and, reaching into a basket, took out a feather like the ones he had in his bonnet and said, "For you, little papoose, an eagle feather." Dolly was so pleased she reached out her arms and he hugged her.

That wasn't the only treasure she received that day. When they visited the Chinese exhibits, a small and delicate looking Chinese lady gave her a pretty little china doll with moveable arms and legs. At noon they enjoyed a light lunch in one of the eating establishments and rested for another half hour on a bench under a palm tree. When Dolly had to go to the bathroom, Andrew asked the guide where the doors leading out to the privies were. To his surprise, the guide informed them they were inside the building. "A chap by the name of George Jennings has invented what he calls 'Monkey Closets' and they are located in the Retiring Rooms not far from where we are sitting," the guide said. "These monkey closets flush away after you are finished."

"You mean to tell me there's no need to empty the commode?" Andrew replied.

"Yes, sir, that's right. Mind you, there is a charge of one penny, but for that price you get a clean seat, a towel, a comb, and a shoe shine. A bargain, if I may say so, sir!"

Although they had to wait in line for a short time, the public toilets were one of the most exciting things they had ever experienced.

"How convenient that would be to have in the winter," Gladys exclaimed when she and Dolly had returned to Andrew and the guide. "It would be wonderful to have one in our new home."

"We shall!" promised Andrew "I shall contact this Mr Jennings when we get home and find out more about his invention."

"I think Auntie Millie must have one in heaven," Dolly said earnestly, causing Andrew and Gladys to laugh.

The afternoon proved to be just as exciting as the morning, but by three o'clock, Dolly couldn't keep her eyes open and fell asleep in the cart. Not wanting her to miss any of the exhibits, Gladys and Andrew sat and had tea while watching other visitors. Most days the admission to the fair was far too costly for working class families, and since this was one of those days, the people they saw were of a higher social standing and were dressed in the most expensive and stylish outfits.

Many of the wealthy visitors were from other countries and were clad in their national attire. Gladys had never seen such colourful garments before, and although she knew she was being rude, she couldn't stop staring at them as they walked by.

Not long after, Dolly woke up, but because Andrew had decided they should stay in London until they had seen all the exhibits, they thought it would be best to go back to the flat.

When the guide returned and heard they were planning on returning the following day, he protested, "But, sir, tomorrow is one of the cheap ticket days. Those in attendance shall be of a much lower class. Not only that, Sir, there will be no guides on duty." Although the man was extremely helpful and knowledgeable, Andrew and Gladys looked forward to being on their own, and the reasonable price of one shilling each for admission made their return the following day that much more attractive.

The next day it rained, and it was such fun to be nice and dry inside the building while looking up and seeing the rain splashing down on the glass roof. "I have always been intrigued by those glass balls with the scenery inside," Gladys said. "Now I know what it is like to be in one."

Some of the exhibits they saw were quite bizarre and the latest in surgical inventions from France were astounding. Splendid carriages of all kinds were on display, some with interiors lined with the softest leather, while others had seats covered with expensive wine and blue coloured fur. There were glass covered stands displaying magnificent works done in gold and silver, caskets full of diamonds and pearls along with the "Koh-i-noor," the world's biggest diamond, all heavily guarded.

But for Andrew and Gladys, the most exciting exhibit of them all was that of Tom's old friend, Willard Sawyer. His velocipedes, or what he referred to as his double-action self-locomotives, were among the most popular exhibits in the palace. He had a variety of models on exhibit from a six-seater family machine to a lightweight racer. His Promenade and Visiting models were even fit to ride while dressed in evening attire, and he had models for ladies, invalids, and children. He also supplied the Crystal Palace with machines for hire, so visitors could pedal around the gardens.

His best velocipede was made with bright iron work, capped and bound with silver, and priced from twenty-five to forty pounds. There were other velocipedes on display that were made in foreign countries, but they were far inferior to Willard's in both technology and engineering. They had no idea that Willard was there, and when Gladys saw him, she couldn't resist throwing her arms around him and saying, "Tom said you would be famous one day!" Before they bid him goodbye, Andrew ordered machines for Gladys and Dolly, and they talked him into ordering one for himself.

At the end of the fourth day, they were all dizzy with thoughts and images of all they had seen and were unusually quiet in the cab on the way back to the flat. They intended to leave in the morning, but Gladys happened to pick up a theatre brochure someone had dropped on the floor of their carriage, and she read that the following night a romantic musical drama titled *O'Flannigan and the Fairies*, was playing at the Little Adelphi Theatre. When she remarked that it was the same theatre in which Millie had performed, Andrew suggested they stay one more night, and attend the performance in her honour. The title seemed to suggest that Dolly would enjoy the play as well, so Gladys insisted she spend most of the day resting.

Andrew left shortly after they had breakfast and didn't return until dinner time. As they were eating, he said, "I took your advice, Gladys, and paid a visit to one of the slum areas they call Old Nichol." Gladys choked on the bread she was eating, and it took a few seconds for her to compose herself. "They are not as bad off as the poor souls in Ireland, but I can see how they need help too. Such living conditions should never be tolerated. I was forced to stop at a bathhouse before I made my way here in order to rid myself of the stench. I shall talk to Lord Cedric and some other friends and see if we can raise some money for them, but the little we will be able to do will be no more than a drop in a bucket, I am afraid."

Gladys wished she had never said anything. Every time the name Old Nichol came up, she feared her past would be discovered. Being able to confide in Millie had helped, but now there was no one she could be honest with. She thought she might confess to Andrew one day, but wouldn't dare do it until the deed to Oaken Arms was in her name.

After dinner, they went to the theatre. The play was a popular one, and they weren't able to get seats close to the stage, but they managed to acquire three in the balcony, which Gladys and Dolly thought were far better anyway. The play was about Phelin O'Flannigan, a man of some means, who believed in fairies, or what he referred to as the Good People. There was a good deal of humour, some lively music, and the play wasn't too long, so Dolly managed to stay awake for the entire performance. Gladys kept picturing Millie in the leading lady's role, and her tears of laughter were mingled with ones of sorrow.

Reluctantly, they left London the following morning. It was a great treat for Gladys and Dolly to have another ride on the train. "Isn't this wonderful, Gamby?" Dolly said after they had settled themselves in their own little compartment.

"I suppose it is," Andrew responded, "but I wonder what other ingenious inventions you will see in your lifetime. Why I have even heard there is a man in France who is attempting to build a flying machine. Imagine that! Maybe Sawyer will try that next."

Chapter Twenty-Five

The trip to London brought Andrew and Gladys closer, but Andrew's feelings towards his daughter-in-law were not altogether paternal. He was extremely fit for a man of forty-five, and Gladys was like no other woman he had ever known. Her lack of education was overshadowed by her intelligence, and he couldn't help but notice that she had a face and a body that would tempt a saint. These feelings began to plague him, especially now that they were planning on living under the same roof.

He hoped that his desires would subside, but unfortunately as time went by they grew even stronger. He prided himself on being an honourable man, so the guilt he felt over his feelings began to weigh heavily on his shoulders, and he had no idea of what to do about it.

The rest of the year passed by quickly as they were kept busy dealing with the building of Oaken Arms. They both wanted the house constructed in the most modern design, which was something of an oxymoron because many of the popular architects were designing homes in a Medieval or Gothic style—a romantic mode with towers, turrets and high crowned gables. As to the interior, they both preferred the modern designer, Joseph Meeks, with his lush, abundant, and cluttered look that was fast becoming known as "Victorian."

By the first of the year, the exterior of the house was almost finished, but there was still a lot of work to do inside. Gladys had Andrew order an Italian made sideboard and chiffonier she had seen when they were at the exhibition in London. She also had a lovely rosewood couch with a spring seat and two elegant, bright blue chairs to complement it, put away at one of the local furniture stores.

Andrew was as anxious, if not more so than Gladys, to move in. He had tried many times to persuade her to move into a larger home that would accommodate a few servants so she would not have to do her own housework, but she always refused. Knowing that his friends expected him to provide Tom's family with the finest, the house she and Dolly were living in was a source of embarrassment, even though he understood her reason for living there.

Gladys was kept so busy shopping for last minute necessities for the manor that it helped take her mind off Millie's death. She was also very active in the church choir—more so than usual since the Reverend Mason's son, Hugh, had returned home from his studies at Cambridge.

Hugh's features were a little too delicate to render him handsome, but he did have a captivating personality and a voice to match. Having just become an ordained minister like his father, he planned to spend six months to a year in Dover before leaving Britain to do missionary work in one of the colonies. It was also rumoured that he hoped to find a suitable wife to accompany him on his mission. A good number of young ladies from his father's congregation would have been more than happy to oblige, but it soon became obvious that Hugh only had eyes for Gladys, and because she couldn't help but be flattered, she thoughtlessly encouraged him.

They both enjoyed singing, and their voices blended so well they were often asked to sing duets, which meant spending time together practicing. Ever since Tom was killed, Gladys hadn't thought about men in a romantic way, but now she found herself having daydreams about what it would be like to make love to another man. Hugh, on the other hand, had been too engrossed with his studies to learn the difference between an innocent flirtation and a serious relationship, and was convinced their friendship would eventually end in marriage.

Until Hugh's arrival, Gladys's life had centred on her father-in-law and her daughter, and although she loved them both dearly, she missed the innocent flirtations she had experienced singing at Scots Inn. Hugh's admiration was a tonic that showed in her countenance and added to her beauty. Hugh doted on her, taking her dining, boating, and horseback riding whenever Andrew or Mrs Grimsby offered to stay with Dolly. Andrew enjoyed spending time with his granddaughter, but he missed Gladys's company, and began to worry that she would decide to marry the young minister and accompany him on his missionary quest. If that were to happen, he would not only lose her, but his beloved granddaughter as well.

The first time Gladys invited Hugh to dinner, she also invited Andrew, who was determined not to like the young man. However, he found his company enjoyable and was pleasantly surprised when Hugh didn't attempt to convert him or behave sanctimoniously. Another thing that surprised him was that the young man shared his sentiments toward the poor Irish families. As much as it bothered him to admit it, Andrew thought he would make Gladys a good husband, but the concept of living the rest of his life without her and Dolly was disturbing.

In spite of his fears, Andrew continued to look after his granddaughter while Gladys and Hugh enjoyed their time together until the day she came to his office to ask if he could stay with Dolly while she and Hugh went to see a performance by Dickens at a local theatre.

Andrew was aware Dickens was in town and that he and his friend Collins, another writer, were staying at Camden Crescent while they were working on a story titled, *Bleak House*. When he learned that Dickens had offered to do a reading at the theatre, he purchased three tickets and planned on taking Gladys and Dolly to see the performance. The disappointment he felt when Gladys told him she intended to go with Hugh Mason prevented him from answering for a minute or two, and Gladys could tell by his silence and the look of disapproval on his face that he wasn't happy about it. Suddenly she realized how much she had taken advantage of his good nature during the last few months.

"Oh, Andrew, I am truly sorry," she apologized. "You have been staying with Dolly so often lately, and here I am asking again. I shall tell Hugh that I am unable to go."

"Perhaps you can leave Dolly with Mrs Grimsby," Andrew replied, rather sharply.

Gladys was taken aback. Ever since their trip to London, she had felt that her future was secure, and smugness, instead of gratitude, had begun to show in her character. Now Andrew's cool response sent a shiver up her spine. She was not yet mistress of the manor, so she smiled at him sweetly and said, "I would much rather be going with you, Andrew, but Hugh asked me, and I said yes without realizing it might bother you."

Her smile was all it took. Andrew not only offered to look after Dolly, but gave her the tickets he had purchased. After she left, he slumped down in his chair feeling like a defeated fighter. He was ashamed of his lack of backbone and wished he hadn't given in. Gladys had him twisted around her little finger, and now he would spend another evening trying his best not to be jealous. He tried going through some papers on his desk, but couldn't concentrate. Finally, he shoved them aside cursing out loud, "Damn her! It is high time I put my foot down." He decided to no longer stay with Dolly in the evenings, thinking that perhaps if Gladys had to stay home, Hugh might decide to find another girl to court. But in truth, he knew that once a man had fallen under Gladys's spell, no one else could compare.

Andrew was a member of Dover's newly formed Chamber of

Commerce, as was his solicitor, Randolph Mansfield, and one evening, after their meeting, Randolph suggested they go for a drink at a men's club they often frequented. They were comfortably settled in a pair of large, stuffed, leather chairs enjoying the smooth taste of their brandy when Randolph brought up the subject of the deed to Oaken Arms. "I have those papers you wanted drawn up and ready to sign, Andrew, but before you do, I want to be certain you know what you are doing. I can understand how determined you are that Rose and her children never inherit the property, but Gladys is still young and attractive, and there are a lot of scoundrels out there who would like nothing better than to get their hands on such a large estate."

"Up until the last few months I thought I knew exactly what I wanted, but now I'm not so sure," Andrew answered with a frown.

"What is it, old boy? Anything I can help you with—in strictest confidence of course."

"It would be a relief to talk to someone, I must admit," Andrew confessed. He took the time to light a cigar and have a drink of his brandy before he could think of what to say. "I have someone in my life that I care for very much."

Randolph didn't answer for a minute. He had heard rumours about Andrew and his daughter-in-law and had considered them nothing but gossip, but now he realized that they might be true.

"Are you saying what I think you are?"

"Yes, I suppose I am, although I haven't even admitted it to myself before, but yes, yes, that is exactly what I am saying."

"Well now! I can understand how you are smitten with her—she's a most attractive young lady, but she is a lady, and you already have a wife, even if she is an estranged one."

"About that; what do you think my chances are of obtaining a divorce?"

"Well, let me think." Randolph thought for a while then he raised his eyebrows and continued, "You do have some influential friends in high places and others in, ahem, low places. A propitious combination, if you get my meaning."

"I fail to see your point."

"Well, you are aware that the only grounds for obtaining a divorce are by reason of adultery, are you not?"

"I am. But I would never stain Gladys's reputation with such an act."

"Oh no, dear boy, I did not mean for you to commit the act."

Andrew looked confused for a second before he realized what his friend meant. "You must be joking! Rose is happy with things just as they are. I give her a generous allowance and she prides herself on belonging to a wealthy family. She would never jeopardize that."

Randolph shrugged his shoulders; then he signalled the waiter to bring two more brandies before answering, "You may be right, but I shouldn't be surprised that if the right man were to come along and throw a little flattery in her direction, the chance of a discreet affair just might tempt her."

"Good God, Randy, you have met the woman. You must be joking!"

"Not at all, and if you take a minute to think about it, I am certain you know one or two less savoury acquaintances who would be only too happy to do you a favour, for a price of course." Randolph then tipped his head and winked. "What do you think?"

Andrew looked at Randolph for a second, expecting him to laugh. When his expression didn't change, he exclaimed, "You are not serious, are you?"

"I am. Mind you, it would have to be someone with a great deal of charm to fool that wife of yours, and I doubt you will find a man with that sort of talent who is willing to do such a thing, no matter how much compensation you are offering."

They sat in silence and enjoyed their drink for a while before, Andrew, who had been mulling over what his friend had said, inquired, "Even if I could arrange such a thing, would it not be dishonest?"

"How honest was she when she pretended to be a kind and loving woman and duped you into an unhappy marriage?"

"I suppose that's true, but I would have to be pretty desperate to stoop to her level."

"You sounded to me as though you were."

Andrew thought for minute then nodded his head and answered, "Yes, by God, I am."

Randolph had noticed how attractive Gladys was and he knew how much younger she was than Andrew, so the thought occurred to him that perhaps the infatuation might be one-sided. Hoping Andrew wouldn't take offense, he asked, "You might be in love with Gladys, Andrew, but does she feel the same about you?"

"I have no idea, but I can only hope she does. Damn it, Randy, I may be an old fool, but I can't help it. Do you think Tom would be disgusted with me?"

"No, I'm sure he would appreciate the way you have taken care of his family. The kindness you have shown toward them is quite perceptible. Anyone could tell you would be a good husband to Gladys and a wonderful father to her daughter. And I daresay you are still man enough to provide the girl with a sibling or two, right?" Randy, said with a grin.

"Thank you, Randy, I needed that. But the thing is, Gladys has a suitor—the Reverend Mason's son, Hugh. He has returned home ordained and full of enthusiasm about sailing off to save every heathen soul in the Colonies. Egad, why cannot these missionaries with their 'I'm holier-than-thou' attitude realize they often do more harm than good?"

"I'm afraid I cannot agree with you there. They are out there in the wilds risking their lives doing what the good book tells them to. But then, you were never much of a churchgoer, were you?"

"No, I never was and shan't ever be, but to get back to Gladys, if she does decide to go with him and take my granddaughter, it would break my heart."

"Yes, I can see it would. However, you must be practical, and in case she does go off with the Mason lad, it would be a grave mistake if you were to put Oaken Arms in her or her daughter's name before they left."

"I suppose you are right."

"Of course, you could prevent her from taking your granddaughter to another country, but I don't think you can legally stop Gladys from going."

"I would never separate them, no matter how much it hurt

me. However, that is my problem," Andrew said as he rose and held out his hand. "Thank you for listening to me, Randy. You are a good friend, and I appreciate it."

"Anytime, Andrew. Anytime. I think we should let things ride as they are for a time until we see what the future brings. I also think you should let your daughter-in-law know how you feel."

"We shall see."

Gladys had really begun to enjoy Hugh's company. As part of his training, he had spent a year in the Colonies, and the stories he told her fuelled her imagination. She recalled the exhibits with the handsome Indian chief and the pictures they had on display of the wide open plains and snow-capped mountains. She could picture herself in such a romantic setting where she could throw caution to the wind—along with hoops and corsets—and jump on the back of a wild mustang, dressed in a pair of buckskin breeches, and ride for hours without seeing a fence or a hedge. She even fantasized about being at Hugh's side as he visited the Indian villages and taught them to be civilized.

She couldn't imagine saving any souls though, because she thought her own might need saving more than the natives, but she had heard that the weather in Canada was exceedingly cold in the winter, so perhaps she and Hugh could teach them to build warm houses with fireplaces to prevent them from freezing to death. As much as she dreamt about a life in the wilderness, the days she spent at Oaken Arms planning for her future home meant more to her than any fantasy, and although she didn't tell Hugh, she knew in her heart that she would never leave England with him.

All sorts of confusing thoughts were on her mind in the following weeks, mostly because Andrew's moods had become unpredictable, which worried her. Then one day she had a visitor who threatened her very existence. She was bent over digging in her garden when someone touched her shoulder. Looking up, she was forced to put her hand over her mouth to stifle a scream. The man standing

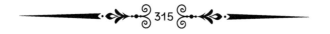

above her was the filthiest and most decrepit looking man she had seen since she discovered Mr O in front of Scots Inn. Getting to her feet, she asked him in a shaky voice what he wanted.

"It's me, missus. Rod O'Brian. Don't you remember?"

Gladys wanted to close her eyes and have him disappear, but she knew it was impossible. "What do you want?" she blurted out rudely.

"I brought you this here," he said as he took a dirty little bundle out of his pocket and handed it to her. She recognized the piece of cloth immediately. It was the one she had wrapped Sally's cameo in. Her hand was shaking as she took it from him.

"Pa give it to me before he passed on. He said I was to get it to you whenever I could. I caught a ride with that fellow what brings girls like our Ellie to work for folks. Da told me what happened to you and made me swear on the St. Michael's medal he wore around his neck that I'd not tell a soul. When I asked for you and our Ellie at the Inn, I was told she moved away and that you lives here. Da told me how well off our Ellie was now and I was spectin' her to help me and my kiddies out. They's in a bad way, missus. Then when I asked for you, I didn't let on I knew you or that you come from the same place as me, and you can believe that."

"Thank you, Rod. That was kind of you," Gladys said in a much kinder voice, but she didn't know what else to say. They both stood staring down at the ground for an awkward few seconds. Gladys wished he would just go away, but he made no move to leave.

Finally, he said, "You see, missus, I don't have a ways home, so I could use some money. Me wife an' kiddies is starving, and I could of sold that there pin, but Pa made me swear I'd give it to you."

Gladys told him she could give him a little, but that she didn't have much. She told him to wait where he was. Then she hurried into the house to get all the money she had and to make sure that Dolly was still playing upstairs and hadn't seen Rod. While Rod was waiting for her to return, he began to realize how afraid she had been when she saw him, and he realized that he had a good chance to return home with money enough to buy food to last his family for a very long time.

When she came back, she gave him a handful of notes. "Here, this is all I have in the house," Gladys said. "Thank you for bringing me the broach, but now I would appreciate it if you were to go before someone sees you here." It was more money than he had ever had in his hands, but he wasn't about to leave until he tried to get more.

"Just a minute, missus," Rod said as he reached out and grabbed her by the arm as she turned to leave.

"How dare you touch me," Gladys said angrily, "If you are not careful, I shall call for a constable, and you will spend the rest of your life in jail."

"I wouldn't be too hasty if I was you. They's still looking for that poor Mr Gaylord, you know."

"What has that to do with me?" Gladys demanded.

"Well you see, Pa didn't just tell me about the pin. He told me about you an' Mr Gaylord too."

Gladys knew she was beaten. "What do you want? I told you I have no more money."

"I'm sure you could get more, missus. I'll be staying in the park down the road, and I'll expect to see you tomorrow when it's dark with twice this much," he said as he held up the notes.

"That is blackmail! What would your father have to say to that?"

"I spect Pa would understand that me little ones means more to me than me conscience. You'd best be there, missus," he said, as he turned and left.

Gladys felt as though she had been kicked in the stomach. Her legs were shaking as she went into the house and sat down to think. She knew it wasn't Mr O's fault, and she certainly could not blame Sally for giving her the pin, but now she almost wished she had not helped Mr O when he came to the inn looking for Ellie. She had come so far since running away from the slums, and now she might lose everything. She knew that even if she could get her hands on more money, Rod would be back for more every time his children were hungry. Not that she could blame him. For Rod, finding her was like finding the pot of gold at the end of a rainbow.

Once Gladys became mistress of Oaken Arms, she could afford to give him money from time to time, but that wasn't about to happen for a while yet, and he had made it clear that he wanted money the next evening. If he did as he threatened, and went to the police, she would be thrown in jail or even hung, and chances were that Dolly might be sent to an orphanage. The cook at Scots Inn had lived next to one of the orphanages and she told Gladys how helpless she had felt when she saw the gaunt and sad little faces peering out of the barred windows.

After she put Dolly to bed, she went to the kitchen and without thinking, pulled out the cutlery drawer and stood staring at the largest and sharpest knife she had. She tried to envision the knife in her hand as she stabbed poor Rob. It was the same hand that held the pillow over Millie's face. She slammed the drawer shut, made a pot of tea and sat at the kitchen table throughout the night.

Somehow she managed to get through the next day while keeping up a cheerful front for Dolly's sake, but once she had her tucked into bed and was sure she was sound asleep, she put on her cloak, took the knife from the drawer and left the house. On the walk to the park she tried to convince herself that what she was about to do was justifiable. She reasoned that she had just as much right to fight for her child as Rod did for his. Gladys also knew that if she were caught it would make no difference whether she had murdered one or three. She could only be hung once. As she entered the park, Rod stepped out from behind a tree. "Here I am, missus. Have you got me money?" he asked.

Gladys answered, "Right here." As she came closer to him, she was about to draw the knife when he said, "I'm really sorry I has to do this, honest I am. But me little kiddies are that hungry, they won't last more'n a week."

For an instant, Gladys could picture Rod's starving children, sitting in a dark, cold room, waiting for their da to return with something for them to eat. Even after all the years she had lived on the outside, she still recalled how horrible that feeling was, so she kept the knife hidden and said, "Rod, I am sorry. I really do not have any more money. I suppose you will just have to believe me, or turn me over to the law."

"That wouldn't help me little ones none, missus. I won't give you away; don't worry none about that. We'll just have to make do with what you gived us an' hope things get a lot better."

Gladys said she wished there was something she could do, and they said goodbye; but as she was walking away, she had an idea and called out to him. When he came back she said, "How would you like to get your family out of Old Nichol?"

The next day she went to see Andrew. "Andrew, I want to talk to you!" she said as she walked into his office.

"Well, good afternoon to you too."

"Oh, I am sorry. It is just that I wanted to talk to you about something so important it could not wait."

Andrew's chest tightened. He was afraid she was going to tell him that she had decided to marry the preacher. "Go on then, what is it?"

"Did you really mean what you said about helping some of those poor people living in the London slums?"

"Of course, I did. I am not in the habit of saying things I do not mean," he answered with relief.

Gladys told him she had met a beggar in the park, and he told her a sad story about his children starving to death. She said she insisted to giving him money even though he tried to refuse it, saying he wasn't a beggar, but was looking for work. She also said that if they could find him employment, he could take his family out of Old Nichol and save their lives.

"That is a brilliant idea, Gladys. You know, the last time I was talking to Cedric he said that Charlie, his stable boy, was in his seventies and the job was becoming too much for him. I wonder if this poor chap knows anything about horses."

"Why it's odd that you should say that, because I remember him saying he was fond of all animals, and he even said he wanted to work on a farm, but he was afraid to apply for a job looking as shabby as he does," Gladys replied.

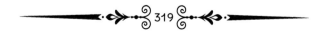

"Well then we shall have to clean the fellow up before taking him out to Sorensons."

They left immediately for the park where Rod was waiting. Andrew was appalled when he saw the sorry state the poor fellow was in, but the Rod they took to meet Lord Cedric the following day looked nothing like the man they had met in the park.

Rod and Charlie the stable boy got along very well, and when Andrew took Gladys and Dolly to visit the Sorensons a month later, she was delighted to see Rod had moved his family into one of the outbuildings close to the stables. Poor Rod had three children when he left Old Nichol with Gladys's cameo, but when he returned to get them, one had succumbed to starvation and the two who survived, a boy of eleven and a girl of seven, were in very poor condition, as was his wife, Emilene.

Although it had only been a few weeks since they had left Old Nichol, their eyes were bright and they were smiling—an expression rarely seen on their faces before they came to Sorenson Hall. Charlie's wife, Nora, having no children of her own, had taken the O'Brians under her wing, like a broody hen with motherless chicks.

Chapter Twenty-Six

Rod O'Brian and his family were the first of four families Andrew and his benevolent friends brought to Dover from the ghetto known as Old Nichol. Rod was doing well working as a stableman for Lord Sorenson, and Andrew, being acquainted with most of the ship's captains, was able to find jobs on a ship for two more of the men. The fourth found employment in the brewery. Only one family had been brought to Dover at a time, since it took a great deal of effort to get them settled. Accommodation had to be found and help needed to aid them in adjusting to a different lifestyle—a style far better in most regards than what they were accustomed to.

The only negative aspect they had to contend with was that they now lived in a world where people were pigeonholed into separate classes, and, unfortunately, the class they were in was one of the lowest. In the ghetto some were more destitute than others, but they all enjoyed the same rank, thus were free to openly express their opinions. Now they were obliged to forfeit that privilege and live a life of servitude. As Rod so aptly put it, "Mind you, I'd not want to go back there, but as bad as it were, there's lots I still misses 'bout it!"

Even though Rod's presence in Dover posed a certain threat to Gladys, she didn't worry about it. She knew how thankful he was and trusted him to keep her true identity a secret. On their arrival in Dover, the families were taken directly to an outbuilding on Lord Sorenson's estate where delousing remedies and tubs of hot water awaited them. Helping rid the families of lice and grime was a heart-wrenching chore for the volunteers, but even worse for the frightened victims who had to suffer the embarrassment of stripping down and exposing their naked, skeletal bodies—most covered in ugly sores. Fortunately, Jim Thornberry, a local doctor and humanitarian, not only donated his services, but also supplied the medications needed, along with soothing salves and creams.

Andrew, Randolph Mansfield, Lord Cedric, and Hugh Mason managed to see to the grooming and clothing of the men and the boys. Hugh was happy to be of help, considering it a practicum for his upcoming missionary work. Gladys, Mrs Grimsby, and Priscilla Mulberry, the girl who had looked after Millie, took care of the ladies, girls, and infants. By the time Gladys had settled Millie's accounts and paid for her funeral, there was little left of value except bolts of material and a few pieces of furniture. She gave the furniture to Rod, and she and Priscilla used some of the material to make frocks for the females.

Gladys knew what to expect when she and the other two women bathed the young girls, but she pretended to be just as shocked to see how emaciated they were. It brought back so many bad memories of when she was a little girl, although, in comparison, she had fared much better, thanks to her friend Sally.

Gladys found Priscilla was pleasant company and someone she hoped would eventually take Millie's place as a confidant, so when Andrew offered to hire her as a nanny, Gladys agreed. "If you find you get along well with her, perhaps she can move in with us at Oaken Arms," he suggested. Surprisingly, Gladys was not that taken with the idea. Puzzled, he asked, "I thought you were becoming quite fond of her."

"I am, but she has had no formal education, and shouldn't a

nanny, or governess, be able to teach her ward as well as care for her?"

"Of course, you are right. So she should. Well then, perhaps you could train her to be your lady's maid."

"That's a wonderful idea. Do you suppose she could stay with me until we move? That way I could have her trained by then, and she could help me around the house and look after Dolly whenever I need her."

Andrew knew this would mean Gladys could spend more time with Hugh Mason without having to ask him to stay with Dolly, but he couldn't think of a good excuse to refuse and so he agreed.

As Christmas drew near, Gladys appreciated Priscilla's help. The girl not only helped with the housework, but she looked after Dolly while Gladys went about town with Hugh and their friends, carolling and wassailing. Wassailing had begun in England in the 1400s, when a group of well-wishers went from door to door with a wassail bowl full of hot spiced ale. After they passed the wassail around, they were rewarded with drink, money for the poor, and Christmas goodies, all gladly given since it was believed to bring them good luck in the New Year. As they went from house to house, they sang the wassailing song.

The day before Christmas, Andrew, Gladys, Dolly, and Priscilla went to Oaken Arms to look for a Christmas tree. It was a cloudy day, and as they were tramping through the woods, it began to snow, adding a festive ambience to the scenery. Gladys remembered Sally describing what a forest looked like to Toughie and her, but even though she had a lively imagination, the forest she pictured was no-where as lovely and mystical as the one she was walking through this day.

When Dolly pointed to a tall, bushy fir tree, Andrew laughed and said it would never fit into their parlour. A few minutes later he spotted a little Scots Pine and, tapping her on the shoulder, said, "Look over there, my little turtle dove. See that poor little tree? It looks so sad."

"Why is it sad, Gamby?"

"Well, you see, it is quite an honour to be chosen as a Christmas tree, and most people choose only the great big ones, so that poor little fellow is probably sad because no one will pick him."

Dolly, taking the story to heart, ran up to the tree and exclaimed, "I think you are the most beautiful tree in the whole forest, and I would love to have you for my Christmas tree." After Andrew cut down their tree, Priscilla was delighted when they found a small one for her to take home. Gladys had insisted the girl take a few days off over the holiday to be with her parents. Andrew cut boughs off some of the other evergreens and they all returned to the buggy with arms full of greenery. Everyone had rosy cheeks and high spirits as they climbed in and pulled the fur rugs over their knees. Andrew had attached bells to the horses' harnesses, and as they were riding home, the lively jingle brought on a chorus or two of a Christmas carol. The pungent smell of the pine and the other greenery lying at their feet, along with the soft, white flakes of snow falling on the horses' backs, left them all with a memory to treasure.

Once the tree was set up in the parlour, Dolly was allowed to stay up past her bedtime to help decorate it. She had worked very hard helping her mother and her grandfather make the decorations, and Gladys thought it only fair to allow her to take part in putting them on the tree. They used dozens of candles, dried fruit, and walnuts that looked like little mice after they glued on tails and ears made from leather. These they hung on the tree in little cradles that Gladys crocheted. They made dainty little cone shaped containers made from old greeting cards that Gladys filled with delicious sugar plums.

Andrew had bought some very dainty and intricate pieces of miniature furniture to hang on the tree as well. This seemed odd to Gladys, but never having a tree before, she thought he must know more about decorations than she did, and Dolly was delighted with them. Unbeknownst to Gladys and Dolly, Andrew had purchased the furniture to fit a dollhouse that he intended to give to Dolly on Christmas morning. It was even more special because it was made in the likeness of Oaken Arms by a talented craftsman Andrew knew.

The gift he bought for Gladys was a pretty glass ball containing winter scenery that she had seen and admired in a jewellery store window. He hoped it would remind her of their visit to the Great

Exhibition since she had mentioned it when they were there.

They had never exchanged gifts before, but this year seemed special. Gladys made a silk shirt with ruffles and intended to give it to Andrew from both her and Dolly, but Dolly was determined to buy her own presents and begged to go shopping. Their shopping trip took most of a day. Nothing she saw seemed to suit her, and Gladys was just about to lose patience when Dolly exclaimed. "Oh, look, Mama, look at that pin. It's a dove. I must buy that for Gamby, so he can think of me whenever he wears it."

The tiny silver dove was on a stick pin and had a little diamond eye. The pin was stuck in a cravat that was on display in a tailor shop window. The cost was more than Dolly had saved, but when the tailor saw how desperately she wanted it, he reduced the price and even gave her the cravat to go with it.

Andrew also took Dolly shopping, and they spent the entire day going from store to store enjoying the decorations and the crowds. They had dainty sandwiches and fancy cakes in a small tea shop and then had their tea leaves read by a plump, blonde-haired, fair-skinned lady whose gypsy-styled costume looked comically out of character. Uncannily though, she did predict that they would soon be moving.

It was a wonderful day for them both, and after Dolly found some lovely pearl earrings for her mother, Andrew asked, "And what do you want Father Christmas to bring you, my little turtle dove?"

"I shall like anything he brings me, Gamby. A book, or a frock, or even an umbrella! I expect it would be nice to have an umbrella of my very own. But I am far more excited about what I am giving you and Mama. You will never, ever, guess what I have for you. It is simply the best present ever, and you are going to be so happy when you see it." Andrew laughed then lifted her up and hugged her so hard, she cried, "Gamby, you're squishing me."

Putting a tree in the house at Christmas was a fairly new custom in England, but putting greenery about during the Yuletide was an ancient tradition. Gladys and Dolly had never had either before, but Millie had always hung as many boughs and holly around her house as she could afford to buy. In Old Nichol, nobody could afford such frivolity, nor was there easy access to unclaimed greenery, so Gladys was not in the habit of following these traditions, until Andrew intervened. Andrew had cut so many branches for them that the house was filled with greenery. As Dolly described it, "Every time I come inside, it's just like going outside."

After Dolly hung her stocking on the mantle and Andrew read her the poem, "'Twas the Night before Christmas," she went to bed and fell asleep in minutes. Gladys tried to convince Andrew to stay the night, offering to move Dolly in with her so he could have her bed. She said it would be nice if he was there to see Dolly have her stocking in the morning. Finally, he agreed, but said he had to take care of his horse and buggy first and would return as soon as he could.

He told Gladys to give him her key and to go to bed after promising to lock the door before he retired. This way he was able to return home to pick up the dollhouse and Gladys's present before taking his horse and rig back to Bob Hennessey's along with a big ham and some candy for Bob's little ones. Bob, in turn, not only delivered Andrew and his presents to Gladys's, but helped him place the dollhouse beside the tree. Before taking his leave, he and Andrew enjoyed a generous glass of whiskey and toasted one another for a very merry Christmas.

Andrew didn't get much sleep—the bed was far too short, and besides, he was so excited thinking about what Dolly would say when she saw the dollhouse, that his eyes refused to stay closed. Worried she might not like it, he cursed himself for not talking it over with Gladys before he had it made.

He needn't have worried. Dolly was so pleased with it that she jumped up and down and screeched with joy—an unusual show of emotion for her. The gentleman who made the dollhouse had never made one so large and detailed. It measured four feet in height and about the same in width with a depth of eighteen inches. The front of the house opened to allow a view of the entire three floors. It also had two big bay windows and a balcony on both the second and third floor. "Oh, Gamby, it looks just like Oaken Arms!" Dolly cried.

"Now how do you suppose Father Christmas managed such a thing?" he said laughing. Dolly suspected that her grandfather was the one who had bought the dollhouse, but because Gamby and her mother seemed to enjoy pretending, she didn't want to spoil their fun. After opening their gifts, they had a hurried breakfast, then left for church. Andrew even consented to go with them. "Just don't be surprised if your God strikes me dead when he sees me there," he warned. After church, they were invited to Sorenson Hall for Christmas dinner and the evening. Hugh had been invited as well, but because he had to attend the evening church service, he wasn't expected to arrive in time for dinner.

Not surprisingly, the Sorenson children were allowed to choose their own Christmas tree. As a result, the fir they chose was so tall that the only place it could stand upright was in the ballroom. It was a beautiful deep green colour, but because there were quite a few bare spaces, Lord Cedric found it necessary to have his handyman drill a few holes and add more branches. No one seemed to notice that the added branches were not from the same species of tree, but many remarked on its pleasant and unusual fragrance. As for the decorations, with the aid of a ladder, the handyman had managed to hang ornaments on the highest branches and tie a star to the top, but most of the decorations on the tree were only as high as the children could reach.

There was also a decorated tree in the servant's hall. As was the custom in the Sorenson home, the servants were allowed to invite their families to join them for Christmas dinner and the evening. Of course, their celebrations didn't begin until the Sorensons and their guests finished their meal and retired to the ballroom. Although the servants were expected to work longer hours during the holiday, they were always left with enough energy at the end of the day to celebrate. Having more than a few musicians among them, it seemed as though they were all born knowing how to sing and dance. At times, their lively music was so loud that it could be heard over the music played in the ballroom by the musicians hired by Lord Sorenson.

Fifty guests, plus Lord and Lady Sorenson and their three children, sat down to Christmas dinner in the large and ornate dining room. They began the meal with a serving of raw oysters followed by bowls of clear turtle soup. There were roasted turkeys and geese, and legs of tender lamb, roasts of beef with all the trimmings including caramel coloured gravy, horseradish, applesauce, and cranberries. There were vegetables of every kind: potatoes cooked with sprigs of aromatic mint leaves, beetroot cut into little cubes and dotted with butter, deep yellow coloured squash mashed and seasoned, and carrots, all set out in the Sorenson's best English china. At each place setting there was a fancy wrapped keepsake, and displayed on a small table were a number of small gifts of gratitude for the Sorenson family from their guests.

After all the courses, a delectable assortment of pies, puddings, cakes, and tarts was brought out, along with various cordials. When everyone had eaten until they could hold no more, and all the toasts had been made, it was time to retire to the ballroom where the musicians were waiting to start playing for the dance.

For the first hour, the children enjoyed taking part, although they did more hopping about than dancing. They soon tired and began to act silly, falling down and bumping into people, so Lady Madeline sent for their nanny, who, after allowing the children to shake hands with all the guests and bid them a very Merry Christmas, marched them off to bed. Dolly was invited to spend the night with the children and only agreed to stay after Gladys promised to come for her early the following day. Dolly was anxious to start playing with her new dollhouse.

Andrew was an experienced dancer and danced with most of the ladies, but it was Gladys he preferred as a partner. Hugh arrived just as the dancing began, but the poor fellow had never danced before and wasn't even sure he approved of it, so he just sat on the side-lines looking on with a mixture of distaste and envy. Gladys was amazed at her father-in-law's dancing skills, and when the last dance was over, she gave him a hug and said, "I could dance with you all night long." Andrew, reluctant to remove his arm from around her waist, leaned over and kissed her on the cheek then replied, "Maybe we will do that some time, *ma cherie!*"

"Why Andrew, I think you've had a little too many of Lord Cedric's hot toddies," she replied with a laugh. Pulling his head down, she gave him a kiss on his forehead, and left to find Hugh.

As soon as Hugh saw her approaching, his mood changed, and he greeted her warmly and asked, "Gladys, my dear, I wonder if Andrew would mind if I took you home. I haven't spent much time alone with you tonight, and I thought it would be nice if we could ride home together?"

"I am sorry if I have neglected you, Hugh, but I have not danced in ever so long. I am certain he will not object."

Andrew wanted very much to object, but he didn't; and a short time later, Gladys and Hugh were sitting snuggly in a buggy with a blanket covering their knees. Although it wasn't snowing, it was chilly, and the full moon shining down on the frosty road made it seem as though they were riding along on a magical carpet sprinkled with sparkling diamonds. It was clearly a night made for romance, so Gladys was pleased when Hugh, who had never made any advances toward her before, put his arm around her, and said, "Isn't this a beautiful night?" She nodded, laying her head on his shoulder. "But it is not nearly as beautiful as you," he added as he pulled the buggy off to the side of the road and kissed her.

Gladys thought it was nice, but more like a kiss one would expect to receive from a brother or one's father. Nevertheless, since it was their first, she thought the second one might be more passionate. Instead of a kiss, Hugh surprised her by taking both her hands in his and saying, "Gladys, you know how I feel about you, and I know you are aware that I plan to take a wife with me when I leave at the end of April."

Gladys had known for some time that this might happen, but she had selfishly thought only of her own pleasure and not what she would say when it did. She gave a weak smile and said, "My goodness, Hugh, was that a proposal?"

"Yes, but I am afraid I did it rather clumsily, didn't I? But then I have never proposed before. Oh, dear that sounded foolish too. I should have gotten down on bended knee. I am sorry, Gladys, but I do love you, and I want to share the rest of my life with you."

"But I—" Hugh stopped her by putting a finger over her lips, "I know what you are going to say, Gladys, but you need not worry. Even mother thinks you shall make a fine minister's wife, and she can give you a lot of good advice."

Gladys started to tell him that she needed a bit more time to think about it, but he interrupted again, "Oh, my darling, close your eyes and picture us on board the ship with our Bibles in our hands and our hearts full of love. What joy we shall bring to those poor souls that are living in ignorance and sin. Oh, dear God, I don't deserve to be so happy. Let us pray!"

Then, without pausing, he began, "Oh, Lord in Heaven, thank you for the love this wonderful woman and I share. Grant us the strength and the faith to stand firm in our convictions in the face of whatever iniquities await us. Dear Lord, we humbly ask for your blessing in our upcoming union. Look down on us now on this the most blessed time of the year and give us—"

"Stop! Stop!" Gladys shouted as she pulled her hands away.

"What is it Gladys? Are you ill?"

"No, Hugh, I am not ill! I am angry. You didn't even wait for an answer before you began asking God to bless our union. What union? I have not even agreed to marry you."

Suddenly, Hugh realized how impetuous he had been and apologized. "Perhaps I did get a little overzealous. It is just that we don't have much time. There is the wedding to plan, your passage to arrange, and so many other things we shall have to see to."

Gladys knew she could no longer continue to delude herself. If she ever had any serious thoughts about marrying Hugh, they were destroyed by his weak proposal and his ill-timed prayer. She liked Hugh, but she could never love him.

"Hugh, listen to me. I am really sorry, but I do not love you. The answer is no."

"What do you mean, 'No'?"

"I mean no, Hugh; I cannot marry you."

"How can you say that? We have been keeping company for months now. You cannot do this to me, Gladys! I have made all these plans for us."

"That is just it, Hugh. You have made all the plans, not I. You have never even mentioned getting engaged before, let alone married. I am so sorry, really I am, but there is nothing more to say. Now please take me home."

Hugh felt devastated. Gladys was such a vital part of the future he had envisioned, and now to find out that she was just dallying with his emotions was more than he could bear. For the first time in his structured and passive life, he was overtaken with anger, an unfamiliar emotion that helped ease his disappointment. In a voice as loud as he often used in his sermons, he declared, "Maybe you have nothing more to say, but I do!"

And talk he did. By the time he had finished, Gladys fully realized the damage she had done with her selfish flirtation. Never had she felt such shame and guilt. She tried to offer an apology, but Hugh didn't listen. When he was through talking, his jaws clamped tight and, without another word, he took her home and didn't even offer to help her down from the buggy. There were tears running down her cheeks as she stood and watched his buggy until it was out of sight. She had never intentionally hurt anyone before. She knew what it felt like to suffer a broken heart. She was heart-broken when she left Old Nichol knowing that she would never see Toughie again, and her heart broke once more when Tom was killed. Now she had caused poor Hugh, who had treated her like a princess, to go through the same agony. She looked up at the stars and prayed, "Please, God, help poor Hugh find someone more worthy of him, and I promise I shall never hurt anyone again."

Chapter Twenty Seven

By the middle of January, Oaken Arms was nearing comple-
tion, and Andrew thought they might be able to move in by March.
One day, he and Gladys were there deciding what furnishings they
would need. Although it was raining, the unfinished conservatory was lovely and bright. As they sat on boxes enjoying a cup of tea,
Andrew looked at his daughter-in-law and thought how happy she
looked. He was still worried that if Hugh Mason proposed to her she
might accept. He knew she must feel lonely without Tom, and how
tempting it must seem for her to marry a virile, young man and set
forth on an adventurous journey.

Knowing how disappointed she had been when they had to
cancel their trip to India, he intended to take her and Dolly there as
soon as they were settled into their new home. They could make it
a pilgrimage in honour of Tom, but first he intended to broach the
subject of Gladys's relationship with Hugh, hoping it hadn't become
too serious.

As the recently elected president of Dover's newly formed

Chamber of Commerce, Andrew had been so busy that he hadn't had time to visit with Gladys for a while and was unaware the courtship had ended. "How are things with you and that young man of yours?" he asked, doing his best to sound casual. "I suppose it won't be many months now before he leaves for the Colonies."

A refreshing wave of relief came over him when she answered, "He's not my young man anymore. It ended on Christmas night, and I am sorry to say that it did not end very well." Then she related what had happened and how she had gone to church the following Sunday and been slighted by most of the congregation. Her voice broke as she said, "Even Hugh's mother and father were not that friendly. Hugh left when I came into the church and did not come back for the rest of the service. It was so embarrassing, Andrew, that I wanted to die. I didn't look up, but I could feel everyone's eyes on me. I haven't gone back since, and I really miss singing with the choir."

"Give it time, my dear, they shall soon find out how much they need you and will beg you to return."

"That is precisely what they will have to do if they want me back."

"That's my girl! Wait until we move into Oaken Arms. They shall all want to be your best friend then. No one else hereabouts has such a stately home. Speaking of stately homes, Oaken Arms brings a poem of Felicia Hemans's to mind:

"The stately Homes of England,
How beautiful they stand!
Amidst their tall ancestral trees,
O'er all the pleasant land.
The deer across their greensward bound
Thro' shade and sunny gleam,
And the swan glides past them with the sound
Of some rejoicing stream.
The merry Homes of England!
Around their hearths by night,
What gladsome looks of household love
Meet in the ruddy light!
There woman's voice flows forth in song,

Or childhood's tale is told,
Or lips move tunefully along
Some glorious page of old."

"There are more verses, but I thought those two the most appropriate, especially the line, 'There woman's voice flows forth in song.'"

"It is a wonderful poem, and I promise you, my voice shall be heard throughout the entire house." That day proved to be one of the happiest days of Andrew's life.

When Priscilla learned that Hugh was no longer courting Gladys, she was as pleased as Andrew. She had fallen in love with the young minister the first time she laid eyes on him, but she knew she couldn't compete with a woman as beautiful as Gladys. Now determined to make him notice her, she began taking added care with her appearance and dressing in more becoming attire. She offered flattering remarks about Hugh's sermons, taught Sunday school, and attended all the evening prayer meetings, hoping to impress him with her dedication.

No matter how much Priscilla strived to be attractive, she always felt plain and dowdy whenever she was in Gladys's company, a feeling she couldn't escape as long as they lived under the same roof. After a time, she decided to move back in with her parents, giving Gladys the excuse that she was needed at home. However, just in case Hugh might choose to marry someone else, she left saying that when her folks no longer needed her, she would be happy to return.

Andrew rode his horse into the Sorensons' driveway one day just as a smartly dressed, middle-aged man came out of the stables and greeted him with a warm smile and a wave of his hand as he made his way to the manor. As Andrew dismounted, Rod came out of the stable and rushed over to take his horse.

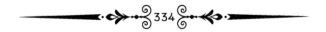

"Thank you," Andrew said pleasantly. It still amazed Rod that esteemed men like Lord Cedric and Andrew would speak to him in such a familiar and kindly manner. He grinned from ear to ear as he took the horse's reins and asked, "Would you likes me to unsaddle 'im, Mr Andrew, sir?"

"I don't think so, Rod. I see his lordship has company and I do not want to intrude. I shall only be staying for about a half hour."

"Just calls out when you're ready, and I'll have him here."

Cedric came out to greet Andrew, but instead of taking him directly to the house, he led him towards the duck pond. "I want to have a chat with you, Andrew, before we go in," he announced.

"My, this sounds mysterious. Nothing wrong, is there?"

"Well, you might think so when I tell you about my guest."

"Ah yes, he gave me a wave as he came out of the stable—appeared to be a decent sort of chap—an old friend?"

"He was, and in a sense still is. He comes from a wealthy family. Nice folks as I recall. His name is Richard Ledingham, and he has had a decent education. We both played on the same cricket team about fifteen years ago. That was before he started gambling. Along with the cards and dice, he's also a compulsive turfer. Bets on any horse that can stand, let alone run. His family supported his habit for quite a few years, but before he managed to deplete their entire fortune, his brother put a stop to it by having their parents put their estate and holdings in his name. Richard would have found himself in debtor's prison if he had not met the Duchess de Artois, a wealthy French widow. After they were married, she managed to obtain a title for him as well. I met her once; a gracious lady, but a good twenty years his senior. A few years after they married, she became seriously ill and passed away."

They were standing under an apple tree and Andrew bent down to pick up an apple that was lying on the ground.

"Here, don't take that one. We leave the windfalls on the ground for the animals. I shall have one of the handymen pick a sack of them off the tree for you to take home, and you can share them with Gladys and Dolly."

"Thank you, Cedric. I'm sure they will appreciate it, but please, continue. I am anxious to hear what happened to Richard after he lost his wife."

"Well, I don't think he was the least bit broken hearted. Mind you, when she was alive, Richard treated the Duchess well. He's not a bad chap really, just has this deucedly bad habit. Actually, it was a blessing she passed on before she discovered he had borrowed so much money on their estate that he has put it in jeopardy. Poor fellow is in debt over his head, and as a last resort, he is going about the country looking up all his old friends trying to borrow enough to bail him out. It seems I was his last hope. I cannot tell you how sorry I was to turn him down. You see, I have lent him money in the past, which proved to be a mistake. I will say this for him though, he took my refusal like a gentleman. Nevertheless, I suspect he is desperate enough to approach whoever he meets with a good story, so beware. But now it is time for you to meet the Duc de Artois."

After being in Richard's company for a half an hour, Andrew found it difficult to believe he had any bad habits. The man was one of the most likable characters he had ever met. Although he was in his late fifties, his countenance still retained an enviable youthful glow, and he had a full head of naturally wavy hair that added to his handsome features. It was easy to see why the Duchess had been smitten. He spoke knowledgably, but not arrogantly, on most topics, and Andrew enjoyed his company so much that his half hour visit continued for two hours. As he was saying his goodbyes, Richard asked if he could drop in to see him the following day, as he was curious to know more about the shipping business. Although Lord Cedric scowled warningly, Andrew couldn't resist consenting.

On the ride home, Andrew thought about what he would say if Richard did ask him for a loan. He could certainly use Oaken Arms as an excuse for a refusal. God knows it was costing enough. But he felt deeply sorry for the fellow and imagining such a vibrant character incarcerated for the rest of his life was depressing. If only he could help him, but, besides Oaken Arms, he was going to have a fair amount of expense settling with Rose and her children. He was almost home when he was struck by an idea that might be a solution to not only Richard's problem, but his own as well.

Rose was taken by surprise the following Sunday in church when a handsome stranger smiled at her across the aisle. She and her children had returned to their pew when Gladys had ceased to attend after her experience with Hugh. Confident that it was a flirtatious smile, she bent her head and returned it with a shy, but coy glance. She was even more flattered when he approached her after the service and said, "Please forgive my boldness, dear lady, but I must say that your beauty distracted me so, I heard very little of the good reverend's sermon." Rose had no idea what she said in return, but it seemed to have pleased the man because he placed his hand under her elbow and offered, "May I escort you to your carriage, or is your husband about?"

It had been so many years since Rose had met a man sensitive enough to display any appreciation towards her appearance that she found herself stammering, "Mm, my husband? I, I, have no husband. Er, I mean, I do have one, but, but he and I, well, we are not together you see."

"How splendid, if you will forgive my forthrightness. Please allow me to introduce myself." He then took off his high hat, swung it across his stomach and announced, "The Duc de Artois, at your service. And, beautiful lady, to whom am I addressing?"

"Rose. Rose Pickwick," she blurted out clumsily.

"Ah, a lovely name to be sure. But I see your cab has arrived. May I send him on his way and have the pleasure of your company in my own buggy?"

Giggling like a school girl, Rose answered, "Oh my goodness! What will people think?"

"They shall think how fortunate I am, to be the escort of such an angel."

"Really, Mr er, I mean, Duc."

"Richard will suffice. You see, my dear departed wife, whom I owe my title to, was the Duchess de Artois. I recently grew weary of the responsibilities that go with the title, and decided to take a holiday incognito. Now, my dear, may I pay the cab driver and dismiss him?"

When they arrived at Rose's home, Richard helped her out of

the carriage and saw her to the door. Then, before taking his leave, he asked if he could call on her the following evening. Rose hesitated, saying, "Although I do not live with Mr Pickwick, I am still married to him, and I am not sure it would be considered proper."

"Surely he would not object to you having gentlemen friends as well as lady friends," Richard protested.

Quickly changing her mind, Rose answered, "And even if Mr Pickwick does object, he has no right to judge me. Especially considering how he flaunts his daughter-in-law about town. It's downright shameful," she shared haughtily.

"A man who would leave such a treasure as you, my dear, is indeed an idiot, and a cad, but let us not spoil our first encounter by discussing your estranged husband. I shall call on you around seven. *Bonne nuit, mon amour*," he uttered, kissing her hand once more.

Rose's heart had never beaten so hard. To experience feelings of sexual desire at her age seemed like a miracle. Her face took on a renewed beauty that even surprised and pleased Richard. As he made his way back to the Sorensons', he began to think that the pact he had made with Andrew might not be as distasteful as it seemed when he first set eyes on Rose.

Richard had exhausted all his potential money lending sources and had almost given up hope of escaping debtor's prison when Andrew came up with a solution. Although a thousand pounds was not enough to satisfy his debtors, it would pay his fare to the Colonies, where he hoped to make a fortune. Lord Cedric had given him a wise bit of advice after refusing to lend him money. As a member of parliament, Cedric knew the Hudson Bay Company was looking for Englishmen to take up land in the recently established Vancouver Island Colony in Canada. There was concern over the amount of Americans showing interest in the area, and the governor wanted to ensure that the largest percent of the colonists were British.

To obtain land, one had only to pay one pound per acre and purchase a minimum of twenty acres. It was also advised that a man bring along five single men or three married couples to help work the land. Richard had no desire to become a farmer but planned on using the money that Andrew would pay him for bedding his wife to build a saloon and gambling establishment. He was convinced that it would not take long before he would be able to pay off his debts and return to his aristocratic life in France.

Of course there was a possibility that his reputation would suffer when he was named in the divorce proceedings, but it was a chance he had to take. Although he was anxious to receive the money and leave, he knew better than to rush the seduction. Such an act might cause Rose to become suspicious, and if he failed to assure Andrew that Rose had committed adultery, he would have no chance of escaping the law.

When Rose told Peter and Mildred about Richard, they were shocked. "How can you be so foolish, Mother?" Richard declared. "We agreed to keep a low profile until our man in London finished his investigation of that wife of Tom's, and here you are acting like a giddy goose over a fancy man. A man who is obviously nothing but a fortune hunter. What on earth is the matter with you?"

"He is not a fortune hunter. He is a Duke! And I cannot see what harm our relationship would do," Rose answered defensively.

"You surely do not believe he really is a Duke? Good Lord, what on earth would a Duke want with someone like you?" he said, then realized how offensive his words were and offered a half-hearted apology. "Er, I mean to say, why on earth would anyone with a title want to court a married woman?"

When Rose began to pout, Peter sent an exasperated glance toward his sister before taking his mother's hand, and adding, "Now, now, Mummy, you know that when that husband of yours moves into his mansion, he has no intention of taking us with him, and I do not think it shall be long before he signs the title of that estate over to that little monster of Tom's. The last time I heard from London, Mr Morgan was certain he was onto something and promised to have some very interesting news for us in a week's time, so until we have something we can use against that woman and her daughter, we do not want to stir up any gossip. If this Richard fellow wants to spend time with you, we shall not object as long as we are with you. Do you understand?"

This arrangement did not fit with Richard's plans, even though he soon won Mildred over with flattery, and impressed Peter by convincing him of his true identity and suggesting the young man accompany him when he returned to France to go hunting at his mountain chateau.

Lord Cedric arrived at Andrew's office one day nearly two weeks after he had introduced him to Richard. Once he was seated in one of the comfortable leather armchairs that Andrew kept in his office and had a glass of whiskey in his hand, he announced, "I say, Andrew, have you heard the rumours about my friend, the Duc, and that wife of yours?"

"You are referring to Richard, are you not?"

"Quite so! What in the blazes do you think the man is up to? Is the woman well off enough to settle his debts?"

"Rose? Not on the allowance I give her."

"Well, there is something going on. He has a way with the ladies and could take his pick, so if you pardon me, what in the devil is he doing with your wife?" Andrew just offered a shrug of his shoulders and Cedric continued, "The man's up to something, and I shall be damned if he is going to do it my town. I shall have a word with him. He is still staying with us, but I shall soon put an end to that."

Andrew rose from his chair, went to the window and looked down on the ships tied up to the wharf. It was a lively scene with sailors loading cargo, cleaning decks, and mending sails, but Andrew's mind was so preoccupied with thoughts of whether or not to tell his friend his plans, that he may just as well have been looking at a blank wall. Finally, he decided to make a clean breast of it. Returning to his chair, he took a good drink of whiskey then quickly confessed to his friend that he was paying Richard to seduce his wife in order to obtain grounds for a divorce.

Cedric, shocked, didn't take this news at all well. As soon as he recovered from his astonishment, he slammed his fist down on the desk knocking over the bottle of Irish whiskey, and barked, "Damn it, man, that is a dastardly bit of work. Why, it is as underhanded as

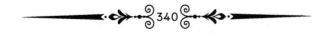

blackmail. Why on earth do you need a divorce? You must be aware that there are plenty of women in this town who would be happy to take care of your needs with no questions asked."

"It is not that simple, Cedric. You see, I want to get married again," Andrew responded quietly.

"That is out of the question. I do not believe in divorce. It shocks me to think that you would do something so devious."

"I can hardly believe it myself, but I am hopelessly in love with someone, and I don't know what else to do."

"My God, man, have you not heard of mistresses?"

"I could never ask her to degrade herself with such a title."

"Who is this woman who is causing you to act like a silly school boy?"

"It's Gladys, and before you go blaming her, she has no idea how I feel."

"Gladys! For God's sake, Andrew. Are you completely out of your mind? I have known you for years, and I never thought you could be such an ass. Gladys must be some sort of temptress."

"I tell you, she is completely innocent and may not even agree to marry me, but if she does, I want to be able to do it without delay."

Cedric tried his utmost to convince Andrew to change his plans but had no success. Finally, throwing his arms in the air, he declared, "Well then, do as you will, but understand this, I shall not condone such actions." Then, shaking his head, he added, "Because of our friendship, I shall do nothing to interfere, but I shall waste no time in evicting that scoundrel. And, Andrew, I warn you, do not count on my influence in the courts to support your case." With that, he walked out the door with his head down and a disturbed expression on his face.

Andrew felt as though he had shrunk a few inches. He didn't even know if Gladys would consider marrying him, and not only had he done something contrary to everything he stood for, but by doing it, he had lost the friendship of a man he had known and admired for years.

On Dolly's seventh birthday, Andrew gave her Tom's collection of books, and among them was Samuel Taylor Coleridge's longest poem, "The Rime of the Ancient Mariner." When she saw it, she begged him to read it to her, but he said it was too bleak a story for such a young girl, and far too lengthy. Dolly knew her grandfather was unable to say no to her for very long, and finally he gave in. From then on, every evening he visited, he read ten verses of what Dolly called "The Poor Old Sailor Story." His voice rose like thunder when he read the lines, "The ship drove fast, Loud roared the Blast, The southward aye we fled," then low and poignant with the words, "And now there came both mist and snow, and it grew wondrous cold: And ice, mast-high, came floating by, As green as emerald."

As she listened to the verses, Dolly could feel the cold wind touching her cheeks, and she felt as though she were part of that crew. Even Gladys waited eagerly for each verse.

He had nearly finished the poem one evening, when he announced that he had to go to Ireland the following morning and wouldn't read the last ten verses until he returned. No matter how much they coaxed him to finish, he refused, saying they would want him to return even more if they had the verses to look forward to.

Chapter Twenty Eight

Before he left for Ireland, Andrew rode to Bob Hennessey's to see if there was anything the blacksmith wanted to send his brother, Nolie. On the way he met Randolph Mansfield, his friend and solicitor, riding in the opposite direction. Nodding his head in greeting, Andrew was about to ride past when Randolph reined his horse to a stop and asked, "Are you going to be in your office this afternoon?"

"No, I am leaving for Ireland in a few hours. What was it you wanted?" Andrew replied.

"Well, I was wondering how things were progressing. Did you manage to find the right man?"

"Right man?" Then Andrew realized what Randolph was referring to. "Yes, yes, I did. It's not something I am proud of though, and I fear I've lost a dear friend by doing it. I have no time to tell you about it now, Randy, but as soon as I return I shall be in touch. Hopefully it will all be taken care of by then."

"Have a good trip."

Andrew nodded and rode on. When he arrived at the blacksmith's, Bob was working on the forge, and Andrew watched as the large, ruddy-faced Irishman pulled a red-hot horseshoe from the coals with a pair of tongs and plunged it into a bucket of water.

The sizzling noise the hot shoe made as it hit the water and the rising steam brought back pleasant memories for Andrew of the times he used to spend with his uncle, who had owned a blacksmith shop in Hastings. Every time Andrew saw a forge, his mouth watered for the taste of the kippers his uncle cooked for him over the hot coals. There were many good memories Andrew had of his childhood, but sitting on a bench eating kippers and listening to his uncle's stories, some quite ribald for such young ears, was one of his favourites.

When Bob finished hammering the shoe into shape, he smiled and greeted Andrew warmly. Andrew informed him that he was leaving shortly for Ireland and asked if there was anything Bob would like to send to his brother. "Sure and that's mighty good o' you, Sir, but it's too far out o' your way. I hate to put you out."

"It's no trouble; I usually have time on my hands before I return, and if you give me directions, I can borrow a horse and rig and it will give me something to do."

"Well, then, I'd be much obliged if you'd give him a letter I was goin' to post. I've put a little in it for him and God knows the poor sot needs it, and I've a bottle in the house that I'll go fetch. Sure and a nip o' whiskey will do him more good than a basket o' taters."

"Save your bottle, Bob. I have one packed in my bag, and I shall even stop and have a drink with him."

"God bless you! Sure an' you're a proper saint you are."

"Ha, I only wish I was. Well I shall miss my boat if I don't get along." Because he wanted it to be a surprise, Andrew didn't tell his friend that the real reason he wanted his brother Nolie's address was because he had made arrangements to bring him and his family back to Dover with him.

The Duc de Artois was becoming exceedingly frustrated. His

debtors were bound to catch up to him any day, and he had yet to bed Andrew's wife, Rose. Mildred and Peter made certain they were present each time he came to call, and he was hardly allowed to sit beside Rose, let alone make advances. Then, one day, Peter announced that he had to go to London and was hoping to return with good news. The evening after his departure, Richard came to visit, bringing along two bottles of sherry. His plan was to see that Mildred become so inebriated she would fall asleep, allowing him the opportunity to seduce her mother. Mildred, however, was not the epitome of innocence that Richard mistook her for and handled her liquor far better than either he or her mother.

He woke the next morning with a throbbing headache, but when he rolled over in bed and his nose came in contact with a soft white shoulder, he silently congratulated himself. Then the owner of the shoulder turned over and smiled at him. It was Mildred. Before he could utter a sound, she pulled his head down between her breasts.

"Oh, my lord," he mumbled between the two soft delights. Then lifting his head, he looked at the buxom young lady, and meekly inquired, "Your mother?"

"Don't concern yourself, dear Richard; she shan't be any the wiser. I doubt she'll be awake for hours yet, so you have plenty of time to seduce me again, and even again."

"What a dear girl you are!" Richard replied, and did just that.

Two days later, Peter returned. He practically spat out his news with excitement as he told them that, after an extensive search, and a good deal of expense, the private investigator had finally, earned his money. "It is just as I thought! She is not who she professes to be. She married Thomas under a false name. She is nothing but a gutter-snipe."

"Is he certain?" Rose asked.

"Almost, but it is up to me to find the last bit of proof we need."

"Oh dear, and how are you going to manage that?" Rose asked.

"A little visit to your step-daughter-in-law, Mother, that is all that is necessary," Peter replied with a smug look on his face, and keeping them in suspense, he refused to say more.

Mildred began to chuckle, then remarked, "When Andrew finds out he has an imposter for a daughter-in-law, it should not take him long to begin wondering who the father of her child really is," as Peter and Rose broke out in laughter.

No one noticed that Richard wasn't as happy with the news as they were. He was worried that when Andrew learned that his daughter-in-law was not who she professed to be, he might not want a divorce, and would cancel their arrangement. Then he reasoned that he may still have a chance to seduce Rose before Andrew found out, and because Andrew was known to be a man of his word, a bargain was a bargain. Peter interrupted his thoughts and solved his problem, saying "Now I think we should be very careful how we handle this. We should probably ask the advice of our solicitor before we begin. However, he always goes to London on the weekends, so I suppose we shall just have to wait until Monday. Mildred, what do you say to a night on the town? I should think we deserve to have a little celebration; don't you agree?"

"Why, I think that is a magnificent idea," Mildred answered, and with a devious smile and a cheeky wink at Richard, she added, "I should not think you and mother would object to having an evening to yourselves now, would you, Richard love?"

Andrew arrived in Dublin on the 5th of March 1852. He managed to settle his business the following day, and because he had to wait for two days before returning to Dover, he had plenty of time to rent a horse and buggy and take his time driving out to the countryside to see Bob Hennessey's brother. He was excited about his plans to surprise the family with the news that he intended to take them along when he returned to Dover. Before he left, he bought a large amount of food to give to the needy he might chance to meet on the road, and a few sandwiches for himself.

Although he was warned that there were gangs of desperate men in the area, and was advised to take along a companion, Andrew, who was very naïve about the dangers involved, preferred to trav-

el alone. Because a great many of the poor had left the country, he looked forward to seeing an improvement over the impoverishment he had witnessed in the past. During the previous year, the census commissioners had stated that they thought Ireland would benefit by the magnitude of starvations, deaths, and immigrations.

As cruel as the statement was, Andrew thought there might be some truth to it, since the immigration to other countries had risen significantly between 1845 to 1851. He surmised that there must now be more food available for those who were left, even though he had heard predictions that the number leaving Ireland was likely to reach 2,000,000 more in the next two or three years, and that was just those leaving for Australia and America. Another 750,000 were expected in England.

He began to believe those predictions as he rode through one village after another and witnessed what seemed to be as many poor souls as he had seen before. Dirty hands reached out from what appeared to be bundles of rags, instead of bodies. Most were too weak to utter a plea. It didn't take long before all the food was dispersed, and he was forced to avoid the towns.

The picturesque scenery with green rolling hills dotted with tidy, whitewashed, thatched-roof cottages and grazing animals was no more. Not a cow or woolly sheep could be seen. Some of the cottages remained, but they were dirty and vacant—occupants having been evicted by their landlords. Bob's brother, Nolie, was fortunate since his landlord had kept him on to help with the work, but he and his family were only given a one room hovel to live in and a small amount of food every day as a wage. It meant that they still had a roof over their heads and were starving to death much slower than most.

Around noon, Andrew came to an inviting stand of small trees beside a little brook. He reined his horse down a little trail to an open spot on the water's edge just a short distance off the road that allowed him plenty of privacy. He managed to find a grassy area for the horse to graze and a shady spot to enjoy his sandwiches along with a drink of clean, cold brook water. Spreading a lap throw onto the grass, he ate his lunch and settled down to enjoy the setting and the peaceful gurgling sound of the brook.

The sordid sights he had just witnessed soon faded as he remembered the Ireland he had visited with his first wife, Dorothy, when Tom was a just a child. They often visited Dorothy's mother, Miriam O'Neill, who lived in a cottage not far from Dublin on an estate owned by Lord Wiltshire. Dorothy's father, Thomas O'Neill, had been the Lord's gamekeeper since he was a young man, and the two had become good friends. Although they joked with each other and enjoyed a drink or two together now and then, Thomas always knew his place and never took advantage of their friendship. He treated his Lordship with as much reverence as did the other servants.

Dorothy was seven when her father went out in the woods one day and caught a poacher taking a rabbit out of a snare. Although Thomas was small in stature, he was a dedicated man and made the fatal mistake of trying to apprehend the thief—a man at least twice his size. The poacher could easily have knocked him down and run off, but he was a bully with a nasty disposition and in a fit of temper, he drew the knife he used to slit the throats of his prey and used it on Thomas. He was caught a few days later and took his last breath with a rope around his neck.

Lord Wiltshire took Thomas's death almost as hard as Dorothy's mother, and he gave her permission to remain in the little cottage for as long as she lived. He also met all her needs, and when Dorothy was fourteen, he was kind enough to send her to a school in England.

By the age of eighteen, she had found employment as the governess for two young girls, children of a wealthy family who treated her as though she was one of their own, even including her in some of their social outings. It was on one of these occasions that she met Andrew Pickwick, heir to one of Dover's shipping magnates. A year later they were married. Tom was their only child, and because Dorothy's mother refused to leave her beloved homeland, they took him to visit her at least twice a year. Although the old lady died when Tom was only six, Andrew knew the boy could describe every detail of the cottage she lived in. They would have gone back to visit Lord Wiltshire, but due to religious prejudice, he had moved to Northern

Ireland shortly after Dorothy's mother passed away.

The Wiltshires were Protestant but managed to live in harmony with their Catholic neighbours even after the Act of Union was passed in 1800, abolishing the independent Irish Parliament in Dublin. This brought the Irish administration under the British Parliament along with the ruling that only Irish Protestants were allowed to be members. For eight years, Lord Wiltshire and his family enjoyed neighbourly gatherings, but then a few new people moved into the neighbourhood, and when they learned that there was a wealthy Protestant and his family living in the area, they let their feelings of animosity and bitterness be known.

Before long, the newcomers even convinced many of the local folks that the Wiltshires were the enemy, even though his Lordship had always argued that the Act of Union was a bigoted act and should be abolished. Soon, his past good deeds were forgotten, and when he realized that even some of his own staff had begun showing signs of resentment toward him and his family, he was deeply hurt. The bigoted hatred toward them finally became so apparent that he feared for their lives, and although it broke his heart to do so, he sold his estate and moved to Belfast.

Now, as Andrew laid back and listened to the murmur of the creek, he daydreamed of bringing Gladys and Dolly to Ireland, and perhaps building a holiday house on a bit of Irish land with a view of the ocean. He could picture them sitting on a bench outside a thatched-roof cottage watching the boats sail by. Thinking of the two he loved so dearly, he took the little pin Dolly had given him from his ascot and kissed it. Then with a full stomach, and his pleasant reminisces of a better time in his mind, he held it tightly in his hand and dozed off.

There were four of them, one carrying a pitchfork and another with an empty burlap sack tied to his belt. All were barefoot and where the bank of the brook was too steep, they walked in the water.

"Here, Mick! Bring the fork. This here's one, I think."

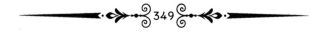

"Naw, Da. See the leaves don't look near like what Ma said. They's far too pointy."

"Tell him to dig it up anyhow, Da," the man called Rory said, "Might be the roots are good as the ones Ma was talking about. We have to bring somethin' home to put in the pot."

"Your Ma said she recalled finding them in the bank along here somewhere; just keep lookin'. We'll find them."

They continued with their hunt until the man called Sean turned and waved at the rest while holding his finger up to his lips. The old man they called "Pa" motioned for the other two to remain where they were while he moved silently forward to see what had drawn Sean's attention.

Andrew was snoring lightly, but as the two men crept closer, a pleasant dream caused him to chuckle. Startled, the men crouched down out of sight and waited. When Andrew began to snore again, they inched forward until Sean stopped, picked up a large boulder and motioned to his father who nodded his consent and waited until his son was standing over his prey. As though sensing danger, Andrew brought a hand up to his face, but the lad brought the boulder down hard before Andrew could open his eyes.

"I hope you didn't do him in, son. Call Mick and Rory while I look to see what he's got in the buggy." With that he walked over to where Andrew had tethered the horse and climbed up into the buggy. "Not much there we can use," he said as he was making his way back. Suddenly he started to run. "God no, don't!" he screamed, but he was too late. Andrew had been impaled with the pitchfork.

"May the saints forgive you, Mick! Ye've gone and murdered the bloke."

"An' ye've put some bloody big holes in that fine shirt he has on," Sean remarked.

Andrew woke to the sound of men arguing. He had the oddest feeling that there was an enormous weight pushing his entire body down into the earth. He tried to focus on his surroundings, but all he could see was some blurry shapes that appeared to be more like spirits than humans. Then, for a split second his vision cleared, and the scene before him caused his heart to ache with sympathy. A naked man, who looked more like a skeleton with nothing but a filthy layer of flesh stretched over his bones, his head, and most of his face, covered in a tangle of dirt-blackened, matted hair, was standing at his feet pulling on a pair of britches—britches that looked vaguely familiar.

Another man in the same emaciated condition nearby was removing the rag he wore for a shirt. Andrew thought he should get up and help them, but the weight was too heavy to allow it. He began to lose consciousness, and as his arm came up in protest it hit the pitchfork that was embedded in his chest. The sharp pain came and ended with Andrew's last breath.

"Jaysus Mick! Why did you go an' kill him? That knock on his knob would'a kept him out 'til we were long away."

"I could see he were a bloody Englishman, Da. Here's us starving and living in a dirt cave, and he's riding around our country like he owns it. What's he doin' here anyway? I'm not a bit sorry I did him in, Pa. When I stuck him, I did it fer my kiddies and fer Ma."

"I know, son. But, you'll hang for it if they catch you."

"Pa's right, Mick. What are we going to do now, Pa?" Sean asked.

"First off we're going to get something to eat. You, Rory, slit that mare's throat. There's enough meat there to feed all our families for a week."

"I'm not about to kill a good horse like that, by Jaysus."

"I'll do it myself then. I'll not go home empty handed this day."

It was Sunday morning and Richard was asleep in Rose's bed when he heard a knock on the door. Rose was snoring beside him, so he slipped out of bed, pulled on his britches, grabbed the rest of his attire and went to see who was calling, hoping to send them on their way and leave before the rest of the family awoke. When he opened the door and saw the caller was a constable, he was all set to go quietly, when the officer said, "Is this the home of Rose Pickwick?"

"Yes, sir, it is."

"Are you a relative of hers?"

"Just a close friend. Is there anything wrong, officer?"

"I'm afraid I have some distressing news."

"Oh dear, I shall see if she is awake. You had better come in," Richard said with a smile of relief as he let the officer in, before leaving to wake Rose.

Rose jumped out of bed with alarm when he told her what the constable had said. "Oh, no, don't let it be Peter or Mildred," she exclaimed as she ran to see if they were in their beds. Richard couldn't help but feel sorry for her, so he dutifully followed along carrying her robe, since she wasn't a pretty sight without her stays. Relieved to find her children safe and sound, Rose woke them and insisted they join her in the parlour to hear what the constable had to report. Her only other living sibling was a brother, Peter's namesake, who lived somewhere in Australia. She hadn't heard from him for many years and surmised the sad news had to do with him.

"It is my brother, Peter, is it not?" she asked the officer with dismay.

"No, Mrs Pickwick, I'm sorry to have to tell you, but it's your husband, Andrew Pickwick."

The constable mistook Rose's sigh of relief as an exclamation of shock, and he took her arm and led her to a nearby seat.

"How bad is it?" Peter inquired.

The constable shook his head. "I am sorry, sir, but by all accounts I can assure you that he did not suffer."

The officer then went on to relate what had happened. When Andrew didn't return that night with the rented buggy, the owner reported it to the police. The next morning a search party was sent out, and Andrew was found a few hours later.

Before the constable took his leave, he asked if they would like him to deliver the news to Mr Pickwick's daughter-in-law, Gladys Pickwick. Peter thanked him but said that it would be much easier for the poor woman if a member of the family was by her side when she was informed of the tragedy. He then assured the policeman that he would see to it in the next few hours.

Gladys always felt at loose ends on Sunday nights now that she no longer attended church. She and Dolly had finished washing up after their dinner when she had an idea. "Dolly, I think we should begin packing. Gamby said we would probably be able to move as soon as he returns. Now you can take these papers and carefully wrap all the pieces of furniture from your dollhouse and put them in the wooden box under your bed. I think I shall begin by packing my ornaments."

Dolly's eyes lit up. "I can hardly wait," she exclaimed. "As soon as we are in our house, Gamby is going to buy me my very own pony!" She took an armful of paper and went upstairs singing, "A pony, a pony, I'm going to have a pony; I shall brush him and ride him, and I shall never be lonely."

Gladys laughed as she went into the parlour to begin her packing. She took down the blue and grey turtle doves and held them against her breast. Memories of their wedding night came flooding back, and she whispered, "Oh, Tom, I miss you so very much." The thought of leaving the house they had been so happy in brought tears to her eyes, and she wondered if she would be as happy at Oaken Arms. She had loved helping Andrew plan and choose furnishings for all the rooms in their new mansion, but now that it was almost completed, she was surprised by the contradictory mixture of feelings she was having.

She knew that being the mistress of such a huge manor would entail a lot of responsibilities, and she feared that when Andrew saw how little she knew about the proper protocol for a lady of such a high station, he might begin to see her for what she really was. Down deep, Gladys also knew that Rose Pickwick was partially right when she said she would always be a sow's ear. Unfortunately, there was still a part of her that liked it that way.

As she wrapped a dainty china cup in a piece of linen, she told herself that once she actually moved into Oaken Arms, she was bound to feel like a lady, or as Rose put it, a silk purse. Then her thoughts were interrupted by a knock at the door.

"Andrew!" she said as she threw the door open. But the man standing there was not her father-in-law. He was a small dumpy, characterless looking fellow who held out a pudgy hand that was as soft and white as a lady's, and said, "I am Peter Pickwick."

His tone was so pompous, she almost laughed, but good manners prevailed, and she, reluctantly, offered her hand. Instead of shaking it, Peter grasped it firmly, turned it over and saw the scar on her palm. "Aha! Gladys Tunner, I believe."

Gladys snatched her hand back, her face turned deathly white, and she had to hang on to the door frame to prevent falling. "I have no idea what you are talking about," she stammered.

"Oh I believe you do. The Gladys Tweedhope you claimed to be died when she was a baby in a place called Old Nichol, but then you know all about that because you came from that same place."

"Even if I did, I cannot see what that has to do with you."

"Come now, even you must be aware that it is a crime to marry someone under a false identity."

Terrified, but trying not to show it, she asked, "I still cannot see that that is any of your business. What is it you want with me?"

"First off, I want you and that bastard of yours out of this town."

Dumbfounded, Gladys stood staring at the man for a few seconds, thinking she must be dreaming, but then she straightened her back and glaring at him, replied, "How dare you call my daughter a bastard. I think your step-father will have something to say about that."

"I think not!" he said, then making a noise that sounded more like a snort than a laugh added, "he is legally my father and not my step-father, but that's of little consequence since he shan't have anything to say about anything anymore, that is, unless he says it from his grave."

"What do you mean from his grave? Andrew is in Ireland and

will be home anytime now."

"Ho! You call him Andrew. Now I know what sort of sinful acts have been going on here. Well no more of that. I am not in the least sorry to tell you that your father-in-law, or should I say 'lover,' was robbed and killed three days ago in Ireland."

Gladys was so shocked by the news that the insinuation went unnoticed, "I don't believe you."

"Well, you can believe it, or not, but Andrew Pickwick is dead. Now it is I who owns his estate, including that mansion he has built." Gladys, still in shock, stood with her mouth hanging open as he continued with his tirade, "And just to show that I am not as hard-hearted as you may think, if you leave Dover, I shall not say anything about your crime. But if you do not, I shall personally see to it that you are thrown in jail and that brat of yours is put in an orphanage."

Although Peter had no idea how serious a crime Gladys had committed, he talked with such certitude that Gladys believed him.

"But where can we go? If you cannot consider my welfare at least think about the welfare of my daughter, and I might add, your niece."

His reply came sharp and direct, "Do not call her my niece. She could belong to anyone for all I know, and as for where you can go, you can go straight to hell or crawl back into the gutter where you belong." Gladys almost slammed the door in the man's face, but she was in need of further information, "Very well, we shall be gone in a month, but when is Andrew's funeral?"

"That is none of your business, and if you do find out, I warn you, do not think of attending it."

Gladys's reply was swift, "That is not only cruel, but it is despicable!"

"Oh, is that so?"

With that, he turned and departed.

As soon as Gladys closed the door, her legs gave away, and she sank to the floor with a loud cry of anguish.

Dolly was on her way downstairs when she heard her mother cry out. "What's the matter, Mama?" she asked, as she knelt down and put her arms around Gladys.

"Oh, my darling," Gladys sobbed, "it's your Gamby."

Chapter Twenty-Nine

Dolly refused to accept the news that her grandfather was dead. Gladys tried to explain how he had met with an accident and was now in heaven with Tom and Millie, but she persistently argued, "Mama, do you remember our turtle dove poem? Gamby will come back, Mama, you shall see."

During the next few days, Dolly ate very little and spent most of her time looking out the window, but Gladys had too much on her mind to worry about her. They had less than a month to pack and leave, and when they found somewhere to live, it was imperative she find employment. She had only enough money to rent a flat and keep them fed for about two months. Women barmaids had become unpopular, since the general consensus was that men were far better suited for the job, so it was unlikely she would be able to find that type of employment. She probably could find a job as a housemaid, but it would be impossible to work ten to twelve hours a day and look after Dolly as well.

Andrew's friend and lawyer, Randolph Mansfield, was also

shocked when he heard of his good friend's death, but the manner in which he received the news caused him as much anger as grief. Early Monday morning, Peter Pickwick came to see him, and without any show of respect or feeling, announced that Andrew had been robbed and killed. He then had the audacity to ask if Andrew's will had been changed. Randolph knew that it hadn't, but told the greedy young man that he would have to wait until the official reading to find out.

He had never been so tempted to commit a crime as he was that day. It would be so easy to forge Andrew's name on the new will that left half of Andrew's estate, and Oaken Arms, to his daughter-in-law and his granddaughter, but in the past few years the handwriting experts had become so proficient at detecting false signatures, he was afraid of being found out. Two days later his friend, the coroner, who also shared a dislike for Peter Pickwick, dropped by his office and gave him something to take to Andrew's granddaughter.

At first, Gladys greeted Randolph warily, not knowing who Peter had talked to and what he had revealed, but when she saw how earnest the lawyer was with his offer of sympathy, she relaxed. He was the first visitor they had since Andrew had been killed, and it was comforting to finally have another adult to talk to and to share in her grief. Randolph, pleased he could be of help, stayed and visited longer than he had planned. He also wanted to spare Gladys the humiliation of attending the reading of the will in the presence of the rest of the family and told her that Peter Pickwick, as the only male heir, would inherit most of Andrew's wealth, which included Oaken Arms. The townhouse was left to Rose, along with a generous yearly allowance.

Surprisingly, she showed no signs of emotion over what seemed to be very poignant and devastating information, but Randolph reasoned that she might be so upset over the injustice of it all, she didn't know what to say. He knew it would be of little comfort, but decided it only fair to tell her what Andrew had hoped to accomplish on his return home.

"Although it does you little good now, Gladys, I want you to know that Andrew had me make out another will in which you and Dolly were the main beneficiaries. He intended to sign it as soon as he returned."

"I knew he intended to put both our names on the deed to Oaken Arms, Mr Mansfield, and I suppose when the shock of his death wears off, I may feel anger and resentment toward him for not seeing to it before he went away, but right now I just feel sad. I am also terribly afraid. Everything we had is gone, and I don't know what to do."

"I can sympathize with your situation, and I wouldn't blame you if you were upset with him. Mind you, he did have a reason for putting it off. I don't know if you were aware of it, but he was trying to obtain a divorce."

"No I didn't, but I know he was not fond of his wife, or her children for that matter," she replied.

"That's true, but that wasn't the reason he wanted the divorce. Andrew confided in me before he left, and I am confident he wouldn't mind me telling you this now. He loved you very much and intended to ask you to marry him."

"Oh!" Gladys's surprise was evident.

"You had no idea how he felt?"

Gladys shook her head. "I loved Andrew, but not as anything more than a father-in-law." She gave a small disparaging laugh, and added, "I suppose that is one thing to be thankful for. I would have had to say no to his proposal."

Randolph suggested that she contest the will, especially since he would be happy to testify that Andrew had a new one drawn up and intended to sign it, along with the deed for Oaken Arms, on his return to Dover. When she declined his offer, and said she was going to be leaving Dover in a week or two, and had no intention of ever returning, he could hardly believe it. Gladys could tell he was puzzled, but she didn't dare mention Peter's visit or offer an explanation. She did, however, inquire as to when and where Andrew was to be buried. Randolph replied that Rose and her family were insisting that both Gladys and Dolly not attended the service.

"That is a shame! Dolly deserves to be there for her Grandfather's burial."

When Randolph suggested she should protest, she informed

him that she wanted nothing more to do with the family. He was about to inquire why, but the tone of finality to her statement changed his mind, and he agreed to do whatever he could. Randolph was a good lawyer, and through the years had developed a good sense of perception. Therefore, he could tell when someone had something to hide. He liked Gladys the first time he met her, and as much as he wanted to know what it was that prevented her from accepting his offer, he also knew that it was none of his business.

Putting his hand on her shoulder, he said, "If you ever need my services, Gladys, I will be here, and I shall take your case free of charge—not only for your sake, but for Andrew's too. He was a good friend." Gladys hugged him, and he was about to leave when he noticed Dolly sitting quietly beside the parlour window and remembered he had something to give her.

Calling her to him, he said, "Dolly, your grandfather loved you so dearly that he told everyone he met that you were his little turtle dove. He showed all his friends the little pin you gave him; he was that proud of it. Now you know that some bad men robbed and killed your grandfather. Well they took all his clothes and even his watch and fob, but there was one thing they did not take. Do you know what that was?"

Dolly's solemn face looked up at the lawyer as tears began running down her cheeks. This was the first time anyone but her mother had told her that Gamby was dead, and her belief in his return was shattered. Unable to answer the man, she just shook her head.

"It was something he had clasped tightly in his hand like this," Randolph held his clenched fist out for her to see. "Something he prized more than anything else in the whole world." Then he opened his hand.

"Oh, Gamby!" Dolly cried, as she took the little dove pin. "Mama, Gamby didn't forget me. See, he saved this just for me, so I would know how much he loves me, even if he couldn't come back."

Once again, Randolph told Gladys to let him know if she wanted to contest the will, hoping she had changed her mind. She thanked him again and said she would think about it, but she knew that would never happen. If it wasn't for Dolly, she might have stayed in Dover and taken him up on his offer. Having lost everything she had worked for, it might be worth the gamble, but she loved her daughter too much to take that chance.

Not long after Randolph had gone, Bob Hennessy arrived. Tears ran down his cheeks as he hugged Gladys and Dolly and expressed how sorry he was. "Sure and I'm so ashamed. Andrew did so much for the poor folk over there, and then it was some o' them that murdered him."

"There are bad people everywhere, Bob. Besides, I remember Andrew telling me how destitute they were, and when a man has to watch his children die of starvation, I guess he will do anything to save them. The men who killed Andrew must have been that desperate."

"That's not reason enough for what they did, but thank you, Gladys. Sure and I think you're as much of a saint as himself."

The blacksmith was shocked when Gladys told him that Peter had inherited all of Andrew's properties, and that she and Dolly had to move. "Sure and we just has a small home, but you and your young one are more than welcome to share it with us," he offered. Gladys knew he barely made enough money to keep his wife and five children in food and clothing, so she thanked him, and, lying, said that she had a friend in Sandwich she could stay with.

Bob stayed and talked a while longer reminiscing about the good times he shared with Andrew. Then, a look of apology crossed his face as he said, "I hates to mention it, Gladys, but that good for nothing, Peter, came by my shop this mornin' and wanted to know what horses and buggies I had o' Andrew's. I told him that he couldn't touch any of them until he showed me some official proof they were his. It should be yourself that has claim to Andrew's two horses and buggy, not him."

"Thank you, Bob, but everything, even Andrew's horses, belong to Peter now. I do have a bill of sale for Tig and the shay, so when he comes back do not include them with the rest. Just wait a minute while I find it so you will have proof." Gladys went back into the house, got the paper down from the top of the china cupboard and took it out to him. "We will be leaving soon, so I shall be by to pick them up."

Before Bob had mounted his horse, a delivery wagon arrived. One of the two men sitting on the driver's bench climbed down and inquired if this was the home of Gladys Pickwick. When Gladys said it was, he turned and called out to the other fellow, "Go on, son, get her unloaded."

The wooden crate he took out of the wagon was about two and half feet long and two feet tall, but by the sounds of the grunts and groans the delivery lad made getting it into the house, it appeared to be fairly heavy. Gladys asked the driver what it was, but he had no idea; so after they left, she asked Bob if he would mind staying to help her open it. He found the tools needed for the job in the back shed then started to remove some of the nails. "I wonder what it can be," Gladys said, and she called Dolly to come and see the strange container.

"What do you think it is, Mama?"

"I really have no idea."

"Sure and it's come a fair way," Bob said as he read a label on the top of the crate. "All the way from America. Here now, there's a name on the side. 'Singer,' I think it is. It must be some musical instrument."

Gladys looked puzzled. "I really have no idea, Bob, but the only way we are going to find out is to open it."

A few minutes later, the crate was open disclosing a sewing machine like the one Gladys had seen exhibited at the fair. "Oh, Andrew!" she exclaimed. "Look, Dolly, Gamby must have ordered the sewing machine from that nice man, Mr Singer, who we met at the exhibition in London."

Bob thought it was a lovely piece of machinery and was curious to know how it worked, so Gladys found a piece of cloth, threaded the bobbin and the needle then proceeded to sew. Amazed, Bob scratched his head and exclaimed, "Sure and that Singer fellow must be the cleverest bloke in America."

Before Bob left, Gladys had him re-crate the machine, since they would be moving soon. "Peter is not getting his greedy hands on this," she vowed.

The following day, she knew she had to have a talk with Dolly and try to explain a few things, because she had begun asking questions. The most upsetting was, "When are we going to have a funeral for Gamby like we did for Auntie Millie?" Instead of making up a false story, Gladys decided to tell her the truth about how Andrew's wife and adopted children had forbidden either of them to attend the funeral. Then she promised they would visit Andrew's grave later and have their own little service.

Dolly also wanted to know when they were going to move into Oaken Arms, so Gladys explained that Gamby had died before he had a chance to put the house in their names, and as a result, they could never move into the house, but would have to find another place to live.

Dolly knew that losing Oaken Arms was as sad for her mother as it was for her, so she put a hand on one of Gladys's cheeks, kissed the other cheek, and said, "Don't feel sad, Mama; it would not be the same without Gamby there anyway." They held each other and rocked back and forth, crying.

Gladys decided to go to Hastings to see if she could find a place to live, and if there were any jobs available. She was hoping that a seamstress might hire her if she told her about having a sewing machine. They were ready to leave for the train station the following day when Lady Sorenson arrived. She greeted both Gladys and Dolly with hugs and a great deal of sympathy that turned to tears when Dolly showed her the stick pin and clenched it tightly in her fist to show how Gamby had saved it from the bad men. Lady Sorenson remarked how lucky she was to have such a brave and thoughtful grandfather and received Dolly's first smile in days.

"Is Lord Cedric with you?" Gladys asked as she went to look out the window after Dolly had gone upstairs to put the pin safely away in a little cedar chest in her dollhouse.

"No, my dear, Rod drove me in. He dropped me off here and has gone on an errand for Cedric. He should be back in an hour or so. How are you and Dolly coping?"

"We are managing to carry on. I think it is harder for Dolly, but even so, I have to admit that she's more of a comfort to me than I am to her."

"I can believe that, she is such a remarkable child. I must apologize for not coming sooner, but if I may be frank with you . . ."

"Of course you can, Lady Madeline," Gladys answered, although she guessed that her ladyship had heard the news, and was afraid of what she was going to say.

"I'm afraid that Cedric thinks you were a bad influence on Andrew, Gladys."

"Me? A bad influence? My heavens, what on earth did I do to cause him to think such a thing?"

"Well shortly before Andrew left for Ireland, Cedric went to visit him. It seems he had heard that one of our old acquaintances was seen in the company of Andrew's estranged wife, Rose. Since Cedric knew the man was a gambler and in dire need of money, he wanted to find out if Andrew knew about it."

"And?"

"I wish I did not have to tell you this, Gladys, but I feel I must. Andrew told Cedric that he was going to give the man a large sum of money to seduce Rose, so he would have grounds for a divorce."

"That cannot be true!"

"You did not know?"

"I certainly did not!"

"And did you not know that Andrew intended to marry you?"

"I only learned that yesterday when Andrew's lawyer, Randolph Mansfield, came to see me. He said that Andrew was going to ask me to marry him as soon as he returned. I had no idea he felt that way. I loved him as anyone would love a generous and kind father-in-law, but that is all. In any case, I would have had to say no if he did propose."

"I knew it! Cedric did not believe Andrew when he said you knew nothing about his plans. Forgive me, Gladys; I should have come to you sooner. Now when are you moving into your lovely new home? The move should help keep your mind off that terrible tragedy a little."

Gladys felt that she could no longer carry on without confiding in someone; she confessed, "Lady Madeline, we will not be moving to Oaken Arms."

"What on earth do you mean?"

"What I'm going to tell you now may end our friendship, but I desperately need to talk to someone and there's no one else to turn to. You see, I am not who you think I am." Gladys only intended to disclose a little of her past, but telling the truth was so refreshing that she didn't stop talking until she had told it all, including the incident with Gaylord, the landlord, but excluding her part in Millie's demise. She finished her confession by telling of Peter's visit and why she had no recourse but to leave town.

The awkward silence that followed caused her to feel she had made a mistake. Finally, she blurted out, "You must think I'm a horrible person, but for Dolly's sake, please, please, do not tell anyone. If you do, I may be sent to prison."

"Sent to prison? Oh, you poor dear. In spite of everything you had to go through, you managed to survive. You most surely did. And not only have you survived, my dear, but you have become a beautiful and gracious lady. For that, I salute you!" her ladyship replied. She rose from her chair, took off her beautiful feathered bonnet, waved it across her tummy with a flourish, and bowed. When Dolly came downstairs, both women had their arms around each other and were laughing.

Rod came soon after to pick up Lady Sorenson, and as she was leaving she said, "I wish there was some way I could help, but I do not think that stubborn husband of mine is about to change his mind." Gladys knew her ladyship was trying to say that she would no longer be welcome as a guest of the Sorensons.

After Lady Sorenson left, Gladys thought it was too late to go to Hastings so decided they would go the following day. She happened to glance out the window just in time to see Lady Sorenson's buggy pull up in front of the house again. Worried, she ran out to see what had happened. Lady Madeline said she had barely left when she remembered overhearing her housekeeper discussing a friend who had been the housekeeper of a Mr James Hornsby, a well-to-do widower and owner of an estate near the town of Sandwich. The housekeeper had fallen and broken a hip and was not expected to recover. The widower was looking for a replacement, and Lady Sorenson thought Gladys might apply for the position. "I shall be happy to give you a recommendation, dear. What do you think?"

"That is most kind of you, Lady Madeline. If you can give me his address, I shall go there as soon as possible."

"I will ask Annie and write it down for you. Rod will deliver it tomorrow."

"A housekeeper's job would be ideal, if the man is willing to provide accommodation for both of us," Gladys answered.

"Splendid! Now we just have to pray that the position is still open."

Gladys was a child of Old Nichol and she instinctively knew that she and Dolly would survive. They had each other and that was all that mattered. Millie had once told her that life is made up of chapters, and, when you finish one, you go on to the next. She didn't know what waited for them, but it was time to go on to the next chapter.

Acknowledgements

Nancy O'Neill, my daughter and mentor. I couldn't have written this novel without you.

Mike O'Neill, my son-in-law, for keeping my computer alive.

My son, Danny, and his wife, Karen, for their love and support.

My big brother, for many lunches and love. I miss you, Bruce.

My niece, Lorna White, for her encouragement and love.

My friend, Patricia Piercy. I wish you were still here to say, "I told you so."

My neighbor, Louise Waterman, for proofreading.

Ken McLeod, for his advice and encouragement.

Gilliian Koster, for believing in my story.

Derek Hanebury, for his advice and encouragement.

To all the staff at Amberjack Publishing, for your expertise, patience, and kindness. Thank you for publishing my novel.

Lastly, the encouragement I received from all my dear friends and relatives while writing this book helped keep me going, and although I don't have room to mention you all, I want you to know that I am grateful to each and every one of you.

About the Author

Born in Vancouver, B.C. in 1927, Betty Annand has resided in the Comox Valley on Vancouver Island since the age of ten. Widowed since 2002, she has enjoyed doing volunteer work at her church, the local hospital and a local theatre, where she writes and directs plays for the seniors group. She resides in the house that she and her husband built sixty years ago and enjoys spending time with her family, who still live on the island. She is the author of three non-fiction books, *Growing up in the White House*, *Voices from Bevan*, and *Voices from Courtenay Past*. *The Girl from Old Nichol* is her first novel.

Gladys' story will continue in the forthcoming release, *The Woman from Dover*.

CPSIA information can be obtained
at www.ICGtesting.com
Printed in the USA
LVOW08s0514171116

513299LV00003B/3/P